The Essenc

ROB SINCLAIR

THE ESSENCE OF EVIL

CANELO

First published in the United Kingdom in 2019 by Canelo

Canelo Digital Publishing Limited
57 Shepherds Lane
Beaconsfield, Bucks HP9 2DU
United Kingdom

A CIP catalogue record for this book is available from the British Library.

Print ISBN 978 1 78863 502 8
Ebook ISBN 978 1 78863 501 1

Look for more great books at www.canelo.co

Printed and bound in Great Britain by Clays Ltd, Elcograf S.p.A.

For Josh

Prologue

She sprinted through the darkened street, glancing over her shoulder every other step – little more than an instinctive reaction as she could see next to nothing in the blackness behind her. At first she'd been screaming, but now she couldn't find her voice. She was too out of breath, and together with the stabbing in her throat from having already bellowed with such force, she was rendered mute.

Her bare feet felt wet and slippery on the cold stone underfoot. Was it moisture on the ground, or was her delicate skin rubbed clean off and bleeding from constant pounding on the rough surface? It didn't matter. She wouldn't stop running. She couldn't.

A fearful shiver ran through her. Not because of the cold but because of the ominous thoughts – memories of what she'd already been through – that were still crashing through her mind. The cool dank space that she could see so little of because of the bright light always blinding her. The binds around her wrists and ankles, locking her in place and giving her no chance to protect or defend her vulnerable body. The cruel words of her captor, the gruesome end planned for her.

She stumbled as those horrors swept through her in a sudden onslaught.

And she was damn sure *he* was there behind her now. She couldn't let him get her. She couldn't go back to that place. She had to get away.

She didn't spot the uneven paving slab. Her big toe cracked into the edge of it, the jolt to her momentum sending her wobbling. Before she knew it her legs had gone from underneath her. Her face was speeding towards solid ground. She managed to reach out her hand in time, saving her head from a horrific smash. Her wrist buckled under the weight of her body. She rolled, the back of her head smacked into the pavement and the shock of pain ran right through her.

There was no time to recover.

She hauled herself back to her feet, head throbbing, disorientated. She grimaced as she felt the wet patch at the back of her head. Blood? She had no idea he was there until he clattered into her from behind and sent her crashing forwards to the ground again. His weight pressed down on her, knocked the wind from her lungs and sent her brain into a heightened panic – if that was even possible. She struggled to free herself but managed only to wriggle onto her back.

'Going somewhere?' he snarled, the white of his gritted teeth just about visible in the thin moonlight. How she longed for that bright light now so that she remained blinded to his features.

He leaned back, his legs pinning her arms by her sides, then threw a fist into her stomach, sapping any remaining defence she was trying to muster. He stood up and grabbed her hair in his hand, began to drag her away. She writhed and kicked and filled her lungs to try and scream. Before she could manage it he wrapped an arm around her throat. He squeezed hard, choking her attempt to raise the alarm.

The skin on her back and side scraped painfully on the pock-marked surface as he dragged her over a step, through a garden gate, behind a thick bush.

'You shouldn't have run,' he said, his voice now calm, almost warm.

Horrific thoughts crashed through her mind as she heard his voice echoing in her mind. All of the things he'd said he'd do to her. She had to fight. She had to give it everything she had.

She kicked and she bucked. She tried to reach up to dig her fingernails into his face, but he blocked her every move.

She heard a noise.

He heard it too. She could tell because of the flinch in his eyes. Someone was coming. A far-off car? A pedestrian on the street?

He thrust his hand towards her. She jolted, her chest constricted sharply. She couldn't catch her breath at all. Looking down, she could just make out the glint of metal, sticking out from her gut.

He withdrew the knife, slowly, assuredly. Then slid it back into her flesh a second time. The razor-sharp blade glided into her abdomen effortlessly. Looking up, she saw him staring down at her with morbid interest.

'You shouldn't have run,' he said again.

Then she heard another unexpected sound. Closer now. A banging noise. A door opening? Her eyes darted off to the side. A light flashed on, so bright it burned into her retinas and she squinted and looked away until the throbbing in her head subsided.

She heard shouting, but her confused and drifting brain couldn't decipher where the noise came from or what the words were.

After a few seconds she finally felt able to open her eyelids again. The light was still on, but was no longer glaring. For a moment she wondered if she was back in *that* place. But no, it felt – and smelled – different here. She was still outside. It wasn't that same blinding light that now tormented her thoughts, but a security light at the front of someone's house, just a few yards away. She was lying in the small front garden. She looked up at the man standing over her. Not *him*.

He'd gone.

'My god,' the man said. 'Don't move. I'm going to get help.'

He turned away.

'No!' she managed to cry out. 'Don't... leave me.'

She mustered all of her strength to reach her hand upward towards him. He lifted his hand out to her. Their fingers brushed.

She didn't have the strength to hold on.

Her arm flopped down to her side. Her eyes slid shut as everything else around her faded to nothingness.

Chapter One

Dani's nerves slowly grew as she wound her car through the leafy streets of the Birmingham suburb of Moseley. The sun was only just beginning to make a lacklustre appearance as it poked over rooftops and its rays filtered through dense trees just showing the first signs of autumn colour. It was thirty minutes until the onset of the morning rush hour and the roads were still quiet. Dani turned onto Rose Hill and parked her car in one of the few available spots on the crammed road.

She turned off the engine then took a deep breath before she put her hand to the door. As she stepped out into the chilly morning air she caught a brief glimpse of her reflection in the side mirror. She grimaced at what she saw. The call had come in more than an hour before her alarm was due to go off. She'd had barely any time to get ready before leaving the apartment. Her well-laid plans for the morning had been well and truly sidelined, and the only option had been to throw on her clothes and tie her messy hair back before darting out.

With her hair pulled back tight across her head there was nothing she could do to hide the three-inch-long mark above her ear where her hair had refused to regrow, the lumpy patch of bare flesh right there for everyone else to see.

There was nothing she could do about that now. At least this way she wasn't hiding, she guessed.

She walked briskly down the street. Beyond the jam-packed parked cars, covered in beads of early morning dew, two long rows of Edwardian semi-detached houses were packed tightly together. Some of the houses appeared downtrodden almost to the point of being beyond saving, their gardens unkempt and overgrown, some filled with all manner of rubbish. Many of the other houses though had clearly been treated with more respect, their original features carefully preserved, their small front gardens neat, lawns and bushes trimmed.

As Dani walked along the pavement she noticed the bumper-to-bumper cars reflected the diverse condition of the houses, with banged-up old Fords and Renaults and Rovers parked next to much newer and shinier BMWs and Mercedes. The street was a clash of character and background and culture and class, much like the entire confused neighbourhood, which sat somewhat awkwardly between some of the wealthiest but also some of the poorest areas of Britain's second city.

With the sun continuing its slow rise, the bright rays of low sunlight peeking through the gaps in the buildings and the trees shone directly in Dani's face as she walked, making her already stabbing headache even worse. She winced and held her hand up to her face to shade her eyes.

Even with the glare of the sun and her squinting eyes, it wasn't difficult to spot where she was headed because of the gaggle of people that were gathered – police officers, paramedics and also several members of the public. Blue and white police tape stretched right across the street, blocking access to pedestrians and traffic. Three marked police cars and an ambulance were parked up in front of the cordon as Dani approached. One or two of the pedestrians looked at her questioningly as she strode up.

The uniformed police officer who moved quickly to intercept Dani had a similar expression, until Dani whipped out her ID and held it aloft. The PC nodded then stepped away as Dani scuttled under the police tape. To her right, beyond a low metal garden gate, and tucked behind a privet hedge, was a seven-foot high white tent. Dani headed for it.

She walked past three forensic specialists, dressed head to toe in white, who were crouched low on the street and in the small front garden, searching for footprints or fibres or body tissues or fluids – any evidence that could be of importance. They'd come to the scene surprisingly quickly. Dani had requested their presence based upon the sparse information that had been relayed to her on the phone earlier, and they had clearly lost no time in attending the scene. She ignored them for now, and they all ignored her too as they focussed on their painstaking searches.

Dani continued towards the tent.

'DI Stephens,' Dani heard someone call out.

She stopped and turned and saw an unfamiliar man walking up to her – late twenties, she guessed, and wearing a long thick grey overcoat. A newbie DS, Dani thought. His youthful face held a carefree expression rather than the worn-down look of many more experienced officers. His face was kind though, with big deep brown eyes, a pinched nose and a dimpled chin.

He held out his hand.

'I'm DS Easton,' he said.

She noticed Easton stare up at her hairline, above her ear. She wondered how much he'd already heard about her. Dani shook his hand. 'First names are fine. You can call me Dani.'

'Sure, I'm Aaron then.'

'Nice to meet you, Aaron. So what can you tell me?'

Dani already had a brief idea of what had happened from the earlier call she'd taken from her boss, DCI McNair, and the follow-up with the PC who'd first been on the scene, and she'd been expecting Easton to be ready and waiting for her. In fact McNair had suggested Easton would be assigned to all of Dani's cases going forwards. He was the new Jason, basically. Dani felt herself deflate a little at that thought, though she had nothing against Easton. She had no preconception about how good he was at his job or what he was like as a person even. She would soon find out.

'The victim is female,' Easton said. 'Late teens, early twenties. No ID or any personal possessions found on her or nearby. She's… well, you'll see for yourself.'

His inability to hold her eye suggested Easton was rattled by the experience of seeing the victim. He was a DS on the Homicide team so it shouldn't be the first time he'd attended a murder scene and she wasn't massively impressed with his reaction.

'Are the homeowners here?' Dani asked, looking up at the house they were standing by, which she noted was one of the better kept ones on the street.

'Yeah. Husband and wife are both in the house still. And their dog.'

'You've spoken to them?'

'Yeah. The dog doesn't speak much though.'

Dani felt herself smile but she quickly resumed a neutral expression. Easton reached in his pocket and withdrew a notebook, holding it up almost victoriously.

'Spoke to the husband for a few minutes before you showed up. He and his wife are both pretty shaken. Mr and Mrs Mondy. The husband found the victim. He was getting ready for work just after five. Heard a noise. Opened the door to see a figure, standing over the victim.'

'A figure?'

'That's what he said. The front light came on but it was still dark and he couldn't give any useful description – tall, short, fat, thin, male, female. Anyway, the killer scarpered. Mondy went to the girl. But there was nothing he could do.'

'Have you ruled them out?'

'As suspects? I dunno.'

'You *dunno*?'

'My gut says they've got nothing to do with it. Not subtle, is it? Stabbing someone in your front garden.'

'Subtle? Subtlety is rarely a word I've used when describing murder scenes. Their reaction should have told you a lot. Next time make sure you're still alert and have your brain switched on.'

'Yes, ma'am,' Easton said, his voice sullen but stern, his face just starting to crease with anger. She hadn't intended her words to come out quite so coldly, and inwardly she cringed at her own brusqueness, but she said nothing of it. 'I don't think they've got anything to do with this. I've spoken to them, I saw how shaken they were. Unless you're trying to tell me otherwise.'

Dani held his eye for a few seconds. 'Ok. Good. So what else?'

'The body is still in there.' Easton indicated to the tent. 'The pathologist too.'

Dani nodded. Although a pathologist would perform a forensic post-mortem on every murder victim, there generally wasn't a need for one to be called to a scene. Not unless there were particularly unusual circumstances – a badly decomposed body, for example. That call was the Senior Investigating Officer's to make. As SIO on this case, Dani, perhaps feeling rusty after so long on the sidelines, had wanted to err on the side of caution for this one, particularly given some of the details relayed to her earlier.

'Who's the pathologist?' she asked.

'Jack Ledford.'

Dani groaned inwardly. Well, perhaps her decision to call out a pathologist was about to come back to bite her. He was sure to tell her straight if he felt his time was being wasted unnecessarily.

'Ok, so tell me what you know so far.'

'The victim was stabbed twice,' Easton said. 'Both times in the torso. Looks like she was first attacked out on the street.'

Easton pointed over to a small pool of dried blood on the pavement slabs, from which a thin streak of blood wormed away through the gate to where the white tent was erected.

'And what does that tell you?' Dani asked.

'The blood trail?'

Dani nodded.

'It's not massive. Perhaps she wasn't stabbed there, but there was some sort of attack or fight. She's got a nasty gash on her head which maybe explains the blood on the street. Then either she was dragged from that spot by the attacker or she crawled from there into the garden herself.'

'Which do you think?'

'I'd say she was dragged there.'

'Why?'

'Because of the grazes on her back. It looks like the two stab wounds were then delivered in the garden, given the amount of blood there.'

Dani nodded and tried to show no reaction to the grim words. His instincts seemed sound enough at least.

'Let's go and see what Ledford has for us then.'

They headed to the white tent and Dani discreetly pulled across the opening, trying not to let the gawkers by the police tape get a view of the inside.

Ledford was in his sixties, bald but for wispy white hair around the sides, a pair of glasses perched on the edge of his pointed nose. He was crouched down by the curled up body of the young woman. The victim's face was contorted in a hollow death stare. She was only partially clothed, in knickers and a tight-fitting strappy top. She wore nothing on her feet. Her skin was dirtied and blotchy and covered in scratches and scrapes. There was a large pool of red underneath the body. Dani noticed rings of reddened flesh around her wrists and ankles.

She clenched her teeth, trying her best to contain her reaction to the horrific sight, particularly given how she'd been less than impressed with Easton's reaction just moments before. For her, it brought back a whole host of painful and very personal memories.

A crime scene photographer was standing over the corpse, looking at the small screen on his camera.

'Ok, that's me done,' he said to Ledford. He nodded to Dani and Easton, then made his way out.

'Jack, it's good to see you,' Dani said.

Ledford said nothing, didn't even react to Dani's voice, just carried on whatever he was doing. It was a frequent habit of his and one of his many oddities. Ledford was something of a hermit, someone who really was pretty damn useless at interacting with still breathing human beings. Dead people, on the other hand, he was quite excellent with.

After a few seconds Ledford straightened up and used the knuckle of one of his gloved fingers to push his glasses up his nose.

'Ah, DI Stephens. You're back.'

He didn't sound particularly moved in any way by the fact.

'First day,' she said. 'Not exactly how I'd planned this morning in my head.'

Dani looked over at Easton and wondered again whether he already knew the full story of her period of absence. Most likely he did. What he hadn't read in the papers would have been passed through the police force on the gossip merry-go-round. Ledford didn't say anything more on the subject of Dani's return and that was fine by her.

'What are your early thoughts?' Dani asked.

'Well I don't think this was an accident,' Ledford said. 'Nor do I think the young lady did this to herself deliberately.'

Dani wasn't sure if Ledford was trying to jest or if he actually felt it important to point those obvious facts out to her, such was his manner.

'What about cause of death?'

'You know you'll have to wait for the post-mortem results before I can give you a full answer on that.'

'Of course. But what's your gut?'

'Perhaps not the best choice of words, DI Stephens.'

Dani noticed Easton smirking, whether at her expense or because of Ledford's stiff and humourless manner, she wasn't sure.

'She's been stabbed twice,' Ledford said, 'and given the blood loss and what I can see of the wounds, one of those blows severed an artery – the abdominal aorta, most likely. Though it could have damaged the inferior vena cava too, which is actually a vein, rather than an artery. It's a damn big vein though, so even though blood runs through it with a lot less pressure, if you damage it you've still got a big problem. I'm sure you know that already, though.'

Yes Dani did know, but she said nothing.

'It seems highly likely therefore that blood loss was the cause of death,' Ledford concluded.

'Any idea about the weapon?' Dani asked.

'Nothing's been recovered,' Easton interjected.

'A smooth blade,' Ledford said.

He bent back down and lifted the blood-covered fabric of the dead woman's strappy top up over her midriff to reveal the fatal wounds.

'You can see from the incisions to the skin…' Ledford pointed to the largest of the wounds, a gaping hole in the woman's mid-section, '…that the wounds are neat, with little tearing. Which would be consistent with a smooth blade. A carving knife, something like that. About one and a half to two inches wide, at least five inches long.'

'Any defensive wounds?'

'It's hard to say at this point. There are lots of wounds. A gash on her head. Grazes, scratches. Dirt under the fingernails. Possibly from being dragged on the pavement, but we'll need to wait to match skin, blood and participle samples to conclude that. You'll also note the marks on her wrists and ankles.'

'She'd been tied up,' Dani said. A statement. She'd already known about those marks which were the key reason why she'd asked for a pathologist in the first place. She held back the rising nausea at the thought of the poor woman's ordeal.

'Very likely,' Ledford said. 'Again, we'll test for fibres on her skin and clothes, under her nails, see if it gives any clues. I'd say, given those surface wounds, that she'd been bound for only a short period. One to two days. And she also appears quite well nourished.'

'But that doesn't really tell the whole story,' Dani said.

'No, it doesn't. She could have been held, unbound, for who knows how long, and it's also possible that those marks have nothing whatsoever to do with her death. Forensics can only give you so much. You're the detectives, DI Stephens and DS Easton; it's for you to properly evidence the many whys and wherefores.'

'Of course, Jack. You'll let me know when the post-mortem results are ready?'

'You'll be among the first to know. I believe DI Fletcher is joint SIO too, though, isn't she?'

'She is?' Dani said, looking to Easton as if for his reassurance but he simply shrugged.

Ledford frowned. 'Well, you tell me. I'll send the report to whoever I need to.'

'I'll let you know,' Dani said.

She and Easton headed back out to the street. The number of bystanders along the police tape had grown in the intervening minutes as neighbours on their way to work had become side-tracked by the titillating events.

'What are you thinking?' Dani asked Easton.

'She was kidnapped. God knows who by or why. Somehow she escaped. She ran. The killer caught up with her. Maybe he meant to kill her, or maybe he panicked. We know he was disturbed by Mr Mondy.'

Dani said nothing. Easton's theory certainly seemed logical enough, which worried Dani, because that meant the death wasn't just a random act of violence like so many of the murders they dealt with, but was cold and calculated.

'If that's true she must have been held somewhere near here,' Dani said.

'Possibly. Though she could have escaped from a vehicle.'

Dani looked over at the gaggle of onlookers, still growing by the minute, then at the houses across the road. Many of them still had curtains drawn. At more than one though, she thought she could see people peering out through the windows to get a glimpse of the goings-on. Nosy neighbours. Always the same.

As Dani stared over at the house opposite she thought she saw a figure in a darkened upstairs room. Just the outline of a person standing close to the window, but in the unlit room they were nothing more than a dark shadow. After a few seconds the figure faded away to nothing and a chilling shiver ran through Dani. She continued to look at the spot for several seconds but saw nothing more.

Was she seeing things now?

No, that really would be a first. She wasn't mad. And she didn't believe in ghosts. Either someone had been there, trying to be discreet, or it was simply a trick of the eye.

'She had nothing on her of significance?' Dani asked.

'No ID, no purse, no phone, no jewellery.'

'We need to identify her. We need to know where she was held. We need the murder weapon.'

'So what do you suggest?'

'Let's see if we can trace her last movements. Find out which streets around here, which homes, have CCTV. We may identify her, the killer, a vehicle, something that we can begin to track.'

'I'll get on it now.'

Dani looked over again at the house opposite. No, that was no trick of the eye. There was the figure again, the outline even thinner and less visible than before, as it was now further back from the window – almost imperceptible in the shadow of the room, but definitely there.

'We should also send a team out doing house-to-house around here,' Dani said. 'We could have more witnesses. She may even have been held close to here.'

'I'll get a DC on the case right away.'

'Not yet. Let's get the ball rolling ourselves first,' Dani said. She looked over at the house opposite again. 'Come on, follow me.'

Chapter Two

Dani and Easton headed up the pathway to the front door of the house. The unkempt garden, weed-filled paving slabs and the paint-peeling wooden window frames were quite the contrast to the Mondys' home opposite. Dani wondered whether this house was even occupied or not.

They reached the worn-looking front door and Dani rang the bell. They waited a few seconds but there was no response from inside. Dani rang again, then stepped back and looked up to the window on the first floor where moments before she'd seen the ominous figure. There was nothing, no one there now.

Still no response to the doorbell.

'Wait there, I'll check around the back,' Dani said.

She headed to the rickety side gate, opened it, and walked along the narrow passage to the back garden. A glazed door led into a dilapidated kitchen that looked like it had been last modelled in the sixties. Dani put her face close to the glass. There were no signs of anyone there, but the house was definitely lived in. Fresh fruit and vegetables sat on the kitchen counter. Cups and plates were neatly piled up by the sink, ready to be washed.

'Anything?' Dani called out to Easton.

'No,' he shouted back. 'There's no one home.'

Yet Dani was certain there'd been someone, or something, in the upstairs window. She looked across the messy grass of the narrow back garden. The six-inch long stems were trodden down in a neat line leading from the back of the house and over to the fence in the far corner.

'Easton, come here.'

She continued to stare over at the footprints as she listened to Easton approaching behind her.

'What is it?' he said.

'Have you got any gloves?'

She turned to him and he reached inside his coat and produced a pair of blue latex gloves. Dani slipped one on.

'Over there,' she said, indicating the footprints in the grass as she grabbed the door handle with her gloved hand.

She pushed down. The latch on the door released and she nudged the door open. She glanced at Easton. He gave her a determined look. She stared inside the space in front of her. Thick and musty warm air billowed out from the inside. Dani stepped in. The smell of stale air filled her nostrils.

'Wait down here,' Dani said to Easton. 'Shout if you see or hear anything.' He nodded in agreement. Dani moved forwards through the kitchen towards the hall, straining her ears for any sounds from within. 'Hello?' she called out. 'This is the police.'

No response. Dani walked along the hallway, glancing into the old-fashioned dining room and the lounge that led off from it. No one in there. No one in plain sight anyway. As she reached the foot of the stairs, Dani looked over the picture frames along the wall leading up the stairs. Many were several decades old, black and white portraits.

'Hello,' she shouted again.

She heard a creaking floorboard from an upstairs room. Dani held her breath as she listened. Her heart was drumming in her chest. The fabric of her blouse pulsated with each beat.

Another creak.

'Easton, get over here,' Dani called, sounding panicked, her thin nerves getting the better of her.

Easton came up to Dani's side. He had the second glove over his left hand, and was clutching a bundle of envelopes. Dani looked at the plastic window of the top envelope.

'Mrs Staunton, are you home?' Dani shouted. 'It's the police.'

Footsteps sounded above.

Dani braced herself, then flinched when a figure appeared at the top of the stairs and she had to fight to push the memory away.

'What on earth are you doing in my house!' croaked the doddery silver-haired lady who came into view, a thick pink dressing gown wrapped around her.

Dani let out a relieved sigh. She turned to Easton and was sure she saw him wipe away another smirk.

–

Thirty minutes later Dani was back in her car, heading through thick traffic to Birmingham city centre. She never had got to the bottom of who, or what, she'd seen in the upstairs window of June Staunton's house. The old lady had sworn she'd been asleep until she'd heard the doorbell ring, but had been groggy and tired and it had taken her several minutes to muster the strength to get out of bed. She had no idea why the back door was unlocked, was adamant she would never leave it like that, and had no idea why there were footprints on her lawn.

Dani had checked the upstairs, claiming that she wanted to get a better look at the crime scene from the higher vantage point, but other than the unlocked back door and the prints in the grass, there was no other sign of anyone else having been there, intruder or otherwise.

Had the figure in the window been there at all or was Dani now seeing things? That wouldn't be a good turn of events.

It was clear Mrs Staunton was rattled by the whole experience, particularly given the murder scene across the road, but Dani decided she had more pressing matters to attend to. Easton was competent enough to deal both with the old lady and the team of forensics who Dani had ordered do a sweep of the house to find any evidence of an intruder. Though she suspected Easton believed she was making more out of the situation than she should have been.

Whatever. Better to be anal than to miss something that could prove useful.

It was gone ten a.m. when Dani parked up in the city centre. As she headed towards the glass-canopied entrance to West Midlands Police headquarters she found herself slowing in her step as unwelcome thoughts wormed their way front of mind. As much as she'd longed to be back doing the job she loved during her long road to mental and physical recovery, there was no doubt she was incredibly apprehensive about now being back. Even though she was damn sure she needed the routine of her work in her otherwise empty life, she'd rarely felt as vulnerable as she did now that she was here.

She pushed the doubts away as best she could and continued across the road. The backs of her heels were already rubbing painfully against the tight-fitting new shoes she was wearing for the first time that day. Was it because they were new though, or because her feet had softened, given that it was so long since she'd worn anything other than trainers or flip-flops? With every stride she took the hard edge of the new leather wedged further into her broken skin and what with that, and the still rumbling doubts, a large part of Dani wished she was at home, wearing tracksuit bottoms and lounging on the sofa. Again.

No, come on, that's not you. This *is you.*

She headed on inside and glanced around. Everything was different inside the HQ foyer. The large open space had been revamped and it now looked like the entrance to any modern corporate office block. There was an oversized, round reception counter plonked in the centre where three security guards were seated – though Dani noticed there were seats and computer screens for four. These weren't desk sergeants like you'd get in a normal police station, just hired-in security staff for what was, essentially, mostly an administrative office, though the building also housed the Force CID Homicide team for the whole of the West Midlands.

Dani made her way up to the middle of the three security guards, the only one she recognised from the last time she'd been in the building over two years ago. She'd said hello and goodbye to him probably hundreds of times but knew him only as Bill.

'Morning,' Dani said, smiling widely when Bill clocked her.

'DI Stephens!' he said, his pouty face brightening. Bill was plump and bald, probably edging towards sixty, with a warm and kind face. 'Long time no see.'

'Tell me about it.'

'You're back?'

'First day.'

Bill looked up, to the spot above her ear, and his smile faded. He quickly averted his eyes.

'I heard about… you know. I'm glad you're ok.'

Dani didn't say anything to that. Out of the corner of her eye she saw the other two guards look over at her, intrigued by Bill's words.

'I was told you'd have a new security card for me.' She placed her old one on the counter. Not only had the whole front entrance and reception area of HQ been refurbished, but the security system was upgraded too, both here at the main entrance and for the car park, which was why she'd had to park across the street as she'd not yet received a fob for parking. Now a row of electronic gates beyond the foyer led into the building proper and Dani was, so far, still on the outside looking in. Not quite one of *them* again, yet.

'Let me see,' Bill said, pushing himself backwards on his swivel chair and over to a drawer. 'I don't remember seeing anything for you, though.'

Bill rifled through the drawer but came back up with nothing.

'No, sorry, DI Stephens. No one told me you were coming back today. We can get you sorted out with one though, I'm sure.'

'Not your fault,' Dani said pleasantly, but she felt agitated. It wasn't like McNair had forgotten she was coming back. After all, she'd had the rude awakening hours before. 'Do you have a visitor pass or something I could take? I know where I'm going.'

'Sorry, I know who you are and everything, but I'm not allowed to do that. I can call your supervisor? He'll be able to come and escort you through.'

'She.'

'What?'

'DCI McNair. Helen McNair.'

'Ah, right, yeah. I'll call her now.'

Bill picked up a phone handset and Dani moved away and went to sit down on one of a row of leather chairs that made up a small waiting area. In front of her was a glass coffee table with a selection of newspapers and magazines. Among them was a pamphlet for the West Midlands Police force, the front cover illustrating – through a series of small glossy photos – some of the force's bigger recent busts, together with various community schemes they were involved in. Dani didn't bother to pick it up. She didn't need to see stories of the public faces of the force. The jolly PCs always ready to help an old lady across the road with a smile and a wave. What she saw in her job was far too grim and sinister to ever make it into a corporate style newsletter.

Dani looked back over to Bill. He'd finished on the phone and was now talking to someone else – a man in his sixties dressed in casual clothes. Bill looked confused and a little disgruntled, like the man was asking him to do something he couldn't. Dani watched them for a few seconds, trying to figure out what they were talking about, trying to get her detective brain firing again. In the end, coming up with nothing much, she turned away and looked expectantly at the security gates and the corridor beyond.

Not long after, she saw a familiar face approaching from the other side. DI Susan Fletcher. At one time Dani would have gone so far as to say they were friends; they occasionally socialised outside of work, although Dani had sensed in the past that Fletcher had a bit of a bee in her bonnet about Dani being seemingly favoured by the top brass above the other DIs in the team. It was an unspoken angst, and one which had never resulted in any kind of open disagreement. That had been more than two years ago, though, and Dani hadn't seen Fletcher at all for months now, once the initial well-wishes had dried up. Not that Dani had tried contacting Fletcher since then either.

As Dani watched her colleague she felt a pinch of grievance. Dani had taken the early morning call and hotfooted it out to the crime scene in Moseley, but Ledford's throwaway comment about Fletcher being joint SIO on the murder case had rattled her, though if it was true, the decision would have been McNair's not Fletcher's. Either way, Dani was sure she would soon be brought fully into the loop.

Fletcher touched a small plastic card to the reader on one of the gates and the low glass doors slid open. She walked through and smiled when she saw Dani.

Dani got to her feet and smiled back, but that smile faltered when she noticed Fletcher's hand smooth down the fabric of her dress around her waist. Fletcher had always been slim, like Dani was, but there was now a clear bump on her belly. She was pregnant. Maybe five, six months. Dani felt a lump in her throat. Dani had always seen Fletcher as a close peer. Career driven but grounded, they'd shared so many similarities. But just how far had their lives now drifted? Fletcher had the looks. The charm. The job. The husband. The home. And now a child.

What did Dani have?

Not that she was jealous. More disappointed in herself, and the way that her life had turned out so differently to how she'd expected it would.

As Fletcher came up to her and reached out to hug her long-time colleague, it was almost impossible for Dani to stop the welling tears from flowing.

Chapter Three

'Murder. A simple word. A simple concept. Stop any passer-by in the street and they could tell you what it means. But you have to pay close attention to the definition to really understand the word.'

Professor Steven Grant paused for dramatic effect and looked around the grand lecture theatre. The room in the redbrick building on the University of Birmingham campus could hold close to two hundred people, but today there were barely forty. And half of those looked on the verge of sleep.

'Murder,' he said again. 'Can anyone give me a definition?'

Many faces in the room remained blank. Just three hands went up. Grant chose the young man sitting on the back row.

'The unlawful premeditated killing of one human being by another.'

Grant was actually impressed, even though it was a simple question.

'Thank you,' he said. 'So let us think about that. Unlawful. Because there are circumstances where a human being can take the life of another lawfully. Which circumstances?'

'War,' someone shouted out.

'Yes. And?'

'Capital punishment,' said a young woman on the front row. Grant held her eye for a second.

'Yes. Anything else?' No more volunteers this time. 'In particular circumstances, self-defence might be lawful killing too.'

One or two nods.

'Ok, and the next part of the definition: premeditated. Because killing someone accidentally or through negligence or otherwise unintentionally isn't murder. Murder requires some level of intention and forethought, whether it's days, weeks, months, or even just seconds.'

Another pause. No reaction from the room.

'And the final part? The killing of one human being by another. An animal killing a human isn't murder, just like a human being killing an animal isn't. Cruel and unlawful, very possibly, but not murder.'

Grant stared out at the room, from student to student, assessing who was paying attention. Not many of them, it seemed. The first year undergraduates in front of him were a mishmash from the law, psychology and other social science degree programmes on offer at the university. The module Grant was leading was relevant for all of their studies, but he could count on his fingers the number of students who sat through his lectures with genuine interest.

What more did these overprivileged, self-important millennial brats want from him? Perhaps they'd spotted the criminology module (which, to be fair, was heavily weighted towards the macabre, given Grant's area of expertise) in the university brochure and seen an opportunity for morbid voyeurism, a chance to learn about some of the most gruesome crimes in modern history so they could revel in the horrific potential of human beings while chatting away to their chums over a pint of beer or a glass of cheap wine in the pub, and were now disappointed that they were actually there to learn.

Grant would admit there was plenty of the gory side of criminality to come in his lectures, but he was there to do a job, not to provide social ammunition. He was there to teach these cretins something useful that they could take forwards to whatever jobs they thought they'd be getting at the end of their three years of mostly partying and lazing around watching daytime TV.

'Murder,' Grant said again. 'It's a simple word, with a seemingly straightforward definition. Yet a wide spectrum of circumstances and actions can lead to murder. The big question, the one we will be coming back to again and again here, is what makes a murderer?'

Grant took another pause as he began pacing. This time it was more to fill time than anything else. He still had two minutes on the clock.

'The question is too wide and vague for us to possibly give a sensible answer. Nonetheless, we all think we understand murder. We know what a murderer is, don't we? *We* are not murderers. We are *normal* human beings. Murderers are something quite different.'

Grant stopped moving and stood and glared out at the students.

'Aren't they? Would you know a murderer if you saw one?'

A few twitches from the crowd. Grant locked eyes with a male student on the second front row who had neatly coiffed hair and thick-rimmed glasses. He at least looked like a classic studious type. He was twitchy, as though he wanted to say something but was too shy to speak up in front of the others.

Grant scanned over the rest of the rabble, the mostly blank faces. No one was going to enter the debate now, not when it was so close to the end of the lecture.

'Ok, that's all for today,' Grant said.

The shuffling of bums and the slamming of folding seats was instantaneous and echoed through the large room barely a second after the words had passed Grant's lips. The lecture theatre would be deserted before he could even say 'suggested reading material for next week'.

Grant shook his head. When had he become so cynical anyway?

He detached his laptop from the wires on the podium then moved behind and over to his brown leather satchel and shoved the computer in. He picked the satchel up and turned, then jumped when he saw one of the students standing right there in front of him. Grant quickly realised he recognised this girl. She'd been sitting on the front row, one of the few who seemed enthralled by Grant's words. For three weeks now she'd sat on the same seat, keenly scribbling in her notebook in between long bouts of staring at him. Not the distant and uninterested stare that many of the other students gave, either. A stare which, as flattering as it was, terrified him.

'That was fascinating,' she said, and stuck out her hand. 'I'm Jessica Bradford.'

'Thanks,' Grant said, giving her hand a brief shake.

Grant looked across the room. It was now empty except for him, Jessica and another female student who was at the far end, at the top of the stairs, propping open the exit door and looking down at Jessica impatiently. Her friend, he realised.

'Criminology is a subject that's always interested me,' Jessica said. 'Though I guess it's not an easy subject to get into.'

She said it almost apologetically, as though it was her fault that most of her fellow students were idiots.

'I think a lot of your friends are going to find that out the hard way.'

'I don't think it helps that the class is so early on a Monday morning. I think you drew the short straw there.'

'I've been doing this for a few years,' Grant said. 'Believe me, when you're lecturing first year undergraduates there's never really a good time. At least half of the students are always asleep or deeply distracted, picking their noses. I count myself lucky to be teaching something that's at least vaguely interesting and accessible. I pity the maths tutors.'

Jessica gave a little laugh and looked coyly down at her feet. Grant smiled and looked back up to Jessica's friend who rolled her eyes at her friend's awkward performance. Grant felt like he was about to be asked to dinner or something. In fact, he was terrified of being put in a compromising situation, or even an innocent situation which could be even remotely construed as compromising.

Why was that his immediate thought?

'I was hoping you could sign this for me,' Jessica said, taking a paperback from her book bag.

Grant looked at the book. The edges were frayed, the front cover bent, the pages yellowed. The book was not just a few years old but well used. Grant smiled again, with genuine surprise and warmth, when he realised what it was.

He looked at his own name, then at the title; *The Essence of Evil*.

'Where on earth did you find that?' he asked.

'I've had it for years. I told you, I've always had an interest in the subject. I don't know why.'

Grant took the book from her hands and quickly leafed through it. He'd not had one of his students bring him a copy in years. He noticed that she'd used pencil to underline sentences and circle whole sections on many of the pages. This wasn't just an interesting read for her, but a learning tool. Grant was impressed. Perhaps there was hope after all.

He took a pen from his shirt pocket and went to the title page. He scribbled his signature in big letters and made a brief dedication in her name. When he handed the book back Jessica beamed from ear to ear.

'Thank you so much!' she said. 'My mum will be so jealous. She knew you, back in the day.'

'Really? Where from?'

'From Durham uni, when you were first studying. Before… you know.'

'Wow. A long time ago then.'

'Her name was Elizabeth Fonte then.'

The name meant nothing to Grant so he just smiled and nodded.

'Say hi to her from me,' he said.

Grant checked the clock on the wall. A nervous reaction. He didn't have anything to get to but he was now feeling increasingly uncomfortable by her fan-girling. The last thing he needed in life right now was the affection of a teenage girl and all the risks that could bring.

Jessica looked over her shoulder at her friend, who gave a clear 'come *on*' look.

'I really appreciate it,' Jessica said, clutching the signed book to her chest. 'And I was wondering... I'd like to come and see you in your office when you're free.'

Grant frowned. 'How do you mean?'

'I had an idea for a thesis subject that I wanted to talk to you about.'

'Thesis? You don't need to be thinking about that just yet.'

Jessica looked thrown by that.

'But I do admire your eagerness. Come over after noon today, if you like. Otherwise it would have to be tomorrow.'

'No, that's great! I'll see you then.'

Grant watched Jessica turn and tootle off up the stairs and out of the lecture theatre with her stroppy friend.

Private tutoring to a keen nineteen-year-old? What could possibly go wrong?

Chapter Four

Day 71

The snarl on his face is pure rage. Animalistic and sinister. He bares his teeth like a rabid dog. This is a man I've known my whole life, but I don't recognise him at all right now. And I'm terrified. Terrified of what he's going to do. Terrified of what he's already done. Terrified that I shared a womb with this person. My twin brother, Ben. Terrified that I grew up with him, that I've known him for more than thirty years and have never understood or suspected what lay beneath.

The phone is in my hand. I need to call for help, but I'm too scared to move. Not just scared for myself but for Gemma, upstairs. For the kids. At least they aren't here tonight.

I can't even look at the phone properly to make the call as I can't take my eyes off him.

Then he lunges forwards. My defence is pathetic. It happens too quickly and I'm too shocked. I try to outmanoeuvre him; to get him into an arm bar and subdue him. I'm trained for this shit. But I can't stop this man. This animal. He grabs my head and slams it against the doorframe. The next second I'm on the ground. My head throbs with pain and confusion. Blood clouds my vision.

I realise he's standing over me but I'm too dazed to do anything other than stare into his cold and heartless eyes.

I see the stone ornament in his hand. I see it hurtling towards my head. The heavy object smashes into my skull with a horrific crack and squelch…

–

My head shoots up from the pillow. I'm panting. Sweating. It takes barely a second for me to figure out where I am. The hospital. Where else?

The memory, the daily nightmare, still flickers away even though I'm now awake. The look on his face. The sound of the impact. The feel of it... so strange because it wasn't pain, but almost a warm, wet feeling, like someone was enveloping my brain with a cosy towel.

Slowly I manage to push the thoughts, the memories of Ben and what he's done, away.

I've been in here for ten weeks now, and every day starts with this same routine, the same nightmare for me. But today is going to be different as it's the first day I'm making an entry in this diary. Just another of the many elements in my seemingly endless road to recovery.

Seventy-one days. That's how long I've been in this damn hospital already. Just over ten weeks ago, at the hands of my twin brother, I suffered a traumatic brain injury. TBI for short. A cerebral contusion that caused severe damage – bruising – to the frontal lobes of my brain. That's the area of the brain that governs my speech, personality, movement and memory. The doctors say what comes next is unpredictable, though it's likely I'll never fully recover.

Short and long term memory loss. Short attention span. Mood swings. Depression. Confusion. Restlessness. These are just a few of the symptoms that will pervade my rehabilitation, possibly the rest of my life.

I'll never be the same as I was and nor will my life, even though the doctors say I've made incredible progress already. In the last few weeks I've already had to relearn how to breathe on my own without a ventilator, to eat and drink without pipes, to walk, to talk again. I'm officially a TBI survivor now.

Often my body still feels next to useless, as though it doesn't really belong to me, and even now as I write here, the pain in my fingers and my hand and my arm and my head is immense. I'm concentrating so hard on such a seemingly simple task.

Yet the biggest hurdle that remains in my bid for recovery isn't physical, but mental – I need to learn how to be me again. That will be my hardest task. Perhaps an impossible one.

I'm lucky to be alive. Or so I'm told. I don't feel lucky...

I remember those moments when Ben tried to kill me with absolute horrific clarity, yet memories of the events leading up to then, and the weeks that have followed in this place, are so much more patchy. Non-existent in places, though things are coming back to me all the time.

The best way that I can describe it is that my memories of the last few weeks are like rivers and streams. The smaller, more distant streams are just snippets. Someone's voice, calling my name, but no image to go with it. A vision of a recognisable face, without any sounds or context.

The streams sometimes connect, sometimes become longer and clearer; eventually the streams in my mind form rivers that are longer still and flow more naturally. I remember conversations, I remember moving, I remember doing things. But how much of it is real and how much is my mashed-up brain playing tricks on me I just can't be sure. And it scares me.

I'm told that much of what I said and did in the first few weeks after I woke from my induced coma was incoherent. I talked nonsense. I had no idea where I was or what had happened. Frequently I thought I was still in the middle of a murder investigation. That the culprit was hiding in the hospital and I was undercover and had to go from room to room looking for him. Other times I was at the police station. I'd been knocked down by a madman trying to escape. I had to get back up, to run after him before he got away.

I guess that's not too far from the truth really.

Any time I got over-excited, or refused to return to my room, I'd get more and more angry, more and more uncontrollable. I'm told several doctors and nurses were needed to physically restrain me, such was the power and focus in my body and my demented mind. Frequently I was strapped to my bed so that I couldn't hurt others, or myself.

I can't pinpoint where my memories, those rivers, actually tell the truth of what I've been through over the last ten weeks. My thoughts now, my actions, feel lucid and rational. At least to me. Yet that doesn't make this experience any less frightening.

Above everything I feel isolated here. Alone. I don't want to be in this place, physically or mentally, anymore.

I cry myself to sleep every night, and every time I wake I've just relived the moment my deranged twin brother tried to kill me once again.

With no end in sight to this pain and suffering, I just don't know where I can go from here.

Was I really worth saving, for this?

Chapter Five

Dani and Fletcher walked side by side through HQ. The well-worn corridors were a world away from the brand spanking new foyer, and, as in the past, were pervaded by a musty smell that Dani knew well but couldn't describe. Despite the familiar territory, it felt anything but a usual day, and Dani felt not only alienated but disorientated too by the clash of familiar and unfamiliar.

When she moved through into the open-plan space used by the Homicide team on Force CID, Dani tensed up. She looked around the room, at the faces. A lot of people paid her no attention at all. Some smiled and greeted her, like they would a long-lost friend. Others simply looked on with curious fascination at the copper back from the dead.

Some of the people Dani didn't recognise, most she did. Especially the man who stood up at his desk and stared over at her expectantly. Jason. He smiled, and opened his mouth to speak, but Dani, feeling her heart lurch, turned away from him and carried on to DCI McNair's office with her head down. She cursed herself inwardly for acting like such a schoolgirl, but she'd realised as soon as her eyes met Jason's that she really wasn't prepared for *that* conversation yet. Today was tough enough already.

-

Ten minutes later Dani was sitting in McNair's office on the fourth floor of HQ, looking out at a new, gleaming glass office block above Snowhill Station. Where had that sprung from?

The door opened and McNair came into the room. HQ and the buildings around it may have changed but McNair had somehow found herself stuck in a time warp. She looked the same now to Dani as she had ten years ago when they'd first met: a smart but not exactly tailored blue suit, short grey hair, droopy eyelids that hid otherwise beady eyes, and a forehead with lines that deepened whenever her temperature rose. Which was often.

Dani had never had a big problem with her hard-nosed boss. The way Dani saw it, McNair's often fiery temperament was something of a necessity. McNair, now in her early fifties, had joined the force when it was a different beast. In those days the only way for a female officer to be taken seriously and get ahead was to be a ruthless ball-buster; to be not as hard as the men, but harder. Times had moved on, thankfully, and now more and more female officers were taking senior positions, though in many ways the male-centric atmosphere remained.

Dani had never seen herself as a McNair apprentice, a future ball-buster, though she knew many of her male – and some female – colleagues had previously believed that to be the case, largely due to the fact that she'd been so career focused and one of the youngest DIs on the force when first promoted. Plus she was unmarried, despite being closer to forty now than to thirty. Clearly there must be something seriously wrong with any such woman. Or she must be a lesbian. That was the other common idiotic assumption that Dani had endured over the years – not helped by the fact that she drank beer and watched sport. The truth was that she'd been too focused on her career to have met a decent man to settle down with. Until Jason. But look at how that had turned out.

McNair came forwards and Dani got to her feet and shook her boss's hand.

'DI Stephens, it's good to have you back,' McNair said, her face betraying no emotion as she went around her desk and sat back down.

'It feels good to be back, ma'am,' Dani said, cringing inwardly at her use of the formal title, which was becoming less and less common. She herself hated it when others addressed her as ma'am, it made her feel like a batty old woman.

'And I'm sure there are plenty on the team who will be glad to see you've returned.'

Dani noticed a twinkle in McNair's eye. Was she talking about Jason? Or maybe Dani was reading too much into her words.

'Take a seat.'

Dani did so and noticed McNair's eyes narrowing as she inspected Dani, as though weighing up whether or not she approved of what she saw. Dani looked away and around the sparse office. There were no picture frames, or knick-knacks, or personal effects of any kind. Just shelves crammed with ring binders and books about good policing and other such theory. Two large aerial shots of Birmingham hung on the walls.

'I'm sure it's been a hell of a time for you,' McNair said.

'Not the best two years of my life, that's for sure. But I'm back. And I just want you to treat me like anyone else.'

'Of course,' McNair said, though the unease on her face suggested something different. 'You'll fit right back in here, no problems.'

'I'm sure I will too.'

'I know you've been cleared by the...'

'Shrink?'

'Well, that wasn't the word I would have used. I know you've been cleared by the *shrink*, but I want to hear it from you too.'

'I'm fine. Really. The amount of meds they've got me on I'm virtually indestructible.'

Dani laughed nervously. McNair didn't even flinch. Dani wondered whether her words had been the wisest. Would the higher powers look upon her ongoing medication with raised eyebrows?

'I'm guessing you think I'm ready too, otherwise you wouldn't have been calling me so early this morning,' Dani said.

Thinking again about how Fletcher was involved in the Jane Doe case, though, she wondered whether perhaps McNair didn't really think she was quite ready after all. Should she ask about that?

McNair held Dani's gaze until Dani looked away, out of the window.

'Is there anything I need to know?' McNair asked.

'About what?'

'About… you know. Traumatic brain injury. Any precautions we need to take, any—'

Dani had never seen McNair look so uncomfortable. Like a mother trying to explain sex to a teenage son.

'All you need to know is that I'm here.'

'I understand TBI is something that people rarely fully recover from, I—'

'I don't need, or want any special treatment,' Dani said, realising she sounded as irritated as she felt. 'Please. I just want to get my life back.'

McNair held Dani's eye for a few seconds before giving a slight nod. Then she reached down to a drawer and took out some papers. She pushed the small bundle across the desk.

'You could say it's good timing. You probably noticed Fletcher is pregnant.'

'I did.'

'She's only got two weeks until she goes on leave.'

Which would likely place her at way more than five or six months, Dani decided, despite the still manageable looking bump.

'To ease you back in I've teamed you with Fletcher. You'll be joint SIO on some of her recent open cases.'

'And today's Jane Doe? Given it's a new case, I thought—'

'Yes, that too. We need to ease you back in. Fletcher is good enough and smart enough to give you the space you need.'

Dani found herself nodding. As imperfect as the tag team sounded, it was clear McNair had already decided on it, so it would be useless to try and persuade her otherwise.

'Fletcher will give you the lowdown on the cases. I'll also be assigning some of her workload to DI Barnes.'

'DI?'

McNair nodded in confirmation.

DI Barnes. Jason. He'd been barely a DS when Dani had first been promoted to Detective Inspector. They'd worked closely together for years, Dani as Jason's supervisor. They'd been an item for six months when she'd been hospitalised. Even though she'd not seen or spoken to him in months now, how could she not even know he'd been promoted? She wasn't sure whether she was more angry at him or at herself for not knowing.

Now, as a DI, Jason was her peer. She should have been happy for him. He was a decent guy and good at his job. No, he was great at his job. For some reason though, Dani felt a little betrayed. By Jason or by McNair, she wasn't sure. It riled her that the world had moved on so quickly while she was stuck in place. A dark place at that.

At one time she'd been the rising star on Force CID. Not anymore, it seemed.

'Tell me what you know from this morning.'

Dani did so, giving both the facts, and also the hypothesis of the young victim having been kidnapped and held hostage before escaping. McNair said nothing as Dani talked.

'So what next?' McNair said when Dani had finished.

'We'll know more when the post-mortem is completed, and when the local searches are done. Forensics will take a while longer. In the meantime we need to get working on identifying the victim.'

'I agree. We'll organise a press conference, probably for later today, to hopefully get some leads.'

'We should also pay a visit to Missing Persons.'

'I'll leave that to you,' McNair said.

An awkward silence followed and Dani wondered if she was missing something.

'Anything else?' McNair prompted.

'No. I'll keep you posted.'

Dani got to her feet and headed for the door.

'Oh, and DI Stephens.'

Dani stopped at the door.

'I'm glad you're… ok.'

Dani said nothing to that.

Chapter Six

The knock on Grant's office door came a few seconds before a minute past twelve. 'Keen' didn't quite do justice to Jessica Bradford's level of enthusiasm, it seemed. Grant pushed the clutter of papers off his desk, stuffed them into a drawer and got up from his chair. He walked across his meagre office that was only just big enough for the battered pine desk, two chairs and one bookcase. He opened the door and there was Jessica, with her chaperone once more. The friend looked Grant up and down, an air of hostility about her.

'I guess I'll see you later then, Jess,' she said.

'I'll call you when I'm done. We'll get lunch.'

'Sure.'

Her friend – Grant had no idea of her name – sauntered off, leaving Grant feeling like a fifteen-year-old boy who'd just been scrutinised by a crush's mate. At least he'd passed the test, it seemed.

'Come in,' Grant said.

Jessica walked into his office, and he shut the door behind her and indicated the seat in front of his desk.

'So what can I do for you?' he said, walking around the desk and taking his own seat.

'I had an idea for what I want my thesis to be about. I thought maybe we could discuss the concept.'

'It's very early to be thinking about that, Jessica.' He noticed a flash of unease on her face at him quashing her enthusiasm. 'But it's good that you're so keen. So what's it about?'

'Murder.'

Grant felt himself tighten up, though he should have guessed this would be the case.

'That's a pretty wide subject.'

'Well, not just murder. I want to really challenge the common thinking of what makes a person take another's life.'

'Nature versus nurture?'

'Yeah, I guess.'

'That's a pretty vast subject too.'

'I know, of course it is. The debate has been going on for… like, ever.'

'So what's your take going to be?'

'I want to explore whether some people really are just born that way.'

Grant nodded, though he was having a hard time figuring how her 'take' on the subject was in any way intriguing or different.

'Are there some people,' she said, 'who, no matter what their upbringing, what happens to them in life, would still end up as killers?'

'I'd say that happens a lot,' Grant said. 'Many murders are simple crimes of passion. Seemingly normal and otherwise law-abiding citizens flip.'

'No, that's not what I'm getting at. Those sorts of murders are caused by pressure, and they are usually just one act, at one time. What about people who have no pressure? No motivation like revenge or hate, or even any other real causal factors?'

Grant interlaced his fingers and sat back in his seat while he studied Jessica for a few moments. She held his gaze the whole time.

'Well, what do *you* think?' Grant asked.

'I really don't know. I don't know the subject as well as you do yet. But I was hoping you could help me. Teach me.'

'Do you want to know what I think, or what I'd be prepared to write down in a scientific paper? The two answers might be surprisingly different.'

Jessica looked slightly put out by that response.

'What you really think,' she said.

'Ok,' he said. 'There are eight billion people in this world. Many more billions have lived and died here. Every single one of those billions is different in some way. Different DNA, different geography, different language, different culture, different upbringing, different experiences. There are infinite possibilities therefore as to how each person will turn out. And really, while as psychologists or criminologists or sociologists we love to put each one of those people into brackets, into defined groups with defined characteristics, I'm just not sure that it can work in every single case.'

Jessica looked at him quizzically like she wasn't quite sure of his point.

'So you do think some people are just inherently bad right from the start, no matter what?' she said.

'I do.'

'Do you know of anyone who you'd put into that bracket then?'

Grant thought again.

'Dennis Nilsen, perhaps?' Jessica prompted.

Grant raised an eyebrow. He was impressed with Jessica's knowledge. Though he wasn't sure 'impressed' was really the right reaction to a young student who took a fascination with serial killers.

Nilsen was one of the UK's most infamous murderers, convicted in the 1980s of murdering six men, but believed to have killed many more. And he hadn't just killed, but had performed rituals with the bodies. For days and weeks after death he bathed them, dressed them and did who knows what else before eventually dissecting them and disposing of the remains.

'Apparently,' Jessica said, 'in one of the interviews after he was arrested, when he was asked about why he'd murdered the men—'

'He said, "I'm hoping you will tell me that".'

Jessica smiled. 'And he also spoke about how he felt no thrill or happiness in killing people. He wasn't doing it for kicks. He simply felt compelled to murder. So don't you think he fits the mould of a born killer?'

'In many ways I'm absolutely sure he does,' Grant said. 'His crimes were abhorrent, and even he couldn't justify them in any logical way. But, I think there were still triggers in his life that made him like that. I'm not sure he was born that way.'

'Such as?'

'Such as bereavement when his grandfather passed when he was a child. His closet homosexuality which, in that day and age, left him isolated and resentful. If you read his interviews with the police you can see how his sexuality severely damaged his ability to generate what we would consider normal and healthy relationships with others, both sexual and non-sexual.'

Jessica looked slightly disappointed again, not because she disagreed with Grant but because he'd so easily knocked back her suggestion.

'Although,' said Grant, 'you have to be wary of analysing these people with hindsight. It's easy to look for the faults and the triggers in their past and put two and two together. Which then clouds the issue of whether they really were born killers, inherently evil, or if environmental factors led them to kill. It's a difficult subject to analyse.'

'But you did say you believed such born killers exist.'

'I do.'

'But you have no proof? You don't know of anyone who fits that profile?'

Grant looked away and thought about that question for a good while.

'No,' he said, eventually. 'But that doesn't mean they aren't out there.'

He noticed a look of disquiet on Jessica's face. He sensed she was about to say something else, but then his phone jumped up and down on the desk. He grabbed it and glanced at the screen.

'Sorry, I've got to take this,' he said. He got up from the desk and turned and walked to the window, looking out over the car park below. 'Hi,' Grant said as he accepted the call.

Mary, Grant's wife, didn't say anything and for a couple of seconds he thought her call had already gone through to voice-mail. But then the sound of breathing came down the line.

'Mary, what's wrong?' he said.

'Steven, please come home. I really need you. It's Ethan.'

'What's he done now?' Grant said through gritted teeth, already feeling anger rise.

He turned and saw Jessica staring. She quickly looked away.

'Please, can you just come home?'

'Ok. I'm on my way.'

Chapter Seven

Dani checked her watch. Time to go. She got up from her desk and packed up her things, keeping her head down as she did so. Since she had arrived, one or two of her colleagues had come over to say hi, but she'd deliberately kept the conversations to the point, and hadn't yet built up the courage to properly chat to anyone. Now she just wanted to get out to her next appointment at Missing Persons.

As she made a beeline for the exit she sensed the approach from her right. She was glad when she looked up and saw it was Fletcher, not Jason.

'You're off to Harborne?' Fletcher asked.

'Yeah. How—'

'McNair mentioned it.'

Dani resisted rolling her eyes.

'I can come with you, if you like.'

No. That really wasn't what Dani wanted at all. She didn't need a chaperone, or a watcher, or a helping hand. She just wanted to be left alone. No, more than that, she wanted to prove herself, if she was just given the space. But she also didn't want to ruffle feathers so soon after her return.

'Fine,' Dani said.

–

Dani drove. To start with the two DIs were somewhat cheery and chatty as they caught up, but the initial novelty of seeing each other after so long quickly wore off and awkwardness crept in. The *massive* elephant remained in the room – or car. Sooner or later they'd have to talk about it. And that would be the case with every one of Dani's colleagues.

Dani glanced over at Fletcher and caught her staring at the scar, much like Bill and Easton had earlier. Christ, how long was she going to have to deal with this? Yeah, it was only her first day but did everyone have to be so damn obvious?

'I'm glad you're ok,' Fletcher said, quickly looking back to the road. Dani gritted her teeth. How many times had she already heard that same line today? 'I don't know how I could've coped with... what happened.'

'I don't have a choice but to cope,' Dani said, putting her foot down as the light turned green.

'You were lucky.'

'No. Not really.'

'Just be glad that he got what he deserved, eventually. And that was all down to you.'

'What he deserved? I'm not too sure about that.'

'He can't harm anyone now.'

'But the problem is, Susan, the damage has already been done.'

–

They soon arrived in Harborne, just a few miles from the centre of Birmingham. Dani parked up in the staff car park and stepped out, eyeing up the building in front of her. It looked like a bog standard 1980s redbrick office block, and dominated the otherwise residential street that was crammed with simple terraced houses. The station was bustling with activity. The sprawling building housed not just the local nick for the suburb, but also several of West Midlands Police's administrative and specialist teams, Missing Persons among them.

DI Gregory, a slightly overweight man in his forties with thin hair on top of his head but an almost impossibly thick goatee beard covering his chin, met Dani and Fletcher outside. The three shook hands. Gregory didn't let on that he recognised Dani, though she could see that telltale look in his eyes that told her he knew who she was. The Homicide and Missing Persons teams worked closely together, most often when an unidentified body was found. But Dani hadn't met Gregory before, and Fletcher too had said in the car that she didn't know him, suggesting he was a recent addition to the team.

Gregory escorted them inside and up the stairs to the third floor.

'I've asked one of my DSs, Jane Carr, to join us too,' he said as they headed across the somewhat outdated open-plan office space. 'She's much more into the detail than I am on a lot of the cases.'

They moved through into a smaller enclosed office, which contained three desks with a round meeting table in the middle.

'This is Carr's office, along with the other DSs on the team. I think the others are both off out somewhere so we'll camp in here for now. Carr was grabbing some stuff from the printer. Please, take a seat.'

Dani and Fletcher did so, and sure enough, a moment later Carr appeared in the doorway. Dani and Fletcher got to their feet and shook hands with the new arrival. Dani stared at Carr as they all took their seats. Carr was a few years younger than Dani and a similar height and build, though with long, straight red hair and a face that was dominated by freckles. There was an eagerness about her, in her expression and her mannerisms. She was basically the copper – keen and dedicated and destined for great things – that Dani used to be. That Dani still wanted to be.

'DI Stephens briefly explained on the phone what you're after,' Gregory said, 'but you'll probably need to be a bit more specific if you want us to give you anything useful.'

Fletcher opened her mouth to speak, but Dani jumped in. 'Initially all we need is a list of any missing persons cases from the last six months that involved a female, fifteen to thirty years old.'

Dani had deliberately set the parameters to ID her Jane Doe wider than strictly necessary, not wanting to miss anything by going narrow.

'You'd be surprised how many hits that simple search gets,' Gregory said.

'How many?'

'Hundreds. People go missing in all sorts of circumstances. Young, old, male, female. Something like two hundred thousand a year across the country.'

'But most turn up soon after?' Dani said. 'We're only interested in the ones still missing.

'Most do. If they're not found within the first forty-eight to seventy-two hours, then the chances that they turn up alive diminishes significantly with every day that passes. Statistically speaking, at least. I'm sure you know all this, though.' Dani and Fletcher both nodded. 'Some turn up months or years later, but generally not. There's often a story with the people who remain missing. Problems in their lives, whether it's drugs or alcohol or work or relationships.'

'Or they've been killed,' Dani said.

Gregory just shrugged at that.

'Here's the list that matches your search,' Carr said, passing two sheets of A4 to Dani. There weren't hundreds, as Gregory had intimated, but there were still a lot more than Dani had expected. She stared at the list of names for a few moments. Next to each one was various bits of information including the date last seen, date of birth, an address, and a brief physical description. Dani honed in on four in particular, based on their ages and the dates they'd gone missing. One had disappeared just a few days ago.

'And all these are missing without a trace?' Dani asked.

'Mostly, yes,' Carr said. 'Of course we put extra effort into the cases where it looks like we can actually do something. And for those people we see as being particularly vulnerable. Children, et cetera.'

'And the others?'

'We do what we can,' Carr said. 'But we're not a big team. We can't devote endless resources to cases where we simply have nothing useful to go on. By that I mean where the disappearance was out of character and out of the blue, and where there hasn't been any kind of evidence of movement since. Often you find sporadic mobile phone usage. Or use of credit cards, that sort of thing, even if just for a short period of time. For many cases, though, there isn't a sniff of where the people went, or why.'

'Technically speaking, a person can be declared dead when they've been missing seven years,' Gregory added, 'so these are all active cases.'

'Or earlier, of course, if there's some evidence of death but no body as such,' Carr butted in. 'Like in a plane crash or something similar.'

'Thank you, DS Carr,' Gregory said, his tone not particularly friendly. 'My point was that as a team we'd consider many of the people in these cases to be dead much sooner than seven years. From our point of view there really isn't any justification in spending time on these problem cases even after a few weeks. At least not without new information.'

Dani wondered why Gregory had felt the need to point that out again, as though justifying why his team was unable to locate these people. She didn't feel he was wrong for doing so. The weight of knowing they couldn't realistically do anything to help these people was the same weight Dani had felt countless times in her career when she knew there was a killer out there that they had to catch, but hadn't yet.

'What can you tell me about Grace Agnew?' Dani asked, pointing to the name on the sheet.

Carr shuffled through the papers in front of her and found the profile she was looking for. She turned it around for Dani to see. There was a small colour picture attached. It certainly looked to Dani like it could be the same person as her Jane Doe. Female, young, blonde. But there were probably another twenty on the list that also fitted that bill.

'Twenty-six years old,' Carr said. 'Has been missing for nearly three weeks now. She lives in Bournville in a rented apartment with another young lady. She went out for a few drinks with a group of friends after work. She took a train home from Birmingham with one of those friends, Victoria Neville, who'd got off the train at the previous stop, University.'

'So you know Grace Agnew got off the train in Bournville?' Dani asked.

'We think we can identify her on CCTV leaving the station, yes. We can't be conclusive because the cameras didn't capture her face very well, but the height, build and clothing match what we know about her.'

'And? Was she alone?'

'Looked to be alone, yes. And it doesn't appear that any of the other people in shot were following her. We've been able to locate and speak to most of them without finding anything of interest. Her home was less than half a mile from the station, but there are no cameras around there once you get out onto the streets. She left the view of the cameras and just... disappeared.'

Dani looked over to Fletcher whose brow was furrowed into a frown.

'And you don't think that's suspicious?' Dani said, her exasperation poorly concealed. 'A young woman alone at night disappears from the streets and no one's heard or seen from her since? I'd say there aren't that many possibilities really.'

'Who said we don't think it's suspicious?' Gregory said, quite defensively. 'We take every case we get very seriously.'

'But this matter hasn't been passed to Homicide, has it?'

'Why would it?' Gregory said. 'We have no evidence that she's been killed.'

'No, but the set of circumstances would tend to suggest something bad has happened to her, wouldn't you say?'

'I'm not sure what you're trying to get at here, DI Stephens,' Gregory said, his patience all but gone. 'We're doing everything we can with this, and with every other case, and we absolutely involve other departments when we have a reason to do so. By which I mean when we have *evidence*. I'm afraid for we don't have anything so far for this case.'

'Unless you're here to tell us otherwise,' Carr added, hopefully.

Dani sighed and sat back in her seat. Looking at the details, it was obvious that this woman had most likely come to harm. Wasn't it? Was it her Jane Doe? Maybe. Maybe not.

'There are three other cases in the last two months of females in their twenties disappearing at night within five miles of Birmingham city centre,' Dani said, realising that she was thinking out loud and making connections in her mind that really weren't all that well-founded.

'Look, DI Stephens,' Gregory said. 'I have a feeling I know the dots you're trying to connect here, and it's your call as to whether to go there and whether you want to waste time and effort in the process. If you have evidence that these people have been kidnapped or killed, and if you have evidence that the disappearances are in any way connected, then please tell us, and we'll help in any way we can. But currently, based on what we know, there simply isn't anything that we can do for these people.'

'And to ease your mind further,' Carr said. 'We do look for patterns in the data, all of the time. Locations, timings, age, sex, race, lifestyle. If we felt there was any connection here, any reason to believe these people had been killed, and by the same person, we would already have alerted you.'

Dani said nothing to that.

'Can we take those?' Dani asked, nodding at Carr's bundle of papers.

'Of course,' Gregory said. 'The full details of each case is in the HOLMES system too. CCTV, the lot.'

'Ok,' Dani said, getting to her feet. 'Thank you both for your time.'

'We're here to help,' Gregory said, his words at odds with his tone.

–

'So what do you think?' Fletcher asked Dani as they walked back towards the car.

'That we need to check all of these out. Speak to friends, family to see if any of these women is our Jane Doe.'

'Is that all you're looking to do? Or are you trying to suggest there's a link here between some of these other cases?'

Dani didn't answer that.

Fletcher checked her phone.

'Shit. I really need to get back to HQ.'

Dani raised an eyebrow. 'Anything I should know about?'

Fletcher went to say something but stopped herself. 'No. It's nothing, really.'

As if on cue Dani's phone buzzed too. She lifted it from her pocket. It was Easton calling.

'You carry on,' Fletcher said. 'I'll get an Uber back.'

'You sure?' Dani asked, holding the phone up to her ear, her finger hovering over the button to accept the call.

'Yeah. Don't worry.'

Fletcher turned and headed off without another thought. Dani answered the call.

'You're not going to believe this,' Easton said.

'I'm not?'

'The old lady. Mrs Staunton. She found a bruise on her neck. I'm no doctor but I'm pretty damn sure it's from a syringe. She was drugged.'

'I'm coming now.'

She pulled the phone away from her ear and looked back over to Fletcher who was wobbling along the road towards the high street, one hand on her belly.

'Are you sure you don't want a lift?' Dani shouted.

Was it her imagination or was Fletcher being deliberately shady? Wanting to butt in on Dani's new case but unwilling to be open about what else she was up to, even though McNair had suggested Dani should be sharing her colleague's workload? Or Maybe Dani was just being overly sensitive given how vulnerable she was still feeling about her return to her old life.

'I'm fine,' Fletcher said, not turning around.

Dani shook her head and pushed the thought away. The truth was, right then she was more focused on what Easton had just said anyway.

She opened her car door, sank down into the driver's seat and fired up the engine.

Chapter Eight

The sun cast a warm glow over the campus grounds as Grant rushed out of the building and across to his car, providing a sightly complement to the orange, red and brown hues of autumn colour in the many trees. Grant loved the old university campus, with its foliage and grassy fields and large traditional brick buildings, though on this occasion his mind was heavily distracted from the phone call with Mary.

He walked quickly around the groups of students milling about. He noticed eyes on him, people staring. Smirking too? He wasn't sure. Grant always felt as though people were looking at him, that they whispered about him as soon as his back was turned. The ex-celebrity who'd faded from the limelight to be just like every other schmuck.

Or was it his field of expertise that marked him as an outsider? An oddity?

Perhaps it was all just in his head. His own insecurities showing through. These kids, after all, were probably still shitting in nappies back when Grant was a somebody; would they really care enough to even give two hoots about him now?

He reached the car park, took the key from his satchel and climbed into the driver's seat of his battered Mercedes. He'd bought it new ten years ago and had never seen the point in changing it. The car did what it needed to do. People didn't buy houses every couple of years (well, some cretins who liked wasting money did) and similarly cars weren't a fashion accessory to Grant. They were a functional device and nothing more, no matter how much his wife had tried to persuade him to update.

The tired engine rattled to life and Grant headed out of the campus. As he drove away he became aware that he hadn't told any of his colleagues where he was going, or that he probably needed cover for his next lecture. That would have to wait. He was too fired up, too distracted to deal with that now.

Grant found his way to the A41 then sped along, heading away from Birmingham and towards his house in the leafy village of Knowle. The traffic in the middle of the day was light and he was soon turning onto his street. As he approached, Grant saw the front gates to the property were open. He drove through and parked the car on the gravel driveway. Mary's Honda was there, as was Ethan's motorbike. Feeling renewed anger at the sight of his son's loud and brash machine, Grant stepped from the car and crunched across the gravel.

The house was grand, redbrick. He and his wife, Mary, had bought it some fifteen years ago, at a time when Grant's prominence and earning power had only just started to wane. Back then it had felt like they belonged in the overtly wealthy neighbourhood, but more recently Grant had come to feel like something of an imposter, a feeling certainly not helped by their snooty – and often snoopy – neighbours.

Grant realised, as he drew the key from his pocket, that the weathered oak front door was already ajar. He slowly pushed it fully open then stepped inside.

'Mary?' he shouted out. There was no response. 'Annie?'

No response still, though he'd already assumed his teenage daughter wasn't in. She rarely was, though there was no doubt she was a good kid compared to their son.

Grant wiped his shoes on the doormat and continued across the wide, wood-floored hallway. Mary would normally scold him if she knew he hadn't taken his shoes off, but that was of little concern right now. He moved through into the large sun-filled lounge that looked out over their expansive lawned garden. The room was empty and Grant was about to turn back around when he spotted movement outside the windows.

Ethan. He was facing away from the house. A cigarette dangled from one hand. His phone was clasped in the other, held up close to his chin the way youngsters often did, not realising that the whole world *didn't* want to hear their discussions broadcast on loud speaker.

Grant balled his fists in anger. How sad it was that the mere sight of his son could do that now. Years of pent up anger and frustration were barely below the surface anymore. The worst of it was, many outsiders would probably say father and son were as bad as each other. Grant was aware of how angry he was already.

Yet he wasn't the one who routinely stepped well beyond the boundaries of reasonable behaviour. At least not without provocation.

'Mary!' Grant shouted out again. There was still no response but Grant now heard a creaking floorboard directly above, in his and Mary's bedroom.

Grant turned and headed for the staircase. He took the steps two at a time and then bounded along the landing to the master bedroom. The door was closed. He reached out and turned the handle. It was locked. He banged on the door.

'Mary, it's me. Open the door.'

He heard nothing for a few seconds.

'Mary?'

Then there was the sound of shuffling inside. It took an age for her to come from wherever she'd been. The bed, the en suite? Eventually he heard the lock being pulled back and the handle came down. The door inched open and Mary peeked out, holding the door open only a crack as though she was dubious of who was really on the other side and was ready to slam it shut if needed.

'Mary?'

He saw Mary's shoulder's slump, not in dejection but in relief. She opened the door and Grant could now see her fully. Tears were running down her cheeks, her eyes were bloodshot. The skin around her left temple was deep red and heavily swollen.

Grant's heart jumped in his chest. He grabbed his wife and pulled her to him.

'What's he done now?' Grant asked. His question was rhetorical, and Mary must have sensed that because she didn't even attempt to answer.

Although Grant wanted to stay and comfort his wife, his anger got the better of him. He let go of Mary. She took one look at his face – the fury on it – and knew what was coming.

'No, Steven, please. Don't!'

It was too late. Ignoring her pleas, Grant stormed back out of the room, down the stairs and into the kitchen.

Out in the garden Ethan was still yakking away on the phone. Grant flung open the patio door from the kitchen and Ethan spun around at the unexpected noise. His eyes narrowed when he spotted Grant.

'Dad.'

'You little—'

Grant swiped at the phone in Ethan's hand and it clattered onto the patio slabs, breaking into pieces.

'What's wrong with you?' Ethan shouted.

Grant grabbed his son by the neck and pushed him back two steps, more or less taking him clean off his feet. For a couple of seconds a panicked look swept across Ethan's face, but it was more surprise than real fear.

'Get the hell off me!' Ethan yelled, finding his feet. With one hand he yanked Grant's knuckles from around his neck and with the other he sent a balled fist towards his father's face.

Grant saw the punch coming and was able to duck enough to dodge the blow. He barrelled forwards and slammed into Ethan's chest. Ethan stumbled back and fell to the ground, landing on the pieces of his shattered phone. Grant got to his feet and stood over his son, snarling like a dog.

Ethan gritted his teeth, his eyes pinched with disdain. He was exactly the same height as his Dad at five ten, and he weighed about the same too. At only nineteen, though, he was lean and muscled in comparison to Grant, in his mid-forties. Yet as he stood over his son, what Grant lacked in youthful athleticism and strength he more than made up for in bubbling anger that seemed to be growing with each escalating indiscretion his son delivered at their door.

'Stop!'

At the sound of the shriek both men froze, but they didn't turn. Their eyes remained fixed on each other, both prepared for an attack.

'Just stop! Both of you.'

The exasperation in his wife's voice knocked the edge off Grant's rage. Really, what was he going to do? Pummel his son into the ground? It was hardly the best reaction, given it was his son's anger and miscreant nature that had catapulted them into this position in the first place. But someone had to put Ethan in his place.

'You've gone too far this time,' Grant growled.

'Me? What the hell about *you*?' Ethan clambered back to his feet and dusted himself down. 'You just assaulted me!'

'Are you taking the piss? *Look at her!*'

'I should call the police,' Ethan said.

'Maybe you should. Then you could explain why your mother has a black eye.'

'She came at me! Just like you did. You're mad, both of you.'

Grant turned around and looked over at Mary. She didn't react at all to what Ethan had said. Her lack of protest suggested maybe Ethan's words weren't entire fabrication.

'See? Told you. Self-defence, that is.'

Ethan was now smirking, though how he could find the situation in the least amusing, Grant had no idea. Did he actually get off on doing this sort of thing to his parents, who'd only ever loved him and wanted the best for him?

'If you *ever* touch her like that again…'

'You'll what?' demanded his son.

'I'll tear your damn head off.'

Ethan scoffed at that, and Grant clenched his fists again, trying to not rise to the bait.

'You know what?' Grant said, fighting to regain his cool. 'Just get out of here.'

'I only came for some of my stuff. You can't keep my stuff.'

'What stuff?'

'My clothes. My things. You can throw me out but you can't just take everything off me.'

Grant once again looked over at his wife for confirmation.

'Seems you've already given most of it away, though,' Ethan spat.

'We thought you didn't want it,' Mary said. 'It was just a bunch of old clothes.'

'Ethan, just get the hell out of my sight.'

'Fine, whatever. But you two owe me.'

'We don't owe you anything.'

Grant reached out and grabbed the sleeve of his son's jacket to pull him away. Ethan snatched his arm back and then turned and trudged towards Mary and the house. She was still crying and she moved to the side and hung her head as her only son stomped past her.

Grant kept pace behind, determined to see Ethan off the property before he went back to comfort Mary. He followed his son through the house and out the front door. Ethan began moving towards his motorbike but at the last second he stopped dead as though having a sudden change of heart. Grant stopped too and felt himself tense up again. Ethan turned around.

'Look, Dad, I need some money. Just a couple of hundred quid. I was going to sell my old things for it, but I can't do that now, can I?'

'Go, Ethan.'

'You're such an arsehole.'

'Takes one to know one.'

Just then Mary pushed past Grant and went up to Ethan.

'Here. Take it, then leave,' she said. She grabbed Ethan's hand and smacked a bundle of notes into his palm. Ethan didn't even thank her; he just looked at Grant and gave him a knowing smile.

Grant couldn't hold it together any longer. He went for his son. Leaping forwards, he balled his fist and swung back his arm and… never saw the punch from Ethan coming. Ethan's fist crashed into the side of Grant's head and before he knew it he was on his back, staring up at the blue sky.

'No!' Mary screamed, running over to her husband.

'You two are both fucking mental,' Ethan shouted.

Grant propped himself up on his elbow as Mary crouched down by his side. Ethan jumped onto his bike and fired up the engine. The raucous exhaust spat out a cloud of fuel vapour onto Mary and Grant, and Ethan tugged on the throttle, making the back wheel skid and kick up gravel as the bike lunged towards the front gates.

Only then, with Grant prone on the ground, did he notice his neighbour, Ed Francis, out across the street, doing a pretty bad job of pretending to prune a bush.

'Fuck's sake,' Grant said, turning away from Francis in disgust. He and Mary were already the talk of the street because of the numerous 'incidents' caused by their son recently, when he'd still been living with them. Even now he had supposedly left, he was still causing embarrassment at every turn. But being embarrassed in front of the neighbours was the least concerning aspect of the situation. Their son was out of control and becoming a bigger problem by the day.

'Are you ok?' Grant asked Mary, when Ethan's bike was out of sight.

She just shook her head and broke down once more. Grant got to his feet and pulled his wife into him, cradling her right there on the gravel. The neighbours could stare all they wanted. Sod them. None of this was his doing, or Mary's – it was Ethan's.

'I hate him,' Mary said. 'God, sometimes I really hate him. My own son.'

Grant just shook his head, not knowing how to respond to her words which cut right into his heart.

'No,' he said. 'No, you can't.'

'But I do,' Mary pulled her head back and looked into Grant's eyes. 'And do you know the worst part? I hate *myself* even more for feeling like this.'

Grant didn't say anything to that. What *could* he say?

He heard sirens. A few seconds later the flashing of blue lights was visible over the garden wall. The police car came into view at the gates and crunched to a stop on the road outside. Grant felt himself deflate further, if that was even possible.

His line of sight passed from the two police officers who emerged from the car and back across to the other side of the road. Ed Francis's hedge clippers lay on the tarmac, next to a pair of garden gloves, and Grant watched as his neighbour scuttled back towards his front door, glancing over his shoulder in disapproval as he went. Whether it was Francis or one of the other neighbours who'd called the police, Grant didn't know. One thing was for sure, though: within seconds there would be curtains twitching everywhere.

Chapter Nine

'What the hell was that all about then?' Easton spouted as he and Dani drove away from June Staunton's house.

Forensics had combed through the old lady's home and garden, taking whatever pictures and samples they saw fit. A technician had swabbed Mrs Staunton's neck, checked her body for other unusual marks, and taken a sample of blood and urine. The investigators had remained on site for several hours, by which point Mrs Staunton was not just terrified but shattered as well. Her son, a not exactly spritely young man himself, had been there when Dani arrived the second time around, giving his mother some much-needed comfort.

'I really don't know,' was all Dani could say to the question.

'It has to be the killer, don't you think? He was in there. With her. But why?'

Dani shivered at the thought of that shadow at the window. Had the killer of the Jane Doe really been so brazen as to have gone from the murder scene and broken into the home to drug an old lady so he could spy on the police?

And was spying really his plan or had there been another reason for drugging Mrs Staunton?

'He had the sedative with him already,' Dani said, thinking out loud.

'You're assuming that's what Mrs Staunton was injected with.'

'To be precise, we're assuming she was injected. We don't know that for sure yet either.'

'Fair enough.'

'But if she was, and if the culprit is the same person as who killed our victim, then…'

Dani lost the train of thought. As focused as she was, her brain simply wasn't yet used to working this hard again. But what on earth had they stumbled over?

They arrived at the gated address in the upmarket area of Little Aston, several miles north of Birmingham, an enclave of serious wealth just beyond the border of Birmingham City Council, but well within West Midland Police's jurisdiction. Grand residences on private roads were well hidden behind security walls and fences and sweeping manicured gardens.

'You sure this is the right place?' Easton quizzed, looking out of his window.

'Sat nav says so.'

'I heard Julio Romeu lives around here somewhere.'

'Julio who–lio?'

'New signing for Villa. You're not a football fan?'

'A big fan in the past. Kind of lost track recently, though, for obvious reasons.'

'Yeah. A lot of my mates were the same after we got relegated.'

Dani smirked but didn't say anything about the fact that he'd misunderstood what she'd thought was a pretty clear point.

'I still make appearances, though,' he continued. 'Habit as much as anything. Nice to do something with my old man too.'

'Probably half the team live around here somewhere,' Dani said. 'They've certainly got the money for it.'

She pushed the button and the window slid down. She pressed the intercom on the redbrick wall. After a few seconds a croaky male voice answered.

'DI Stephens from West Midlands police,' Dani said. 'We spoke earlier. About your daughter.'

'Come on in.'

The intercom clicked off and a moment later the wrought-iron security gates effortlessly swung open. Dani slowly turned the car along the twisting tarmac. After a hundred or so yards a glorious mock-Tudor house came into view.

'Bloody hell,' Easton said. 'He does what again?'

'Her, I believe,' Dani said. 'He's a property developer but apparently she was chief exec of some pharma start-up back in the nineties. Sold it for nearly nine figures to one of the big boys about ten years ago.'

Dani vaguely remembered reading about it in the local press at the time. The story of a self-made mega-rich local businesswoman was one that had hit a note with Dani at the time, given her desire to make a name for herself as a young female, even though by that point she'd already decided to dedicate her career to the police force rather than to the corporate world.

'I wonder what they've got in there,' Easton said, nodding over to the quadruple garage that was separate from the house, and which, with its dormer windows in the sloping eaves, was probably bigger than most regular detached homes.

'Dead bodies?' Dani said.

Easton gave her an eye roll.

'I was thinking more like Ferraris and Bugattis.'

'Yeah. Those too.'

Dani parked on the gravel turning circle next to an elaborate fountain, though the water was switched off. She grabbed the papers as she and Easton got out and crunched across the yellow stones to the canopied front door.

'Butler or maid?' Easton said, quietly.

Dani didn't answer. She pressed on the bell and a couple of seconds later the front door swung open to reveal a smartly dressed, pot-bellied man, with deeply tanned skin and cropped silvery hair and beard.

Dani glanced to Easton who just shrugged.

'Peter Agnew?' Dani said.

'Yes, yes, please come in.'

Dani and Easton did as they were told, heading into the expansive wood-panelled hallway that was topped off by a five-foot-high polished suit of armour, complete with ornamental sword.

'Please, come through to the drawing room.'

Dani was sure she heard Easton snigger but she just kept her eyes ahead as they followed Agnew through into the thirty-foot-long drawing room. Basically a posh lounge, Dani decided.

A bleached blonde lady with a skin tone slightly darker than her husband's, suggesting many weeks spent somewhere a lot sunnier than England, got up from the sofa and came over. In figure-hugging cream trousers and a sequinned top she walked with the confidence of someone who was worth as much as she was.

'Linda Agnew?' Dani said, holding out her hand. The woman nodded and gave her a firm handshake. 'I'm DI Stephens. This is my colleague DS Easton.'

Formalities were briefly completed before all four took a seat. The Agnews sat together on a three-piece brown leather sofa. Dani and Easton took opposite armchairs.

'I explained briefly on the phone what this is about,' Dani said.

'About Grace, yes,' Peter said.

'I'll get right to the point. Last night we found the body of a young female in the Moseley area of Birmingham.'

'You think it's our Grace,' Peter said. His wife sniffed and dropped her head onto his shoulder.

'It's possible. The pictures I'm about to show you are quite graphic, but please, if you could take a look and tell me if you think this is your daughter.'

Dani leafed through the photos she had in her hand and took out the two least gruesome – head and shoulder shots that showed the victim from slightly different angles, and gave little indication of her horrific injuries. Unpleasant as it was, showing the Agnews these carefully selected photographs was the least distressing way at this stage for them to either identify their daughter or rule out the possibility that the body was Grace.

She got up and handed the pictures to Peter. He took them with shaky hands and his brow furrowed as he stared at the pictures. Linda whimpered. Peter seemed frozen.

'Mr and Mrs Agnew, is that your daughter?'

'No,' Linda said, her bloodshot eyes looking up from the pictures to Dani. 'No. It's not. I've never seen her before.'

'You're positive? If there's any doubt, we can arrange for you to view the body, so you can be doubly sure. We'd have to do that anyway in order to complete a formal identification.'

'No,' Peter said. 'We're absolutely sure. That poor woman is not Grace. I've never seen her before.'

He put the pictures down onto the coffee table and took his sobbing wife in his arms.

–

Twenty minutes later the crying had stopped. Mr and Mrs Agnew had taken on a hard-nosed resolve as the four of them sipped coffee in the country-style kitchen that looked out over the enormous rear lawn.

'I'm sorry we had to put you through that,' Dani said, before taking a sip of rich coffee.

'You're just doing your job, Detective,' Linda responded. 'We'd already built ourselves up for the worst.'

'We're both just in shock,' Peter added.

'You've probably been over this with the Missing Persons team, but can you think of any reason why your daughter has gone missing? Anywhere she might now be?'

'I'll be honest with you, we haven't always gotten along,' Peter said. 'We loved her dearly, but she wasn't an easy child. We haven't been close for some time.'

'But she's not a child now. She's twenty-six years old.'

'She's still *our* child. And she was immature for her age.'

'Peter, that's not true at all,' his wife scolded, her distaste at his comment clear.

'What are you talking about?' he said. 'She dropped out of university three times. She couldn't hold any job for more than six months before getting bored or sacked or both.'

'Because you were always so stable in work, right?'

'I did just fine, thank you very much,'

'But you never exactly had a strong work ethic. She's more like you than you realise. Stubborn. Single-minded. Easily distracted because you're always thinking about the next project.'

Peter said nothing to that. They stopped their bickering. Linda gave Dani an apologetic look.

'What about friends?' Easton asked. 'Have you spoken to them? Is there anyone you think we should be speaking to?'

The Agnews both thought about that question for a while.

'The thing is, we really didn't know her group of friends that well,' Linda said. 'Not recently at least.'

'Recently?' Dani asked.

'She's been living over in Bournville for the last eighteen months or so. We really haven't had much contact with her since then.'

'It was her boyfriend. That's why she moved over there. We only met him twice but we never liked him.'

'But they split up anyway. About six months ago, I think. She moved into a bedsit with someone she didn't even know.'

Peter Agnew shook his head in disbelief. About which part of the story Dani wasn't quite sure.

'Is there a reason you didn't get along with him?' Easton asked.

'Because he was a lowlife piece of scum—'

'Peter!'

'Well he was! Thought he was the bees' knees because he almost had a shot at a football career at one point, but he was just a loser. We were glad when she kicked him into touch. We thought maybe she was finally going to get herself straightened out. We begged her to come back home to live with us. She was distraught about the break-up. But typical, stubborn Grace, she was determined to do things her own way.'

Linda tutted and shot her husband an unimpressed look as though the stubbornness and their daughter's poor decision-making was entirely his fault.

'What's his name?' Dani asked. 'The ex.'

'Paul Reeve. We told the other detectives all about this too. They surely would have spoken to him by now.'

'I'm sure they did. I'm just making sure we're all aligned.'

Dani finished her coffee and indicated to Easton for him to do the same. They put their empty cups down on the oak worktop.

'We won't take any more of your time.'

'I'll see you out,' Peter said, putting his own mug down.

'It was nice to meet you, Mrs Agnew.'

She sniffed at that. 'I don't mean to be rude, DI Stephens, but you're a homicide detective and I really hope we won't ever meet again.'

Dani said nothing to that.

-

'A penny for your thoughts?' Dani asked Easton minutes later as they were driving back towards Birmingham.

Easton looked up from the papers he was holding and sighed as he thought about his answer.

'Odd couple,' was his only response.

'I admit, they weren't quite what I was expecting.'

'Just goes to show, money really doesn't buy happiness.'

'Still, if they offered me fifty million I wouldn't turn it down.'

'True. What do you reckon about this Paul Reeve?'

'That Missing Persons should speak to him, if they haven't already. We only went to the Agnews to see if we could ID our Jane Doe. It's not our job to find Grace.'

Easton huffed and shuffled through the papers he was holding for a few seconds.

'Apparently mis-pers did contact Reeve. Looks like nothing came of it.'

Dani sighed, then the car fell silent. Dani's brain whirred with thoughts, but she really didn't have many answers. She looked at the clock on the dash. Nearly four p.m. The day was quickly catching up with her, she realised. She'd been due to take her pills more than an hour ago but had forgotten. It wasn't like her to not keep to her regimen. She relied on the medication more than she would ever have wished, and first day back on the job she felt she needed them more than ever.

With the thought planted in her mind, Dani felt a stinging pain in the front of her head. As she drove on, her vision intermittently blurred to white. Then her hands began to shake on the wheel. She squinted, pushing the growing feeling of nausea away, trying to refocus on the road ahead.

'Dani? Are you ok?'

'Yeah, fine,' she said, his voice bringing her back around, out of the fog.

What the hell was that?

'So what do you reckon?' he asked.

Dani's mind finally cleared. She took a gulp of air. 'That I've no idea what's happened to Grace Agnew, but it's really not our concern right now. We've got three other missing persons that could be our Jane Doe. We need to check them all out. We have to find out who she is. Otherwise we may never find out what happened to her.'

Chapter Ten

Thoughts of the last few months cascaded through Dani's mind as she splashed her face with cold water, hoping it would do the trick of reinvigorating her. She'd just downed the pills she should have taken nearly two hours ago, and taken some extra painkillers to try and quell the growing throbbing in her head. It was nearly five p.m. She could call it quits for the day. No one would mind, would they?

But then she wouldn't be doing herself justice. She still had a job to do. She hadn't gone through nearly twenty-four months of rehabilitation for nothing. She'd gone through it to prove she could still be *her*. Could still be DI Stephens.

'What doesn't kill you makes you stronger,' she told herself out loud, before heading for the exit.

Dani stepped outside the toilet and spotted Easton casually leaning against the corridor wall, waiting for her.

'You sure you're ok?' Easton asked.

'Piss off, Easton,' Dani said, storming past him. She was angry, even if she knew it was only because she was afraid he'd spotted her vulnerability.

He set off by her side, not in the least perturbed by her response.

'We've known each other for less than a day,' Dani said. 'I don't need you checking up on me. If there's a problem, I'll damn well tell you.'

'Yeah, I get that sense from you. You don't exactly hold back, do you?'

Dani ignored that comment. She knew that her irritability was just one of many side effects of that damn TBI, but she didn't feel like trying to justify it each and every time she snapped at someone unnecessarily. She carried on walking quickly along the corridor and through the Homicide team's office. The floor was already emptying for the day, but Fletcher was there, standing just outside McNair's office. The DCI was next to her, pouring water from the cooler into a little plastic cup.

'Stephens,' McNair said looking up. 'Where the hell have you been?'

'Ma'am?'

'I told you earlier. We're having a press conference. We needed you to help prep.'

'You didn't tell me what time,' Dani said.

'I didn't?'

Dani looked to Fletcher who was unable to meet her eye. Dani remembered the call she'd taken earlier in the day in Harborne. Not for the first time she wondered if Fletcher was deliberately holding back on her. But why even bother? It wasn't as though Dani was much competition to her at the moment.

'Well, too late now,' McNair said. 'We had to work around you. Come on, Fletcher.'

Fletcher just shrugged and set off alongside McNair. Dani scuttled behind.

'Where exactly have you been all day anyway?' McNair quizzed, sounding less than impressed, though Dani had no idea why.

'We were with forensics at the murder scene,' Easton said. 'Then at the house of Mrs Staunton across the road. We think the killer may have snuck in there.'

'Then I went to Missing Persons with Fletcher,' Dani said.

'Then to the house of Peter and Linda Agnew to see if we could ID our victim,' Easton added.

McNair looked around, an eyebrow raised. Was that an impressed look? The activity list certainly sounded like a lot to cover in one day.

'And?' McNair said.

'And everything's in the balance at the moment,' Dani said. 'We weren't able to ID our Jane Doe. Yet. But we do have some other possibilities to check out.'

'Then we go ahead with the press conference as planned,' McNair said.

'So how are we playing this?' Fletcher asked.

'You and me, just like we planned,' McNair responded. 'Stephens, Easton, you can sit this one out.'

'Ma'am, don't you think I should be up there too?' Dani protested. 'I'm SIO. And for continuity? Fletcher won't be around much longer.'

At Dani's words Fletcher frowned and began gently stroking her bump, as though what Dani had said was somehow offensive to her unborn child.

'Good point,' McNair said. 'But…'

McNair looked Dani up and down, clearly disapproving of something.

'But you're too recognisable right now, Stephens. Because of… you know. I don't want the press's attention to focus on you and your brother rather than this case.'

'That's bloody ridiculous!' Dani said, and the glare McNair gave in return showed Dani had just earned herself another black mark. But how was she supposed to act? And how was she ever supposed to get back to just being a normal detective if everyone was always going to treat her with kid gloves now?

'If it's continuity you want we could always have Easton up there too,' McNair offered.

Dani was even less happy about the prospect of giving her podium position away to a DS.

'Ma'am, I agree with Stephens,' Fletcher said to Dani's surprise.

Dani welcomed the intervention, though she realised it only made Fletcher seem even more righteous and in control.

McNair looked at Fletcher and sighed. 'Very well. Stephens, me and Fletcher. Easton, you're sitting this one out. But,

Stephens, you're there to take questions on this case only. If anyone talks about… you know—'

'Understood,' Dani said, still angry, but accepting she'd got the outcome she wanted.

Though as it turned out, Dani wasn't so sure about that. Yes, she wanted to be up there in front of the cameras, as the Senior Investigating Officer, because she wanted so badly to get her life, and her career, back on track. But when McNair opened the doors a moment later, and Dani saw the gaggle of reporters and photographers, and the cameras started flashing incessantly, almost blindingly, Dani immediately felt nauseous again.

For the first ten minutes the press sent an inevitable barrage of questions Dani's way, largely related to her fuck-up of a brother, and Dani was soon feeling as dazed as she was depressed. McNair, increasingly angry with the reporters, successfully shot down each and every attempt to steer the conversation down that path, and finally questions were being fired relating to the dead body found that morning.

'Have you identified this young woman?' came a clarifying question from a reporter from the *Birmingham Mail*.

'No,' McNair said. 'I think we've made that clear already, which is one of the reasons for holding this press conference. The sooner we can identify her, the sooner we'll be able to properly target the investigation and catch her killer.'

A lengthy back and forth began as to the nature of the killing and whether the police believed it was random or targeted, whether it was a crime of passion or a planned attack, whether it was gang-related or not. Anything that came Dani's way she answered as blandly and as safely as she could, though all the talk of killers and victims started to trigger thoughts of her own dark past, and her mind began to fog over.

'DI Stephens, this is your first case since returning to the force following the successful murder conviction of your brother?' came a question from a smartly dressed male reporter Dani didn't recognise.

'Correct,' Dani said.

'Please, I thought we were done with all that,' McNair interjected, sounding as pissed off as she looked.

'Sorry, but this is related,' the reporter said. 'DI Stephens, have you been put onto this case because it shows similarities to the types of case you worked in the past?'

'I'm not sure what you mean,' Dani said.

'I'm talking about serial killers. Do you believe this could be someone who has killed before?'

'Yes,' Dani said. 'Based on some of the circumstances, I'd say that's very possible.'

There was an immediate hubbub in the room as a myriad of hands were thrown into the air. Dani realised her mistake almost as soon as the ill-thought-out words had passed her lips, but by then it was already too late.

She looked over at McNair. All that was missing from the raging look on her face was steam coming from her ears and nostrils.

Dani sank even lower in her chair. For months she'd wanted to break free from her isolation, get out of her apartment and back to her job and her old life. But in that moment, she simply wished she was cooped up once more. Despite her earlier protestations, perhaps she simply wasn't ready for this level of pressure.

Maybe she never would be again.

Chapter Eleven

'What the hell were you thinking?' McNair blasted as she stormed after Dani.

Dani said nothing, just carried on away from the conference room, back through the corridors towards Homicide's office. She knew Fletcher and Easton were also in tow. Well, they wouldn't want to miss out on this slanging match, would they?

'Stephens. I'm talking to you! What was that all about?'

'What was what about?' Dani said, coming to a stop and turning around.

McNair stopped too. Her face was creased in anger. Fletcher and Easton were a couple of steps behind, pensive looks on both their faces.

'You spouting crap about serial killers! I told you to only take questions on *this* case. Our Jane Doe. That was it.'

Dani returned her boss's glare. 'Which is exactly what I did.'

'Don't be so ridiculous. You basically confirmed to the press that we're looking for a multiple murderer!'

'That's not what I said! I think you'll find the question was, *do you believe this could be someone who has killed before?*'

'And you bloody well said yes without even thinking!'

'Because that's what I think.'

'But that doesn't mean you have to tell the bloody press!'

'Why not?'

'Seriously? I was really hoping for a different answer from you. Something like, your brain injury means you've got no filter now. That despite your media training and all of your other case management training you now spout crap without thinking it through and there's nothing much we can do about it.'

Which kind of was the truth, though Dani wouldn't give McNair the satisfaction of agreeing.

'Sorry to disappoint you,' Dani said.

McNair was now incredulous. 'Can you imagine the backlash we're going to see tomorrow? You've taken a simple local murder case and turned it into a national media frenzy!'

'I said what I thought.'

'Based on what evidence exactly?'

'How about that our victim had most likely been kidnapped and then imprisoned somewhere before she escaped and was murdered? We don't know when she was taken or how, where she was kept even. In my mind, someone who undertakes such pre-planned and meticulous and frankly dire behaviour is likely to have committed previous offences. How—'

'You're putting two and two together, even with those assumptions.'

'We also have several other young women who've gone missing in West Midlands recently who fit a similar profile to our Jane Doe, who may or may not be dead already.'

McNair's look soured further. 'What are you—'

'And how about the intruder at Mrs Staunton's house? Not satisfied with killing Jane Doe, the perp heads across the road, seamlessly breaks into a house, drugs the occupant and then stands watch over our crime scene investigation before vanishing into the ether. Again, that suggests to me a repeat and calculated offender.'

'*Suggests* being the correct word, Stephens. That's not evidence; it's wild fantasy. You have no evidence those other women are dead, and certainly not at the hands of the same person. You have no evidence that the intruder at that house, and the killer of Jane Doe are the same person, or that they're even in anyway linked.'

'But it's possible! And quite frankly them being the same person is more likely than it being a coincidence.'

'In *your* opinion.'

'Yes, in my bloody opinion. I am a detective. I do get to have one.'

'Dani,' Easton said, tentatively coming over to her and putting a reassuring hand on her shoulder. 'Perhaps we should head off for the night. It's been a long day.'

Dani opened her mouth, ready to tear into him, but managed to hold herself back. Just.

'I think that's a very good idea,' McNair said, sounding calmer herself, though her eyes remained pinched with distaste. 'Get some rest, Stephens. We'll talk about this in the morning.'

Dani said nothing else, just turned and walked off.

–

As she headed up the stairs of her apartment block, Dani's head was still pounding despite the earlier medical intervention. Until the press conference her first day back on the job had gone by without serious incident, but now she was jaded and mentally shattered and wondered if the damage done with McNair was at all repairable.

She was also angry. Had Fletcher asked for Dani to be at the press conference just so she could be made a fool of? Dani had never seen Fletcher as the conniving type but perhaps she now felt her position was under threat with the prospect of several months away from the force, in the same way that Dani was feeling threatened coming back after so long on the sidelines.

After the argument, McNair and Fletcher would no doubt have taken themselves away to confer and swap notes. Dani was back on the force, but she felt like she was already being marginalised.

When she exited the stairwell on the sixth floor, she noticed the door to the apartment next door – Mrs Miller's – was wide open.

Most of the inhabitants in the twelve-year-old apartment block overlooking the canals were young couples or young professionals. Dani lived in one of four apartments on the top floor, the 'penthouse' level, as it had been sold to Dani when she'd bought the place, just a few months before the financial crash hit in 2008. Up on this level there was just Dani, Mrs Miller, and an engaged couple who Dani knew both worked for a big accountancy firm, but she couldn't remember either the name of the firm, nor of the man and woman. They were rarely about anyway, seemingly working all hours and regularly away from home. The only other apartment on the floor – a three-bed monster that probably was fit for the title of penthouse – had been empty and on the market for more than four years, the seller unwilling to budge from the price he'd paid for the pad when the block had been brand new. So it was generally just Mrs Miller that Dani saw out and about on floor six.

Mrs Miller was in her seventies, a true cat lady. She'd been married once but her husband had run away with his mistress some twenty years previously and she'd never re-married or even put herself back into the dating game as far as Dani knew. She was harmless enough, if a little senile, but for some reason she'd never liked Dani.

Perhaps it was because Dani was a police officer, or because she was in her mid-thirties and lived on her own. It certainly wasn't because Dani was a loud or obnoxious neighbour in any way.

Dani peered into Mrs Miller's apartment as she walked past, intending to give a smile and a greeting if she saw her neighbour. Mrs Miller was standing just away from the door, wearing a thick light blue bathrobe and holding a shabby ginger cat in her arms.

'Hi,' Dani said.

Mrs Miller squinted her eyes and nodded.

'I thought you were the Tesco man,' she said.

'What? No. Didn't see anyone coming up either.'

'Idiot's probably got himself lost again.'

And with that the door was slammed shut.

'Delightful,' Dani muttered under her breath.

She carried on to her apartment and when she'd stepped inside and locked the door behind her she leaned against the wall and let out a long sigh. After taking off her shoes – with great relief – Dani stripped off her work clothes and slung on her pyjama bottoms and a hoodie. Then she went to look for more medicinal relief. She opened the bathroom cabinet and stood there staring at the bottles.

In the end she decided against it. She'd had plenty for one day. She wanted something else. She moved to the kitchen. In the fridge was a bottle of wine she'd put there the previous night but not opened. On her meds she was ok to drink, but knew that her alcohol tolerance was seriously diminished. Consuming too much, she'd been told over and over, was yet another factor that drastically increased the risk of her having seizures.

Putting better judgment to one side she took the bottle out and found the corkscrew. As she was taking the cork out she recalled a documentary she'd seen not long ago where overweight and unfit couples were put through the wringer over their diets and exercise regimes. One couple had got into the habit of sitting in bed together every night with a bottle of wine each, not talking to each other, just drinking – him straight from the bottle and her from a protein shaker. Dani had thought their routine was both sad and weird and more than bordering on casual alcoholism, but all of a sudden she could see the appeal.

In the end though, Dani opted for a regular wine glass and only half-filled it with wine. She was still standing in the kitchen, enjoying the first sip, when there was a knock on the front door. Dani frowned and put the glass down. The outer doors to the apartment block were securely locked so visitors had to use the video intercom to gain entry. Perhaps it was Mrs Miller?

Dani walked back through from the kitchen to the front door and peered through the peephole.

Jason. What the hell was he doing there? And how had he got into the building? Dani wondered whether she should just wait it out and see if he disappeared, but after a few seconds he reached forwards and knocked again.

'Dani, I know you're in there.'

Dani cursed under her breath but she knew the best thing to do was just to open the door and get this over and done with. She did exactly that before she could talk herself out of it.

Jason smiled when he first saw her, before frowning as he looked down at her pyjamas and hoodie.

'What do you want, Jason?' Dani said, sounding harsher than she'd intended.

Jason didn't bat an eyelid. He'd long gotten used to the new, angrier Dani, a personality he surely wouldn't have fallen for. She noticed Jason look over to his left, towards Mrs Miller's apartment. Dani leaned her head out into the corridor and saw the Tesco delivery man was now there, unloading crates of food. Mrs Miller was standing by her doorway with a deep scowl on her face as she stared over at Jason suspiciously.

'How did you get up here?' Dani said, turning back to Jason.

'The door was open,' Jason said. 'Can I come in?'

Dani once again looked over at her neighbour who was still giving her the evil eye, as though Dani were operating an illegal brothel and Jason was a degenerate punter rather than her ex-boyfriend who'd been living there not all that long ago, having moved in with her after she'd come out from hospital to help look after her during her ongoing recovery.

'Yeah. Probably best if you do.'

Dani stepped back and Jason followed her in, shutting the door behind him. He'd obviously been home from work already before coming over because he was now dressed in trainers, jeans, v-neck jumper and his faithful leather jacket. Jason was tall – six foot four – and on the bulky side of lean. His appearance and his kind manner were what had drawn Dani to him in the past. They had drawn many women to him, Dani knew. Not that he was a player. He was kind and modest.

Jason didn't make a move to take off either the jacket or his shoes, and in the end the two of them just stood awkwardly in the small hallway, a couple of feet away from each other.

'I don't think she likes me too much,' Jason said.

'Mrs Miller? I don't think she ever did. Don't take it personally, she doesn't like anyone much. Except for Philip Schofield, I think. And sometimes the Tesco guy. But not that one.'

Jason smiled and Dani nearly caught herself doing the same thing. Nearly.

'It's really great to have you back at work,' Jason said.

'Yeah,' Dani said.

There was another awkward silence.

'I'm glad you're ok.'

'Who said I'm ok?'

'Well, I mean, you're back now. That's a good thing, right?'

'Jason, why have you come here?'

'Because I wanted to see you.'

'And now you've seen me. So is that it?'

'No. I wanted to talk to you too.'

'About what?'

'About us.'

'I'm not doing this now.'

'Why not?'

'Because I can't.'

'You can't just ignore me forever, Dani. It's been months already.'

'I'm well aware how long it's been.'

'I still care about you.'

'I'm not sure we even know each other anymore.'

Jason looked hurt.

'I'm sorry,' Dani said, hanging her head, not wanting to look him in the eye. He'd done nothing wrong, really. The problems between the two of them were all down to Dani and her stupid messed-up brain. Well, and her damn murderous brother who'd caused the injuries in the first place.

'Why do you always push everyone away from you?' Jason said. 'I can help you through this. I *want* to help.'

'I don't need your help!' Dani shouted. 'I don't need anyone's help. Jason, I'm sorry, I am, but I think you should go.'

'That's it?'

'I need more time.'

'I've given you plenty of that already.'

'Just go.'

Jason shook his head, disappointed, and angry too, she could see. He felt like the aggrieved party, but he wasn't really. Dani was the one whose life remained in disarray. If Jason really wanted to help, he just needed to suck it up and wait for Dani to find her old self again. If she ever could.

When the silence had dragged on long enough, Dani reached forwards and opened the door. Jason held his ground a few seconds as though weighing up whether he would fight any more. Eventually he just turned and walked out, leaving Dani slightly disappointed that he hadn't tried harder, even though she'd meant what she said about needing more time.

After she'd closed and locked the door, Dani went back to the kitchen and over to the fridge for the bottle. She plonked the wine down on the counter, then opened up the cupboard again. Sod it, she was going to need a bigger wine glass after all.

Chapter Twelve

Day 90

'Dani,' the woman says.

I hear her voice but my head feels foggy and although I know I'm awake, I don't want to open my eyes.

'Dani, it's Lucia. It's time to eat.'

Lucia. One of the nurses in the rehabilitation ward. She's from Poland. In her thirties, plump and matronly with a stern face but a kind and safe manner about her. When I first met her I struggled to understand her English, her accent was so thick. Apparently I would repeat the words she said, taking on a Polish accent myself in a strange attempt to converse with her, much like a toddler might. Much to the amusement of others. I wasn't trying to amuse them, just trying to do what they wanted me to – talk, communicate.

I finally find the strength to open my eyes. Lucia is sitting by my bed in her dark blue uniform. She has a tray of food in front of me. A tuna salad. Tomato pasta. Apple pie and custard. Orange juice.

'Can you manage?' she asks.

'Yes,' I say.

I take the dessert spoon and plonk dollops of custard and pie onto the tuna salad then take a few mouthfuls. Next the orange juice goes into the pasta bowl to form something akin to a minestrone soup. I take big mouthfuls of salad, then soup, not bothering to chew if I don't have to. I don't know why I eat like this. It's a habit now, even though I know it's not right. The thing is, I can't smell or taste the food I'm eating. Apparently I probably never will recover those senses properly. Mixing the foods together – starter, main, dessert, sweet, savoury, whatever – is merely my means of getting the meal over with more quickly. Eating is a necessary inconvenience for me and nothing more.

A familiar face appears at the door. His tall frame takes up most of the doorway. Jason.

He smiles at me. I do my best to smile in return.

Jason's is the first face that I remember seeing among the jumbled mess of memories from my time in hospital. At first I was glad to see him. It took away just some of my angst to have him by my side, made me feel just that little bit more safe and secure. Now, weeks later, I'm not so sure.

We'd only been dating for six months before I was brought here. We didn't even live together, though I did love him. But there were never any vows between us, no 'till death do us part', or 'in sickness and in health'. He has no obligation to stand by me now. Why does he even want to? I'm not the same person he fell in love with. I'm just a burden.

I don't get many visitors here. My parents are both long dead. My father died of a heart attack while he was out gardening. My mother died from a stroke caused by her rapidly worsening dementia barely a year later. My only sibling — my murderous twin brother — is locked up, in part for trying to kill me by smashing my head against a doorframe before bludgeoning me with a stone ornament. Yes, all of this is because of my brother — Ben. My brother, Ben, who married my best friend, Alice. My brother, Ben, who killed Alice in a fit of rage when she threatened to leave him over his affair with another woman. My brother, Ben, who hid that secret for years, remarried, had another child, and was seemingly as normal as anyone else until he flipped again and went on a killing spree which culminated in him trying to murder both me and his new wife, Gemma.

So no, I don't get many visitors here. One or two colleagues from the police have been to see me, but they haven't returned. There's Gemma, my sister-in-law, and her kids — one of whom is actually Alice's, but was only a baby when she was killed — but she only comes every few weeks. In truth we never got along that well, and after what happened with Ben, there's an unease between us that may never pass, even though we were both victims of his. Yet other than her and Jason, there really is no support network around me.

So why does it annoy me so much that Jason keeps butting in? I can't describe why but I resent that he wants to help so much. I wish I didn't feel like that.

'I'll continue my rounds,' Lucia says, then gets up and heads for the door.

'How are you doing today?' Jason asks.

'I'm fine.'

'I brought you these.' He holds up a bag of jam doughnuts. 'Your favourite.'

The nurses have encouraged him to bring extra food in for me. I've lost two stone in bodyweight and my metabolism remains heightened as my brain tries in vain to recover.

'They were *my* favourite. You may as well have brought a bagful of mud.'

'Still, the sugar'll do you good.'

'I'm not hungry now,' I say, pushing the tray of nearly eaten slops away.

'Maybe later then.' Jason moves to the bed and puts the bag down. He pecks me on the forehead.

'I don't want them later!' I snap. 'I can't taste a damn thing anyway, so what's the point? You have them.'

Jason just smiles and sits down, not rising to it at all. I'm told that my irritability and unconscious outbursts are down to my damaged frontal lobes. I'm angry, a lot. I blurt things out, angrily, like someone with Tourette's might. But despite what the doctors tell me, most of the time I think my anger has nothing to do with my broken brain; it's because people just don't listen to me. They treat me like an incompetent invalid, or like they'd treat a two-year-old. They make decisions for me, tell me what to do and what to think and what to say.

I just want to be listened to and trusted again.

'Have you seen the physio today?'

'Yes.'

'And?'

'And nothing. He wanted me to use that bloody hand bike again. What's the point?'

I'm able to walk unaided now, but my body lacks coordination still. Writing in this diary helps not just my brain but my dexterity, even though it leaves me with pains and cramps most days. Likewise, the hand bike is one of the many exercise machines designed to help me build up muscle again and regain 'normal' motor skills.

But it's tedious, and I hate that they tell me when I have to do it and for how long and then sit there monitoring me and assessing me, rather than just letting me do things for myself. Yet it surprises me that my motivation to get better is so low. I was always such a determined person.

Once again, evidence of the new Dani, courtesy of those bloody frontal lobes.

'I'm really tired. I could do with some rest.'

'Sure thing. Do you want me to hang around? Or come back later?'

'No. Just go.'

For a second he looks crestfallen, but the look is gone in a flash and the next moment he appears relaxed and smiley again. It pisses me off even more that he won't just say what he's really thinking, that he treats me like this, as though nothing is ever a problem. Everything is a damn problem. Look at me!

He leans forwards and pecks me on the forehead again.

'I love you,' he says.

I say nothing, just shut my eyes and keep them closed until I'm sure he's out of the room.

Chapter Thirteen

When her alarm went off the following morning, Dani wanted nothing more than to crawl into a dark, quiet space and hibernate. One day back on the job and she was already drained. The bottle of wine certainly hadn't helped, and as she found the strength to open her eyelids despite her pounding head, she resoundingly regretted having been so weak.

She dragged herself out of bed and showered. Afterwards she stood in front of the mirror, staring at her reflection. At the scar above her ear. At first, when the stitches were still present, the deep wound over her fractured skull would ooze a sticky fluid, and she could barely bring herself to look. Then, when the stitches had gone, the whole area around the wound had remained a patchwork of red and black and purple and yellow for weeks. Still, Dani had held out hope that the damn thing would go away. But other than the patch turning silvery there'd been no change, no improvement at all, for months. *This*, the scar, the bald patch, was now her permanent reminder of what had happened.

Dani growled in frustration and reached out to open the mirrored door of the cabinet. For a couple of seconds she stared at the various bottles of pills in front of her. She'd already taken the anti-seizure tablets she needed. What about the anti-depressants? Painkillers? She knew from recent experience that she could seriously take the edge off how she was feeling. With a strong enough dose she could glide right through the day ahead and be none the wiser to it all.

No. Not today. She was a DI once again, and she was determined to prove to herself that she was recovering well enough without needing all the pills.

She grabbed a hair band from the shelf and slammed the door shut.

'Get out of my head,' Dani said through gritted teeth, glaring at herself in the mirror.

She reached up and pulled her hair back, then wound the hairband around to make a tight bun. She'd had her mousy brown hair dyed lighter two days ago, and had felt pleasantly energised about the new look. She had also bought a new suit and new shoes for her big first day back at work. New look, new Dani. That was the theory. That had all been blown to crap the day before with the rude awakening from McNair. Now the clothes and the look all seemed silly and pointless. Like she was pretending. A fraud. And who really gave a shit anyway?

She spent a couple of minutes putting on some light make-up then sighed and turned away from the mirror. She grabbed her suit jacket from the bed then moved out into the hallway and slipped on her battered old work shoes. The new ones she'd worn yesterday had cost her over a hundred pounds but had left her with painful blisters on both ankles. She really didn't need that aggro on top of everything else.

She was on her way to the front door when her phone began buzzing on the hall table. Dani grabbed it. Looking at the screen, she frowned.

Gemma?

–

An hour later Dani sat on a park bench as her niece and nephew raced about in the play area at Sutton Park. Chloe was five. Harry ten. It was half term and Gemma had been let down by her child-minder and couldn't get out of the morning meetings she had planned in the office. Dani was surprised Gemma had thought of her. She was sure she wouldn't be first on the emergency list, even though she was technically family.

McNair had been accommodating enough about the situation, and Dani had promised to make the hours up. Perhaps she'd already had enough of Dani following the press conference. Dani wouldn't admit it to anyone, but having slept on it, she was now feeling more than embarrassed about what she'd said – not just to the press, but to McNair afterward. All she'd wanted was to get back to the job she loved. Already her boss and colleagues probably thought she was a crazed idiot.

'Good job,' she muttered to herself.

She'd left Easton following up as best he could with the families of the other missing persons cases. If all went to plan she'd be back at work by lunch. Not that she was itching to get back there, only to make a fool of herself again. Plus, the unexpected time with her niece and nephew was a refreshing change. She only wished she made the effort to see them more often. She'd barely seen them for months after her injury. Hadn't really wanted to, in honesty. Like many things in her life, she'd not been able to find pleasure in their company anymore, instead feeling like they were just unnecessary hassle. She cringed inwardly at the thought. She knew it was wrong to have felt that way, to still feel that way at times, yet that was simply the way her brain was wired now.

Chloe came whizzing up to Dani on her scooter.

'You look funny today.'

'Funny?'

Chloe pursed her lips and cocked her head, looking pensive.

'Your hair's different. And your clothes.'

By which Dani assumed Chloe meant she was more used to seeing her aunt dressed in jogging bottoms and hoodies. Comfort wear.

'I was supposed to be at work this morning,' Dani said. 'You remember what I do?'

'Yeah. You catch the bad guys.'

Dani smiled. 'I certainly try my best.'

'Did you know we have the same surname?'

'I know. Perhaps one day you could be Detective Stephens too.'

'No. I'm going to be an astronaut.'

'Wow. Can I come to space with you?'

'No. You have to be really strong. You're too fragile now. Mummy said so. You might break.'

Dani laughed even though she wondered about how that conversation between mum and daughter had gone, and what Gemma's intention had been.

'Where's uncle Jason?' Chloe asked.

'He's at work.'

'Mummy said he's not your boyfriend anymore.'

Dani sighed. 'No. He's not.'

'I like him.'

'Yeah,' Dani said.

'He's big and strong. Maybe he could come to space with me.'

'Maybe you should ask him.'

Chloe looked away coyly. A second later she was whizzing off again. Feeling more at ease than she had in ages, Dani watched them both intently for a few minutes. In many ways she wished she lived in such a world of innocence like they did.

Harry bounded over, his cheeks reddened from his non-stop activity.

'I'm starving,' he said. No pleasantries like his talkative sister, just straight to the point. An undoubted Stephens characteristic. 'What have you got to eat?'

It was barely eleven a.m. but Dani didn't care. They sat down in McDonald's and Harry pulled out his Big Mac as Chloe dove straight into her Happy Meal box for the toy.

'Yes!' she said. 'I really wanted this one.'

'Must be your lucky day,' Dani said, taking her burger out of its box.

The three of them tucked into their food in silence for a couple of minutes.

'Have you been to see Dad?' Harry asked with a mouthful of fries. The question, coming out of the blue, knocked Dani. She wondered how much the kids knew about what had happened. She'd certainly never had a conversation with them about it. Nor had she spoken to Gemma much about it. In fact, she'd talked to pretty much no one about it. She certainly wasn't going to be the one to explain to Harry that his father had killed his biological mother all those years ago in a fit of rage, covered up the crime, then years later when his life of lies and deceit was steadily unravelling, decided to go on a killing spree which included trying to kill his twin sister and Gemma – his new wife, mother to Chloe. Even Dani couldn't make sense of that, never mind a ten-year-old and a five-year-old.

'No. I've not seen him at all,' Dani said. 'Why do you ask?'

'I really want to see him. But Mum says no.'

'Why do you want to see him?'

Harry looked down at his food, his sorrow clear. 'Because he's my dad. I miss him.'

Dani looked from Harry to Chloe. She seemed oblivious to the conversation. She'd only been three at the time, perhaps she couldn't even remember Ben properly. But Harry had been eight. Not only would he remember Ben but he probably knew most, if not all, of what had happened from one source or another.

'Prison isn't a nice place for kids,' Dani said, realising she was treading on thin ice. This was really the last subject she wanted to be thinking about, and she didn't want to put her foot in it and say something she shouldn't to a ten-year-old.

'That's what Mum says too. But it's not fair. I know what he did, but…'

'But?'

'He was a good dad. I wish he was still here.'

Dani really didn't know what to say to that.

'Do you think he's a really bad person?' Harry asked.

'I think there's good in him,' Dani said, her own words shocking her.

Did she really mean that? Or had she only said it in order to ease the suffering of a child?

88

'But you're his twin,' Harry said. 'Aren't you both the same? It's not fair that he's stuck in there and you're out here.'

Dani was by now feeling a build-up of mixed emotions; regret, sadness, but also anger. What did set her and Ben apart? She'd asked herself that same question countless times during her recovery. She'd never got to a satisfactory answer. Was it just bad luck, bad judgment that had led to his fate? Or if there really was something wrong with him, something in the way his brain was wired that had turned him into a violent criminal, then was Dani not affected by that too? How long before she snapped like he had?

'I just feel sorry for him,' Harry said. 'He must be so lonely in there. He can't do anything. Ever again.'

'I can go and see him. For you. If you want me to.'

Once again the words passed Dani's lips without any real fore-thought and she immediately regretted them, even though she'd contemplated plenty of times whether seeing Ben could be a good thing for her. Wouldn't it help her recovery if she were to face him head on? Ask him all of the questions she *had* to know the answers to, in order to understand what he'd done and why?

'I think he'd like that,' Harry said, smiling.

Dani sighed and looked away. What had she just done?

Moments later her phone was ringing. It was Easton.

'I need to take this. I'll be back in a sec.'

Dani got up and headed towards a quiet corner in the restaurant.

'Yeah.'

'We've had a breakthrough. A call to the hotline about the press con.'

'Seriously?'

'Yeah. A friend who thinks she knows the vic. She's coming to the station in an hour.'

Dani looked at her watch. Gemma was due to take the kids back in forty minutes.

'I'll be there.'

Chapter Fourteen

It turned out Dani had plenty of time. Having already pushed thoughts of her murderous brother to the back of her mind, she dropped the kids off with Gemma five minutes early and hotfooted it back to Birmingham with ten minutes to spare, only for Rebecca Hargreaves to be nearly forty-five minutes late. That wasn't too big a problem. While they waited, Dani and Easton sat in an interview room and swapped notes on what they knew so far. Which was little. The post-mortem of Jane Doe was yet to be completed. There were no results from forensics. Easton had managed to speak to only one of the families of the other missing women that Dani had pinpointed, but had again drawn a blank in identifying their murder victim. Which meant a lot of the waiting time was spent with Easton talking about football and his alternative fantasy life as a football agent. He was certainly enthusiastic, if a little naive, and at least there was no talk about the press conference the previous day, or any of Dani's other problems, for that matter.

When Rebecca Hargreaves finally arrived, she wasn't alone, bringing a friend – Laura Finlay – for support. While Dani would object to such a companion in a more formal interview, she wanted Rebecca to be open and at ease so didn't question it. Dani knew that the DCs on her team were more than capable of carrying out an interview like this one, but she was still feeling rusty and thought it would be good to immerse herself in the nitty-gritty of the investigation, until she felt properly acclimatized to her job once again. If that point ever came.

Easton brought the two young ladies to the room. Rebecca was pale, her skin almost translucent. The only colour anywhere on her face were her bloodshot eyes, and the dark eye make-up surrounding them. It was clear she'd been crying. Dani, in a strange way, felt optimistic, seeing Rebecca so distraught. It suggested that perhaps this was a fruitful lead after all.

'Rebecca, thank you for coming to see us,' Dani said, getting to her feet. 'I'm DI Stephens, please take a seat.'

Rebecca looked around the room nervously as Easton came and sat down next to Dani. The two young women took their seats somewhat awkwardly. Easton had briefed Dani on the small amount of information he had found about Rebecca on her Facebook profile, so she knew she was twenty-one and a waitress in a bar. She looked younger than twenty-one, though, maybe only sixteen or seventeen, with a painfully thin frame and long spindly arms and legs. Her eye make-up was so dark it was like looking into two black holes. Her straight hair was a clash of black and pink and blue. Dani thought the look would be described as 'emo' although she wasn't sure what that meant, exactly.

Her friend sported a similar look. Both girls' eyes had thick bags underneath them and they were twitchy, not really focusing on anything. Together with their swollen nostrils and overall washed-out appearance, Dani felt she knew what it all added up to. There were no needle marks on these girls' arms, so Dani doubted they were heroin addicts, but they probably took all manner of other substances, legal and illegal: alcohol, nicotine, cannabis, coke, meth, ecstasy.

Dani noticed Rebecca's eyes fix on the one-way mirror.

'There's no one behind there,' Dani assured her.

'Are you recording this?' Rebecca asked.

'No. This isn't a formal interview, Rebecca. Not yet.'

'Not yet?'

'We're at an early stage of the investigation. We'll take notes of what's said here, of course, but there's no need to take a full recording. You have nothing to worry about in speaking to us today, we're not here to trick you. We just want to find out what you know. We can take a formal statement at a later time if we think it necessary.'

'I just can't believe she's gone,' Rebecca blubbered and started sniffing and spluttering into her tissue.

Laura reached out to rest her hand on Rebecca's arm and her friend grew in strength slightly. Dani pushed a composite picture of Jane Doe across the table. It was too soon to show these two anything more graphic. And anyway, it was the composite that had been used for the press conference the previous day, together with a grainy CCTV image they'd found, and managed to blow up, of the young dead woman running scared through the streets.

'Who do you think it is, Rebecca?'

'Natalya. It's Natalya. I know it's her.'

'What's her full name?'

'I don't... know.'

Dani and Easton shared a questioning look.

'Then how did you know her?'

Rebecca looked at Laura as though searching for reassurance as to what to say. Laura just nodded.

'We were friends. We hung out with the same group of people.'

'But you don't know her full name?'

'No, I already said that.' Her tone was now defensive.

'Do you know where she lived?'

'I can give you the address. She lived alone. She was from Romania. At least I think she was. She doesn't have any family here.'

'When did you last see her?'

'The weekend before last. The Saturday night. She was in the bar where I work. She came in most weekends.'

Rebecca gave her friend that same look again. Dani's mind buzzed as she tried to think of how to eke out whatever secrets the two girls were clearly hiding.

'Which bar?' Dani asked.

'Neptune.'

Dani knew it. A late night bar in Digbeth that was something of a dive; dark, dingy and loud. And that was just the punters.

'Do you know why anyone would want to hurt her?' Easton asked.

That look again.

'Rebecca. Look at me,' Dani said. 'Not at Laura. Do you know who killed her?'

A tear escaped Rebecca's eye.

'No. I really don't.'

'But you do know something. Don't you?'

Rebecca sighed, exasperated. 'Look, Detective,' she said, sounding more in charge all of a sudden. 'She's an escort. Ok?'

'Escort?'

'I'm sure you know what I'm getting at.'

'And you two?'

'It's good money.'

'And did she have any regulars?'

'Of course she did. We all do.'

'And how about a pimp?'

Laura scoffed. 'That's not how it works. We're not seedy back alley prostitutes. We organise everything ourselves.'

There was a slight pause in the conversation as Dani gave the girls a chance to defuse slightly. She had no need to rile them, she just wanted them to tell her what they knew.

'Is there anyone at all who you think could have done this to Natalya?' Dani asked.

Laura looked at her friend. Rebecca looked frozen.

'Go on,' Laura said. 'Tell them.'

'There's one guy. Creepy as hell. It could be nothing. I don't want to get him into trouble for no reason.'

'Rebecca, if he killed Natalya then I wouldn't say that's no reason.'

'Ok, ok. This guy, he's been hanging around all the time. But only the last couple of months. I don't know much about him, just that he wanted Natalya to see him. You know, properly see him. He wanted to take her out.'

'And did she go out with him?'

'I think so, yeah. It happens all the time. These guys forget what the whole deal is, they want us to be their girlfriend all of a sudden.'

'But she did go out with him?'

'I warned her not to. I told her how messy it could get.'

'Do you know his name?'

'I just know he's called Jimmy.'

'Just Jimmy?' Easton said. 'Like it's just Natalya?'

Rebecca glared but said nothing.

'Ok. And what do you know about this Jimmy?' Dani asked.

'Becs isn't involved in any of this,' Laura stated, her tone acidic.

'In any of what?'

'Laura,' Rebecca said, turning to her friend and giving her a pleading look which Dani read to mean *shut the hell up*.

'Girls, just be straight with us. Tell us what you know. Who was Natalya mixed up with?'

'Jimmy deals coke,' Laura said, matter-of-factly, as though it was something she'd always disapproved of and she was now pleased to be spilling the beans.

Rebecca hung her head.

'I mean, he isn't… he's not a gangster or some big shot like that. But he used to buy coke, sometimes E, off someone he knew and sell it to his mates and… well, us.'

'How did Jimmy get into that?' Dani asked.

'I don't know,' Rebecca said. 'I honestly don't know. I've barely spoken to him before properly.'

'But you think Natalya's death has something to do with him?'

'Makes sense, doesn't it?' Laura said. Rebecca stared down at the table, not engaging. 'I mean, that's a pretty messed-up world to be involved in. We're not saying Jimmy did it. But what if it's because of him?'

'Rebecca? Do you know who could have killed Natalya?' Dani asked again.

'I've told you what I know.'

'Who supplied Jimmy?'

'I've no idea where he got the stuff. But I do know he got into trouble because of it before.'

'How do you mean?' Easton said.

'He was thrown out of the bar, a few weeks ago. He was with Natalya at the time. Some other guys turned up and a fight broke out. The bouncers sorted it all, turfed the lot of them out. That was the last time I saw Jimmy.'

Easton and Dani turned to look at each other. The conversation was certainly taking an interesting turn. Dani was now regretting setting up the meeting in such an informal way. She wasn't far from stopping proceedings right then and starting over.

No, don't rattle them. Just carry on, see what else these two can give. Carry out the formalities some other time.

The slight nod Easton gave suggested he was thinking the same thing.

'Can you give us anything else at all so we can try and track this Jimmy down? An address?'

'I've no idea,' Rebecca said.

Laura shook her head.

'What did he look like?'

'I dunno really. He was tall. Looked athletic. Square jaw, stubble. He was handsome but… there was always something off about him.'

'Natalya told me he was a footballer. Not like Premier League or anything. I think it was Tamworth he played for. Used to, anyway.'

Dani and Easton looked at each other, both clearly thinking the same thing. Easton riffled through the file he had on the desk with the info on the missing persons he and Dani had been perusing before Rebecca and Laura had arrived. He found what he was looking for.

'Do you recognise this man?' Easton asked, pulling a photo out of a plastic wallet and pushing it across the desk. It was a large colour picture of Paul Reeve – the ex-boyfriend of the missing Grace Agnew. Dani had read in the profile that Missing Persons had pulled on him when they were investigating Grace's disappearance that he used to play for Tamworth football club.

Both girls stared at the photo.

Rebecca frowned. 'Yeah,' she said. 'That's him. That's Jimmy. How did you know?'

Chapter Fifteen

Following the confrontation with Ethan the previous day, Grant hadn't bothered going back to work, instead spending the time at home with Mary. Their daughter, Annie, was staying at a friend's house until late into the evening. Grant had called Professor Langley, his boss at the university, who knew about the recent stress and trouble Ethan had caused Grant and his wife, and had been happy to help Grant rearrange his diary for the rest of the day and find cover for the two lectures he was missing. Grant had been a diligent worker for years so he felt he had a decent amount of goodwill with Langley, though he would avoid testing exactly how far the goodwill would stretch if at all possible.

It turned out, as Grant had guessed, that the police who had arrived on the scene moments after Ethan had scarpered were called by one of the neighbours, who'd reported a domestic disturbance. The two PCs, who Grant felt were somewhat out of their depth, had initially treated Grant with outright contempt, believing him to be the culprit of the disturbance, and of the clear bruising to Mary's face. The officers had split Grant and Mary up while one of them chatted quite forcibly to Mary, trying to persuade her to come clean about her husband and press charges against him. The officer with Grant had toed a similar hard line, and seemed reluctant to believe his account of events, given the absence of the mysterious Ethan who had escaped from the scene in such timely fashion. The police had been called to the house more than once recently because of disturbances caused by Ethan, not to mention the other misdemeanours they had on record for him, from drunken assault to possession of drugs to speeding, but none of this seemed to influence their view of Grant as the likely guilty party. It was true that this was the first time that Ethan had been violent to his mother, which as far as Grant was concerned was a new low.

Only after some time, and when the officers had conferred, did they finally come to accept that they'd misread the situation. Both were then apologetic, but still determined to make an arrest, and it had taken a lot of persuasion by Grant and Mary to get the officers to agree to not take the matter any further. Neither Grant nor Mary wanted Ethan arrested and banged up, however increasingly despicable his behaviour was. Plus, Grant knew he himself wasn't wholly blameless for the fracas, given he had lunged at his son. Ethan wouldn't get another chance though – not from the police, and not from Grant and Mary.

Once the police had, somewhat reluctantly, headed on their way, Grant and Mary had sat in the lounge for hours, sometimes in silence, sometimes talking about the good times, Annie – their teenage daughter – and her plans for the future. They talked a bit about when Ethan was younger and a seemingly normal boy. Unsurprisingly, they'd dwelled on the bad too, discussing what had gone wrong and what they could do to change the nineteen-year-old man Ethan had become.

At his relative young age could they still change him?

The answer was that they had to try.

Annie hadn't arrived home until after ten p.m., by which point Mary was already in bed, and Grant hadn't the heart or the strength to explain what had happened to her. The following morning his daughter had left for school before Mary was up, and Grant reluctantly headed off to work. The day passed by in a blur, and he found himself unable to properly concentrate, so he left work earlier than usual and arrived home minutes before Annie returned from school, just after four p.m.

Following less than thirty seconds of chat with her dad, she promptly locked herself away in her bedroom, once again without seeing Mary. Her lack of social interaction with her parents was nothing more than would be expected of a fifteen-year-old girl, Grant and Mary had previously decided. She wasn't another Ethan-sized problem in the making, just a teenager who preferred the company of her friends and her music and her phone to her boring and clueless parents. Really, Annie was a sweet girl and plenty mature enough for her age.

So just where had everything gone wrong with Ethan, then? It was a question Grant had asked himself constantly for a while now. Ethan had never been particularly troublesome as a younger child – he was simply a typically boisterous boy who enjoyed playing rough and tumble and tormenting his little sister. Only when he was fourteen had he changed from a hyperactive boy to an out of control young man with a beef against the world. There had been no one catalyst, no spark, no trauma or suffering or loss which had caused his degradation from boy to loser. Ethan was just Ethan.

Grant still lived in the vague hope that perhaps his son would grow out of his arsehole stage. That he'd find a good job and a nice girlfriend, and would settle down and become a real man. As the days and months wore on, that dream felt further and further from reality. But it was still a dream that Grant clung to. Largely because he couldn't fathom how the current situation would ever end with a positive outcome.

How much further into the mire could they spiral?

'Shall I fix us some pasta?' Mary said, coming into the lounge.

He saw the look of despair still on her face.

'Sure,' Grant said. 'Honey, you have to believe that this isn't our fault. It just isn't. We tried everything to get things right with him.'

'Did we?' Mary asked. By now the swelling around her eye had turned purple, the eyelid was swollen almost shut.

'You know we did.'

Ethan had been aggressive towards them both before, and he'd bordered on violence, squaring up to his dad more than once. But he'd never lashed out at them like he had the previous day.

Certainly never hit his own mother. That was a new low from which Grant struggled to see a return.

Mary shook her head. 'I used to think that too, but it's just not true, is it? It can't be. If we'd really tried everything, then *that* wouldn't be our Ethan.'

In reality Grant felt the same; that he and Mary were the ones to blame.

–

Thirty minutes later Grant and Mary were sitting at the breakfast table in their lavish country-style kitchen, silently eating bowls of penne arrabbiata, a favourite of Grant's. The irony wasn't lost on him that the literal translation of the fiery sauce's name was 'angry'.

As Grant began to wipe his empty bowl clean with a piece of bread, Annie finally made an appearance in the kitchen doorway, some fifteen minutes after Mary had called her down.

'Mum!' Annie shouted, when she saw Mary's face. 'What the—?'

'Come and eat your tea, sweetie,' Mary said, the look on her face suggesting she was as embarrassed by the bruise as she was sad or angry.

Annie stormed over and plonked herself down on a chair, her cheeks reddening.

'Why didn't you tell me something was wrong? What happened?'

'We didn't want to worry you.'

'What's going on, Mum? Why have you got a black eye?'

Mary looked over to Grant for help.

'Ethan came over yesterday,' Grant said.

'Ethan hit you?!' Annie shrieked. 'That piece of sh—'

'Language!' Grant shouted.

'Sorry,' Annie said, hanging her head. 'I just can't... I can't believe he'd do that. God, I really hate him.'

Mary shook her head. 'Don't say that. He didn't mean it.'

'Yes he did,' Grant said. 'He knew exactly what he was doing. Don't you stick up for him now.'

Mary huffed and got up from her seat. She snatched Grant's empty bowl away from him and padded over to the Belfast sink that looked out over the large back garden.

'Why would he do that?' Annie asked Grant, quietly.

'Best not to think about it. He certainly won't get away with it again. The police wanted us to press charges.'

'The police were here again? Why are you only telling me this now?'

Grant didn't really have an answer for that. Mary said nothing, doing a good job of keeping herself out of the conversation.

'Why didn't you press charges?' Annie asked.

'Because he's still our son. Your brother.'

'Are you sure about that? Maybe he was swapped at birth or something.'

Annie smiled mischievously and Grant reciprocated.

'I can still hear you both,' Mary snapped from the sink, clearly not impressed.

'Seriously, Annie, don't worry about Ethan. We'll deal with it. And he would never hurt you.'

'You reckon?'

'Of course,' Grant said, but as soon as the words had passed his lips he realised there had been an edge to Annie's response. 'Wait, what do you mean? What has he done to you?'

Annie shook her head and looked down at her food.

'It's nothing,' she said.

'Just tell me.'

She said nothing.

'Annie, damn it, tell me!'

Grant's raised voice made Annie jump and Mary rushed over and put her arms around her daughter.

'Don't you take this out on her,' Mary said.

'Fine! I'll tell you. Even though I told him I wouldn't.' Annie paused and looked away. 'You know where he's staying now, right?'

'With a friend, that's all he told us,' Grant said.

'His name's Jimmy,' Annie said. 'He's way older than Ethan, like twenty-five or something. He's a complete…'

She paused again and looked at her dad. Clearly she'd thought twice about whatever word she'd been about to use.

'…Oh, I don't know, he's just so sleazy and slimy, and horrible.'

Grant was vaguely aware of Jimmy because he'd been to the house once or twice to pick Ethan up in his car when Ethan had still lived there. He was an out and out loser, as far as Grant was concerned – cocky and arrogant. Probably one of the popular kids back in his school days. Such kids sometimes forgot to grow up.

'What is it, Annie?' Grant said.

'Look, I can't say much, because I wasn't there, but Jimmy is always taking girls back to his place; he thinks he's a real stud. My friend, Olivia, slept with him.'

'With Ethan?'

'No! With Jimmy.'

'She's only fifteen!' Mary blasted.

'I know! But he picked her up in a bar. Maybe he didn't know.'

'What? Wait, since when have you—'

'I wasn't with her, Dad. I don't go to bars. But Jimmy doesn't care how old they are. He's so creepy. Apparently Ethan was there too. In the bar, and in the apartment. He's always there. They're like a sleazy duo. Their place is a proper bachelor's pad. They both take different girls back there all the time. That's what I was told, anyway.'

Grant shut his eyes, trying to block the unwelcome images that were forming in his mind. What on earth was wrong with Ethan?

'All the boys at school think it's hilarious,' Annie said. 'They're always making fun of me, calling Ethan a paedophile.'

Grant squirmed at the word. The more he heard, the more he felt queasy. He didn't know what to say. Mary looked similarly frozen.

'He's not. Is he, Dad?'

'No, Annie, of course he's not. That's a horrible thing for them to say.'

'I just wish he'd grow up and get a life,' Annie said, and Grant truly was with her on that one.

The doorbell chimed and Grant looked over at Mary. He didn't know why but he was filled with nerves all of a sudden. Was it the thought that it might be Ethan at the door? Or the police again? He really didn't know.

'I'll get it,' he said.

Grant walked through the hallway towards the front door. It was still light outside and as he approached he noticed out of the porch window who was standing on the front step. Ed Francis. The nosy neighbour.

What was he doing there? Come to gloat about the police's appearance yesterday? Or to find out some more of the details, some juicy gossip to pass on to the other busybodies in the street?

Grant shook his head to clear his thoughts before he opened the door.

'Hi Steven,' Francis said, peering over Grant's shoulder. 'Not a bad time, is it?' he asked, and it sounded like he hoped the answer was yes.

'Course not,' Grant said, acting relaxed and nonchalant. 'Why would it be?'

'What? Oh, no reason.'

Grant resisted rolling his eyes. What had Francis expected him to say? To give him all the gory details of yesterday's incident with their out of control son?

'Yeah, anyway,' Francis continued in his annoying southern wide-boy accent, 'the reason I popped over was, I noticed the other day, when you were cleaning out your garage, that you had a set of golf clubs in there.'

This time Grant had to try *really* hard not to roll his eyes. Was there anything this guy didn't see?

Francis stopped talking and Grant wondered what he was waiting for.

'Yeah. And?'

'Oh, I just wasn't sure if you're still a golfer or not.'

'I was never much of a golfer, to be honest, but I play every now and then.'

'Great. The thing is, I just joined a new club. You know the Belfry?'

Did Grant know the Belfry? That world-renowned golf club just down the road that had hosted the Ryder Cup four times? Oh yeah, that rang a bell. Even someone who didn't know a birdie from a bogey had heard of the place. This was typical Francis. The guy and his wife had only moved to the area a couple of months ago but from the little Grant could make of the two they were out and out show-offs. Fancy cars, fancy clothes. Fancy golf club. Always trying to rub their wealth in other people's faces. Perhaps that was why Francis was always snooping about the place. He was determined to make sure he was the most overtly rich and fashionable person on the street.

Grant had no idea what Francis did for a job. He was younger than Grant was, probably in his early forties. He didn't seem to have a regular office job, never left the house first thing in a suit or anything like that.

Snoopy neighbour? *Look who's talking*, Grant thought, realising then how much attention he'd been paying to Francis over the last few weeks.

Takes one to know one.

'Yeah, Ed, I know the Belfry.'

'Awesome. Well, you know, if you fancy a game? I don't know that many people down there yet, but I could introduce you to some of the crowd. Would be good to get to know you a bit better, us being neighbours and all.'

'I'm a bit busy this week to be honest,' Grant said.

'Oh, right, yeah. But I've actually got a game first thing tomorrow, eight a.m. I noticed before that you're normally around Wednesday mornings, aren't you?'

Grant clenched his jaw for a couple of seconds. Francis was right. Did he miss anything? Wednesday was Grant's quietest day, and he usually either worked from home all day or headed to the university only after lunch.

'Yeah, ok, why not?' Grant said, surprising himself somewhat, but in a way it felt easier to just agree and get Francis to bugger off. 'Would be good to dust the cobwebs off the clubs.'

'Nice one,' Francis said, looking over his shoulder to Grant's old Merc. 'We can pop over there in my Range Rover. Only had it a couple of weeks though, so we'll have to be careful not to get it too muddy, but there's plenty of room in there for the two of us and our bags.'

'That's no way to talk about my wife,' Grant said.

Francis didn't seem to get the joke. Really Grant wasn't sure why he'd even attempted the humour. Was it because on some level he was trying to impress the flash Francis?

'I'll pick you up just after seven?' Francis said. 'That'll give us time to get down there and warm up a bit.'

'Not a problem, I'll see you then.'

Grant went to push the door closed and Francis once again looked over Grant's shoulder, no doubt looking to see if there was anything of interest happening within the madhouse.

There wasn't.

Grant shut the door and returned to the kitchen. Annie had already disappeared and Grant felt a little uneasy that the awkward conversation with her had been left unfinished. Mary was just finishing cleaning up.

'Who was that?' Mary asked, looking slightly suspicious.

'Ed Francis.'

Mary raised an eyebrow.

'He wants me to play golf with him. Tomorrow.'

'What did you say?'

'I said yeah, why not.'

Mary glowered at him, her eyebrow crawling up her forehead as she showed her disapproval.

'Just remember what happened the last time you played, Steven,' Mary said.

Grant sighed. 'Of course, darling. How could I possibly forget?'

Chapter Sixteen

Dani had concluded the interview with Rebecca and Laura, securing their reluctant agreement to return to view the body. Even though they weren't family, and didn't even know the dead girl's full name in order to provide a definitive ID, at least if they formally confirmed that Jane Doe was who they thought, the investigation could be honed. After swapping thoughts with Easton and sending him off to follow up on the snippets of info they now had for their potential victim, Dani headed straight from the interview room to McNair's office to update her.

Although they'd spoken briefly on the phone earlier, Dani hadn't seen her boss at all since after the press conference the previous day, and as she knocked and waited outside the door, she wondered whether she would still be in disgrace.

'Come in,' came McNair's raised voice.

Dani opened the door. McNair had a neutral look on her face. Not a bad result, Dani figured.

'I need to update you,' Dani said.

'Go ahead. Sit down.'

Dani did so. The room fell silent as Dani wondered whether to just dive in or to say something about their argument.

'So?'

Well, if McNair was happy to gloss over it, then so was Dani.

'We have a lead. Two, actually. We have a name for our Jane Doe. Natalya. Easton and I have just been speaking to two of her friends.'

'Natalya? Natalya what?'

'That's the thing. We're not sure yet. It's possibly not her real name at all. From what we've learned she was an escort, and very possibly an illegal immigrant from Europe.'

McNair's face screwed up, the way it often did. 'This is a lead?'

'I genuinely think so. We have an address for Natalya. Easton is on it. But there's more. We were given the name of a guy she was known to hang around with. Jimmy. But—'

'Just Jimmy? What is this, Stephens?'

'Just bear with me. Yes, we were only given the name Jimmy. But we were told he's a low-level drug dealer.'

'You think that's what this is about?'

'Possibly. But there is a link to another missing woman.'

Dani saw McNair's features pick up.

'Yesterday we attended the house of the parents of Grace Agnew who went missing near central Birmingham very recently. We thought maybe she was Jane Doe, but her parents were adamant she isn't. There's no hint of where Grace has gone. When we asked the parents what they thought could have happened to Grace, they talked about her lowlife ex-boyfriend. A Paul Reeve.'

'Finally, two people with surnames.'

'And we've found his ID. We got a picture of him. When we showed it to Natalya's friends…'

Dani left that one dangling, wanting McNair to fill in the blank herself.

'Jimmy is Paul Reeve?' McNair said.

'It seems so.'

'Which means we have one dead woman and one missing woman, linked to the same man.'

Dani held back a smile. 'Exactly.'

–

The debrief with McNair had gone about as well as Dani could have expected. McNair agreed Reeve was a solid lead. Once they'd tracked him down, they'd bring him in for questioning. Dani wanted to lead that herself. But even if they found Reeve straight away, she was done for the day. He could stew in a cell overnight. She was on her way out of HQ, moving towards the lifts when Easton sidled up to her.

'Quite a day,' he said.

'Yep,' Dani said, carrying on walking.

'But we made some decent progress.'

'We're getting there.'

'You live around here, don't you?'

'Just the other side of town.'

'It's pretty late, but… if you want to grab some food before you head back? I've got no plans.'

'No football tonight?' Dani said.

'Well, yeah, if you're interested, we could go to a bar that's got it on.'

Dani stopped walking and Easton stopped too.

'DS Easton, are you asking me out on a date?'

Easton looked flustered all of a sudden, like a nervous schoolboy. 'What? No, I—'

'I'm joking,' Dani said. 'Relax. Sorry, Easton, but I've learned the hard way not to mix business with pleasure. No offence. But thanks for asking.'

Easton looked more embarrassed than anything else.

'Sure thing. See you tomorrow, Boss.'

Dani smiled, then headed on to the lifts.

She was walking through the near empty basement car park when she heard footsteps behind her. She tensed and glanced over her shoulder. She should have known.

'Jason,' Dani said, continuing to walk towards her car as he jogged up to her side.

'Another long day,' he said.

'Yep.'

'I was thinking. About what you said.'

'What did I say?'

'You're right. We don't really know each other anymore.'

Dani stopped walking, Jason did too. She turned to glare at him.

'And? What's your point?'

'That I'd really like to get to know you again. If you'll just let me. Let's just start over. From the beginning.'

'Pretend the last two years hasn't happened? I'm sorry, but that's not possible.'

'Dani, just give me a chance, please. We'll go and get a drink. Some food. Come on, what do you say?'

Dani thought for a few moments. It was barely sixty seconds since she'd turned down Easton's offer. In reality, a stress-free evening drinking and talking football with him was probably far better for her than sitting and skirting around major issues with Jason. But did she really want another night in all alone?

She let out a long sigh. 'Fine,' she said, before she could talk herself out of it.

She left her car where it was and they headed to a nearby pub. It was quiet, with most of the office workers who frequented it having already headed home for the night. It was only Tuesday after all.

When Dani ordered a large glass of red wine Jason gave her his best disapproving look, but he quickly realised his mistake and wiped it away.

'I hear congratulations are in order,' Dani said when they'd taken a seat in a leather-clad booth in the corner of the bar. She raised her glass and chinked it against Jason's.

'Yeah,' he said. 'Thanks. To be honest, with you gone there was a bit of a gap. Too much work, not enough DIs.'

He looked a little sheepish as he said it.

For the next few minutes their conversation was mostly about their jobs, but there was only so much policing that the two of them could take, and soon their conversation turned away from work. Perhaps it was the alcohol, but Dani quickly discovered – or was it rediscovered – just how engaging Jason was. She'd shut him out for so long, but with her defences down the mood was relaxed and their chat free and easy. Somehow Jason managed to ask Dani all manner of questions, without ever putting her on the spot. He also seemed careful to steer clear of the one subject that Dani was dreading talking about.

But after two large glasses of red wine and a steak sandwich, he apparently just couldn't help himself. If only he'd quit while he was ahead. Instead he wanted to talk about *them*. Again.

'You know, I blame myself for what happened,' Jason said.

'You blame yourself for my brother trying to kill me?

Jason looked twitchy all of a sudden. Dani just wanted to get off the subject.

'No, Dani. I'm talking about us. I should have listened to you. My heart was in the right place, and I just wanted to be there for you. But I know now that I pushed too far. I should have given you more space.'

Dani said nothing to that. Was he really to blame? Would they still be together now if he had taken more of a back seat role during her period of recovery, or would she just have resented him for that too? Who knew, but in a way she was even angrier with him now for trying to turn the situation around and make it about himself.

'Maybe it just wasn't meant to be,' Dani said.

Jason looked hurt by that.

'I don't believe you,' he said, sounding more angry himself now. 'I know the real you. Yes, you've changed, but *she's* still inside. This facade, the armour you've got now, it's just on the surface, and it doesn't stop me wanting you. It never will. I get your injuries have changed you, have changed the way your brain is wired, but the same Dani is still in there. I know it. I see it even now.'

Dani's eyes welled with tears, but she held it all inside and didn't say a word, determined to not let the chinks in that armour show.

But why was she so determined to do that?

She picked up her wine and downed the rest of the glass, then looked at her watch.

'It's been a long day,' Dani said.

'Yeah,' Jason said. He finished off his drink too, reading the message loud and clear.

'Thanks for the drinks,' Dani said.

'Anytime.'

Somewhat grumpily Jason headed off to catch a train back to Wolverhampton – where he now rented an apartment alone – before the service stopped for the night. Given the wine she'd had, Dani left her car at HQ and walked back through the city to her apartment. It wasn't that late, just gone ten, and there were plenty of people still out and about. Still, Dani felt jittery as she walked alone in the dark, uneasy, as though there were eyes on her. Perhaps it was her first two days back on the job catching up with her, but as she carried on, her nerves continued to build.

When Dani turned the corner onto the narrow road between two new apartment blocks that led to her building – a quieter and darker street than she'd come from – she picked up her pace and began looking behind her every few steps.

Sure enough, after a few yards, a dark figure appeared around the corner behind Dani, and she felt a wave of panic flooding through her. She walked faster still, looking around twice more as she moved.

The figure was alone. A man, or a woman? Dani couldn't quite tell in the darkness, and because of what looked like a long overcoat that masked the figure's frame. The person wasn't walking particularly quickly. It could be absolutely nothing, Dani realised, but she was spooked.

She ran – no, sprinted – as fast as she could towards the door to her apartment block, reaching into her pocket for the key fob. She looked back again. The figure was still there, still moving calmly but assuredly with a measured step. No alarm. No hurrying. Yet wasn't the person even closer to Dani now than before?

Who the hell *was* that?

Dani turned back, flew the last few yards and lunged towards the security door. She pressed the fob against the keypad, heard the lock release, flung open the door and raced inside. She pulled the security door closed without daring to look outside – she just wanted to get to the safety and comfort of her home. She let go when she felt the magnets lock in place.

Stairs or lift? They were both in the same place, and Dani darted over and banged on the call button for the lift several times. If the lift wasn't already on the ground floor she'd take the stairs.

Luckily it was right there. The doors opened. Dani was already inside and slamming on the button for floor six before the doors had even finished opening fully. Despite her repeatedly pressing the close button, they shut painfully slowly.

'Come on!' Dani said through gritted teeth.

The dim orange street lamp outside by the canal cast a tall but unidentifiable shadow through the glass doors and across the foyer. Dani stared at the shadow, looking for movements. She strained her ears for any sounds of the security door opening.

As the lift doors edged closed, the shadow began to take the shape of a person, and Dani heard the security door wheeze open.

She heard footsteps, slow at first then getting faster. Her heart was bursting in her chest as the lift doors finally closed and the mechanical motor chugged into life.

Even though she was finally on the move, Dani remained panicked. She watched the numbers on the little digital screen. One, two, three, four, five…

'Come on!'

Six. The doors opened and Dani sprinted across the corridor to her door. The key was in her hand but it took her several rushed attempts to get it into the lock because she was shaking so much. When she finally stepped into the dark apartment she kicked the door shut behind her, turned and pulled the latch over.

A shiver ran through her as she switched on the hall light. Her eyes darted around what she could see of the darkened apartment beyond.

Everything seemed quiet and as it should be.

Dani slumped down against the wall.

What the hell had just happened?

She held her head in her hands. She was out of breath. Her pulse was racing. Beads of sweat covered her brow, tears were streaming down her cheeks.

Dani sat there, in silence, while her breathing and her heart and her mind calmed, listening for any sounds from out in the corridor.

None came.

It was only then that Dani realised how alone and vulnerable she felt. She thought about calling someone. But what would she say? And who would she call, anyway? Jason? Gemma? Easton?

Dani shook her head, annoyed at herself for being such a mess.

After a few minutes she finally found the strength to get back to her feet.

She headed straight for the bathroom cabinet.

Chapter Seventeen

Day 122

I'm only half awake as I lie in the hospital bed, alone in my room. There's a knock on the door.

'Come in,' I say.

The door opens and Gemma, my sister-in-law, is standing on the other side. I'd say it's a welcome surprise as she hasn't been here in weeks, but the look of anger in her eyes soon puts paid to any pleasantries.

'What the hell is wrong with you?' she shouts, tossing the newspaper that she's clutching at me.

The paper slaps down onto my chest.

Gemma stares at me aghast. I glance at the paper. A copy of the Daily Mail. I look at the date. It's today's. I pick the paper up, and straighten it out to look at the front page. I'm left staring at a picture of myself. In my hospital bed. Inset is a picture of Ben, my brother.

'What is this?' I say, feeling my hackles raise.

Jason has told me that the national press have taken an interest in my story. Well, my brother mostly. It's not every day that a multiple murderer is caught in Britain. Ben's trial is now in full swing. Jason has warned me off speaking to any reporters, though really he didn't need to. I wouldn't want to speak to them anyway.

'I don't understand,' I say as my eyes scan over the first few lines.

'Yeah, well I bloody do. How much did they pay you for this sensationalist crap?'

'No,' I say, shaking my head, as the reality slowly starts to sink in. My thoughts begin to blur as though my memories are suddenly cracking. I remember the doctors cautioning me. My brain, in its bid for recovery, continues to create false realities. I no longer pace around the hospital looking for the mystery madman, but I'm still easily confused. I see things that aren't really there, have conversations with non-existent people or can't remember anything about real conversations with real people. I feel it now. Confusion. It's taking over and I squeeze my eyes shut, trying to focus, to gain some clarity.

'This wasn't me,' I say, but even I'm not so sure I believe those words.

'No? Then how the hell are they quoting you? It's one thing to put yourself out there, but how dare you bring me into this?' Gemma slams. 'And my children? How could you do that to them, you evil b—'

'Get out!' I yell at Gemma, though I'm not angry with her. I'm angry with myself. 'Just get out. Leave me alone.'

'My pleasure,' Gemma says. 'And you leave me and my kids alone. Got it?'

Gemma storms out. I pick up the paper. It rattles in my hands, which are shaky from the adrenaline surging through my blood. I read the whole article.

I'm such an idiot. I really don't care that much about my own image, but Gemma is right. I've broadcasted the story of my niece and nephew's murderous father to the nation. I've brought them into it.

And the worst part is that I've no memory of the interview. Who did I speak to? When? Did they trick me or did I just willingly give them everything they needed for the prized scoop?

What is happening to me?

Chapter Eighteen

Dani awoke from her drug-eased sleep just after seven in the morning. Not surprisingly she felt anything but refreshed. Even though the fear and panic of arriving home the night before seemed distant and nothing more than an irrational overreaction, the unhappy end to the couple of hours she'd spent with Jason was still playing on her mind.

She checked her phone, saw there was a message from him.

> Thanks for tonight. Sorry how it ended. It was great to see you.

She tutted and scrolled up the page to see the other texts from him that were still on her phone. He'd last texted her three months ago, though she guessed the lack of contact since then was more down to her than him. Once again she didn't bother to reply. Instead, she checked to see if there was any update on Paul Reeve. There was none. Did that mean they hadn't found him yet?

She got up from the bed and set about getting herself ready for the day ahead. When she was showered and dressed and appropriately medicated, she closed the apartment door behind her and headed towards the stairwell. She was soon out in the street and walking alongside the canal towards the revamped Brindleyplace area in central Birmingham. She headed past the closed bars and restaurants, through the looming glass-fronted International Convention Centre and then onward past the oddity that was the newly erected Library of Birmingham, that to Dani basically looked like a gold-cladded chimney and had cost two hundred million pounds at a time of supposed austerity. Still, at least it looked better on the inside.

From there Dani headed past chugging dump trucks and cranes and booming diggers, in the midst of further redevelopment around the area known as Paradise Circus – yeah, real paradise – and onto Colmore Row, heading towards HQ. But HQ wasn't her destination. Not yet anyway. Dani had set Easton up to track down Paul Reeve. She would have happily been involved in that herself, but there really was no need to cause a fuss so soon after returning to work by not keeping to her agreed programme of rehabilitation. So instead she would go to an appointment that she really didn't want to have to keep, but had no choice about. Not if she wanted to continue as a DI under McNair's watch anyway.

The psychiatrist's office was on Newhall Street, off Colmore Row, so was at least convenient for getting to HQ afterwards. Dr Scholz, one of countless psychiatrists Dani had seen over the last two years, was a German-born man in his fifties. He'd lived in England for nearly thirty years but his roots were still obvious in his heavily accented English. He reminded Dani of a professor-type from a bygone era, with his thin hair, round glasses and wispy moustache. He was always immaculately dressed and groomed, yet there was little warmth in Scholz, and Dani had never really opened up in their sessions in the way she was expected to.

Which perhaps explained why she was still having to see him after some six months, even though she'd now been cleared to return to work. Her continued therapy was just one of the conditions McNair, on the advice of Scholz, had insisted upon, until it was deemed Dani was of sound enough mind to halt both the sessions and her anti-depressant medication. Dani often wondered whether she would ever reach that point.

She arrived outside the old redbrick Victorian terrace ten minutes early for her appointment and headed inside to the reception area that was decked out in modern and largely bright white decor – was it modern or just clinical? She sat on a blue plastic chair in the small waiting area while the young receptionist filed her nails. Every so often she glanced at Dani for a few seconds as though she were trying to figure out what was wrong with this clearly deranged woman. At least that's what Dani thought.

Scholz poked his head around his office door bang on the hour and ushered Dani through. His office was pleasantly inviting compared to the reception area, with book-filled shelves, ornaments and various colourful paintings on the walls. As well as the two plain metal chairs in front of his desk, there were two armchairs plus the obligatory chaise longue. Dani had never taken to lying down during these sessions. Instead, at Scholz's invitation to sit where she wanted, Dani opted for one of the seats at the desk. Would Scholz draw any conclusions as to her mental wellbeing from that simple choice alone?

Probably yes. He wouldn't be able to help himself.

'How are you, Dani?'

Scholz sat on his own chair – comfortable leather – put his elbows on the desk and clasped his hands together.

'Fine. I'm back at work now.'

'That's good. And you're coping ok?'

What was she supposed to say in response to that question? That since returning to work she'd gone to bed in tears two nights in a row? That she'd needed both alcohol and pills to help her sleep and to keep her feeling close to sane? That she'd seen a mysterious shadowy figure at a window at a murder scene? That last night she'd thought she was being stalked by the same or possibly another shadowy figure that may or may not have really been there? That she'd nearly had a full-blown panic attack over that?

Of course she wasn't fucking ok.

'Yeah. It feels good to be back,' Dani said.

'I saw you on TV the other night.'

'Yeah.'

'Can't be easy being put straight back into the limelight. Especially on a murder investigation.'

Dani shrugged. 'That's my job.'

Scholz said nothing to that, just sat and studied Dani for a few moments. Their sessions together had blown hot and cold over the past few months. Sometimes Dani would remain placid, almost detached, just trying to stay calm and compliant so that she could get the session over without raising any questions in Scholz's mind. Other sessions became more heated, with Dani defensive and up for a fight over what she felt was Scholz's and the police's agenda of trying to make her out to be goods damaged beyond repair.

Today Dani was strongly hoping she could keep calm. She simply wanted to ride over this and get out in one piece, then get on with the day ahead.

'Have you been taking your medication?' Scholz asked.

And then some, Dani thought, but she didn't say it. 'Just as the doctor ordered.'

'That's good. Often patients struggle a little at first when we reduce the dosages. So taking less hasn't caused you any problems? Heightened sadness? Anxiety attacks? Anything like that?'

Reduced dosage? Well, about that…

'Believe me, not every day is a party, but I think I'm doing ok, under the circumstances.'

After that, the conversation got down into the nitty-gritty of Dani's life over the last few days, but particularly how she had been impacted by being back at work. The session was going quite well, Dani thought. Then Scholz raised the subject of Jason. He asked how Dani had coped with seeing her former lover for the first time in months. She clammed up from there. Jason was far from the cause of her problems, but the subject of their failed relationship was still one of the sorest, and saddest, in her mind, even if it was she who'd ended it – and it felt particularly raw after last night.

'I'd really like you to try something for me, for the next phase of our therapy,' Scholz said.

Our therapy?

'Try what?' Dani asked, hoping they were moving on from talking about Jason.

'Pardon my forwardness, but I think it's really important that you stop closing your mind off from what's happened to you. It's the only way you'll be able to properly move forwards.'

'You mean you think I'm in denial?'

'That would have been a more succinct way of putting it, yes.'

He was probably right, but Dani didn't want to agree and give him the satisfaction of knowing that.

'What I'd like to see the next time we meet is that you've taken steps to confront some of your demons, so to speak. The worst thing for someone in your position to do is to internalise their problems.'

'Are you still talking about Jason?' Dani said, feeling frustrated that he was a subject that needed discussing at all.

'In part, yes. If you were to ask me my personal opinion, I'd say that pushing away someone like Jason who cares about you is probably not helping you right now. Having a support network is very important and I'm not sure why you're so determined to get through this alone.'

'Just as well I didn't ask for your personal opinion then,' Dani said, and she saw Scholz squirm slightly at that. He looked at her questioningly, as though waiting for her to apologise for her abruptness.

'Sorry,' she said, not really feeling it. 'You can blame my irritability on my damaged frontal lobes. Or the meds. Take your pick.'

'Don't worry, Dani. I know you're still struggling with the changes in your personality.'

Did he?

'Actually I do get where you're coming from,' Dani said.

Scholz raised an eyebrow at Dani's perhaps unexpected acquiescence.

'Which is why I've arranged to go and see Ben.'

Scholz looked shocked at that.

'You said I need to confront my past,' Dani said, when Scholz failed to say a word.

'I did. I'm actually pleasantly surprised by this, Dani.'

'Believe me, there's nothing pleasant about the thought of going to see my brother.'

'No, I'm sure there's not. But I really do think that it will help you in the long run. May I ask what led you to this decision?'

Dani let out a long sigh. She thought about Harry and Chloe. Was a part of her doing this for them, or would saying that just be a smokescreen? Until yesterday, Dani hadn't known how on earth her visiting her murderous brother in prison was ever going to help her relate to the real world with more purpose again. What she'd thought she needed was to erase him from her life one hundred percent. Remove every single memory and every single facet of his existence from her mind. But really, didn't she need some sort of closure for herself?

'I saw my niece and nephew yesterday.'

'That's good. I'm glad you're able to spend time with them now.'

'Harry brought it up. I saw the hurt and the confusion and the anger in his eyes as he talked about Ben. He doesn't even have the option of confronting his father. Gemma won't allow that. He's effectively being placed in denial because of someone else's wishes.'

'I'm sure she's looking out for her child's best interests.'

'I'm sure she is too. But wouldn't it do him good to be able to see his dad and to ask him all the questions that a ten-year-old must have?'

'Perhaps. I can't say, as I've not met him.'

Dani sniffed at the vague and unhelpful response.

'On the other hand,' she said, 'you're right. The only person stopping me from moving on is me. Seeing him is something I now know I *have* to do.'

Ben was still on Dani's mind as she made her way on foot from Scholz's office to HQ. Out in the fresh air her anger rose again as she continued to think about her brother, and she shook her head, trying to clear the thoughts of him from her mind. Yes, she would see him, but she still had a job to do in the meantime. She couldn't let him dominate her life, nor could she let her constant irritation sour her return to the force.

She walked down Colmore Row, past St Philip's cathedral, the pavements busy with suited workers piling into their offices. Dani would normally arrive at HQ well before the morning rush got into full speed, and she dodged and occasionally bumped into the frustratingly slow movers as she stormed along. Just before she reached Snowhill station, Dani ducked into a Waitrose store to grab a strong black coffee that she hoped would help to calm her mood.

She waited in line at the self-service machine. On a rack to her left she spotted a small pile of *Birmingham Mail* newspapers from the night before. Unsurprisingly, the picture on the front cover was of Monday night's press conference. McNair, Fletcher and Dani sitting in a row. McNair was in mid-speech, her hands gesticulating. Fletcher looked cool and composed. Dani looked like the proverbial rabbit in headlights.

The headline stated that the police were desperately trying to identify a murder victim, but that clearly wasn't the whole story detailed in the fine print because Dani could also see the caption underneath the picture. Rather than giving her the plain old title of DI Stephens, the hacks had done exactly what McNair had suggested they might.

> DI Danielle Stephens, twin sister of serial killer Ben Stephens, back with Force CID following her horrific attempted murder ordeal.

Dani cringed and shut her eyes for a few seconds. It was one thing having to deal with her problems, but having the whole world watching her… Why was she even putting herself through this?

Maybe she should walk out of the shop, go home, pack her bags and head off to the deepest, most remote countryside and grow potatoes or something.

When she opened her eyes again it felt as though all eyes in the store were on her. Like everyone had seen the newspaper and knew who she was. Like they were judging her, talking about her, trying to decide if she was a mental case like her brother or not.

With the walls closing in, and Dani's heart pummelling her ribs, she moved up to the coffee machine and pressed the button for a black americano, adding an extra shot for good measure, even though she was sure the extra caffeine was probably not what she really needed. She was shakily putting the lid onto the paper cup when she felt someone moving up behind her. Dani half-turned.

'I'm so sorry,' the woman said. 'I didn't mean to startle you.'

'That's fine,' Dani said, only giving the blonde woman a cursory glance. Whoever she was, Dani didn't really want to engage.

'I thought I recognised you from the paper,' the woman said. 'You're Danielle Stephens, aren't you?'

'Yes,' Dani said, moving away from the woman and the machine. She needed air.

'I—'

'Why don't you just buy the damn paper?' Dani said, voice raised. 'I'm sure that'll tell you everything you need to know about me.'

Dani carried on her way, not looking back to see the reaction on the woman's face. She moved over to the self-scan tills, keeping her head down. The shop felt stifling; she needed to be outside. She swiped her card against the pad then strode for the exit, avoiding eye contact with anyone else.

Only when she was out in the cool morning, taking deep lungfuls of autumn air, did it strike Dani that maybe she'd just blown a potential lead. The whole idea of the press conference, after all, was to obtain information related to the murder. What if the woman who'd approached her knew something? She could be another friend of the victim or a witness of some sort. And Dani had been more concerned about her own public image than bringing a murderer to justice.

Too late now. As Dani glanced around, and back into the shop, she didn't even know which of the many people in sight it had been. Banishing the thought that she'd messed up, Dani continued outside and turned left to head the short distance to HQ. The entrance was in sight when her phone rang. She lifted it from her pocket. Easton.

'You need to get over here right away,' he said.

'What is it?'

'Paul Reeve. He's dead.'

Chapter Nineteen

Grant had to admit, Francis's Range Rover was actually damn nice. The quality of the interior was sublime. There were splashes of chrome everywhere, and anything that wasn't shiny was draped in cream leather, edged in thick stitching that had more than likely been done by hand. Quite how many cows had been skinned to fit out the car, Grant didn't know, but he was sure it was many. Regardless, he was impressed. And a little jealous. Perhaps it was about time he had an upgrade after all?

'You work over at the university, don't you?' Francis said as they hurtled along the M42. The needle on the speedometer edged past ninety, though the car felt like a cocoon from the outside world and there was no sense of the speed of the machine.

'I do,' Grant said. 'I'm a professor.'

'Criminology, right?'

'Yes.'

'So basically you're into serial killers and things.'

Grant looked over at Francis, who was staring straight ahead at the road.

'That's been one of my main areas of focus over the years, yes.'

Francis shook his head. 'Man, I don't think I'd have the stomach for that.'

'It's not to everyone's taste, I'll admit,' Grant said.

'I never read your book.'

Grant had wondered how long it would take for the conversation to steer to that. People were always so predictable.

'Not many people would these days,' Grant said. 'That was all a long time ago.'

'*Essence of Evil*. That was it, wasn't it?'

'It was.'

'So you don't stick by it anymore?'

'Stick by it? I'm sure much of the psychoanalysis I wrote about still applies, but what happened to me, the backdrop of that book, was a long time ago. I'm a different man to who I was when I wrote that.'

Grant felt little emotion as he talked about his dark past. He'd long come to terms with what had happened to him. Following that disturbing period had come something of an awakening for him, the writing of his book as much an exercise in catharsis as it was the research and analysis of his profession that it appeared to be to everyone else.

'What do *you* do, anyway?' Grant asked Francis.

'Not too much these days. Just a bit of consulting every now and then.'

And that was all Grant got from his neighbour, and although intrigued by the vague answer, he didn't bother to question for more. He hadn't wanted Francis prying into his personal affairs so why would he do the same to Francis?

They arrived at the Belfry a good half hour before tee off. The place was buzzing with activity, as the resort included not just three golf courses but a hotel and large conference centre too. There was certainly a hell of a lot of money on display, Grant noticed – flash cars and flashier men with their outrageous golfing garb here, there and everywhere. Not many women about. Perhaps they were all in the adjoining health spa. It was the exact opposite of the type of place that Grant felt comfortable in, but he was there now and he'd do his best to enjoy it.

After ten minutes on the practice putting green, Francis and Grant made their way to the first tee where their two playing partners were waiting.

'Alright boys,' Francis said, slapping his hand into the palms of both the men.

'Greg, Eric, this is Steven Grant, my neighbour. Steven, this is Greg Wilander. He's some big ass partner over at PwC – you know, those clowns who earn shitloads of cash for dishing out everyday advice that no one needs.'

Wilander stepped forwards and shook Grant's hand.

'You're only saying that because you can't afford me,' Wilander snorted, and Grant thought he appeared flattered by Francis's laddish banter.

'Twelve hundred quid an hour?' Francis said. 'I can think of far better ways to spend that sort of money than on you.'

'But you've never tried me, so how could you know?'

Francis winked at Wilander before turning to the other man.

'And this is Eric Baxter, he's a Chief Super over at West Mids police.'

Baxter gave Grant an unconvincing smile and a bone-crushing handshake. Grant reciprocated, though he was feeling somewhat out of his depth in this group of men.

'Hey Bax, you and Grant here have probably got a lot to talk about. This is Professor Steven Grant. You know, the guy who knows everything there is to know about murder.'

Grant felt his cheeks flush, but Baxter appeared unimpressed with the revelation.

'I thought you looked familiar,' he said, his eyes narrowing. But that was all he said.

The foursome took their shots from the first tee and soon they were off, trudging around the sodden golf course. Although the day was sunny and dry, the cold autumnal night had left the ground thick with moisture and the low sun could do nothing to alleviate the situation. The bottom of Grant's trousers were soon sopping wet – not helped by the fact that on each of the first three holes his tee shots were wayward, landing in the long grass of the rough.

By that point Grant already felt something of an outsider among the four. Francis may only have lived in the area for a couple of months but he clearly already had the attention of the other two men – both senior figures in the community, in their own ways. Grant couldn't really figure how that had happened.

Why did Francis have such a hold, other than because he was cocky and arrogant?

Wilander was an extrovert like Francis, Grant noticed, but Baxter was more measured – as Grant had found many senior police officers to be over the years. Baxter, in his fifties, Grant guessed, was a true silver fox with bright grey hair that sat somewhat uncomfortably with his tanned skin. Grant was sure Baxter was a ladies' man. There something about his look, and although he was reserved he was clearly full of confidence and self-importance. He didn't wear a ring on his finger – probably divorced following a mid-life crisis that had involved him putting his penis into a much younger version of his wife.

Or perhaps that was just an unfair assumption by Grant, brought on by the fact he felt out of his depth with these confident men. Regardless, Grant felt wary around the senior officer, whose eyes were forever on the move as he weighed up the integrity of everyone and everything around him.

You can take the man out of the police, but you can't take the police out of the man.

'You two really should get together, you know,' Francis said to Grant and Baxter as they walked along the fairway, as though he were an expert matchmaker.

'I don't know,' Baxter said. 'No offence, professor, but we've had your type in before.'

'My type?' Grant said, naturally offended.

'No disrespect, but there's a big difference between the theory and actually policing a murder investigation.'

'I don't doubt that for a second,' Grant said. 'But understanding the psychology of a killer can still be important in finding them.'

'Yeah, you must have watched *Cracker* before, Bax?' Francis added, as though it was a miraculous insight.

'In my experience it's not important at all,' Baxter said. 'Deranged serial killers don't really exist in the real world. Not like you see on the telly all the time, anyway. They're one in a million. Most homicides we deal with are far simpler than you see on *Silent Witness*. Gang violence. Domestics.'

'You're doing yourself an injustice there, mate,' Francis said.

'No, just telling it straight. But if we do find ourselves with a crazed multiple killer on our hands who leaves no trace of evidence, you'll be the first to know, professor.'

'I'm flattered,' Grant said, trying his best to not sound agitated.

'You'd better watch it, Bax,' Francis said, sniggering. 'I think the prof is going to drop you in a vat of acid now. He knows all the tricks, don't forget.'

Baxter smiled at the joke but Grant sensed the policeman wasn't in the least amused. Quite why he'd felt the need to belittle Grant, he didn't know.

By the end of the sixth hole Grant's golfing rustiness was showing: he was already several shots behind the other three, and feeling more and more riled by his poor game. His mood wasn't helped by the fact that he was becoming increasingly alienated from the group who were often left chatting among themselves while Grant was off trying to find his ball.

The others said nothing about Grant's poor game. At least not initially. But then the inevitable comments started. *Your knees are too bent. Your back's not straight. The club's too far away. Your feet are too wide.*

Grant was getting more and more angry, not just with them but with himself too. This was the very reason he'd stopped playing golf regularly in the first place. Despite his introvert nature, Grant was a massively competitive person and he couldn't stand that he wasn't as good as he wanted to be at the game. Some people were able to scuttle around a golf course with the worst-looking swing in the world – a real hit and hope style – and still record scores way better than Grant, who'd taken lessons for years to try to develop a swing that resembled 'correct' form. He just couldn't get it right though. At least not to his satisfaction.

On the twelfth hole Grant's second shot landed in a deep bunker next to the green and his heart sank.

'Hard luck, mate,' Francis said.

Grant prepped himself for the next shot while the other three stood over their balls, each of them already on the green.

'Make sure you take a lot of sand,' Wilander called.

'Nice and hard,' Francis said.

Baxter said nothing, just stared.

Grant looked down at the ball and imagined the little puckered object was Francis's head. Then he swung the club down at speed and crashed the club face into it. He topped the damn thing. The ball jumped up the side of the bunker, sped across the green, rolled up a ridge on the other side and landed straight in another bunker.

There was an awkward silence from the other three, who must have by now sensed that Grant was about ready to explode. He stomped his way across the grass, not looking any of them in the eye.

'More sand this time,' Wilander said.

Grant clenched his fists as tight as he could as he walked past. He reached the ball and squared up and this time imagined the ball was Wilander's face, complete with his bleached white smile and that arrogant glint in his eye. Grant swiped at the ball angrily but this time went too deep, talking way too much sand, and the ball jumped all of two feet in front of him then rolled back down the slope of the bunker back to his feet.

Without thinking Grant took another angry swipe and this time topped the ball again and it scuttled across the green back where it had come from, rolling straight into the opposite bunker for a second visit.

Grant couldn't hold it in any longer. He roared in anger and hurled the club across the green. The spinning metal projectile whizzed past Wilander's face, missing him by only inches.

Wilander's face soured. 'You throw that at me?'

'What? No,' Grant said, stepping out of the sand.

Baxter said nothing. Just glowered at Grant with contempt.

'Quite a temper on you there, mate,' Francis said, his face showing his disapproval at Grant's lack of etiquette – a golfing faux pas of grand proportions. Grant really couldn't give a shit.

He only hoped he could contain his rumbling anger for the rest of the game.

Perhaps Ethan wasn't so different to him after all.

Chapter Twenty

'What happened?' Dani asked Easton as she stared at the bloodied and near naked body of the man in the corner of the lounge. There were splashes of blood on the oak flooring and magnolia walls. Other than a colossal TV with DVD player and extravagant sound system, plus a single three-seater sofa, the room was strangely sparse with no other furniture or knick-knacks.

'You mean what happened to him?' Easton responded, an eyebrow half-raised as though Dani's was a dumb question.

'No. With you. How did you get in here?'

The ground floor apartment in Edgbaston was one of three inside a grand Edwardian semi-detached. At one time the building and the whole street would have been well-to-do. In recent years, as the city had expanded, the area, so close to the city centre, had become another confused neighbourhood, much like Moseley, with clashing cultures, various ethnic backgrounds, religions, languages, immigrants both legal and illegal and both wealthy and poor inhabitants. Judging by the size and quality of the building, and the apartment, Dani guessed that it was towards the higher end of the properties on the street.

'This was one of two addresses we could link to Reeve,' Easton said. 'The first was over near Harborne, but it's now rented out to a young couple who claimed to not know him at all. There was no answer here when we rang and knocked on the door. DC Constable decided—'

'DC Constable?'

'Yeah.' Easton said, straight-faced.

'Detective Constable Constable?'

'Yeah.'

Despite the situation Dani found herself stifling a smile.

'He's upstairs at the moment, checking out what the neighbours have seen and heard.'

'So?'

'So Constable tried the handle.'

'For what reason?'

'You'd have to ask him that.' The tone of his voice made it clear he felt unnecessarily challenged.

'And?'

'It was unlocked.'

'So you decided to enter, just like that?'

'I think we had reasonable cause, given what's happened.'

Easton was certainly on the defensive. That was fine. Dani was pushing him, she had to make sure the judgment to enter the premises was sound. Even though there was a dead body here, the police had entered effectively on a whim. She'd have done the same thing – in fact she had done so over at June Staunton's house – but that didn't mean everyone would see it the same way, and the key thing was making sure that Easton had a sound and justifiable explanation.

'Hindsight is a wonderful thing,' Dani said. 'So what do you know?'

'Very little. I mean, it looks like it's our guy, doesn't it?'

Dani looked at the blood-smeared face, which certainly bore a close resemblance to the picture they had of Paul Reeve, aka Jimmy.

'The paramedics confirmed the death,' Easton said. Dani nodded. A medically trained person confirming death was a procedural necessity, even if it was damn obvious Reeve would never be getting up again.

'What happened before they arrived?' Dani asked.

'We checked the body first, to see if he was alive. After we called it in, we checked the rest of the apartment to see if anyone else was here. But other than that we haven't touched or looked for anything. I called forensics, just like you said, then waited for you to arrive.'

'Ok,' Dani said, deep in thought.

'Do you think we should call the pathologist too?'

Dani mulled that one over for a moment. She moved to the body and squatted down onto her haunches.

'Stabbed to death, it looks like,' Dani said.

'I agree. There're at least two puncture wounds to the gut. Massive blood loss. But also abrasions and bruises to the face, arms and torso.'

Dani sighed. Cause of death seemed clear enough, and even though she could well imagine Ledford's response to being called out to the crime scene if he felt it unnecessary, she feared that the case might be bigger than even she had thought. They'd wanted to speak to Paul Reeve in relation to the murder of Natalya, and he also had a clear link to another missing woman – Grace Agnew. Plus he had two stab wounds to the gut, the same injuries which had proved fatal to Natalya.

What the hell was happening?

'Call Ledford. Maybe he'll pick up on something here that we won't. I'd rather be safe than sorry.'

'I'll do it now.'

Easton headed off into the hallway. Dani slipped on the pair of blue latex gloves she was carrying in her pocket.

The dead man in front of her was wearing nothing but a pair of black boxer shorts. His body was covered in blood, and although he had other scrapes and cuts, there didn't appear to be any serious wounds other than the two in his belly.

She looked over his hands. There was grime under his nails. Together with the scrapes and bruises on his body, he'd definitely been involved in a fight or struggle at some point, but it was possible those marks had been inflicted at an earlier time. Hopefully Ledford could provide some clarity on that.

Dani looked around her. Other than the blood smears in the room, there were no obvious signs of a struggle. She thought about moving the body to inspect for other wounds on his back. She didn't. Ledford would soon be there and he'd want to do things his own way.

Instead Dani straightened up and took a look around.

There was nothing else of interest in the lounge so she headed out to the hallway. The apartment had two bedrooms, both with en suites, and a large kitchen/diner. Everything was neat and ordered, expensively fitted but with little by way of warmth or homeliness. No ornaments or photo frames or art on the walls. One of the bedrooms had a single bed, with a bare mattress on top and an empty wardrobe. Dani walked into the other bedroom which had a much grander king-size bed, with mussed up shiny bedclothes on top.

She moved over to the large chest of drawers nestled next to an ornate dark wood fireplace. The first drawer contained t-shirts. Expensive t-shirts at that. The second contained similarly pricey clothes. The third down was something of a dumping ground with all manner of correspondence and stationery and forms and records. Dani picked up a utility bill, just a couple of weeks old. It was addressed to Mr J Colton.

She rifled through the other items and found several other letters addressed to J or Jimmy Colton, including a mobile phone bill, a credit card statement and a letter about a gym membership. Then she found a bank statement. A little over five thousand pounds was the balance just a few weeks ago, though the ins and outs over the period shown were several times more than that.

'Mr Paul Reeve,' Dani said out loud as she looked at the addressee.

'What have you got?' Easton asked. His unexpected voice made Dani jump. She spun around. Easton was casually hanging in the doorway.

'Jesus, Easton, why are you sneaking up on me like that?'

'Sorry, didn't mean to startle you.'

'Over here.'

Dani went back to her search. She lifted up a plain white envelope and found underneath it three passport photos from a square of four. The man in the picture was definitely Paul Reeve. And Dani was sure it was also the same man who was now lying dead in the other room.

'What's with the false name, do you think?' she asked as she stared at the photos.

'Who says it's false?'

Good point, Dani thought, but didn't say. They'd already confirmed that Paul Reeve was a genuine identity, and had assumed Jimmy was just an alias he used. But was there really a Jimmy Colton too? If not, then Paul Reeve, or someone else on his behalf, had gone to a hell of a lot of effort to create the fake identity. It was way more than just using a different first name to chat up girls in bars. Why?

'Constable is still off speaking to the neighbours,' Easton said. 'Forensics are outside, just getting kitted up. Ledford will be here within the hour.'

'Thank you.'

'I've also got an address and a phone number for Paul Reeve's parents. So what now?'

Dani shut the third drawer and opened up the last one. Socks. Boxer shorts. Neatly folded and designer branded. Dani frowned. She stuck her hand into the drawer and pulled the underwear aside. Sure enough, the drawer was shallower than the other three. She felt around the edges. It wasn't a false bottom. Dani slid the drawer back slightly then tilted it up and pulled it back out, lifting it off the runners. She looked inside the unit's carcass.

'Bloody hell,' she said.

Easton crouched down beside her.

'Bloody hell indeed,' he said, as Dani gazed inside the drawer unit. More specifically, she gazed at the myriad little plastic bags of white pills and powder. There were also two brick-sized lumps covered in brown tape.

'I think we know how he could afford this place then,' Easton said.

Chapter Twenty-One

'What exactly do we know about Paul Reeve?' Dani asked Easton as they drove from Edgbaston and across to Shirley where Paul Reeve's parents lived. Her question was as much a refresher for herself as it was a means of learning new information. They'd already scoured what data they could on Reeve but Dani was struggling to put the pieces of his life and death together in her mind.

'Twenty-two years old,' Easton said. 'A former semi-pro footballer for Tamworth football club. Apparently everyone thought he'd make it to full professional when he was younger, but a knee injury saw all that come to an end when he was still a teenager. You'd be amazed how many careers fall apart at a young age like that.'

'You're speaking from experience?'

'Not me, I was never that good. But more than one of my mates had professional contracts when they were younger, that never worked out. And afterwards, they're left with nothing. Clubs don't care, the agents walk away with their cut and move onto the next one to bleed dry. In my eyes the clubs and the authorities need to do more to protect these kids and make sure they have something even if their premier league dreams don't work out.'

She looked over at him and was pleasantly impressed with the determined look on his face. She'd assumed his spouting about football agents before was just the pipe dream of a football fanatic, but perhaps there was more to it than that.

'And what's Reeve been up to since?' Dani asked.

'Odds and sods. Worked in his dad's business for a while. Some sort of building contractors, from what I can gather. More recently he'd been working as an apprentice plumber for one of his dad's mates, and doing night classes.'

'Though he had quite the side business going.'

'Either that or he had a serious coke problem.'

'We have to assume his death could be related to the drugs.'

'Seems the obvious answer doesn't it… but I sense you're not convinced by that?'

'No. I'm not. Though I don't really know why.'

Dani took a left turn, leaving behind terraced rows of mainly Asian-inspired shops and eateries and onto a quieter and wider residential street.

'Take this right,' Easton said after a few hundred yards.

Dani did so, then stopped soon after at a red light at a busy crossroads flanked on one side by a petrol station and on the opposite by a grand old pub building that had been remodelled as a trendy bistro. Together with the leafy streets and the imposing period houses it was certainly a homely and relatively wealthy area. The lights turned green and Dani pulled away.

'It should be just down here on the right,' Easton said, craning his neck.

Dani turned, then after a hundred yards she pulled the car to the side of the road outside the unassuming detached house on a quiet suburban street. It seemed nice enough, not all that upmarket, but close enough to more affluent areas to make the residents feel like they'd made it in life. Plus the residents could still claim to come from the borough of Solihull, of course.

Matthew Reeve opened the door to Dani and Easton. In his forties, he was tall and athletic with a wide chest and a face that was dominated by a heavily chiselled jaw. Dani had her ID card at the ready and did the introductions. They'd called in advance to prep the parents about the reason for the visit and Matthew said little, just ushered them inside. His wife, Barbara, was in an armchair in the floral-inspired lounge. She looked sunken and hollow. In Dani's experience it was the way all mothers looked when they learned of the death of one of their sons or daughters. Even Dani, who'd suffered more than most, couldn't quite imagine what that pain must feel like.

'Please take a seat,' Matthew said.

Dani and Easton sat next to each other on a three-seater sofa. Barbara offered them hot drinks – as a courtesy more than anything, Dani decided, and both she and Easton politely declined. Matthew sat in a chair next to his wife and reached his hand out onto hers. She didn't react at all. In fact Dani hadn't even seen the woman blink yet. She could quite easily have passed for a waxwork.

'We attended an address this morning on Rotton Park Road,' Dani said. 'We believe that's where your son, Paul, lived?'

'Yes. He did. Does,' Matthew said.

'I'm very sorry to have to tell you that the body of a young man was found there. We have reason to believe it was your son.'

Dani noticed Barbara Reeve flinch, but she held herself together.

'We'll need you to come and perform a formal identification of the body at a later time, but for now it would be useful if you could provide confirmation based on a photo of the deceased. The picture I'm about to show you… this won't be easy for you, but I'd like you to tell me if this is your son.'

Dani nodded to Easton who took out his phone, found the close-up of the dead man's face, and passed the phone over to the Reeves. Matthew took it in his hand, took one glance and looked to his wife. She was staring at him. He nodded to her, and she flicked her eyes to the screen for just a split second before she whipped them away again. She broke down in tears.

'Mr Reeve, is that your son?' Dani asked.

'Yes.'

'You're absolutely sure.'

'It's Paul,' he said as a tear escaped his eye and ran down his cheek.

The foursome remained seated in the lounge. For minutes no one had moved. Dani and Easton were giving the Reeves the time they needed to process the death of their son, but Dani wanted to push on. There were questions she needed to ask. If they'd let her.

'What happened to him?' Barbara asked, looking up at Dani.

'It's too early for us to say exactly. But we think he was murdered. Stabbed.'

'How? Why? Who would do that to him?'

'Those are some of the questions we were hoping to ask you,' Dani said.

With that, Barbara's expression turned from hollow to scathing in a flash. Dani wondered whether her words had been misconstrued. She braced herself for the outburst that was surely coming. She'd seen it many times in family members who'd just learned of the death of a relative: consumed with pain and anger, they needed to vent, and the police were an easy target. Dani knew better than anyone how venting and raging was a by-product of trauma. She would try to remain as placid as she could. Barbara Reeve had lost a son and she needed support.

'So you don't know who did this?' Barbara blasted. 'What good is that? You should be out there now, catching my son's killer.'

And then, as quickly as the anger had come, it was overtaken with sadness and Barbara bowed her head and sobbed.

'So you think this could take a long time then?' Reeve asked. He betrayed no emotion, though he seemed strained as though he was bottling it up to try and stay strong for his wife. Eventually it would explode out of him, Dani knew. It always did.

'It's possible,' was all Dani said to that. 'You have to understand that we're at a very early stage of the investigation.'

'But you have no suspect?'

'I'm afraid we don't yet.'

'Wait a minute,' Barbara said. She jabbed a finger towards Dani in something of a eureka moment. 'I know you.'

Matthew Reeve raised an eyebrow and looked over to his wife. Dani felt Easton staring at her too and she tensed up, waiting for Barbara to carry on.

'I saw you in the paper, quite a while back, but then the other day as well. You're that detective who was almost killed.'

She turned to her husband for confirmation. He looked back at Dani, his eyes now beady as he tried to place where he might have seen her before.

'I'm right, aren't I?' Barbara asked.

'Yes,' Dani said.

'Hell of a thing to come back from that.'

'It was. But I'm back nonetheless.'

'They caught the guy, didn't they? The one who did that to you?'

Barbara pointed again. Dani knew she was indicating the scar. By now Dani's blood was rushing, and the room felt stifling. Given the press conference and the headline in the local paper, she had to expect to be recognised. She just wished it didn't make her feel so useless and… angry. Why did it make her feel angry, exactly?

Was a smaller part of what Ben had stolen from her a sense of anonymity? It was true that in the past Dani had been a private person, a detective devoted to catching the bad guys rather than being in the limelight. Now, no matter what she did in her career, Dani would always be known as the woman who was almost killed by her serial killer brother.

Dani clenched her teeth.

'It was your brother, wasn't it?' Barbara said, not yet reading the signs, as everyone else in the room cringed and just willed her to shut the hell up.

'Yes,' Dani said, her hands, her feet, her legs, now trembling as she struggled to contain her emotion. But she fought through it and when she spoke, she sounded calm and collected, almost detached. 'My brother. My twin in fact, if you must know. He did this to me.' She touched the scar. Ran a finger along its length. Remembering. 'He tried to kill me. He didn't succeed. And now he'll spend the rest of his life behind bars. I stopped him, just like I've stopped dozens of killers in the past. And I'll do everything I can to find your son's killer too.'

The room fell silent. Reeve nodded as though impressed with Dani's resolve. Barbara just held Dani's stare, her face giving nothing away.

When the tension grew unbearable, Dani sprang to her feet, fished her phone out of her bag and looked at the screen at the imaginary call coming through. 'If you could excuse me a minute, I've just got to take this.'

She strode for the door without waiting for a response.

Chapter Twenty-Two

Dani took several gulps of fresh air as she stood outside the Reeves' house, trying to rein in her irritability. She wanted nothing more than to be amenable and sympathetic to the parents of a young man who'd just been found murdered, but despite her best intentions, the mention of Ben and her past had a habit of bringing the worst out in Dani. The last thing she needed was to be butting heads with the parents of the deceased, but she'd felt about ready to explode at Barbara Reeve for bringing up her ordeal.

She took two more lungfuls of air and held her body rigidly in place, until the trembling stopped. Satisfied, she made her way back into the house.

As she walked through the hall she stopped to look at the gallery of family photos hanging from the wall and up the side of the staircase. She'd noticed them on the way in, but hadn't been given the chance then to take them in properly. There were various holiday snaps and professional photos of the Reeves taken over the years. Paul Reeve featured in many of them. He was tall and lean with chiselled facial features – much like his father. His squared chin, protruding brow and dark stubble made him look older than his age. In many ways he was handsome, but there was an unpleasant glint in his eye. Rebecca had said he was creepy; the Agnews had said something similar too. There was simply something… off about him.

Paul wasn't an only child. There were even more pictures on the wall of a guy Dani could only guess was Paul's older brother. He was not as tall, nor as athletic as the now-deceased youngest son, but the firm family favourite, Dani decided. As kids he was the one always in his mother's arms on the holiday shots, where Paul was often off skulking to the side. The brother was the one with a wide and happy smile, compared to Paul's frowns and pouts. The star photo of the gallery by far was of Paul's brother wearing graduation garb from Aston University. No such picture of Paul existed.

'That's Anthony,' Barbara said, her unexpected intrusion startling Dani.

Dani turned to Barbara who was standing in the lounge doorway, her face drained, her eyes welled with tears.

'He's older than Paul?' Dani said, quickly recovering.

'He was. Ant's dead too.'

'I'm so sorry,' Dani said, her words edged with genuine shock.

'It was a car accident. A lorry driver, asleep at the wheel on the M6, ploughed into his car. Four years ago this December. Ant and his girlfriend both died that night.'

'That's terrible,' Dani said, surprised that Barbara was holding herself together as well as she was.

'The guy'll be out of prison next year, they reckon,' Barbara said. 'Good behaviour. Our Ant had good behaviour all his life… where'd it get him? No one can give him a get out of jail free card.'

Dani didn't know what to say. She felt immensely sorry for Barbara and Matthew Reeve, to have lost not one but two adult sons, and in such a short space of time.

'They're lovely photos,' Dani said, thinking about how she could steer the conversation somewhere useful. She wanted to find out more about the brothers. More about who Paul Reeve was, and what had got him killed.

'Yeah, well, that's all I have of my boys now.'

Barbara turned and padded off towards the kitchen.

'Are you sure you don't want a hot drink, detective?' she called without turning back.

'Black coffee, please. Strong.'

'But not strong enough,' Barbara called back. And Dani thought she knew what Barbara meant by that. What she would do for a vodka on ice…

She huffed at her own immature thought and moved away from the wall of photos and back into the lounge. She took the seat next to Easton again.

'We were just talking about Paul's football career,' Easton said.

'Your colleague here,' Matthew said, 'he's got his head screwed on all right. If only Paul had known someone like this back when he was a youngster.'

Dani looked over at Easton, impressed by the compliment. He flicked his eyebrows in a self-satisfied manner.

'Paul was good, wasn't he?' Dani asked, looking back at Matthew.

He half-smiled and shrugged. 'He loved his football, but… oh, I don't know. Of course it would have been great for him to play for the Villa – that's my team, his too – but you need more than just talent. A lot of it's luck. Right place, right time. Even without the injury, it would have been tough, but… we'll never know.'

Dani sensed plenty of tension in Matthew Reeve, and she had the feeling that it wasn't all related to the news about the death of his son. There was something else underneath, as though Paul's failed football career had long been a bone of contention in the family. She thought back to the photos on the wall. Of Paul's distance in the pictures, and of the elder son's graduation. How far back did all the strain go?

'So what did Paul want to do with his life, after football was out of the picture?' Dani asked.

'Well that was the problem, wasn't it? He had nothing to fall back on. We told him all along he needed a backup. We wanted him to go to uni, like Ant, but Paul was having none of it. In the end he came away from school with nothing.'

Barbara came back from the kitchen with a tray of steaming mugs and her expression turned from amenable to hostile when she heard what her husband was talking about. She pretty much slammed the tray down. Two of the cups spilled over in the process.

'Don't you dare talk about my Paul like that.'

'I was just answering their question,' Reeve said, his hackles rising too.

Barbara dished out the drinks and Dani took a long, deep inhale of her treacly black coffee, the hot vapour renewing her focus.

'How was Paul in himself when he realised his football dream was over?' Dani asked. She felt Barbara giving her daggers but she kept her focus on Matthew.

'It changed him,' he said 'He wasn't himself anymore. I mean, he was depressed. Maybe not… you know, not like…'

Matthew looked away from Dani as though he was treading on territory that was too close to her own position.

'…he wasn't diagnosed with it or anything. He wasn't on Valium or Prozac or any of that nonsense—'

Dani tried her best not to react, though she was sure Matthew was insinuating that she *was* on all that nonsense. Which she was, but that wasn't the point.

'—but he was definitely different. Different to the boy we knew.'

'You took him on at your company?' Easton asked.

'He needed a job. He was still living at home through all this but we wanted…'

Matthew trailed off again, unable to say what he'd intended. Barbara was kind enough to finish her husband's sentence.

'What my husband is trying to say is that he wanted our son out of the house. He thought Paul was a useless sponge. He gave him a job just so Paul would have enough money for us to get rid of him for good without us worrying about him living out on the streets somewhere like a bum.'

Barbara glared at her husband but he just looked straight ahead at Dani. He remained impassive but the slight twitches in his facial muscles suggested he wasn't far from breaking down. Dani thought he was probably now severely regretting the many run-ins he'd had with his son. Whatever his emotion, he held it in.

'You say Paul had changed,' Dani said. 'How did he take Anthony's death? You said, Mrs Reeve, that Anthony died nearly four years ago. Wasn't that about the same time Paul stopped playing football too?'

'Paul was as devastated by Ant's death as we both still are,' Matthew said. 'But if you're trying to suggest he got his leg broken in three places on the football field, jeopardizing his whole career, just because of Ant... I mean...'

'Sorry, I'm not suggesting anything like that,' Dani said, holding her hands up. 'I just want to understand what could have been going on in Paul's mind. How he changed and why.'

'He was only a kid when he had the accident. Not quite nineteen. It took months and months to get him back on a pitch but a good while more for him to realise he would never make it. Was it the injury or just his head that changed? Who knows. Either way he was lost in life. He had enough reasons to be.'

By now Matthew Reeve was answering almost in monotone. Barbara, meanwhile, was simmering. She looked furious but was holding her tongue. Dani hadn't wanted to upset them, but they clearly were very troubled. Could this be because she was close to something that the Reeves wanted to keep tight to their chests?

Should she push on or call it a day?

'Mr and Mrs Reeve, do you know of any reason why someone would want to hurt Paul?'

Dani decided to push on. She wanted to know what they were hiding, but she would do it as softly as she could.

Barbara scoffed. Matthew didn't react.

'What on earth are you trying to suggest?' Barbara asked.

'Most people are killed by someone they know,' Easton said, and Dani was glad he had taken the baton. 'We don't yet have any suspects for Paul's murder but chances are it was someone he knew. We're just trying to find out about your son, his habits, his friends, so we can find leads to follow. Had he made friends with anyone you disapproved of? People who were mixed up with—'

'Just stop right there!' Barbara shouted, putting her hand up. 'This is *my son* you're talking about. He was a good boy.'

'Did you know he dealt drugs?' Easton asked. 'Cocaine. Ecstasy. Perhaps others.'

Barbara's cheeks flushed. Dani could tell Matthew was clenching his teeth.

'Yes. We did know,' Matthew said. His wife shot him a look but it was too late to stop him talking. 'It goes back a long way. A couple of months before his injury, Paul was suspended by the club for two weeks. For possession of cocaine.'

'He was just a kid then,' Barbara said in her son's defence.

'But after the accident he started taking it. He thought it was helping him recover. In mind, at least.'

'Do you know where he got it from?' Easton asked.

'No. He never told me.'

'But you know he started dealing too?' Dani said.

Matthew shook his head, in shame, perhaps? 'He's my son. It's my job to know. He had more money than he had any right to have, given his low-level jobs. It had to be coming from somewhere.'

'Did you ever find out where?'

'No. And that's the truth. I've no reason to lie about that.'

Dani nodded. She believed him.

Over the next few minutes the conversation trailed off. Dani tried asking the same questions in different ways, hoping for a different, and more useful answer, but the Reeves remained steadfast in not giving away anything more about their son's criminality. They had no reason to hold back, Dani ultimately decided, figuring it was time to move on. They also said they had never heard of Grace Agnew or Natalya.

'Just one more thing before we leave you,' Dani said. 'Have you ever heard of Jimmy Colton?'

'Jimmy Colton?' Matthew said, his face screwed in confusion. 'Why?'

'We believe he may be an acquaintance of your son's.'

'You think he might be the one who did this?'

'We don't know yet. Have you heard that name?'

'No,' Matthew Reeve said, before looking to his wife for confirmation. She shook her head. Their reaction to the name seemed genuine enough.

Dani checked her watch. 'I think we should probably get out of your hair. Unless there's anything else?'

Dani knew she and Easton didn't have any further appointments to get to, but she sensed they'd pushed enough. The Reeves' lack of response to Dani's question gave their answer, and Dani and Easton were soon back in the car, heading towards Birmingham.

'Well the Reeve house is one unhappy place to be,' Easton said.

'You think they were being straight with us?'

'Straight-ish. They probably know more about their son's problems than they're letting on, but I don't think they're holding back to be deliberately obtrusive.'

'Yeah. I felt the same. And I'd say they've never heard of those women before, nor Jimmy Colton.'

Did that suggest Jimmy really was just an alias of Reeve's rather than a real person? Maybe, maybe not.

'We've already got Reeve's mobile phone, right?' Dani asked.

'Yeah. Recovered at the crime scene. There was also a tablet and a laptop there.'

'Good. We need to scour through his records, dig as far as we can into his life. His friends, his contacts. See who's in the mix that shouldn't be. Remember, he's our murder victim, but we also have to treat him as what he is; a criminal who's linked to the death of one woman and the disappearance of another.'

'You think that's what he is?' Easton said. 'Not just a victim but a suspect too?'

'Maybe he killed Natalya. Maybe Grace Agnew too, but one thing is clear, he didn't kill himself. Regardless of Reeve's role here, there's still at least one other party out there we need to identity and find. Reeve was a dealer. That's an angle we have to cover.'

'Do you think there really is a Jimmy Colton too? If so, he could be our guy.'

'I honestly don't know. But you can be damn sure that I'm going to find out.'

Chapter Twenty-Three

Grant arrived back home not long after six p.m. The game of golf had taken the four men through until lunchtime, and afterwards they'd settled in the bar for the obligatory stodgy food and pints of beer. Grant's day had never quite recovered from his tantrum on the twelfth – either in a golfing or a social sense – but he'd had little choice than to tag along after the game; it was that or call a taxi home, which almost certainly would have been a questionable move in the other players' eyes. He decided instead to suck it up and try and make the day as least bad as he could.

It was fair to say he hadn't particularly warmed to either of Francis's friends much. Baxter was a seriously cantankerous man who Grant failed to hold any sort of relaxed conversation with, and Wilander's head was so far up his own arse he must surely be forever eating his own shit. Francis, for all of his laddish bravado, was actually the one that Grant had felt most at ease with. Which was quite a turn-up, given how Grant had felt towards his neighbour at the start of the day.

'We play every Wednesday,' Francis said as they were pulling into his driveway. 'Sometimes at the weekend too if there's a tournament or social going on. You're always welcome.'

'No. Thanks for offering, but I think I need a few more lessons before I put myself through that again.'

When the engine shut off, Grant opened his door, got out, and went around to the back of the car.

'You just need to relax and enjoy it more,' Francis said, coming around from the driver's side. He clicked a button on his key fob that sent the boot lid gliding effortlessly and silently into the air. 'None of us is that good, really.'

'Yeah, I'll let you know,' Grant said.

He pulled his clubs from the Range Rover's cavernous boot, slung the heavy bag over his shoulder, said goodbye to Francis then lugged his gear across the street back to his house. When he reached the front door he slapped the bag down onto the gravel and headed inside. He'd put the clubs away later, he just wanted to get inside and slump down for a while.

Before he'd finished taking his shoes off his attention was caught by the sound of giggling in the kitchen. He looked over at the shoe rack and noticed a pair of three-inch stilettos there, with fancy sequins along the straps. They weren't Mary's or Annie's. Unless one of them had been on an impromptu shopping spree.

'Mary, I'm home,' Grant called out.

'In here, Steven,' she called out, followed by more muted laughter.

Grant walked through to the kitchen. Mary was there, standing over the breakfast counter with a cocktail glass in her hand filled with pink liquid. She was all glammed-up in a knee-length skirt and silk blouse, her hair neatly coiffed, her lips a cherry red and her eyes dark with make-up that nearly covered her bruise.

She wasn't alone. Sat at one of the breakfast stools was a similarly dolled-up woman. Actually, no, she was even more dolled-up than Mary. The make-up on this woman's face was thick, almost like paint, her lips so bright they could act as a beacon, and the figure-hugging top she was wearing revealed several inches of buxom bust that was over-spilling onto the marble counter.

'Darling, this is Julie Francis. Ed's wife.'

'Hello, Steven,' Julie slurred.

Grant nodded and smiled. He was certain that wasn't their first drink of the day.

'Did you boys have fun?' Mary asked.

'Not as much as fun as you two have had, by the look of it,' Grant said.

'Oh, stop being such an old stiff,' Mary said, taking a glug of her cocktail. 'Come and have a drink.'

'Why not?' he said. He took a seat next to Julie and felt her eyes on him.

'Mary tells me you're a professor,' she said.

Grant looked up at Mary who smiled before setting about making his drink.

'I am,' he said.

'You must be damn clever then,' Julie said.

'That's one way to describe it. And what do you do, Julie?'

'Oh, you know, this and that.'

Grant really didn't know, but he didn't say. And he wasn't that interested, even though it did intrigue him that, like her husband, she'd given such a vague answer about her profession, if she had one at all.

'Seems like you two have had a good day,' Grant said.

'We have,' Mary said, reaching over and passing him the cocktail.

Grant took a sip of the drink, which was pretty much pure gin with a smidgen of overly sweet mixer. His eyes watered. On top of the beer he'd already drunk, this was certainly going to make for an interesting evening.

'Julie came over this morning,' Mary explained. 'She was bored at home on her own. She suggested we get some girly pampering.'

'You men were treating yourselves so why shouldn't we?'

That explained the make-up and hair, and the glittering and polished nails that Grant saw both of them had. Quite when the day of pampering had turned into a binge-drinking fest, Grant wasn't sure, but both women were happily slurring their words, and he was pleased that Mary was relaxed and less tense than she had been recently. He'd long got used to her wild mood swings, from way up high to rock bottom, a long-standing problem of hers but one which was exacerbated by Ethan's recent behaviour. Unfortunately, that meant that recently there had been far more lows than highs.

'Sounds like that was a good idea,' Grant said. 'You both look great by the way. Bottoms up.'

He held his drink out and the three of them chinked glasses. Julie knocked back the rest of her glass then checked her jewel-encrusted designer watch. Whether the jewels were real or cheap knock-offs Grant didn't know, but it was ostentatious bling regardless. Like husband, like wife.

'Look at the time, Mary. I'd better get back to babs. He'll be wanting a foot massage after all that walking about chasing balls.'

'Yeah, Mary,' Grant said. 'How about that?'

'Ha, think again,' Mary said. 'Haven't you got any work to do today at all?'

'No rest for the wicked.'

Mary set her drink down and guided Julie out of the kitchen. Grant watched them both sauntering and swaying away. Julie turned and looked at him coyly before she moved out of sight. He heard more giggling from the hallway before the front door finally opened and then closed, and Mary returned to the kitchen.

'That was different,' Grant said.

'Tell me about it.'

'She seems… nice.'

'She's mad,' Mary said. 'But a lot of fun.'

'That's one way to describe it.'

'Yeah, well you can fix your eyes back in your head now, Steven.'

'What do you mean?' he asked, feeling his cheeks flush.

Mary looked at him and raised an eyebrow.

'Where else was I supposed to look?'

'How about at me?'

Mary twirled around and blew a kiss at Grant.

'Yeah, when you put it like that.'

Grant got up from his stool and moved over to Mary. She turned away from him and he put his arms around her waist and pressed his lips against the back of her neck. He saw her skin go goose-pimply when he lightly kissed her.

'How was Ed?' she asked.

'Not as much fun as his wife, I'd say.'

'You didn't have a good time? Oh, Steven, you didn't spoil it, did you?'

Grant said nothing. Was he that obvious?

'That temper of yours.'

'It wasn't that bad. Actually Ed was surprisingly ok. Better than his mates at least.'

Grant kissed Mary on her neck again and she let out a satisfied sigh and pushed back so her body was tightly pressed against his.

'So come on,' Mary said. 'What gossip did you get?'

'Gossip?'

'About Ed and his wife. What's the story?'

'I didn't get any of that.'

'Too busy talking about girls and cars no doubt?'

'Something like that. Why do you ask, anyway?'

'Oh, I don't know. There's something odd about those two. She seems nice and all but… they're a bit mysterious aren't they? And the way she talked about Ed. I sensed it's not all good over there. He sounds so controlling of her. I think she appreciated the chance to get out.'

'Certainly looked that way to me.'

'And he's always so leery and staring when I see him. I really don't know what he's about.'

'Who can blame him when he's got such a gorgeous neighbour?'

'Ha, keep working at it, Steven. What does he do, anyway?'

'For a job? I have no idea.'

'She doesn't work at all. I just don't get them.'

'I reckon you're overthinking this a bit, honey. I tell you what, I could really do with a shower. You want to come with me?'

'I've just had my hair and my face done!'

'Ok, well maybe afterwards we could…' Grant kissed Mary again, more tantalisingly this time.

'Not today,' she said, swivelling around and pushing herself away.

Grant sighed.

'Well, off you go then,' she said, giving him a cheeky smile. 'I'll cook us some dinner.'

Grant was about to head off when Mary turned towards him.

'What is it?' he asked.

'What's that noise?'

'What noise?'

'Shouting. Outside.'

Grant stopped and listened. Sure enough, there was the faint but nonetheless clear sound of quite frenzied arguing. A man and a woman. Grant and Mary moved out of the kitchen and through to the dining room to look out the front.

Across the street, on the drive of the Francis's house and in the glare of their security lights, Ed and Julie were in the midst of a raging slanging match. Francis's face was creased in anger. Julie, her back to Grant, was waving her arms around in the air frantically as she gesticulated at her husband.

'What the…?'

'That poor woman,' Mary said.

Julie spun around and, walking on one heel, hobbled away from Francis. She opened the door to the Range Rover and jumped in. Francis moved forwards to try to stop her but a second later the reverse light came on and the car swung viciously backwards in an arc, into the road.

'She's pissed as a fart,' Grant said. 'She'll crash that damn thing.'

Tyres screeched and the Range Rover sped forwards. Francis, holding Julie's other stiletto in his hand, rushed after it and flung the shoe at the escaping car. It harmlessly smacked against the back window. Francis didn't give chase, just stood there huffing at the edge of his drive as his wife tore away in his pride and joy.

After a few seconds, his chest still heaving, Francis turned and glared over at the Grants' house. His eyes moved to the dining room window where Grant and Mary were gawking.

Mary gasped and stepped back, pulling Grant with her, but neither of them could fully tear themselves away and they stood at what they hoped was a safe distance.

'Can he see us?' Mary asked.

Grant didn't know, and he didn't answer, just carried on staring over at his raging neighbour. After a few seconds more, Francis turned, stormed back to his house and slammed the door shut behind him.

'I don't think he's getting that foot massage today,' Grant said, not trying to hide his glee. At least now he wasn't the only guy on the street whose dirty laundry had been aired in public.

Chapter Twenty-Four

Day 146

McNair is sitting by my hospital bed. I'm pissed off that she's the one who's come to see me. Not someone from the CPS, not one of the detectives who's been involved in the case, but my own boss. As though the familiar face will make a difference to what I can remember.

'Dani, do you understand what I'm saying to you?' McNair asks.

'Yeah. That you think there's a chance my brother might get off.'

'No. Not get off. We know he's a killer. But the defence's argument of diminished responsibility has some credibility. We just need to know if you can help. You know him better than anyone.'

'Do I? Other than him coming for me and trying to crack my head open like an egg I remember jack shit. Don't you understand? It's gone. My brain is fucked. Whatever you want from me, it's not in there anymore.'

'I know you're struggling, Dani. But you taking the stand could help make sure he gets what he deserves. Just paint the picture: who he was, what he did. You knew him for years when he was hiding his secret. He killed Alice, his wife, your best friend, then got on with his life like nothing had happened.'

'I'm well aware now of what he did. Clearly at the time I wasn't.'

McNair sighs. 'I know. Just think about it, yeah?'

She gets up from the seat, but pauses as she hovers over me as though she's expecting me to have a sudden change of heart.

Of course, I don't. Eventually she turns and leaves without either of us saying another word.

Later I'm sitting at a formica table in the assessment room, McNair's visit still weighing heavy on my already tired mind. Greg, one of the neurologists, is next to me. Two large beakers are on the table. I've just separated all of the white plastic counters into one, and all of the black plastic counters into the other.

'Very good,' Greg says as he finishes scribbling a note on his pad. 'Now again.'

He picks up a beaker in each hand and empties the counters onto the table, mixing them around with his hand.

I sit back in the chair and fold my arms. I'm tired. I'm bored. My head is raging, at Ben, at McNair. At Greg for making me do this, again. But I'm trying to keep it inside.

I look up. I see McNair standing across the other side of the room. I blink, thinking perhaps it's just a hallucination. I know my brain plays tricks on me sometimes. No. This time I'm damn sure McNair is right there, watching me.

'Dani? Let's do it once more,' Greg says. 'See if you can beat your time again.'

'Beat my time?' I say, my focus still on McNair who's staring at me like I'm her little experiment. Like she's analysing me to see what the craic really is. 'It's not a bloody Olympic sport. Who gives a flying fuck how fast I can do it?'

'I do,' he says, not at all moved by my aggressive response. 'Please?'
'No.'

'This is the last time today. I promise.'

'I don't want to!' I scream, jumping up from my chair.

I swipe my arm across the table and the plastic counters clatter to the ground. I glare over at McNair who hasn't even flinched. I wonder again if she's really there at all.

'Dani, sit down!' Greg says, not shouting, but I can tell for once he's losing his cool with me. His response only fires me up further. I heave and upend the table and it crashes against Greg's legs. He squirms back in shock as two burly porters rush towards me.

My brain is acting on pure instinct now. This anger, the outbursts, it's like a survival mode. I wish there was an off button for it, but so far I've not found one.

I know the nurses and doctors here don't want to hurt me; that I'm not a prisoner, no matter how much I feel like I am sometimes. They just *want to help me. To protect me. Yet somehow as the porters come forwards, I find myself swinging back my arm and balling my fist. I throw a punch into the first man's face and he clatters to the ground, but seconds later the other man has me restrained, pinning my arms. I'm kicking, screaming, writhing. I just want them to get off me, but the more I protest, the harder their response, and the more I protest. It's a vicious cycle my brain won't allow me to break.*

Out of the corner of my eye I spot McNair. She slowly, calmly, turns and walks away. The staff struggle to contain me as I continue to rage. After a couple of minutes of grappling there are three men pinning me to the ground as I continue to buck and twist and shout. A nurse hovers over me. I feel the pinch as the needle is pressed into my flesh. I feel the cold liquid surging through my veins.

A few seconds later I'm genuinely relieved when a sense of calm washes over me and my eyes draw shut.

Chapter Twenty-Five

Thursday morning was grey and grim. Dani couldn't help but think of her time in hospital, of that visit from McNair, of all the pain and anguish she'd been through, as she headed into the office for the early morning team briefing that she'd set up. It wasn't the thought of the briefing that had her mind turning over, but the appointment to visit Ben that she'd be heading to soon after.

At two minutes to nine the dated blue conference room was already full, with more than ten officers clustered around the worn pine furniture. Dani vaguely recognised most of them but couldn't yet remember all of the names of the more junior staff, particularly those from other departments. Easton was already there, as was Fletcher. McNair wasn't, Dani was relieved to see. Although she'd sent her boss an invite, she was well aware that the DCI had an early morning meeting over in Harborne, which Dani had somewhat deliberately double-booked against.

As she closed the door behind her, the room fell into a hushed silence, like it would at school on the first day of term, when a new teacher walked in to start a class. Dani could feel eyes on her. Could almost hear the questioning thoughts, everyone still wary of the copper back from the dead.

'Morning all,' Dani said. 'We'll be ready in a minute.'

She smiled and got some murmured responses in return. Fletcher was standing on her own at the front of the room, cleaning a whiteboard. Dani headed over to her.

'You're leading this?' Fletcher asked quietly.

'I'm happy to.'

'Makes sense. I think you're probably more into the detail than I am at this stage.'

Which Dani would agree with, even if Fletcher's acknowledgement surprised her.

She got the meeting underway. First, she went over the events of the last three days, from Natalya's murder scene, to Reeve's murder and the drugs found in his apartment, to the information given by Rebecca and Laura and the link to Grace Agnew.

'Where are we at with house-to-house for Natalya's murder?' Dani asked when she was done with her initial regurgitation.

'All done, ma'am,' said a smartly dressed DC with designer slicked back hair. DC Constable, the same officer who'd been with Easton at Paul Reeve's murder scene. 'We went to every house over three streets. We've been back since to cover ones who were out. Still a few to go where the residents must be away, but other than the Mondys, we've got nothing new.'

'And cameras?'

'Again, we've covered them all off now. Nothing new.'

'But we had Natalya on one less than half a mile away? We used the image for the press con?'

'It's a mainly residential area,' Easton said. 'There really aren't that many cameras about unless we go out further, but would Natalya really have been running for miles?'

'Probably not,' Dani conceded, though she thought she might come back to it.

'I've no idea how the killer escaped the one Natalya was caught on, but he did,' Easton said.

'And that one camera doesn't give a clue as to where she came from?'

'We're still looking into it, but on the face of it, no.'

Dani sighed.

'And who's working on formally IDing Natalya?'

A female officer at the back of the room stuck her hand up. 'No real luck yet, ma'am. We found no ID at the address taken from Rebecca Hargreaves and Laura Finlay, and no correspondence for our vic, or anyone else for that matter. All utility bills were paid by the landlord who… well, he's a bit dodgy. Took cash, no questions. He couldn't give us anything useful on Natalya.'

'No ID at all at her home? Any evidence that the place was deliberately cleared?'

'No. Sorry.'

'But he did acknowledge that someone by that name had been staying there?'

'Kind of, but he really was pretty vague even about that.'

Dani thought about that for a moment. She didn't like the sound of the situation at all. Was the guy just a dodgy landlord or was he a potential suspect?'

'Bring him in for formal questioning. Find something to caution him with if you need to. Firstly, I want to clear him off as a suspect.'

'Yes, ma'am.'

'And Mrs Staunton. Have we cleared up what happened to her?'

'Still waiting for forensics results,' Easton said. 'Maybe we'll have something today.'

Dani sighed. Other than her relaying to the team her own thoughts and findings, there really wasn't much else to go on. She spent a couple of minutes dishing out further responsibilities. Largely casting the net of enquiries and CCTV searches a little further. Then she was done. She needed to go anyway.

'Are there any further points before we wrap up? Dani asked.

'So we really are looking for a serial killer now, do you think?' piped up one of the young DCs. DC Grayling.

'No,' Dani said. 'We are not toeing that line, either internally or externally. Not officially. But it's becoming quite clear these two murder cases are closely linked, and we can't rule out that possibility.'

There were a few murmurs from the room. Dani was aware that Fletcher was staring at her but she didn't bother to look. Her answer this time certainly wasn't as inflammatory as at the press conference, but would McNair still have disapproved?

'Anything else?'

No one raised their hand this time, and Dani called the meeting to a close. After a quick and largely pointless further debrief with Fletcher and Easton, Dani was soon back in her car, whatever insecurities and aggravations she was feeling about her role in the force well and truly sidelined, and her anxiety levels peaked despite the tablets she'd taken before leaving the house earlier that morning.

When she reached the junction for the M42 she went right over, continuing south on the A435 towards Evesham. She knew the area south of Birmingham relatively well. There were many picturesque towns there that she'd been to over the years. She remembered relaxing Sunday morning strolls with her parents and her brother when she'd been a child, the odd weekend escape to a luxury hotel with Jason.

No, thinking about those times wasn't going to make her much happier right now.

But wasn't it a little ironic it was in that area, much loved by her family all those years ago, that Ben, her twin, would likely spend the rest of his life?

Dani might have known the area generally, but she'd never before been to her destination; HM Prison Long Lartin – a category A prison in a somewhat unusual village setting, where all manner of violent or otherwise highly dangerous prisoners were incarcerated; rapists, murderers, drug dealers, terrorists. Her brother.

When she reached the security gate at the perimeter of the prison complex, Dani explained who she was and was let through into the small visitor's parking area. The prison from here looked like nothing more than a 1970s low-rise office, with blocky features and slabs of concrete interspersed with red brick and blue painted panels.

Dani made her way to the visitor's entrance, pushed open the left of the double doors and moved into line behind two others who were queuing in front of the glass-fronted reception desk. She noticed there were already more than a dozen people crammed into the waiting area, eagerly awaiting the chance to spend some not-such-quality time with their not-so-good loved ones. There were children among the visitors too. They were the ones Dani felt sorry for. But then she wondered again about Harry and Chloe. Did they deserve the chance to come here to see their dad?

When it was her turn Dani walked up to the reception desk and smiled at the uniformed prison officer who was sitting on the other side. He had a grey-stubbled face and droopy eyes that gave him an overall unkempt and tired appearance. Perhaps that was the toll his job had taken on him.

'Morning,' Dani said.

'Morning,' the officer said in return, though the greeting was somewhat forced and his tone was coarse, his face serious.

Dani explained who she was and the officer, whose name tag gave his surname as Abbott, began a long search on his computer.

'Yes, that's fine, Miss Stephens,' Abbott said when he'd finished. 'When the masses get called through you'll need to wait here. The Deputy Governor will collect you separately.'

'Oh, right, yeah ok,' Dani said. Abbott turned to the next visitor in line behind Dani, and she realised she'd get no more explanation from him as to what he meant.

She turned and moved to the four blue plastic chairs that were bolted to the ground underneath a large corkboard, taking the one free chair. Various pamphlets and posters were pinned to the board, mostly outlining in no uncertain terms the dos and don'ts of prisoner visits. Don't bring drugs or alcohol. No knives or guns. Did people really need to be reminded of that?

After scanning much of the board Dani's eyes focused in on a leaflet discussing mental health.

How apt.

When the clock in the waiting area edged past ten fifty-eight, a set of double doors at the far end opened and two uniformed guards came out and began giving heavy-toned instructions to the crowd of people. The guards weren't quite talking to the visitors like they were the scum of the earth, but it wasn't far off. The crowd was quickly shepherded through the doors into the inner sanctum, one guard taking the lead. Soon Dani was the only visitor remaining on the outside.

'Miss, are you coming or not?' the second guard said, staring at Dani suspiciously. 'Last chance.'

'I've been told to wait for the Deputy Governor.'

'Suit yourself,' the guard said, shaking his head as though she were a moron.

He turned and walked through the double doors and they closed behind him, leaving Dani alone. Well, Abbott was there too, but he wasn't exactly the best company.

It was nearly eleven-fifteen by the time a woman emerged from a different set of doors. Grey suit. Grey hair. Pale skin. She looked like she'd been put through the washing machine on a too hot setting several times over. When she smiled, however, there was a certain warmth to her face – a contrast to Abbott's dour expression for sure. Dani got to her feet and the woman stretched out a hand.

'Miss Stephens?' the woman said. 'I'm Anne Cartwright, the Deputy Governor. Please, come this way.'

'Is there a problem?' Dani asked, as she set off in tow.

'Not exactly.'

Cartwright led Dani back the way she'd come, down a short corridor, and soon they were standing in a dreary and dated office that was sparsely furnished and, like the outside of the building, looked like a snapshot of the 1970s, save for the sleek laptop computer on top of the roughed-up desk.

'Is something wrong?' Dani asked.

'No, of course not. I just didn't want to have this conversation with you out there. Some visitors feel uncomfortable with that. You have to appreciate, Miss Stephens, that your brother is among the most high risk and high profile prisoners here. Access to him is heavily restricted, and we won't allow him to be in the visiting hall with the general masses. I hope you understand that?'

'Has he done something in here to warrant that?' Dani said, though she wasn't quite sure why she felt the need to stick up for Ben. They could do what the hell they wanted to him.

'Not at all. This is how we treat all of our highest risk inmates. You'll see Ben in a private room. You can speak to him alone, if you wish, with someone watching from outside, or you can have a prison officer in the room with you. It's up to you.'

'I'd rather speak to him alone,' Dani said, though she wondered if there was really much difference if someone was watching on a screen or through a one-way mirror.

'Absolutely,' Cartwright said. 'We'll need to do some formalities first, and then you can see him.'

The 'formalities' took another twenty minutes. Dani's ID was checked. A full body search was conducted. They checked her jewellery over too, apparently looking for any signs that a key was somehow forged into it. Her pockets were emptied; they checked her shoes. They took a photo of her face, took her fingerprints. She was read a long list of what she could and couldn't take into the room, and of things she could and couldn't do when seeing her own brother.

Hands to be seen at all times. Remain fully clothed at all times. Don't sit on the prisoner's lap. No passing of contraband.

Really? She thought, sarcastically; but what about the weed I brought?

When it was finally over Dani was escorted through corridors and metal-barred doors until finally they arrived outside the interview room. Dani paused. She pushed away the wave of nausea as best she could. Cartwright turned.

'Are you ok?'

'I'm fine.' She took a deep breath. 'Let's continue, please.'

Cartwright didn't look convinced but she turned to the officer by the door, who unlocked and opened it, and ushered Dani inside.

Chapter Twenty-Six

The interview room was much like the ones Dani had been to in countless police stations and prisons in different locations over many years. Ben was already in there, sitting down on one of two chairs in the room, wearing the standard prison garb of blue jogging bottoms and blue jumper. His hands, cuffed together, were on top of the small table in the middle of the room. He looked up at Dani and smiled awkwardly. She couldn't read what the expression meant. Was it friendly? Or was it calculated and knowing? Taunting, even? Again Dani's mind took her back to the hospital and all of the stories she'd read about Ben's crimes and his trial. Diminished responsibility? Yeah right. At least the jury hadn't bought that crap.

The officer who'd shown Dani in waited for her to take her seat and then promptly left, shutting and locking the thick door behind him.

'Well isn't this nice,' Ben said, breaking the silence.

Dani didn't say anything, just stared at him. This was her brother, the same person she'd grown up with, yet he looked so different. There was a coldness to his manner that set this man apart from the one she'd known for so long. His skin was paler too, more creased, his hair lighter, his eyes a dull grey. It was like all of the goodness and colour and vitality had been sucked right out of him.

Had prison done that to him, or was this just the man who'd always been beneath the mask?

As kids the two of them had naturally spent a lot of time together. Not friends exactly – they'd often fought, like many siblings did – but their blood bond had always kept them close. Even as young adults they'd continued to mix in the same crowds. Ben had eventually married Dani's best friend. Alice.

God, poor Alice. He'd killed her. Throttled her to death on their own bed. His first victim. Not his last.

Dani felt a wave of nausea, but she fought against it and it quickly went away. In its place came a rush of memories as she stared at Ben. Some good, many bad.

'You came all this way and you're not even going to speak to me?' Ben said.

But in those first few moments, Dani really didn't know *what* to say. She noticed him stare up at her scar, but he didn't say anything. She didn't react at all. In fact, she almost felt frozen, though her brain was busy, wondering what he was thinking.

'How are the kids?' Ben asked. He shook his head, looking distressed, almost, for a fleeting second. 'I miss them so much.'

'They're fine,' Dani said. 'Though I've not seen them that much recently.' Again, she felt bad. Those kids hadn't deserved any of what had happened. She really should have done everything she could for them. She had no sensible reason for not having seen them more often, other than that she was a selfish cow. Oh yeah, and because for the last two years she'd been suffering the after-effects of brain damage, thanks to Ben.

'Why haven't you been seeing them?' Ben asked. 'They always loved you so much.'

Dani clenched her teeth before answering. 'It's not been easy for me, Ben. But I do see them when I can. I saw them the other day in fact. That's partly why I came. Harry was asking after you.'

'He was?'

Ben's face brightened slightly.

'I'll be there for them,' Dani said. 'Gemma too.'

The brightness faded at the mention of Gemma, Ben's second wife. He'd tried to kill her too, the same night he'd tried to kill Dani. Apparently he blamed Gemma and Dani for everything. Despite his best efforts, both of them had lived.

'They never come to see me,' Ben said.

'Are you in any way surprised by that?'

'I'm still their dad.'

'And you still killed your son's mother, and tried to kill your daughter's mother too.'

Ben gave her a hard stare and Dani matched the look. He broke eye contact first.

'I know you wouldn't come here just for a social visit,' he said. 'So come on, spit it out, what's on your mind?'

'Nothing's on my mind. I thought it might help me to see you. To discuss what happened. My therapist seemed to agree.'

'You're still seeing a therapist?' Ben said, smirking as though he was impressed with the havoc he'd caused.

Dani didn't understand quite what he meant by 'still'. She hadn't been to visit him before so he knew nothing of the rehabilitation she'd endured over the last two years.

When she didn't respond to his taunt, Ben carried on: 'I don't buy it. Not Dani the super-detective. I saw you on TV the other night, you know. Life just carries on as before for you, doesn't it?'

Dani just scoffed at that. If only he knew.

'You're searching for a murderer, right?'

'Yes. We are,' Dani said.

'So what? You've got a mysterious killer on your hands and you're all stuck for answers so you thought you'd come and speak to me to see if I can help you in some way? I'm flattered, really. This is all a bit Hannibal Lecter, isn't it?'

Ben did a mocking impression of Lecter, sucking through his teeth. Dani had to admit, he actually did a pretty good job, but she showed no reaction. And was she there as a detective, or as his sister? Even she wasn't fully sure of the answer to that one.

'Priceless,' he said, his smile wide now. '*You* coming to *me* to help catch a killer.'

'That's not why I'm here. I told you why I came. For me. And anyway, I hardly think you're an expert on the subject of murder. After all, you failed. I caught you and helped put you in here.'

Ben huffed. 'Yeah. You did, didn't you? I'm not sure I've ever properly thanked you for that.'

'No need.'

'So that's it, then. You don't need my help. You've got no update on how my wife and kids are getting along—'

'Your second wife. Your first one is dead, remember?'

'Yeah. I remember,' he said, his eyes narrowing.

'To tell you the truth, Ben, I wasn't sure about this. Until a couple of days ago I never planned to see you again. I didn't think there was anything in the world you could possibly say to me that would help. And sitting here now, I still think that's the case.'

'Seems like you've wasted your time then, Detective.'

Dani shook her head. 'Actually, I'm not so sure about that.'

'Yeah?'

'Maybe this is worthwhile. The thing is… look at you.'

She said the words with genuine disdain. She noticed him clench his jaw, holding back a response.

'You've caused me so much pain,' she said. 'Have caused others so much pain. But you, in here, you can't hurt me anymore. You're nothing.'

She got up to leave.

'Where do you think you're going?' Ben said through gritted teeth.

'Bye, Ben.'

She turned but then jumped when Ben thumped onto the table.

'Sit down, right now!' he shouted.

Dani turned back to him then flinched when Ben lurched forwards towards her. The chain on his cuffs caught and held him back. He snarled and tugged on his restraints.

'You stupid bitch. Who the hell do you think you are?'

The door to the interview room burst open and two uniformed guards rushed in, grabbed Ben and tried their best to pull him back. Ben roared and started twisting and writhing.

Dani looked on in shock. She'd seen plenty of people act batshit crazy before, but to see it in her own brother... where was it coming from?

She took a step back, closer to the door. Then another. Ben locked eyes with her.

'Dani, don't go!' he said, writhing around, trying to shove the guards off him, but his voice now sounded more panicked than angry. 'Please!'

Dani realised she was shaking. She simply didn't know what to say or do.

'Get out of here!' one of the guards shouted over to her, just as the other one pulled out a baton and swiped it down across Ben's back.

'Dani, help me!'

'Go!'

Dani didn't need to be told another time. Her legs feeling like jelly, her head a jumbled mess, she darted out through the open door.

Chapter Twenty-Seven

Dani headed to her car, her legs wobbling underneath her. She sat down in the driver's seat, closed her eyes and let out a huge sigh.

It took a few minutes to fully regain focus, to push thoughts of Ben to the back of her mind, before she felt ready to move on. What worried her most was that she could see so much of herself in Ben. She had thought – or was it hoped? – that her short and often irrational temper, and her occasional violent outbursts, were a result of the TBI. But was that just wishful thinking? Were sister and brother in fact both defective in the same way? Was there some problem in their DNA?

That was the idea that scared her more than anything.

As kids, as twins, they hadn't just been siblings but rivals. Everything was a competition between them; whether consciously or not, they fought over who was the best, the fittest, the strongest, the cleverest, the kindest, whatever. Somehow Dani, a true tomboy back then, had invariably come out on top, much to her brother's general disgruntlement.

Over the years that feeling of inferiority in Ben had gradually worn at their relationship, which had culminated in a period, immediately after their mother had died, where brother and sister fell out of touch completely.

But was all of that the reason Ben had flipped and done the horrendous things he had? Simple jealousy and pent-up anger from a lifetime of playing second fiddle to his sister? Did he consider himself a failure, even though he'd had a spouse and a family while Dani had been too career-focused to have ever settled down?

If that was Ben's only trigger, then there must still have been something inside him to make him capable of the acts he committed, and to allow him to rationalise breaking societal rules so flippantly. Not every jealous sibling goes on a murderous rampage. So did Dani, deep down, share those same killer traits as Ben? And was it simply circumstance which had meant that thus far in her life those traits had been buried beneath the surface?

Trying to take her mind off those depressing and worrying thoughts, Dani checked her phone. She had a missed call and a voicemail. She listened to the message from McNair. Her boss had briefed DCI Fairclough from the Organised Crime team on the deaths of Natalya and Paul Reeve, given Reeve's clear link with the drug world. For now the Homicide team still had the lead, but it could be that Fairclough would soon take over.

Was the explanation for Reeve's and Natalya's deaths really as simple as gangland violence? Perhaps it was, though Dani felt there was something bigger and more sinister at play. After all, Reeve was connected to the missing Grace Agnew too.

Either way, she wasn't impressed that the investigation was slipping from her grasp.

Despite the turmoil in her mind, Dani decided to head straight back to HQ. She could have called McNair back, to air her concerns about Fairclough's involvement, but she'd rather have the conversation in person. She arrived just before one p.m. When she stepped from her car she realised she was still shaky from the abrupt end to the meeting with Ben, but as she walked it subsided and she managed to calm her still swirling thoughts.

Did she feel better for having seen her brother? In a way, yes. She'd meant what she said to him. Seeing him in that place, if only for a few minutes, had helped reaffirm that he really couldn't hurt her anymore. But then the way he'd flipped so easily at the end... that crazed man simply didn't tally with the one she'd known for so many years.

She remained terrified that the same demons that tormented Ben were also now inside her. Over the last two years it had certainly seemed that way. How many times had her brain felt ready to explode, had she been on the brink of losing control? Scratch that, how many times *had* she lost control?

As Dani headed through into the open-plan space of Force CID the place was bustling, not with work but with chatter. Which likely meant McNair wasn't around after all. There was a group of five guys standing by Easton's desk chatting and smiling and being a bit… laddish. Easton was among them, along with DC Constable – his best chum, it seemed – and three others Dani hadn't seen before. They looked to be in their early twenties so most likely were constables or sergeants from one of the other divisions.

Dani headed towards her recently acquired desk, the second to last space in the far corner of the room. She'd previously had one of the best positioned desks, over by the windows. She greeted the group of men in passing. Easton said hi; the others smiled and smirked. She did see that right, didn't she? She heard a snippet of what they were talking about as she moved away. *Murderer. Maniac. Tried to kill her. Now in the clink. Gone mental.*

Dani took her seat and glared over at Easton. He caught her eye and somewhat nervously stepped away from the group and came over to Dani.

'Post lunch gossiping, DS Easton?' Dani said.

Her harsh tone drew stares from the other men and their conversation suddenly became more hushed.

'A possible lead actually,' Easton said, his face creasing slightly at her coldness, though as ever he didn't bring her up on it.

'Yeah?' Dani said, her ears pricking up.

'Do you remember Professor Steven Grant?'

'Should I?'

Easton glanced over his shoulder towards his chums, then back to Dani.

'Seems his son, Ethan, was arrested last night.'

'For what?'

'Driving pissed. He was also found with a pretty big bag of weed on him. They let him out this morning on bail.'

'Ok, am I missing the point here?'

'You really don't remember Professor Grant?'

'No.'

'I mean, I was only a little kid back then, but I still remember the news headlines. You've heard of the Southwell Slicer, haven't you?'

Dani rolled her eyes at the ridiculous name. Why did the tabloids always have to do that? They'd tried the same with Ben too. The Barmy Brummy was the closest moniker that almost stuck, making him sound more like some loony character from a crappy 1970s British comedy than the vile killer that he was.

But as Dani properly digested the words, she realised she did know what Easton was talking about.

'Grant was his last victim,' Easton said, filling in the blanks. 'He was abducted and held in a remote barn for weeks before the police found him. He was the only victim to escape.'

Dani looked back over at the gaggle of men. So had the snippets she'd overheard been about Grant and the Southwell Slicer? Or had they been comparing Grant's fate to Dani's? Whatever. She had to expect a certain level of chatter about her past. It was more the tone they had used, the smiles and sniggering, that riled her. Did they know she'd just come from the prison?

'Grant was already a doctor of criminology back then,' Easton said. 'Apparently the Slicer targeted him for that very reason: because Grant was helping the police with their enquiries.'

'And then afterwards Grant wrote a book all about it,' Dani said. She'd even tried to read it at one time, but had given up halfway through. She had enough of death during her day job.

'And there was a documentary,' Easton said 'Very nearly a Hollywood movie too, apparently.'

'So what has all of this got to do with our case?'

'It seems Grant junior, Ethan, was friends with Paul Reeve. I've got a list of contacts from Reeve's phone and Ethan is on there. He was on our list of people to talk to anyway. Then he got himself nabbed last night.'

'But he's now been released?'

'Yeah. Apparently we weren't too connected there.'

'You mean the lines of gossip didn't quite stretch down as far as the local nick? Shock horror, DS Easton. Do we know where Ethan Grant is now?'

'No. But we have his home address.'

'Ok. Well, if he was on our list anyway, then we'll go to him first. Any idea where Fletcher and McNair are?'

'No.'

Dani rolled her eyes for the second time in a few minutes.

'Let's go then,' she said.

She picked up a pad of paper and slipped it in her shoulder bag. Easton rushed over to his desk and grabbed what he needed. As Dani moved back over to the exit she felt as though the group of young men still had judging eyes on her. She stopped walking.

'Don't you lot have anything better to do?' she snapped.

Silence.

'Well?'

'Yes, ma'am,' came the chorus of half-hearted replies, though none of the men hopped into action.

'Then what are you bloody waiting for? Move!'

Dani stood there, glaring at them until they finally dispersed, then she stomped off.

'That told them,' Easton said, catching up with Dani, an amused grin on his face.

'Easton, don't act like you weren't part of that too. If I see you and your mates having a laugh at my expense again, I'll knock your damn head off. Understood?'

'Yes, ma'am.'

'How many times have I told you, call me Dani.'

'Yes, Dani. Look, we weren't—'

'I don't want to hear it.'

'Sorry, Dani. We were only saying how you and that professor had a lot in common.'

'I said I don't want to hear it.'

'I was thinking, though, maybe that guy could help us. I mean, we've got two dead bodies, perhaps the same killer. Murder is Grant's area of expertise.'

'Yeah. And look what happened the last time he helped the police. He was abducted and nearly killed.'

'And you were nearly killed too. But you still came back.'

'True. And the moral of the story, Aaron, is that some people just don't know when to quit.'

And that was about the most sense that Dani could make of it all.

Chapter Twenty-Eight

They took Easton's Peugeot over to the Grants' house in the upmarket village of Knowle, thoughts of Ben still swirling in Dani's mind, particularly given the history of the family they were about to speak to. Steven Grant too had nearly lost his life at the hands of a deranged killer. Had he ever truly recovered?

The street the Grants lived on was a quiet cul-de-sac with a multitude of individually designed detached houses. None were overly extravagant – the street wasn't filled with footballers or mega-millionaires – but the homes were, in the main, handsome and well-appointed with large front drives and wide and deep plots.

Easton pulled up outside the gates to the Grants' house and left the engine idling.

'So Ethan Grant still lives at home with mum and dad?' Dani said.

'Well I'm not sure a nineteen-year-old could afford this type of place.'

'Nor would a nineteen-year-old choose to buy a place like this even if they had the money. A city centre bachelor pad would be most likely.'

'The police were called out here a couple of days ago.'

'What for?' Dani asked, wondering why Easton had only just chosen to tell her this.

'Domestic incident. The lads were telling me this morning. A couple of PCs came out here following a 999 call. From over there.'

Easton pointed to the house opposite.

'The call was anonymous but the house is being rented to an Ed Francis.'

'Rented?'

Easton shrugged.

'So what happened?' Dani asked.

'No arrests made. Seems the PCs believed Grant was beating up his wife initially. She's got a right shiner, apparently. The Grants both denied it was the professor, claimed the disturbance was down to their son, but that they didn't want to press charges. The PCs didn't believe that to start with, but felt there wasn't much else they could do. The son by then was nowhere to be seen.'

Easton had certainly been doing his homework. Even though she hadn't said it to his face, she was becoming more and more impressed with his ongoing diligence.

'Ok. Let's see who's home. Go up onto the drive.'

Easton drove through the already open gates and parked the car up on the gravel driveway. They stepped from the car and made their way to the wide front door of the house. Dani rang the bell then knocked and waited.

Nothing.

She heard Easton stepping back and crunching across the gravel. She turned and saw he was looking up and across the house for signs of life. He shrugged.

Dani rang and knocked again. They stood and waited but there was still silence from inside the house. Dani was about to turn to head back to the car when she heard the lock on the door release, the door opened and she was looking into the eyes of a woman.

'Mrs Grant?' Dani asked.

The woman looked Dani up and down. In her late forties or early fifties, she was about the same height as Dani with wavy blonde hair, blue eyes and a light dusting of make-up that didn't do a very good job of hiding the black and purple flesh around her eye.

'Yes, I'm Mrs Grant.'

'I'm DI Stephens, and this is DS Easton, from West Midlands Police. Is your son, Ethan, home? We'd like to speak to him.'

'What on earth has he done now?'

'Is he home?'

'No. He's not. He doesn't live here anymore.'

'Oh,' Dani said. She turned to Easton but he just looked back at her blankly.

'This is the address he gave on his arrest forms,' Easton said to Dani.

'Arrest forms?' Mrs Grant said. 'Can you please tell me what's going on here, detectives?'

'Do you think we could come in to talk?' Dani said. Chances were that Mary Grant had nothing of use to add to the whole situation, but they'd made the trip, so they may as well make the most of it. 'We shouldn't take much of your time.'

'Of course,' she said, smiling, though it seemed forced. She stepped to the side and ushered Dani and Easton in. 'Please leave your shoes at the door. I've just finished polishing the marble.'

Dani resisted the urge to smirk at that instruction though she wasn't sure why. She did as she was told, as did Easton. Mary led them through into a lounge whose key feature was a huge stone fireplace. She indicated to Dani and Easton to sit on one of the three brown leather sofas. There was no offer of a drink or anything as hospitable as that.

'So Ethan was arrested again?' Mary said, sitting on the arm of a sofa.

'Last night,' Easton said. 'Drunk-driving. He was also in possession of a not insubstantial amount of cannabis.'

Mary shook her head, in a show of distaste. Whether that was at her son or at the police, it wasn't clear. Either way there was little real feeling in her reaction. She seemed almost detached.

'So why are two detectives now out looking for him?'

'He was released from the station this morning on bail,' Easton said.

'You didn't know this?' Dani asked Mary. 'From what I understood, it was a lawyer who's worked with your husband who filed the paperwork?'

Mary threw her hands up in exasperation and shook her head. 'It's all news to me. Though it's not altogether surprising. Ethan is always getting himself into stupid trouble. But you still haven't explained why you're now out looking for him again, if you had him in custody just this morning.'

'Like we said, he was released on bail. But we're actually here now on an altogether different matter, Mrs Grant. We're from the Homicide team at West Midlands Police, and we're investigating the murders of a Paul Reeve and an as yet unidentified female.'

'Ah, I thought I recognised you,' Mary said, and for the first time – at least the first time that Dani noticed – she looked up to Dani's scar. 'I saw something on the local news about that the other night.'

'We believe your son knew at least one of the two victims,' Dani said, hoping to steer the conversation away from what Mary may or may not know about Dani.

'I remember reading about you a while back,' Mary Grant said, clearly not as keen to let the subject drop. 'When was it?'

'It's been over two years since…' Dani trailed off, not quite sure that she wanted to say anything more.

'Such a terrible thing to have to go through. I should know. You realise my husband is Steven Grant?'

'Yes, I realise that. And the similarities between what happened to him and to me have been pointed out to me today already. Not meaning to be rude, but mine and your husband's pasts have nothing to do with why we're here.'

'Oh, that's fine,' Mary said, seeming to relax now that she'd found some common ground between Dani and her husband. 'I'm sorry for bringing it up. Steven's the same. He hates that people still recognise him for all the wrong reasons.'

'Mrs Grant, do you know anything about Paul Reeve? Was Ethan close to him?'

'I don't recognise the name, to be honest.'

'What about Jimmy Colton?'

Mary paused this time, but still looked unmoved.

'I'm sorry, detective, but the thing is, I really don't know much about Ethan's personal life anymore. For one very good reason. You can see the type of trouble he gets himself into. I don't want any part of it. I have no idea who his close friends are but I do know that most of them are probably no good.'

'Your son did that to you?' Dani asked, indicating the black eye. Well, if Mrs Grant wanted to bring up sore subjects, then so would Dani.

Mary hung her head in embarrassment.

'He didn't mean to. It was a misunderstanding. He's never hit me before. He's just… in a bad place.' Her head shot back up again. 'Wait, you don't think that Ethan actually had something to do with—'

'No, Mrs Grant. He's not a suspect in our investigation at this stage. We have no reason to believe that at all. We just want to speak to him like we want to speak to all of the close friends of the victims.'

'I guess the only thing I can do to help you then is to give you the last address I have for him, though who knows if he's actually there or not anymore. He made me drop some of his things off there a few weeks back but I didn't even go inside.'

'That would be very helpful.'

Mary disappeared and came back a few moments later with a Post-it note that she handed over to Dani.

'I wish I could help more, but we're not exactly on the best of terms right now.'

That was clearly an understatement.

'Thank you for your time, Mrs Grant,' Dani said. 'If you do think of anything else—'

'You'll be the first to know.'

Dani and Easton were shown out, and no sooner had they stepped over the threshold than the front door was sharply closed behind them.

'Yet another interesting family,' Easton said when he and Dani were safely inside his car.

'That's one way of putting it.'

'So we're going straight there?' he asked, indicating the Post-it that Dani was holding.

'I've not got anything better to do. Have you?'

Easton smiled and fired up the engine. Dani stared over at the Grants' house. There was no sign of Mary at the windows. But as Easton swung the car back out onto the street, Dani found herself focusing on the house opposite, because in the upstairs window she could clearly make out a man, standing close to the glass, facing out. Ed Francis, most likely. The same man who'd called the police three days ago, according to Easton. Dani held his gaze. It seemed like he was staring right at her, his eyes piercing and... menacing.

Francis stepped back from the window and his form disappeared into darkness. Dani shivered.

'You ok, Dani?' Easton said, snapping her from her thoughts.

'Yeah, I'm fine.' She squirmed in her seat and focused her eyes back on the road ahead. 'Why?'

'You look like you've seen a ghost.'

Dani huffed. 'No, not a ghost.'

She didn't believe in ghosts. Quite what she'd seen, though, when she'd looked into Francis's eyes, she really couldn't explain.

Chapter Twenty-Nine

'What did you make of Mary Grant then?' Easton asked as they drove back towards central Birmingham, to the address they'd been given in Handsworth.

'Hard to say.'

'Do you really think her son would hit her?'

'I can't see why she'd say so if he didn't.'

'You don't think she's covering for the husband? That's what the PCs initially reckoned, though the Mr and Mrs both denied it.'

'If she was covering for the husband, do you not think she'd say she walked into a door handle or something like that? Why get her son into trouble?'

'Fair point. And he does sound like he's out of control. Drugs, drink driving, assaulting his own mother. Yet on the face of it they seem like such a respectable family.'

'Kind of like Paul Reeve's family then, don't you think?'

Easton nodded. 'Do you think Ethan is more than just an acquaintance then?'

'You mean do I think he could be mixed up in drug dealing too?'

'No. I mean, do you think he could be the killer? It's possible, isn't it? A history of violence, mixed up with drugs...'

'Or he could be the next victim. We can't rule out that there's a multiple killer out there.'

'A serial killer?'

Dani cringed at what Easton said. Serial killer. The words still sounded outlandish and ridiculous, even though she was the one who'd first mentioned the possibility, and even though she knew only too well that such people really did exist. And the life and death of Natalya still worried Dani. Why had she been bound like that? And what had happened to Grace Agnew?

Dani's phone chirped in her bag. She lifted it out and saw the call was coming from a withheld number.

'Yes?' she said, answering it.

'DI Stephens, it's Jack Ledford.'

'Jack, good news I hope?'

'Good? Detective, I've been dissecting human corpses this morning. Young people whose lives were taken away from them quite cruelly. I'm not sure there's much good about that.'

Why did he always have to twist the meaning of her words like that?

'But I do have some results for you.'

'I'll be there right away,' Dani said, before ending the call. 'I need to go to the mortuary,' she said to Easton.

'You want me to come too?'

Dani looked at her watch. 'No. You've got a lead here. Drop me at the mortuary then pick someone from HQ to accompany you and go find Ethan Grant. You're happy handling that, aren't you?'

'Of course. Sounds better than spending the rest of the afternoon with a stinking corpse, to be honest.'

'DS Easton, that's no way to talk about Birmingham's finest pathologist.'

Dani looked over at Easton and he gave a cheeky smile.

The traffic was kind to them and not long after, Dani stepped from the car outside the mortuary. She took a deep breath of fresh air then headed inside, working her way through the corridors of the building to where she knew Ledford was located.

With each step she took the air felt heavier and the smell of rot and death and decay grew. No matter how much bleach, industrial cleaner and air freshener was used, there was simply nothing that could be done to mask the grotesque smell of a morgue – a smell that infected every pore of Dani's body whenever she visited.

She'd only been a fresh-faced DC when she'd witnessed her first post-mortem. She'd felt queasy from the moment the procedure had started but had held firm, trying to be strong and to see the ordeal through. She hadn't managed it. At the point the bone saw crunched its way through the dead woman's skull, Dani had gagged. When the pathologist had then removed the skull cap with a sickly squelching and sucking sound, exposing the cadaver's shrivelled brain, Dani had been physically sick right there on the spot, in the middle of the examination room. The thick lumpy vomit had covered herself, the floor and the pathologist's trouser legs.

That had not gone down well.

Dani had been the butt of jokes for quite a while after that, and she felt like it had taken equally long to get rid of the smell. She'd showered as soon as she could when she'd got home, and three times more that day, but the godawful smell lingered for weeks.

She'd never become used to post-mortems, and didn't know how any person could willingly do that for a job, but as an experienced DI she could at least now bear the sight of someone's brain being removed without spewing her guts.

At least she had been able to at one time, but Dani hadn't been to a mortuary for over two years, and as she opened the door to the examination room and spotted Paul Reeve's dissected body on a metal autopsy table, the wave of nausea that passed over her almost took her off her feet. It was a good job Fletcher had assigned DS Langdon to attend the actual post-mortem that morning.

'DI Stephens,' Ledford said, turning around from where he'd been scribbling notes into a ledger. 'You're looking a little green.'

'I'm fine. You said you had some results.'

'You just missed Fletcher actually,' Ledford said, looking at his watch. 'I thought maybe she or DS Langdon would have given you the results, but I know you said you wanted me to talk through the findings in person. It would have been easier to brief you all at the same time, but so be it.'

'Sorry. I was out on other business. And I didn't know Fletcher was coming.'

'But you told me I needed to speak to you both about this matter? So I called you both.'

'Yes, that's fine. So you've carried out procedures on both bodies now?'

'I have. I don't have full toxicology results on the male yet, but we do know a lot more. Come and have a look.'

Ledford led Dani over to the autopsy table and she looked down at Paul Reeve's now stitched-up body. His skin was as white as the sheet that was dangling off the end of the table. His glass-like eyes stared up at the ceiling.

Now he was all cleaned up, the two knife wounds – one to his side, one to his belly – were clearly visible. The edges around them looked thick and protruded like they were plasticine wounds that had been stuck to him for special effect. Ledford reached across and swiped away the sheet that covered Natalya's corpse on a metal gurney next to them, and Dani winced as she looked at the similarly cut-up remains.

'Both victims died from, to put it into layman's terms, massive blood loss.'

'Exsanguination,' Dani said.

'Yes, very good, DI Stephens,' Ledford said, clearly not that impressed with Dani's knowledge. 'Paul Reeve's injuries were more severe, and it's likely that he was dead within a minute or so of being stabbed. As well as massive blood loss from the two wounds, this wound here, in his gut, severed the abdominal aorta, which is what I mentioned to you about the young woman the other day.'

Ledford poked and prodded at the wounds as he spoke and Dani held back the urge to gag. Ledford looked up at her and must have noticed her squeamishness. He gave her a clear look of disapproval.

'As for the young lady's injuries…'

'Natalya,' Dani said. 'We think her name was Natalya.'

'Ok. As for Natalya, she lasted a bit longer. Like Reeve, Natalya did eventually bleed to death, but the stab wound to her side didn't sever the renal artery, just nicked it really. The blow actually caused quite a lot more damage to the kidney itself, and it was fifty–fifty as to whether she would have died from blood loss or from the effects of the lacerated kidney, which would have poisoned her from the inside. She was still alive when the killer was interrupted, I hear, and probably was for several minutes afterwards.'

'Paramedics pronounced her dead on their arrival.'

'They did, which was close to ten minutes after the 999 call.'

'Would a quicker response have saved her?'

'Possibly, but I'd say it's quite unlikely.'

'What about the other wounds on Reeve? Are they defensive wounds?'

'I'd say some are. It will take me a while longer to properly analyse them all, but I can see that some of the bruises and cuts are probably two or three days old.'

'So he was in a fight?'

'Possibly. Or maybe he played rugby or some other contact sport. Martial arts. Who knows? But there's definite evidence of a struggle in the lead up to his death too. This wound here…'

Ledford lifted up Reeve's right arm, revealing a long deep cut riding up to the elbow. Dani hadn't spotted that back at the apartment.

'…I'd say was inflicted by the same knife that killed him.'

'He held his arm up to defend himself.'

'Most likely. There's also a rather nasty lump on the back of his head. The result of a blunt force blow.'

Dani looked at Ledford. 'What are you saying?'

'I can't be definitive. Perhaps he was hit over the head with an object, or perhaps he fell and smacked his head on something. Closer examination of the apartment may give the answer.'

'There were no objects recovered that looked like they'd been used as a weapon.'

'There is potentially some significance to that head injury.'

'You think he was unconscious when he was stabbed?'

'There's no evidence of him trying to drag or move himself away, either in terms of marks on his hands and fingers for example, or in relation to marks or blood trails in the apartment.'

'And he didn't try to raise the alarm either. But you said he would have died very quickly from the stab wounds?'

'That's true. But thirty seconds, a minute, is still plenty long enough for someone to fight for their survival.'

'So you *do* think he was unconscious then?'

'Whether he was stabbed in the gut first, then took the blow to the head, or the other way around, I can't be sure. Although the result would be the same, it could tell you something about his killer, their motives.'

'What about the dirt under his fingernails?'

'Sent for analysis. I don't know yet whether there's any blood or DNA traces in there.'

'And what about Natalya?' Dani asked, looking over again at the corpse of the young woman. 'The wounds on her wrists and ankles?'

'Not much more to tell than what I said the other day. Those wounds look relatively new, so I don't think they were more than a day or two old. But there were other wounds on her. Scrapes and gashes to her feet from having run barefoot. One hand was badly grazed and there's a graze on her head too.'

Ledford went over to Natalya and pointed out each of the wounds.

'All wounds were very fresh. These happened in the moments before she was stabbed.'

Dani tried to think about the sequence of events. Natalya running. Running away from her killer. The grazes. Then the stab wounds to her front.

'Do you think she fell? That's how the attacker caught her?'

'Fell or was pushed. There were elements of grit and tarmac in the wounds so that would be my conclusion.'

'What about sexual assault?'

'No evidence of violent sexual assault, nor were any traces of semen found in her or on her.'

Dani again flinched at the words, even though it was welcome news, of sorts. There was silence for a few moments as Dani tried to process the information and the significance of it all.

'You look disappointed, Detective,' Ledford said.

'What? No. I just… I expected more similarities in the deaths.'

Because wasn't a single killer the most likely explanation here, given that the victims were linked to each other?

'Similarities? Well, they are and aren't there. Natalya was stabbed in a quite straightforward manner – in and out wounds. She died from blood loss but it took quite a few minutes, I'd imagine. Reeve, on the other hand, took a horrendous blow to his gut. Now, this might surprise you, but in a normal in and out stab wound, it's very difficult to cut into the intestines. A bullet to the gut, well that cuts through anything in its path. But the speed and pressure of a knife is usually too small and the intestines just bounce about and slide around the blade when it penetrates the area. Here, though, we have massive damage not just to the intestines but to the abdominal aorta too. The knife was pulled about inside his body. Now that was no accident.'

Dani shuddered at the graphic words, but tried to remain focused.

'For Reeve the killer wanted to make sure there was significant damage that would result in a quick death,' Dani said.

'That's a hypothesis consistent with the wounds, yes.'

Dani's brain was racing with different thoughts.

'So do you think killing Natalya might have been a mistake? That the attacker didn't want to kill her? Just subdue her? Or that the killer, her abductor, panicked and stabbed her?'

'I simply can't answer those questions with a yes or no. I speak facts, it's for you to put the story of those facts together.'

That was fair enough. They were questions she'd have to just keep in her head.

'These two victims are linked. We believe they knew each other. Which is why I'm keen to understand if they could have been killed by the same person.'

'You know it's not possible for me to draw such a conclusive opinion. And as I've just explained, the wounds, on the face of it, do appear to be quite different in their delivery. But, having said that, based on the nature of the wounds, the damage caused, the size of the incisions, the clean cuts with little tearing, I do think that a very similar knife was used to kill both people. Could it be the same knife and the same person? Absolutely it *could*.'

Dani simply nodded at that and Ledford looked slightly disappointed that his moment of revelation hadn't caused a bigger reaction. Yes, the news was exactly what Dani had been gunning for, but until they had a killer locked up or at least some tangible evidence – the murder weapon, DNA – they were just putting two and two together.

'And the type of knife?' Dani asked.

'Something rudimentary. A kitchen knife perhaps. Something with a long, thin, single-edged smooth blade. I think I said before, one and a half inches wide, maybe as much as two, and at least five inches long. Probably a relatively dull point to it.'

Dani was taking all of Ledford's words in, but as she took a deep inhalation of breath her mind went foggy, queasiness setting in as she stared at the two bodies right there in front of her.

'Toxicology results aren't back yet so that's really all I have for you right now, but you're welcome to take a look at my detailed notes. I was just writing them up.'

What Dani wanted was to go and get some fresh air. She was glad when she heard her phone vibrating.

'I'd better take this,' Dani said. 'I'll wait until you've got the full report completed before I take a proper look. Thanks for your time, Jack.'

'Very well. Just doing my job, Detective.'

Dani grabbed her phone and pressed the green button as she headed back out into the corridor. She took a massive lungful of air as soon as she stepped out, the rush of oxygen together with the still present death smell swirling around inside her and making her feel dizzy for a few seconds.

'DI Stephens,' Dani said as she lumbered along, searching for the exit.

'Dani, it's me.'

Jason?

She was about to end the call, she didn't need *this* right now, but Jason spoke again before she got the chance.

'You need to get over here right away,' he said. 'It's DS Easton. He's been attacked.'

Chapter Thirty

With the help of paracetamol and vast quantities of water, Grant was thankfully feeling more human by the time his final lecture of the day came around at four. He'd woken up earlier that Thursday morning at five a.m. with a stinking hangover. It wasn't like him to drink so much during the week, and especially not like him to have drunk so much so early in the day with those early beers after golf, followed by him and Mary finishing what she and Julie had earlier started. Namely a litre bottle of gin and a bottle of Chablis.

Annie had been faintly amused, though also slightly embarrassed, when she'd returned home from her friend's house to find her parents merrily sloshing the wine in their glasses and the words in their mouths. She'd made the sensible decision to shut herself in her bedroom for the rest of the evening.

Grant and Mary hadn't much minded that. Annie would get over it and Grant knew it was good for him and Mary to both let their hair down, and spend an evening giggling and flirting with each other like they were carefree twenty-somethings rather than middle-aged parents with a violent loser for a son.

Inevitably, though, the alcohol had done its work and by ten p.m. Grant was fast asleep on the sofa in the lounge. He wasn't sure what time he'd dragged himself to bed, but his confused body clock had woken him up at five, and all in all he felt horrendous for it.

He'd left Mary gently snoring in the bed – she always slept better than him, which really riled him – and after a shower and some plain buttered toast he'd arrived at the university campus just after seven. He'd missed out on an entire day's work the previous day so it seemed sensible to catch up on some lost time before the grind started again.

After his first lecture in the morning, when he'd staggered about like a zombie, looking and feeling as ropey as the gaggle of students did, he'd steadily worked through his backlog. Now he just had one lecture to go until finally he could call it a day.

That lecture, a specialist criminology module that Grant had titled Deviance, Youth and Culture, was an optional module that students from a variety of degree subjects, ranging from sociology through to politics, were eligible to take. As with Grant's other modules, the class was generally filled with a mishmash of students from different backgrounds – Birmingham was a renowned multicultural city after all. The one uniting similarity of the majority of the students was their inability to pay full attention to proceedings.

Grant by now recognised the faces of the small group who would actually sit with genuine eagerness, and he knew that one of those students for the module was Jessica Bradford. This would be the first time he'd seen her following the brief fangirl moment earlier in the week.

Which was why he was feeling slightly anxious as he headed inside the theatre and over to the podium. He really didn't want the embarrassment of her swooning over him again.

When he spotted her in her usual position on the front row, she gave him a coy smile and he quickly averted his eyes and tried to clear his head. He carried on through his patter, and was part way through discussing Robert K. Merton's strain theory of deviance – a theory that attempted to explain how societal pressures lead to criminality – when he noticed his phone, which he'd left on the podium, light up with an incoming call from Mary.

He thought about answering. Would the students care? Would they even notice? Grant thought about which of Merton's five responses to strain could be used to describe his action if he did answer the phone. Rebellion, probably, exhibited by people who rejected both cultural and social goals.

Actually, no. Rebellion might be the response that best described the simple action of answering a mobile phone at an inappropriate time, but Grant knew the social response that his reaction to pressure fit perfectly; ritualism. This described the response of people who rejected society's goals (largely because they were unable to achieve them), but still accepted and adhered to society's means of achievement and social norms. Like Grant, people who exhibited ritualism were most commonly found in dead-end, repetitive jobs.

Dead-end? What was he thinking? Many people would consider being a professor of criminology an upstanding and rewarding profession. So why didn't he?

Grant carried on with the lecture but couldn't quite shake the feeling of a lack of fulfilment in his life. He wrapped up the session five minutes early, intent on calling Mary back. As usual the room cleared within seconds. Not fully, though. Jessica came idling up. Her friend, this time, hadn't bothered to wait.

'That was fascinating,' she said.

'I'm glad you thought so.'

'I've had some further thoughts about my thesis. Could we chat about it again when you have some time?'

Grant looked at his watch. 'I really can't today,' he said. 'Perhaps later in the week?'

She looked disappointed, but she had more than two years before she'd need to hand it her thesis. She could surely wait a day or two.

There was a bang at the top of the stairs as the doors to the lecture hall opened. Grant looked up and did a double take when he saw Mary standing there.

'Honey?'

She didn't look happy as she stomped down the steps towards them. Jessica looked from Grant to Mary and back again, looking sheepish all of a sudden.

'I tried calling you,' Mary said.

'I was in the middle of a lecture,' Grant said. He looked at Jessica.

'Let me know,' Jessica said, before turning and, scuttling up the stairs and out of the room, avoiding eye contact with Mary as she went.

'Keen student?' Mary asked, sounding a little aggravated.

'Apparently so,' Grant said, feeling a little embarrassed.

'The police came around again this afternoon,' Mary said, and Grant wasn't quite sure whether he was happy about the abrupt change of subject or not.

'Ethan?'

'Yeah.'

Grant had absolutely no doubt as to which of Merton's responses to strain Ethan most closely aligned with; retreatism, used to describe people who rejected both cultural goals and means, and who committed acts of deviance to achieve things outside of normal society's values. Basically drop-outs. True deviants, some would call them.

'What's he done now?' Grant asked, putting his hand on Mary's shoulder to offer comfort.

'He was arrested last night for drunk-driving and possession. Again. He was released on bail this morning. Apparently your lawyer got him out. You didn't know?'

'What? I had no idea!'

But then Grant did remember that he'd seen a missed call and voicemail on his phone earlier. He'd been in the middle of something else at the time though and, not recognising the number, had forgotten all about it.

'That isn't what the police came over for today, though.'

By now Grant's mind was racing with confusion. Where would the problems stop with that boy?

'So, what then?' he asked.

'They were looking for him in connection with two murders – that woman who was stabbed and was on the news the other day. And a man, too. One of Ethan's friends. Paul Reeve. But they also asked about a Jimmy Colton and what we knew of him.'

She didn't need to say anything more than that. Grant had never met Jimmy Colton, as far as he was aware, nor Paul Reeve for that matter, but given the conversation he and Mary had with Annie the other day about Ethan's no-good friend Jimmy, the police's questions surely couldn't just be a coincidence? Grant put his hand to his forehead and squeezed his temples as hard as he could until the pressure caused a stabbing pain at the front of his brain.

'What should we do, Steven?'

'I think at this stage the real question is; what else *can* we do?'

Chapter Thirty-One

With the sun edging down beyond the high-rises in the distance, Dani looked around as she approached, noticing the police cordon, the ambulance, the three squad cars and riot van that all had their lights flashing, and the collection of yellow-coated bobbies swarming about the place. No sign of Jason now, she realised. Easton was perched on the back end of the ambulance, its doors wide open, his legs dangling. He had a cut above his left eye and his swollen nose was plugged with cotton wool.

'Quite some drama you've caused here, DS Easton.'

'I've always been a bit of an attention-seeker,' he said.

'Can you get up to show me what happened, or do you need a wheelchair?'

'Perhaps a few weeks of paid leave first? I hear the Bahamas is nice this time of year.'

'Easton, get off your lazy arse before I give you something far worse than those two scratches.'

Easton smiled, then got to his feet and he and Dani walked across the street. The police response to hearing of an attack on a fellow officer was swift and strong, as it should be, but on this occasion, as Dani had figured out on her way over to Handsworth, it was also largely unnecessary. Easton was fine. McNair had called a few minutes after Jason and confirmed that his injuries were not serious, which Dani now presumed was why Jason hadn't hung around. Dani had felt massive relief at the news, but then she'd had to suck it up when McNair had openly laid the blame for Easton's attack at Dani's door, for sending him out chasing the lead without her – as though Dani were Easton's mother and should chaperone him twenty-four hours a day. He was a sergeant, for god's sake! And a pretty damn competent one at that. Dani had wanted to remind McNair of that fact, but in the heat of the moment, with McNair giving her the hairdryer treatment, she'd realised it was probably not the wisest move.

'That's the address there,' Easton said, pointing.

Dani took in the largely grubby-looking terraced row. On the ground floor was a small parade of shops; a newsagent, a down-trodden Caribbean cafe, a barber shop and a nail bar. The nail bar looked glitzy and shiny compared to everything else there, clearly the newest and most thriving of the small businesses. Above, on the first floor, were flats, reached by a door from the street, which was standing open.

Looking at the building, Dani felt that this was such a vast world away from the well-to-do village of Knowle with its array of executive homes, where Ethan Grant's parents lived. How had their son wound up here?

'The flat is rented,' Easton said as they stopped by the open door. 'Current registered tenant is a James Colton.'

'You're kidding?' Dani said.

'Not at all. The landlord turned up when he saw the police cars. Mr Assad. He lives across the street. His tenant background checks aren't exactly thorough, given the documents he showed us, so it's still anybody's guess as to whether there really is a James or Jimmy Colton.'

What on earth was the story with Colton? Dani wondered.

'Ok, that's all good info, Easton, but tell me what happened to you. Who did this?'

'I honestly don't know. DC Constable and I—'

'He's here?'

'Yeah, he's over there.'

Dani followed Easton's line of sight to the young man, who was talking to a uniformed female officer. Talking? More like flirting, Dani thought.

'Hard at work, I see,' Dani said.

'Yeah,' was all Easton said to that. 'Anyway, we were just approaching the door here. I was reaching out to ring the bell when the door suddenly sprang open. There was a man standing there. But I didn't get a good look, it all happened so quickly.'

'Any description at all?'

'I didn't really see his face. About my height, build. Blue hooded sweatshirt. White trainers. He looked like a... a normal guy.'

'Age?'

'I really can't say.'

'Well that's pretty bloody useless, isn't it?' Dani said, her harsh tone unintentional.

Easton frowned and Dani shook her head and looked away. Had it really been such a sudden attack, or had Easton been too distracted by something else to have taken notice?

Perhaps he and Constable had spotted a young lady in a short skirt crossing the street, she thought, glaring over at Constable for a second, though she'd come to expect more of Easton than that.

'Are you ok, boss?' Easton asked.

'I'm fine,' Dani said, sounding anything but.

She quickly thought about her pills. When had she last taken them? Standing on the street she could feel her mind fogging over, her irritability peaking, her mood taking on a sharp edge.

'The guy must have clocked us as police,' Easton said. 'These buggers have a sixth sense even when we're not in uniform. We didn't get the chance to say anything. He headbutted me and made a run for it. I was down on the ground and had no chance of catching him.'

'And Constable? He doesn't look injured to me. Didn't he give chase?'

'Kind of funny, really,' Easton said, rubbing the back of his neck nervously. 'As I was falling back, I barged into Constable. He then tripped over an old lady's trolley bag. She was just walking by. Nothing more than bad timing.' Easton pointed to a shaky old woman who was still being consoled by two uniformed officers.

'She must be a hundred and fifty at least. The trolley fell, knocked her to the ground. Kind of like dominoes, or so the gawkers were saying. I mean, I was dazed, seeing stars. Dan, I mean Constable, he went to pick the old lady up. He thought he'd broken her leg or something. She was screaming and screaming.'

'Meanwhile, whoever attacked you had the easiest getaway ever.'

'I know what you're thinking. Keystone cops.'

'You said it, not me.'

'But we did the right thing,' Easton said with absolute conviction. 'I mean, turns out she's fine, but if we'd left that old lady injured on the ground with a smashed leg, the result would've been a massive lawsuit slapped on the Super's desk.'

Easton was probably right about that. Was that approach called damage limitation or plain old rose-tinted community spirit? Dani wasn't sure, but she did know her instincts in that situation would probably have been very different. She would have been up and after the guy in a flash.

'Did you or the PCs find any witnesses?' she asked, looking around at the now largely dispersed crowd.

'There really weren't many. It was quiet. And they all moved on too quickly.'

'What about the old lady?'

'Her description was pretty much the same as mine and Constable's.'

'So you've no idea if it was James Colton or Ethan Grant or someone else entirely who did this to you?'

'No idea. Though the fact he attacked me and ran at all suggests he's up to no good, one way or another.'

'Yeah.' Dani sighed then took a couple of deep breaths to try and get her head straight and focused. It seemed to take the edge of her worsening mood ever so slightly. 'Have you been inside yet?'

'No. Constable has. It's a two-bed flat. Pretty sparse place. Not quite up to Reeve's standards. Mattresses on the floor for beds, not much in the way of furniture or personal belongings, but plenty of booze and cigarettes. Weed too. There's no ID. No post or documents to say who's been living there.'

Dani scanned the area around her. Once again she felt eyes on her from all directions. She shuddered. As ever, with the police cordon in place around the flat, there was a gaggle of eager bystanders on the sidelines, trying to get a good look at proceedings, but it wasn't their keen eyes that had spooked Dani.

She looked over at the houses, flats and shops, trying to place the source of the eerie feeling that was taking hold of her once again, just like it had more than once over the last couple of days. Or maybe it was just her medication – or lack or it – messing up her mind again.

She saw nothing to explain the feeling. No shadowy figures, no ghouls, and yet somehow she felt the same ominous presence as she had on the street outside her flat. At Natalya's murder scene. Even outside Grant's house.

What was wrong with her?

'Right. I'm going to go up and take a look,' Dani said, managing to bring her focus back.

'Shall I come up with you?' Easton said.

'Sure. But probably time to get rid of this lot first, don't you reckon?' Dani asked, indicating the crowds of people and the now unneeded police and vehicles.

'Yeah, ok.'

'But why don't you get Constable to do it. Give him something useful to do rather than chatting up that poor PC. If you're worried about lawsuits slapped on the Super's desk, then that there is one in the making.'

Easton smiled. 'Ok, I'm on it. I'll be up in the flat in a minute.'

Dani finally drew her eyes away from the street and she headed through the open doorway and up the bare staircase to the flat. Once inside she quickly saw that the place was a dive. Why was Ethan Grant living in such a cesspit? It reminded her of the house from *The Young Ones*, the comedy show from the eighties where the central characters, university students, lived in a squalid house, the conditions in it almost as bad as the personal hygiene of its occupants. Really this flat was nowhere near as decayed as that one, but the similarities were there; the ashtrays piled high with butts, the empty beer cans and bottles of spirits, the pizza boxes and takeaway containers half filled with leftovers, and not a clean cup, plate or bowl in sight.

Despite herself, Dani realised she was smiling. She'd loved that show when she was young. Ben had too. At times they'd been just two happy, smiling kids, who revelled in the violent slapstick and foul language of one of their favourite TV shows, huddled together on a sofa together in fits of laughter, tears streaming down their faces.

Dani shook her head, trying to flush from her mind the memories of herself and Ben, angry that she'd slipped back to that mostly happy and far more innocent period of her life.

Or had it only appeared innocent? Had Ben been a monster even then?

Dani stepped over discarded crockery and moved over to the two sash windows in the lounge. One was covered with a makeshift curtain that looked like a plain old bed sheet tacked to the window frame. The other window had a tatty venetian blind. Dani used the tips of her fingers to spread apart two of the slats on the blind and looked down to the street below. A PC was already in the process of rolling away the police tape. Only one of the squad cars remained. Two officers were helping the old lady into the back, probably to give her a lift home. The bystanders were slowly filtering away, disappointed that the fun was over.

Someone caught Dani's attention. A hooded figure standing away from the crowd. Lurking. Clearly interested in what was happening, like the others, but being more discreet about it.

Not quite discreet enough, though.

Was he – at least Dani thought it was a he – the reason for the sinister sensation she'd experienced moments before? Her natural sixth sense, a barometer for danger?

Ok, perhaps that was a bit dramatic, but nonetheless Dani hurried out of the flat and back to the stairs. She raced down them and when she reached the bottom Easton was just moving towards the entrance, his head turned away as he shouted an instruction to Constable. Not looking, he almost collided with Dani.

'Easton, watch out!'

She held her arm out to stop him and their chests bumped. Easton jumped in shock and then rolled his eyes. At his own klutziness, Dani assumed.

'Sorry, Dani. I didn't see you.'

Dani held her hand up and shook her head, showing she wasn't interested in his apology.

Dani discreetly looked over his shoulder to the man across the street who was now half hidden behind a parked van. He was wearing different clothes to the man Easton had described – blue trainers and a grey hooded top, the hood pulled right over his head so nothing could be seen of his face.

'Behind you on your left. By the van, wearing a hoodie. Could that be the guy?' she asked.

Easton glanced over briefly. 'Different clothes but… I really don't know.'

The man casually walked away.

'Come on,' Dani said.

Easton said nothing more but headed off a step behind Dani as they crossed the street. By the time they got over to the other side and around the van, the man was ten yards in front, walking with more purpose.

After a few seconds he glanced over his shoulder. He spotted Dani and Easton.

And he ran.

Chapter Thirty-Two

Dani and Easton sprinted after the man. The pavement they were running down wasn't busy, but it was narrow with terraced houses on one side and tightly parked cars on the other. Any pedestrians, even those walking on their own, would block the man's way, and Dani hoped that would allow them to close the distance. The early evening autumn sun didn't help matters either, the rays poking through buildings in front of Dani blinding her every now and then as she hurtled along.

She could hear Easton's heavy breathing behind her. She wasn't surprised that he hadn't the pace to overtake her. She'd made light of his cuts and bruises but he was still injured. Possibly concussed too. She should really tell him to stop and wait because the last thing she wanted was for him to suddenly collapse because of the exertion. She didn't, though. She was too focussed on the man ahead of her who was striding in athletic motion. Even with her tight-fitting trouser suit on, and slip-on shoes, Dani was no slouch, though. She just needed a bit of luck...

Up front a young mother was strolling with a pram. The man called out to her and she shrieked and pulled the pram as far to the side as she could as he sped past. The slight distraction lost him a yard.

Next up was a junction with a busier road running crossways, cars blasting left and right. A set of traffic lights marked the pedestrian crossing but the man wasn't about to stop and wait for the green light. He slowed his pace a fraction as he approached the road, as though he was about to be cautious and reduce the chances of him being squashed, but then he simply darted out into the traffic.

Cars screeched to a halt, horns blared, and the man had to shimmy left then right to avoid a hefty collision. The bonnet of one car bumped him but he simply glided a half step in the air before landing back on both feet, the contact causing nothing more than a momentary stumble.

Still, Dani gained another two yards because of it, and she would take that. If she could close the gap another three or four yards she'd be within distance to launch herself at him.

With the traffic in the junction now at a stop, she raced right through without being impeded at all. The man ducked left and Dani followed down a narrow alley that soon opened out onto an expansive concrete forecourt. In front were two looming tower blocks.

'Go around to the left,' she shouted to Easton between laboured breaths. 'I don't think he can get out to the right. We'll box him in.'

Dani turned to Easton who nodded before he veered off and Dani continued on. Off to the right hand side a long red brick wall separated the council blocks from the backyards of terraced houses on an adjacent street. Unless there was an alley or a snicket of some sort in that wall then there was a good chance that the man would head left after the tower blocks, and with Easton coming around the side they'd corner him.

Dani's heart beat wildly in her chest, and she was quickly losing pace from the initial sprint. Unlike in the movies, it really wasn't possible to continue at full pelt for minutes on end. Her pace had already dropped to little more than a fast jog, and although the man was slowing too, she was struggling to further close the distance. The jeers and shouts from a group of kids and teenagers loitering in the expansive yard told her exactly what she must have looked like as she huffed and puffed along in her trouser suit.

'He went that way!' someone shouted.

'No, that way. He went inside.'

'Please don't arrest me, miss.'

And, of course, the obligatory, 'Show us ya tits.'

Dani ignored them all. Up ahead the man took the left after the tower block, just as Dani hoped he would, but this meant he was momentarily out of sight. Pumping her arms and legs as fast as she could, but with the build-up of lactate in her muscles now severely hampering her speed and making her legs feel like lead weights, Dani rounded the corner.

Realising the man was nowhere to be seen, she came to an abrupt stop.

Chest heaving, drops of sweat running down her face and down the small of her back, Dani gazed ahead. She heard more calls from behind her but ignored them. A narrow passageway of garages led into the distance, coming to a stop at a T-junction with yet another row of garages off to the left and right. There was no sign of the man at all. Could he have made it to the end and turned already?

There was no sign of Easton either. He should have been coming from the left, around that corner in front.

Moving cautiously, Dani edged forwards, her eyes busy.

She looked up at the concrete tower blocks. Even if the man didn't know this place, or anyone here, he still had the upper hand. Chances were few people around would help the police, if they could avoid it. It was the sad and unfortunate case that in many of the poorer communities in the city there was still a 'them versus us' mentality when it came to the police.

As Dani moved slowly forwards, her senses on high alert, she heard sounds from the flats above. TVs blaring. Babies crying. Talking. Shouting. A door banged, off to Dani's left. She felt herself jump and readied for action but then a middle-aged woman appeared. She looked at Dani suspiciously then carried on her way, walking off in the direction Dani had just come from.

Dani was by now nearing the junction by the garages up ahead. She wondered whether she'd been too hasty in stopping running. Had the man already scarpered, off to the right?

And where the hell was Easton?

That same ominous feeling crept over Dani again, her heart racing for a different reason now. She was scared.

Then she spotted movement ahead. A looming shadow. Her heart raced.

Easton.

Dani would have felt a rush of relief, but he wasn't where she'd expected him to be at all. He was on a higher level. Not alongside the garages where she was, but on top of them. How the hell had that happened? He was no longer running either, as though he'd come to the same conclusion she had; that the man was now hiding.

'Anything?' she shouted out to him.

He shook his head. Dani made it to the intersection and quickly scanned left and right. Off to the left the row of garages formed a closed loop that connected to the tower block itself, which explained why Easton had been forced to come up over the top. Off to the right, where the row of garages ended, the tarmac gave way to a large patch of grass, a children's play area in the near distance.

'Dani, there he is!' Easton shouted.

As the words passed his lips Dani saw him, peeling away from where he'd been hunkered by a garage door, and making a mad dash for the grass ahead of them.

'Shit, it's a dead end up here!' Easton shouted.

Dani growled in frustration. She bounded after the man. She wasn't letting him get away. The man hurdled over the low fence into the play area, and Dani felt sick as tension suddenly filled her. Mums and dads in the play area turned to take notice, concerned looks on their faces. The children carried on, oblivious to the threat.

Please, not that, Dani willed.

She felt relief when the man ran right past the tiny toddlers and jumped the fence on the other side. Dani followed and by the time they were both running down the hill across the open grass, she'd managed to close the distance again, with less than ten yards between them now.

Up ahead the grass ended at a thin line of trees. Dani couldn't see what lay beyond but she could hear the roar of fast-moving traffic getting louder with each step. As she neared the tree line she spotted a chainlink fence the other side, separating the grounds from a dual carriageway. The man was at the fence already. He began to climb. This was her chance.

Dani strained and pushed herself forwards. She thought about leaping through the air to catch him. She may even have done it; her mind blurred at that moment. She reached out, visualising grabbing the man and hauling him back off the fence and to the ground. She shouted out and…

Missed him by only inches. At the last second he managed to clamber up and over the fence, and landed on both feet as he thumped down on the other side.

Dani, who'd been focused only on getting there in time, couldn't stop herself and she slammed into the chainlink fence which crashed and bent and shook. The man, right there in front of her, but out of reach on the other side, looked over at Dani.

Much like hers, his chest heaved from exertion. She could see more of his face now, underneath the hood. His cheeks were flushed red. He had thick stubble that belied his otherwise youthful skin. She starred into his dark brown eyes and he smiled.

What was he doing?

It was an unsettling moment that seemed to last far longer than the fraction of a second it probably really was.

Then the man turned and sped down the bank. Dani grabbed the fence and pulled herself up. Like before, at the road crossing, the man hesitated for a second when he reached the edge of the tarmac, surveying the busy traffic in front of him.

Then he plunged right into the road.

He cleared one of the lanes no problems, but as he was midway through the second lane, a truck blasted towards him…

There was a horrific bang. Tyres screeched. Dani jerked in shock. Her hands let go of the fence and she fell to the ground.

Just like that, the man was gone.

Chapter Thirty-Three

Dani initially froze, unsure what to do, but with her suspect lying in pieces on the road she couldn't rely on the first response team to do the job. She was already on the scene. She *was* the first response. Yet, having scrambled over the fence and having begun to walk across the tarmac towards the chaotic mess, she could already sense that what lay ahead would leave her forever scarred.

The carnage in front of her was devastating and absolute. With the braking and the screeching tyres and the smashing at an end, and the smoke clearing, Dani could see that four cars were involved as well as the large articulated truck that had pulverised the man Dani had been chasing.

Big trucks had big problems stopping quickly, and safely, and although the driver had probably done his best, it was inevitable on such a busy road that other vehicles would be sucked into the mess.

Dani hit the button to call Easton then pulled her phone to her ear as she walked through the destruction, not quite sure what to say or do first. Two of the cars caught up in the disaster were almost unrecognisable; just lumps of mangled, crumpled and jagged metal. What remained of the windows was smeared with blood from the unlucky occupants stuck inside. The other two cars had fared better; their drivers and passengers were already out of the vehicles, surveying the damage, wondering what had just happened to them, and pretty soon likely to be overcome with emotion when they realised how lucky they were to still be walking and breathing.

The call to Easton went unanswered and Dani put the phone away. A second later she heard him call out to her.

'Dani!'

She turned to see him clambering over the fence. She locked eyes with him for a second.

'Call for help,' she shouted out to him before she faced back to the truck driver who was standing by his open cab. 'We're going to need a lot of help,' she said more quietly, almost to herself.

The truck driver seemed the least injured of the many people involved, though by the shaky look of him he was possibly the most mentally damaged.

'I didn't see him,' the driver said over and over again. His face was as white as chalk and he was shaking. 'I didn't see him.'

A plump balding man with rounded facial features which reminded Dani of the Fat Controller from *Thomas the Tank Engine*, he was talking to no one in particular, just staring at the lumps of flesh and bone that used to be a man. As well as the mess on the front of the truck there were streaks of blood and flesh and clothing stretching a good hundred yards across the tarmac behind the vehicle, glistening gruesomely in the warm evening light. The little that remained of the man formed an ugly lump that had been catapulted further down the carriageway even after the truck had finally come to a stop.

Dani reached the driver and, like him, simply stood and studied the carnage in front of her. As she'd walked across she'd expected to feel horror and shock and to be a shaking mess like the man standing next to her. What she actually felt was absolutely nothing. No emotion whatsoever. Dani was numb.

She reached into her pocket and pulled out her ID which she held out in front of the truck driver, her eyes still on the remains of the man she'd been chasing moments before.

'Honestly, I didn't see him. I couldn't do anything.'

'I know. I saw.'

'How...? What... oh god.' He cupped his hand to his mouth and sobbed.

Dani really didn't know what else to say. She shook her head to regain her focus. *First response.* She couldn't just stand there. She

213

had to help. She turned away and walked with purpose towards the group of people from the other vehicles who were busy trying to rescue the occupants of the two more heavily damaged cars.

'Please stay back!' Easton ordered the civilians, holding out his ID. 'For your safety and theirs, stay back. Help is on the way.'

Easton warily and carefully pulled the largely shell-shocked civilians away. Dani moved up to him. Both the male driver and woman passenger of one of the cars were trapped, the front of the vehicle crumpled beyond recognition and their torsos stuck somewhere among the mess.

Dani stuck her head through the broken glass of the passenger window.

'Can you hear me?' she asked, putting her hand on the woman's neck, feeling for a pulse. It was faint, but she was definitely still alive.

'Go check the man,' Dani said to Easton. 'But don't even think about trying to move him.'

The woman stirred and Dani talked to her quietly and calmly, trying her best to get an understanding of what her likely injuries were, but she really didn't even know where to start in helping to get her out. A police squad car arrived moments later, then an ambulance, and Dani was thankful to have the paramedics take over from her. Two more squad cars soon arrived, followed shortly after by two more ambulances. Finally, two fire engines hurtled to the scene.

Minutes later Dani had pulled away from the melee and was standing by a police car, the moment when the man had been creamed by the truck replaying over and over in her mind.

'What the hell happened, Dani?' Jason said, coming up to her side. When had he arrived? Who had called him?

Dani didn't answer. She really didn't know what to say.

'Come on, why don't we get you out of here?'

'No,' Dani said. 'I'm not leaving. Not until I know those people are ok.' She nodded over to where the fire brigade were busy sawing away at the roof of the most crumpled car.

'It's not your fault. You were just doing your job.'

'I'm not even sure that matters,' Dani said, trying her hardest to hold back her tears.

–

More than three hours later, darkness fully descended, but the crash site lit up brighter than day with portable spotlights, Dani was still on the scene, along with a large crew of traffic police who had by then largely taken charge of the situation. Jason had stayed too, and Dani had to admit she was grateful for that. The side of the road consumed by the crash was still closed, and would be for a while longer, but the police had managed to move the gridlocked traffic from behind the crash site one vehicle at a time, having them turn around and drive the wrong way to the nearest junction. The opposite side of the road remained jam-packed with evening commuters leaving the city, the traffic backing up way past as far as the eye could see as natural voyeuristic instincts took over and people slowed to survey the grisly scene.

Dani headed back over to a police car where Easton was busy chatting to a uniformed PC. She'd just taken an update from the traffic officer in charge of the scene. Forensics would be some time yet recording everything they needed before the damaged vehicles could be removed, but the update she'd received had at least told her that there'd been no other fatalities. Yet.

She'd also spoken to McNair on the phone three times to brief her. McNair had been friendly enough, though Dani was sure there would be a lot more grilling to come. She'd be required to give formal statements. There'd no doubt be an inquiry into what had happened.

She really didn't want to think about that right now.

'All good?' Easton said.

'Not exactly,' Dani said. 'Why did he run?' she asked, as much to herself as to Easton.

'It wasn't your fault, Dani. And anyone who asks will get that answer from me.'

His words of support were comforting, but the potential reper-cussions were still worrying.

Anyone who asks will get that answer from me.

But he hadn't seen what had happened. He'd already told her – he was running across the playground when he heard the smash. So was he saying he'd lie for her?

Did she want him to?'

Jason came over and Easton wandered off.

'Maybe we should go. Not sure we're of much use here now.'

Dani wanted to be taking a more active role, but the truth was she didn't know how, yet she was struggling to pull herself away even though she knew the officers on site had everything under control.

'Come on then,' she eventually said.

They walked back to the chainlink fence. The image of the man racing into the road flashed in her mind again and she stopped and squeezed her eyes shut to try and clear it from her mind.

'Dani, are you ok?' Jason asked.

'I really don't know.'

'Come on, let's get back to your car.'

Jason grabbed Dani's arm and pulled enough to get her moving again before he let go.

They traipsed through the dark across the dewy grass back towards the tower blocks. When they reached the row of flats, Dani noticed a uniformed officer stationed outside. Given what had happened, someone would stay there now until the occupants returned or at least until they figured out exactly who was now lying smeared across the dual carriageway.

Dani recalled the scene from outside the flats hours earlier. The man across the street. Why did he run?

'Give me your keys,' Jason said.

'What?'

'I'll take you home in my car. Someone else can get yours for you.'

Dani didn't protest. She handed Jason her car keys and he headed over to the PC by the flat. After a brief exchange he handed the keys over then made his way back to Dani.

'Come on, my car's this way.'

Chapter Thirty-Four

Day 231

I'm eternally grateful to the paramedics, the nurses and doctors who saved my life. To the neurologists, psychotherapists and physiotherapists and all the other -ists who further helped my recovery. But there's no doubt that after those months in hospital, since I've been home I've felt more alone than ever. I've entered a dark place. With the twenty-four hour watch and care of the NHS long gone, I'm struggling, even though I won't admit it to anyone. Least of all to Jason.

He's moved into my apartment now, though we sleep in separate beds, and that's not just because of my unsociable nocturnal habits that include frequent trips to the toilet, together with agonising bouts of insomnia. It doesn't feel like we're a couple; there's no romance in our relationship. He's my carer, however much I don't want him to be.

Since I've come home I've had a letter from the DVLA to say that my driving licence has been revoked. I'll have to go through a full assessment in the future to determine if I'm fit and able to drive again. I don't have a mobile phone. I'm not trusted with one, particularly following what happened with the Daily Mail article. Jason has taken my laptop and changed all my passwords too. I'm not supposed to operate other heavy machinery – what exactly that means, who knows – not even allowed to boil a kettle or use the hob without supervision. I can't be trusted. What if I make a mistake? What if I have a seizure while carrying out these simple tasks?

It's a stark reminder of just how different I am now, in other people's eyes, even if in my own mind I'm still me.

So Jason being here, in my home, is little to do with affection. He's basically here to watch and monitor me, and although I do depend on his company now, I hate that he sees me so differently. That he sees me as an inferior rather than his partner.

I'm sitting on the sofa in my lounge. I'm not dressed even though it's the middle of the afternoon. I was always such a motivated and get-up-and-go type person in the past. Fitness mad, I worked all hours under the sun. That's the main reason I've never settled down, got married, or had kids. I had no spare time.

Now I can't even find the motivation to get out of my pyjamas. I'm told this is normal behaviour for TBI survivors, though certainly isn't encouraged behaviour. But it's not just lack of motivation; it's lack of energy too. I'm tired, all of the time. I can't focus on tasks. Sometimes I fall asleep in the middle of a conversation or while eating. I can walk for all of five minutes before I need to sit down because my head is swimming.

Jason comes into the room with a look of concern on his face.

'When did you last take these?' he says, holding up a box of pills.

I frown. 'When I'm supposed to. I can manage taking a few pills each day, you know.'

'Ok,' he says, in his challenging tone. He's not all smiles anymore, like he used to be back at the hospital. Now he's more like an overbearing parent. 'So tell me, which drugs are these? Anti-depressants? Sleeping pills? Anti-seizure?'

I have a cocktail of daily meds. Anti-depressants because many TBI survivors naturally become depressed with their new lives, many develop symptoms of bipolar disorder, where one day they're manically high, then next they're suicidally down. It's uncomfortable that those symptoms almost perfectly describe my moods. I also take anti-seizure pills because the risk of a brain seizure for TBI survivors is so high, particularly in the twelve months following the initial injury. If you have more than one seizure, you're diagnosed with epilepsy. And I take sleeping pills to try and help my brain rest at night, to ease my insomnia and to help me recover. The more exhausted the brain gets, the more likely a seizure is.

'They're the anti-seizure ones,' I say.

He throws the box over. I catch it and look at the label. I read the name of the drug several times, at first convinced that I am right; that these are the pills I'm supposed to take to help prevent me from having a *potentially fatal brain seizure. But as I re-read the name over and over, my mistake slowly dawns on me, my confused mind making sense finally. It reminds me of a story I heard of another TBI survivor. He went for a walk with a relative shortly after being released from hospital and damn near got himself obliterated by a double-decker bus at a traffic light crossing. He was convinced the red man meant walk. It's common for TBI sufferers to be confused by everyday tasks like this, and for them to suffer further horrendous accidents because of their messed-up minds.*

The brain really is a funny old thing.

'Those are your sleeping pills,' Jason says. 'Have you been taking those in the morning?'

'Fuck's sake,' I say, slamming the box onto the coffee table.

'No wonder you're so bloody tired all the time. Are you sure you've been taking the other ones properly?'

'Well I've not had a seizure so I'd say it's all good.'

He shakes his head in despair and turns to head back out of the room. I know where he's going. He wants to prove his point.

I jump up from the sofa and dart out into the hallway to intercept him.

'Stay out of my room!' I yell as I grab his shoulder and swing him around. 'Just for once let me take care of myself.'

I storm past him before he can think of a response and slam my bedroom door shut. I lock myself in the en suite, then open the cabinet and stare at the pill boxes and bottles inside. Looking at the labels now, it doesn't take me long to figure I've been doing it all wrong, just as Jason suspected.

I feel my bottom lip quiver. It feels like an alien response to me. My psychotherapist tells me I score in the bottom ten percent on the emotion charts they use, in particular my lack of empathy is startling to him. He can't say exactly how much of that is because of the injury and how much I was like that beforehand, though I know in my own mind that I just don't feel much in the way of a range of emotions anymore. Certainly I can't remember the last time I felt truly upset. Bitter and resentful certainly, but not sad.

And the last thing I want to do right now is cry.

I slam the cabinet door shut. In the mirror, I see that tears are welling in my eyes. I don't want that. I'm too strong for that. To fight them off I let out the loudest, most powerful and angriest scream I can muster, and I don't stop until my throat is hoarse and my brain feels like it might explode with rage.

Chapter Thirty-Five

Neither Dani nor Jason said a word as they drove the short distance back to the centre of Birmingham. When they reached Dani's apartment block Jason parked up and they both got out. Dani didn't even think about questioning the fact that he was coming in with her. They headed up the lift to the sixth floor and Dani opened her door and stepped into the darkness. Only then did the emotion she'd been expecting earlier feel like it was brimming somewhere inside, trapped but preparing to burst out.

She didn't want it to. She wanted to keep it locked away as long as she could.

Jason turned on the lights and shut the door.

'Let me fix you a drink before I go,' he said. 'Tea, coffee?'

'Something stronger,' Dani said.

'Wine?

'Stronger.'

Jason looked unsure. 'What have you got?'

'There's some vodka in the cupboard next to the fridge.'

'You sure that's what you want?'

'No, it's what I need. Pour yourself one too.'

'Not really my thing. But on this occasion…'

'Give me a minute.'

Dani headed off to the bathroom and turned on the light above the cabinet. She opened the door and stared at the pill bottles. Dr Scholz's words from the previous morning about reducing her dosage swam in her head. Christ, had that really only been yesterday morning? It felt like a lifetime ago.

Dani grabbed one of the bottles and took two pills out, then stared at her reflection for a second. Angered at herself she snapped the cupboard door shut and dropped the pills into the sink. She had no right to take that medication tonight. No right to try to hide away from what had happened. She deserved to have it playing in her mind.

She found Jason in the kitchen, holding two tumblers. He held one out to Dani.

'I couldn't find any mixers, so just went with ice.'

'Cheers,' Dani said, taking the glass and downing it.

Jason looked a little put out. 'I know I wasn't there when it happened, Dani, but you need to hold it together. Getting yourself shit-faced isn't going to help you.'

'Are you a fucking shrink now?' Dani snapped.

Jason paused, though he didn't look at all put out by her angry response. Dani guessed he was more used than anyone else was to the new, more horrible her. Yet in a way she wished he would pull her up on it. Because she really wasn't sure she liked the new her at all.

'If I need your advice I'll ask for it,' she said.

'Right you are. I thought maybe you wanted some company.' He put his glass down on the counter and looked over at her. 'Well, do you or not?'

'You're not a kid, you can make your own mind up.'

'I guess that's a no then. I'll see you tomorrow.'

Dani said nothing and didn't move, as Jason passed her and made for the exit. She heard him open the door, then a long sigh. When she heard the door close shut a few seconds after, she turned around and headed into the hall, a large part of her wanting to see him standing there in the hallway having had a change of heart.

The hallway was empty and she slumped.

'Why do you push everyone away, you stupid...'

She headed back to the kitchen and stared at the vodka bottle on the side. For minutes she barely moved, her mind consumed with thoughts not just of the young man who'd lost his life out on that road, but of the two murders she was investigating and how all the events were connected. Also sloshing around was her visit to Ben which now all seemed so trivial. Scholz had told her she was in denial. Damn right she was. Not just about Ben, but about so many aspects of her life. How much longer would she continue to internalise all of the shit that had happened to her before she finally erupted?

She snapped out of her thoughts and reached for the bottle. Unscrewing the cap, she moved over to the sink. She hesitated for a second before she turned the bottle up and the spirit glugged out. She grabbed Jason's glass and threw the vodka and ice into the sink.

'No more hiding,' she told herself.

From here, she'd face her demons head on.

Chapter Thirty-Six

Grant had a much better night's sleep than the previous evening, not waking until he was roused by Mary getting up from the bed. He looked over at her and she gave him a friendly smile.

'Good morning.' She looked and sounded fresh and bright.

'Morning,' he said. 'What time is it?'

He checked the bedside clock. His eyes sprang open.

'Shit!' He jumped up from the bed. 'I was supposed to be in for nine!'

He had a performance appraisal meeting with the faculty head. He'd meant to set the alarm but must have forgotten. Mary just laughed as Grant darted off to the en suite shower. He washed quickly and was out a few minutes later with a towel wrapped around his waist. Mary, still only wearing her thin silk nighty that didn't extend much further than her backside, was standing by the window, looking out.

'What is it?' Grant asked as he moved over to the bedside drawer for some clean boxers.

Mary turned to him, a perplexed look on her face.

'Did you see Julie yesterday?'

'Julie Francis? No. Why would I have seen her?' Grant asked, realising belatedly that he sounded defensive.

Mary tutted. 'I didn't mean like that, Steven. If I thought you were screwing our neighbour's wife I'd have chopped your balls off already.'

'Just as well it never crossed my mind then.'

'Ha, yeah. But seriously, I've not seen her at all since they had that bust-up. When she stormed off in his car.'

Grant went over to the window and looked out too. There was definitely no sign of Francis's prized Range Rover on the drive, and come to think of it, he hadn't seen it yesterday morning when he went to work, or when he came home in the afternoon. Mary moved away from the window to fetch her dressing gown.

'Maybe he's got a job after all,' Grant said. 'And he's already gone out.'

'No. He's in. I saw him walk past the window a few moments ago.'

Grant rolled his eyes at that. Was Francis ever more than a metre away from a window? Though he and Mary were both snooping right at that moment too, so who was he to judge really?

When had he and Mary become such nosy sods anyway?

'Maybe she left him,' Grant said.

'Yeah, maybe.'

'Have you not got her number? Send her a text.'

'I did. After that fight. No answer.'

That did sound odd, Grant had to admit.

'Well, if you're that interested then just go over and ask if she's in. Say you want to get your nails painted again.'

'Yeah, I think I might. It just seems strange that she's disappeared like that.'

'Hello, what's this?' Grant said when a Ford Mondeo slowed to a stop outside their front gates.

'What?' Mary said, coming back to Grant's side.

A man and a woman stepped from the car. Both were smartly dressed. The woman was short and the unmistakable bump under her jacket showed she was expecting.

'Police,' Mary said.

Exactly what Grant had thought too. Mary looked as despondent as he felt at the prospect of yet another visit from plod. The two officers opened the front gate and walked up the gravel driveway. Grant's focus moved from the police and back over to Ed Francis's house. As if on cue – well, Francis wouldn't miss this, would he? – the outline of a figure appeared at one of Francis's downstairs windows, a second before the doorbell rang.

Grant looked at his watch. He really didn't need this. He threw on some suit trousers and pulled a shirt from a hanger in the wardrobe.

'I'll be down in a minute,' Mary said, searching for something to wear.

Grant nodded and walked out of the room. He knocked on Annie's door as he went across the landing.

'I'm leaving in five minutes if you need a lift,' he called out to no response.

He did up the buttons of his shirt as he headed down the stairs, then quickly tucked the shirt in before unlocking and opening the front door.

'Mr Grant?' the lady said.

'Yes.'

'I'm DI Fletcher; this is DC Constable.'

'Detective Constable Constable?' Grant said, not sure he'd heard that right, and trying his best to hold back any childish reaction.

'Yes,' the young man said, evidently aware of the funny side, but not in the least amused by it.

'Is it ok if we come in?' Fletcher said.

'What's this about?'

'It's about your son, Ethan.'

Grant stepped to the side and ushered Fletcher and Constable through. Mary, now dressed, was coming down the stairs by the time the officers were both inside, the door shut behind them.

'What on earth now?' Mary said. 'This is the third time this week you lot have been here. And different officers every time. Do you not speak to each other?'

'Sorry. Mrs Grant, is it?'

'Yes, it is.' Mary said. Her tone was sharp, and Grant was a little surprised by that. She came up to his side. 'So?'

Grant checked his watch again. He thought about offering the police a seat, but didn't. He'd rather they just got on with the reason they were there and then left.

'Mr and Mrs Grant, we shouldn't need to take much of your time,' Fletcher said, reading the signs. 'But we need to ask you about Ethan.'

'Your colleagues did that yesterday.'

'I'm afraid something's happened since then.'

Mary rolled her eyes but Grant was feeling nervous all of a sudden.

'Well go on then,' Mary said. 'Ask away.'

'Have you been in contact with your son in the past twenty-four hours?'

'No, why?'

'There was an incident yesterday,' Fletcher said.

Grant felt himself tense up and he gave Mary a look. She obviously wasn't feeling it.

'You gave a colleague of ours an address for your son, in Handsworth,' Fletcher said. 'When police attended the address, Constable here and another officer were attacked.'

'By Ethan?'

'It's not clear yet. But not long after that, two detectives gave chase after a potential suspect and… I'm sorry to say that the young man in question lost his life. A road accident.'

Grant put his hand to his mouth. 'Ethan…'

'No. It wasn't Ethan,' Fletcher confirmed.

Grant heaved a sigh of relief and he heard Mary let out a gasp, though for some reason he couldn't bring himself to look at her at that moment.

'The dead man has been identified by his fingerprints as Dean Harland. Did you know him?'

'No,' Grant said.

'No,' echoed Mary. 'Should we?'

'We're not on good terms with Ethan,' Grant explained.

'I heard that,' Fletcher said. 'But we really do need to speak to Ethan urgently about what happened yesterday. And about the deaths of the two people that my colleague, DI Stephens, was here to talk about yesterday.'

'We already know that,' Mary said. 'Please, we'll let you know as soon as we hear from him. *If* we hear from him.'

'And you have no idea where he is now?'

'We would already have told you if we did,' Mary said, turning to face Grant. He thought she looked slightly flustered. 'Honey, don't you need to go?'

'Yes, I really do. Sorry, officers.'

Fletcher looked at Constable as though questioning whether or not they were done. The slight shrug he gave suggested he was all out of ideas.

'Sorry to have disturbed you so early,' Fletcher said. 'I'm sure we'll be in touch soon.'

'*You'll* be in touch?' Mary said. 'Exactly who is in charge of this mess?'

'I am now, Mrs Grant,' Fletcher said, handing over a card. 'You can deal with me from here on in.'

'Very well,' Mary said.

Grant showed the officers out and then stood there, his back up against the wood frame while he gathered his thoughts. He wasn't sure why, but he felt shaken.

'For a moment... I thought—'

'Don't say it,' Mary said, coming over to him and putting a finger up to his lips. She nestled her head into his chest and wrapped her arms around him.

'Mum. Dad? Is everything ok?'

Mary pulled herself away from Grant and they both turned to Annie, who was halfway down the stairs.

'Yes, sweetie, everything's fine,' Mary said.

Grant didn't say anything to that. There were only so many secrets and lies he could take.

Chapter Thirty-Seven

Perhaps the one positive for Dani when she awoke the next morning was that at least she didn't have a stinking hangover. Still, a quick raid of her painkiller stash was needed before she could even think about the day ahead. She showered and dressed and then made her way outside for what she was sure was going to be a shitty day. Yesterday – the afternoon at least – had been all about doing her public duty as an officer at a horrific road accident. Today, though, she was sure the ramifications of what had occurred in Handsworth would begin to bite.

Before heading off, Dani walked along the street to her car, having spotted it from the window of her apartment. She had no idea who had left it there or at what time, but had found the keys in her letterbox on the ground floor. She put the car into the apartment block's underground car park and then made her way back outside and across the city on foot to HQ.

Inside, the office was busy with people, but quiet on the chatter front. Quite the opposite to the previous day. Dani knew that meant McNair was in. She spotted Jason at his desk, busily typing away. He didn't look up at Dani. Was he avoiding her after their bust-up – their most recent one of many – or had he not seen her?

Easton was at his desk too. He gave Dani an awkward look and got to his feet.

'Boss?' he said. 'Are you ok?'

'I'm fine, for god's sake. Can I not even sit down without being hassled?'

Easton took his seat again, looked back to his computer, his cheeks flushing.

Dani heard McNair's office door open. She slumped. She knew even before McNair spoke who she was after.

'DI Stephens, in here please.'

From across the room, Jason gave her a sheepish look, almost as though he were apologising for what was to come. Dani headed to McNair's office. When she was in the doorway she realised the DCI wasn't alone inside. A silver-haired man was sitting behind the desk.

McNair closed the door behind them and went and stood by the man.

'DI Stephens,' the man said. 'I'm Chief Superintendent Eric Baxter.'

Dani knew the name, but they'd never met. Baxter had been transferred in from another force a few months before. This was quite a way to be introduced to her new big boss.

'Please take a seat,' Baxter said.

He had a pile of papers on the desk which he shuffled about a bit as though he were building up to what he wanted to say.

'I understand you're probably feeling quite bruised by what happened yesterday?'

'Bruised? You could say that, sir. I saw a man being wiped out by an articulated lorry. It's not, thankfully, an everyday occurrence.'

'No, it certainly is not. I'd like to talk to you about the events, though, if I may?'

'On what basis?' Dani asked, looking over at McNair who looked down to the big cheese for the answer.

'How do you mean?' Baxter said.

'Is this a formal disciplinary meeting?'

'Do you think it should be? Do *you* think you've done something wrong?'

'What? No!'

'Then I'm not sure why you said that. This is merely a fact-finding exercise. Though you have to appreciate that this is a very serious incident. A young man lost his life yesterday.'

'If I may, sir, can I ask who the man was? Do we know yet?'

Baxter looked to McNair who gave a slight nod and Dani thought it odd that the Chief Super was looking to her for the answer to the question.

'From a fingerprint ID, we believe the victim was Dean Harland,' McNair said. 'We don't know too much about him at present. His parents live in Lancashire. They've been informed of his death.'

Dani took the information in but didn't react. She didn't know Harland, the name hadn't been on her radar at all. She'd thought perhaps the man they'd chased was Ethan Grant, the same man Easton had been trying to speak with in the first place. But perhaps Ethan was, in fact, the man who originally attacked Easton?

Whatever the explanation, Dani knew there was a story behind those two, and Jimmy Colton too, and that story may or may not link to the murders of Paul Reeve and Natalya.

'Ok. So how can I help?' Dani said.

'Can you please tell me why you decided to visit the address on Wood Road in Handsworth yesterday.'

'I'll have to check timings, if that's important, but I received a call on my mobile phone from DI Barnes advising me that DS Easton had been attacked there. I wasn't given details of the attack at that time.'

'And why was that relevant to you?'

'Because I was the one who sent DS Easton to the address.'

'Why did you send DS Easton to that address?'

'We were pursuing enquiries related to the murders of Paul Reeve and a young woman we know only as Natalya. We were given that as an address for Ethan Grant who was believed to be an acquaintance of Reeve.'

'But you didn't go with DS Easton?'

'No. Is that a problem? He's a sergeant, he's more than capable of carrying out routine enquiries.'

Baxter paused for a moment and Dani sensed he wasn't impressed with her tone of voice.

'Ethan Grant was not a suspect in your case?' he asked.

'He was, and is, a person of interest, but not a formal suspect at this stage.'

'And what happened when Easton arrived at the address?'

'I understand Easton was knocked to the ground when he went to speak to the occupants of the flat. But I'm presuming you'll be speaking to him in more detail as to the circumstances of that? I wasn't there.'

Baxter nodded, not giving anything away.

'And what happened when you arrived?' he asked.

'I established that whoever had attacked Easton had gone, and that the cordon and heavy police presence on the street was unnecessary. I asked for Easton and Constable—'

'Constable?'

'DC Constable. That's his name, sir.'

Baxter looked unsure at that but didn't say anything.

'I asked for Easton to get Constable to clear the cordon. Meanwhile I did a brief search of the flat.'

'A brief search?'

'I'd already been told by Easton that nothing of interest had been found. I simply wanted to take a quick look to see if my impression was consistent with what he had told me.'

'And was it?'

'It appeared so, yes. As I was exiting the flat I noticed that most pedestrians had already moved away but one man who'd remained caught my interest.'

'Dean Harland?'

'It appears so.'

'How did he *catch your interest*?'

'He was just…' Dani searched for the words. She glanced from Baxter to McNair and back again. She sank into her seat. She could tell that whatever she said wasn't going to be good enough for these two.

'He was just, *what*, DI Stephens?'

'He was loitering.'

233

'Loitering? Is that a crime now?'

'Of course not. But I am a detective. He took my interest. He had a hoodie covering his face. He looked out of place, like he was more than just a curious passer-by. It was a gut instinct.'

'And what happened next?'

'I simply wanted to understand who he was. I'd say it was perfectly reasonable to assume he was connected to the flat somehow, that maybe he knew the tenant or that he *was* the tenant.'

'So how exactly did this result in a foot chase?'

'Easton and I, we just crossed the road, we didn't… we didn't do anything. As soon as he saw us moving towards him he ran.'

'Why did you give chase?'

'Because he ran! Why would he run? Unless he had something to hide.'

'Quite an assumption, given that you didn't know who he was.'

'Would you not have made that same assumption?'

'That's not for me to say.'

'No, you just get to pick apart other people's actions after the event.'

'DI Stephens, that tone is not going to help matters. We are not trying to trip you up here. We simply need to establish the course of events.'

'Fine.'

'You were in plain clothes, correct?'

'Yes.'

'At any point did you shout to Mr Harland to inform him that you were police officers?'

'No.'

'Is there a reason why not?'

'In the moment it never crossed my mind. I know it should have. Yes, we were in plain clothes but Harland had been watching the scene. He must have known we were officers.'

'Another assumption on your part, then?'

'Yes, another damn assumption!'

Baxter paused and looked to McNair, as though questioning Dani's sharpness. When he returned his focus to her, Dani held his glare.

'Did you call for backup?' he asked.

'No. I was more intent on catching him.'

'And you didn't request Easton to call?'

'No.'

Dani let out a long sigh and the conversation paused. She could see Baxter was mulling over something. When he came back with the next question it was simply more of the same, and the back and forth carried on in that way for another ten minutes, as Dani painstakingly talked through the events leading up to Harland's death, and her actions in the aftermath.

Her tone with Baxter remained sharp and defensive, though beneath the surface she felt sorrow and guilt bubbling away over the fact that a man had lost his life. She wouldn't let it out now.

When Dani was done with her explanation, McNair leaned over and whispered something in Baxter's ear. He nodded, then turned back to Dani.

'DI Stephens, we're very appreciative of your time this morning. Do you have anything else you'd like to tell us before we consider next steps?'

'Like what?'

'Any mitigating circumstances or other issues that you think are relevant to this discussion, and that you'd like us to be aware of and to consider.'

'Yeah, ok. How about that I wasn't driving that damn truck? How about that I didn't force Harland to run away from us, nor did I suggest or encourage or otherwise force him to run into the middle of a bloody dual carriageway? How—'

'I'll take your sarcasm as a *no* to my previous question. I understand you've recently returned to Force CID after an extended period of absence?'

'Correct.'

Baxter studied her for a few moments, as though he couldn't bring himself to open up the subject matter. He said nothing more, just waited for Dani to finish what he'd tried to start.

'You want to know if my brother attempting to murder me, and the subsequent brain damage that I suffered, for which I've been sidelined from my job for two years, had any bearing on my actions yesterday. Have you any idea how ludicrous that sounds?'

'I'll take that as another *no*,' Baxter said. 'Ok, well if there's nothing more?'

'There's nothing.'

'We'll need a while to consider.'

Dani huffed and got up from the chair. McNair escorted her outside as though Dani had no clue where her desk was located anymore.

'Don't go anywhere,' McNair said to Dani before heading back into her office.

Dani sat back in her seat and let out another long sigh. It was taking all of her strength to stop tears from flowing. She looked across the room. Everyone now had their heads down, even Easton and Jason. They all knew what was coming and no one was prepared to stand up for her.

Not even Easton? Despite what he'd said to her yesterday about the accident not being her fault? Perhaps McNair had already put enough pressure on him to make sure he would turn an eye to the force throwing Dani under the bus.

Bad choice of words, perhaps.

It didn't take long for Baxter and McNair to deliberate. McNair called Dani back in less than fifteen minutes later.

'Please take a seat,' Baxter said.

'I'm fine standing,' Dani said, folding her arms. Defiant to the end.

'DI Stephens,' Baxter began, 'based on the information we have gathered so far, including your own responses to our questions, we believe there is sufficient evidence to require the conducting of a formal inquiry, and that it would be in the interests of all the parties to do so. Given the seriousness of the matter, that a young man has lost his life, and another man is in a critical condition in the hospital—'

Dani winced as she recalled the scene; the occupants trapped in their cars. She was hugely relieved that they were all still alive, whoever they were.

'—I have no choice but to refer this matter to the IOPC, who will determine the necessary investigative steps required.'

IOPC. The Independent Office for Police Conduct. Dani could already sense what Baxter was about to say next.

'I'm afraid, DI Stephens, that pending the results of that investigation, you are suspended from active duty. Is there anything you'd like to say at this stage?'

'No.'

'We'll be in touch in due course with details of the formal process, once the IOPC has considered the steps they wish to take. You'll continue to receive full pay and benefits until the outcome of proceedings is known, though I am obliged to inform you at this stage that it's possible that matters could move beyond disciplinary action against you.'

'Meaning what?'

'I understand the IOPC has already received word from the deceased's legal representatives that they are considering whether Dean Harland was unlawfully killed, and therefore whether there is sufficient evidence for a full public inquiry, and for civil or criminal action to be taken. Do you understand what I'm saying?'

'Yeah. That you might not be happy with just throwing me off the force for doing my job. If it gets you the right slap on the back from the powers that be, you'll be happy to see me in jail too.'

Baxter shook his head. 'DI Stephens, I do hope you'll remain co-operative through this process. It will only hurt your prospects if you choose to do battle with us.'

'Point clearly understood. Thank you for the warning.'

'We'll need your ID before you go. You are to refrain from any and all contact with regards to this matter with other members of the force during the investigation period. DCI McNair will show you out.'

Dani gritted her teeth. 'Understood.'

She turned and put her hand on the door.

'And Stephens?' Baxter said. Dani gritted her teeth as she awaited the parting comment. 'Please continue with your scheduled appointments with Dr Scholz in the meantime. What happened yesterday can't have been easy on you.'

Dani said nothing. Just opened the door and looked out across the team, and prepared herself for the walk of shame.

Chapter Thirty-Eight

Dani was still shaking as she traipsed back across central Birmingham to her apartment, her head throbbing from pent-up rage, but also from immense remorse.

Of course she understood the seriousness of the situation. A man had lost his life. Was that because of her actions? Well, yes, if she hadn't chased him he would more than likely still be alive.

Why *had* she decided to chase him like that? Why *hadn't* she called for backup? It was true that there were many things she could have done differently in the situation. That still didn't mean she didn't feel aggrieved at the way the force had seemingly turned against her at the first opportunity. Had McNair ever wanted Dani back on the team at all?

By the time she arrived home, Dani was all out of ideas as to where she went from here. What she did know was that she was hungry, thirsty and tired. Her only thought about what to do next was to go inside and eat and drink herself into delirium, to curl up into a little ball and lock herself away from the world like she had done for months. There was no doubt she'd come to find a certain safety and calm in solitude.

Dani bought a sandwich, two packets of crisps, three chocolate bars, two bottles of fruit cider and two bottles of white wine from the corner shop, then made her way up the stairs to her apartment, wryly telling herself that she may as well burn a few calories first. It was barely midday but once inside she poured a bottle of cider into a pint glass half filled with ice and took a big gulp, then went and sat down in the lounge to finish off the food.

It didn't take her long. Not long after, she relaxed back into the sofa, in silence, staring out of the window at the sky, greying as a storm approached.

'Where do we go from here, Dani?' she said, then let out a mocking laugh. 'Great, and now you're talking to yourself again, you mad woman.'

Front and centre in Dani's mind was genuine sorrow and guilt over the death of Dean Harland, not to mention the other people caught up in the mess who would be scarred, both mentally and physically. Yet she also felt hurt and betrayed, and angry. Strangely, the one person she was feeling herself pushed closer to in that moment was someone who had hurt and betrayed her more than anyone else. She really didn't know why, but after she'd finished her first bottle of cider she picked up the phone and called the prison.

Of course there was no prospect of either seeing or speaking with Ben that day, but with an appointment to see her brother after the weekend, and little else to do for the rest of the day, Dani fixed herself another drink.

Hours later she was still sitting and sipping in silence when the doorbell rang. She groaned, got up and headed to the hall. She looked on the intercom monitor and saw Jason. She thought about not answering, but really she was intrigued. He was like a boomerang.

'What do you want?' Dani asked, pressing the speaker button.

He held up a hand gripping a bottle of vodka. Grey Goose at that.

'Come on up,' Dani said.

–

'It was a shitty thing to happen,' Jason said.

They were sitting on opposite sofas in the lounge, both holding onto a tumbler of neat vodka with ice. Their third.

'You know what, I really don't want to talk about it,' Dani said. 'I did what I thought was right.'

Jason said nothing.

'What's going on with the case?' Dani asked. 'I'm guessing you've been put on it instead of me now.'

'Fletcher's going to be off any day. McNair needed another DI.'

'What about DCI Fairclough and the Organised Crime lot?'

'To be honest, he's not really too interested. He didn't know of Reeve or Harland or Ethan Grant, said they must only have been small players. He's doing what he can to look into people who may have known Reeve or Harland, but so far he's not given us anything useful.'

'So where's the investigation headed?'

Jason screwed his face, like he'd been asked a hugely inappropriate personal question.

'Maybe we should drop the work talk. Take your mind off it.'

'Whatever. But I want to know what's going on still. It's my case. There's at least one murderer out there and it matters to me that we catch them.'

Jason didn't respond to that, and Dani decided to drop it. The truth was, for once she did feel better having him there. At least this time he wasn't criticising her drinking, and it was surely better to have company for a change than talking to herself.

–

The day passed by in a blur, and even after darkness had arrived Dani and Jason remained sitting and chatting. With the vodka bottle nearly empty and blood alcohol levels soaring, both Dani and Jason had warmed up, the talk between them more natural and open once they'd decided to leave policing problems aside, and with no mention of Dani's other problems.

'Damn, look at the time,' Jason said, glancing at his watch. 'I really should be going.'

'Are you sure? You can stay longer.'

'My last train was ten minutes ago.'

'There's a taxi rank over the other side of the canal, towards Brindley Place,' Dani said. 'Or if you can't make it that far, you can have the spare bed.'

She was glad she'd managed to say the word 'spare', rather than 'your', even if he was the only person to have ever slept there.

Jason thought for a few moments. 'No, I think I've probably had plenty.'

'Fair enough. Probably about time for bed then.'

Dani caught the awkward look Jason gave her and she smiled.

'I didn't mean the same bed,' she said. 'The spare room is all yours, though, if you want.'

'No, thanks, best to just get a taxi and get home. Busy day tomorrow.'

Unlike Dani, who now had nothing to do. They didn't say anything more and both wobbled to their feet then made their way to the front door. Jason slipped on his shoes.

'I know I'm not a shrink,' he said, 'but I am a good listener. If you ever want to talk...'

'I know, Jason.'

'I know it's not the best timing, but I'm glad we did this.'

Dani sighed. This was what she'd wanted for a long time. Just to be able to start over, with no talk of their past life together. Why had it taken such a shitty turn of events at work for it to happen?

'I'm glad we did it too,' Dani said. 'You're always there for me when I need you.'

'I'd do anything for you, Dani. You know that.'

Jason looked at her with a twinkle in his eye. She was alert enough to know she was pissed, that the alcohol was clouding her better judgment, yet she didn't break the eye contact.

A short but awkward silence followed, and then Jason leaned forwards. Dani didn't react or move at all as he planted a kiss onto her lips. He moved back to look into her eyes. Still she didn't break eye contact. He came back for another attempt. He closed his eyes. She closed hers. Their lips touched.

No. This wasn't what she wanted. Not now. Not tonight. Not like this.

'Jason, stop,' Dani said, moving her lips away from his, but a moment later he was kissing her neck gently.

'Jason, for fuck's sake, I said stop!' Dani yelled.

She hauled her knee up and crashed it into Jason's groin, then shoved him away as hard as she could. He shouted out in pain and stumbled back, tripping over his own legs and landing on the floor with a thud.

'What the hell is wrong with you?' he shouted.

'Me? What the hell is wrong with you? The one time I just wanted you to be here for me, Jason. And you try to kiss me!'

'You kneed me in the balls!'

Dani held a hand to her head, exasperated. 'Jason please… I can't do this.'

He clambered to his feet, his hands cradling his groin. His face was lined with anger. He grabbed his coat.

'I know you're not the same person you used to be,' he said, the anger in his voice clear, 'and maybe you'll never be her again, but it's about time you opened your eyes, accepted it and just got on with your life.'

'That's exactly what I'm trying to do.'

'Sometimes I have to wonder, though, is it really the head injury that's made you into… this?'

Dani said nothing, just shook her head. Jason huffed, opened the door and stormed out.

Slamming the door shut, Dani slid down the wall to the floor. Only then did the emotion of the day finally catch up with her. Tears cascaded down her face. She wondered if they'd ever stop.

Chapter Thirty-Nine

Day 408

I've been home for six months now. It feels as though my life is finally on the up again, 'normality' is slowly returning. The darkest days are behind me, though I know I still have a long way to go to full recovery. I have an assessment booked to regain my driving license in two weeks! I'm so excited, like I was when I first took my test when I was seventeen. I have my phone and laptop back. I'm even trusted to boil a kettle of water…

Jason remains in the spare room, though I honestly don't think he needs to be in my apartment anymore. I've already got my sights set on returning to work, maybe in the new year, just five months away. Above all, I feel confident that my old self is still there, and finally winning out.

I've been trying to regain my fitness. I started out by running a couple of miles a day along the canals near my apartment. Within a few weeks I was running five miles a day. Two weeks ago I signed up for the London Marathon. I'll be running for Limitless, a charity for people and families dealing with brain damage.

I've just finished a twelve mile run, my longest yet and as I walk up the stairs to my apartment my legs are like jelly and my head is swirling with exhaustion. But I feel relaxed, and buoyed by my progress.

I'm meeting Gemma for lunch in an hour. I haven't seen her for over a month, and for once I'm looking forward to talking to her, to updating her on where I'm at, both physically and mentally. She's become a great sounding board for me recently. I've never felt so close to her in fact. Jason, on the other hand… we just fight all the time. I'm told it's a common reaction. That TBI survivors will often take out their frustrations on their spouses more than anyone else, then be happy and amenable with others, even strangers. Something to do with safe zones and security and helping the brain to recover by venting. It goes hand-in-hand therefore that some seventy-five percent of TBI survivors get divorced.

But Jason and I aren't even married.

What startles me most is that I don't even feel sadness or regret to know that our relationship is teetering so close to breakdown.

I check my watch as I walk along the corridor. I'd only intended to run eight miles so I'm behind schedule. I have to rush to get out on time.

When I'm ready not long after, I walk briskly through Brindley Place to the French bistro where I've agreed to meet Gemma. I see her standing outside the entrance, checking her phone. She looks up and smiles at me. I'm still sweating from my run, though I've showered and washed my hair. My heart is pounding in my chest. I'm exhausted and looking forward to some food and a tall, cold drink. Gemma puts her phone away. I see her get ready to embrace me.

Then she freezes.

I realise I've stopped walking too. A look of concern sweeps across Gemma's face as she stares at me.

A strange noise rumbles in my ears.

And then everything turns black…

–

It's several hours later when I'm finally aware of what has happened. I'm in a hospital bed. Gemma and Jason are by my side. I've had a seizure. I'm told I pushed myself too far, that it was inevitable. It makes me angry to hear that so soon after the event.

Gemma recounts what happened. How I stopped walking and made a strange gargling noise as my body stiffened then started to shudder out of control. I was frothing at the mouth like a crazed animal. She didn't get to me in time to stop me plummeting to the ground. There's a gash on the back of my head that's been stitched. I bit my tongue too and it is badly swollen inside my mouth.

Beside the embarrassment and anger at myself, my immediate thought as I lay there in the hospital bed is one of immense fear. That just when I *thought I was on top, I've blown it. Perhaps I've just taken several steps back in my recovery.*

And banging my head? Can my brain take any more blows before it packs in altogether? Have I just lost another slice of Dani Stephens?

Did I ever really get her back?

I can hear Jason talking to me, but I'm not processing the words. Then the room falls deathly silent.

My eyes fall on Jason, then Gemma. They share a look. They both half-smile, awkwardly. They look like they want to be pleased about something but don't know if they should.

What on earth could they have to be pleased about?

I only realise what the issue is when my arm reflexively lifts up to wipe my face.

To wipe away the tears that are falling.

Tears.

How long is it since I cried? Since the last time I felt this kind of emotion? In fact, the last time I even came close I tried my hardest to shut it away. This time I don't. I let it come. I let it all out. I sob. I cry. Strangely it feels good to be sad, and the smiles on Jason's and Gemma's faces grow.

Perhaps the old me really is somewhere inside still.

Chapter Forty

It was Tuesday morning and having not seen her brother at all for two years after his incarceration, Dani was making her way to Long Lartin prison for the second time in less than a week. The weekend had passed by in something of a blur. Not a drunken or pill induced blur though. After her most recent bust-up with Jason, Dani had stayed strong for three nights in a row, had even tried her best to wean herself off the pills, like Scholz had advised. The blur was more because her mind was so muddled with thoughts as to how – whether – she could get her life properly back on track again, just like she'd had to after her injury, just like she'd had to after that seizure.

There'd been no word from McNair or Baxter on her disciplinary investigation. Numerous times she'd debated whether to call Fletcher to get an update on the murder cases, but had decided against it.

Easton, on the other hand, had said he'd be there for Dani. Hadn't he? At least Dani had taken that as his meaning back at the crash scene. She'd called him several times, wanting to speak about the case, but he'd not taken or responded to her calls.

Unlike Jason, who was the one person who'd been trying to reach her. Despite what had happened in her apartment he'd called and texted. First to apologise to her, but later wanting to check on how she was. To lend an ear, support her however he could. No matter what happened, Jason was the one person who seemed willing to stick his neck out for her. She'd felt unable to answer or respond to his calls and texts, yet how much longer would he hang around if she kept pushing him away?

Half an hour later Cartwright was once again showing Dani into the interview room at the prison, where Ben was already sitting in wait. Dani took the seat as the door was closed and locked behind her.

'I'm surprised you came back,' Ben said, with what looked like a genuine smile.

'I'm as surprised as you are.'

She could see quite clearly that Ben had a large bruise on his face, around and under his left eye.

'What happened?' Dani asked.

'This isn't a beach holiday, Dani.'

'Someone attacked you?'

'Does it matter to you if they did?'

It did. But she didn't say it.

'So what can I do for you this time?'

Dani didn't answer that. She didn't quite know herself.

'I heard about what happened,' Ben said after a few moments of silence.

'Heard what exactly?'

'It was on the news. You were chasing some chump who ran onto a busy dual carriageway.'

'Nothing escapes the media's eye, does it?'

'So now you've killed someone too.'

Dani opened her mouth but managed to hold her tongue. She met Ben's eye for a few seconds but she really didn't like what she saw and had to break the contact first.

'What does that mean for your job?' Ben asked.

'I don't know yet.'

'They're firing you?'

'Possibly.'

'So you came to your little brother for comfort.'

Ben smirked. Dani didn't.

'The only comfort I get from you is knowing that you're locked up in this place.'

Ben's face fell into an angry frown but he didn't bite back.

'I saw the kids again at the weekend,' Dani said and she noticed Ben's features pick up. 'It was great to spend some more time with them.'

'How are they doing?'

'Chloe's a real natural at sports—'

'Just like you used to be.'

'She's the star of her football team. I went to watch them play over at Wyndley. Harry's not bad either, but he's more into his PlayStation than anything else.'

Dani noticed there was a wide smile on her face as she talked. She'd come to realise that being around those kids was one of the few true bright spots in her life; they were just about the only two people that seemed to be able to bring a smile out of her. Yet even that part of her life she'd neglected.

Ben was beaming back at her and Dani quickly took her smile away.

'I miss them so much, Dani,' Ben said, and she saw cracks in his demeanour begin to take hold.

'They're good kids, Ben. Despite everything. They're going to be fine.'

'I just wish I could see them again.'

Dani didn't say anything to that.

They sat through a few moments of silence, before Ben's face again opened out into a wide grin.

'What?' Dani asked.

'Remember when we were younger. You were always such a tomboy too, just like Chloe is.'

'Yeah. I remember.'

'There was this one time, we were ten, eleven maybe. The lads in school were giving you a hard time. I think you'd just beaten them at long jump or something. They were calling you all sorts, pushing and shoving you.'

'It happened more than once, believe me.'

'This one time, though, I was right behind you all. We were walking out of school and one of the lads grabbed your rucksack and pulled you backwards. You landed on your arse. I was about to rush forwards to confront the guy but you shot back up and clocked him one. A massive right hook onto his chin that sent him down. Pretty much knocked him unconscious. Everyone stood in awe.'

Dani sighed. 'Mickey Farmer.'

'Yeah, that was him.'

'Was there a point to the story, Ben?'

Ben looked down at his hands and sighed. 'I don't know. Just that you always did know how to take care of yourself. And that I hope my Chloe is just like that too. I hope she's just like you.'

Dani could see what he meant by that, though part of her also felt a little uncomfortable that one of Ben's standout memories of her involved her being violent. How much different to Ben was she really? Part of his defence when he was on trial was that he'd acted with diminished responsibility, that he was schizophrenic. The jury hadn't bought that. He'd not been diagnosed with a mental disorder, but surely there was something wrong with the functioning of his brain? Why else would he have flipped like he did?

That was the key aspect of what had happened that continued to worry Dani the most. It wasn't as if her mind was in tip-top shape.

'Can I ask you something?' Dani said.

'Fire away.'

'Why did you do it?'

'Seriously? *That's* what you want to know? Haven't we been through all this before?'

'Yeah, yeah, sure. Alice wanted to leave you. You killed her in a rage because if you couldn't have her, no one could. You quietly held a grudge against me for years after that, supposedly for poisoning her against you. Then one day you flipped and started killing everyone.'

'You make me sound like some sort of nutter,' Ben said with a wry smile.

'You've not exactly helped yourself there. But why *you*, Ben? We're twins. We're virtually the same. We shared a womb. Our DNA is more or less identical. We had the same upbringing. How could *you* do what you did? Because I certainly never could.'

'You really think that's true?'

'I know it is.'

'Then you're wrong, Dani. At one time I thought like you're thinking now. I'd have said the exact same thing. But it's plain wrong. All humans are the same. We're all made of the same stuff, and deep down every single one of us is a potential killer.'

The way Ben said it chilled Dani to the core.

–

She stayed in the interview room for nearly forty-five minutes before their conversation fully dried up. She wouldn't say it was nice, or even rewarding, to be there with him, but her mind did somehow feel more at ease by the time she left the prison. Maybe confronting Ben really was an important step to her moving on.

Having detoured and stopped off for lunch in Warwick, it was mid-afternoon by the time Dani made it back home. She set herself down on the sofa in the lounge. She was all out of alcohol, and had deliberately not bought any more. Sitting on her own for hours on end, she knew how easy it was to turn to the bottle for comfort, but she was determined to break the habit.

After sitting in silence for a few minutes she grabbed her laptop and opened it up and navigated to West Midlands Police website. She headed into the portal to gain access to the intranet, typed in her details then held her breath as she hit return. Would they have suspended her access?

She sighed in relief moments later when the screen refreshed and she realised she was on the inside. Feeling her heart rate building, as though she were a hacker who'd just hit gold, she entered into the HOLMES 2 system which detailed all of the force's cases. It took her a few moments to set up a simple search to look for any new murder cases. There had been two in the last couple of days, but neither seemed in any way related to the deaths of Reeve or Natalya.

Similarly, none of the new missing persons cases jumped out at her.

Nonetheless, Dani carried on her search, looking into various cases both familiar and otherwise, reading notes and interview transcripts and all manner of other information contained within.

By the time she had finished her fruitless search it was dark outside, and the only light in Dani's apartment was coming from her laptop screen and the orange glow of streetlights outside.

Dani sat back and sighed. A shuffling noise from out in the hallway caught her ear. Dani frowned, set the laptop down and walked out of the lounge. In the hallway her eyes moved down to the bottom of the front door where the edge of a piece of paper was poking into her apartment. Dani rolled her eyes. Each of the apartments had letterboxes on the ground floor, but that didn't stop canvassers from regularly sneaking into the building and pushing their junk straight into people's homes.

Dani moved over to the door and bent down to pick the paper up, ready to go through the motions of tearing the leaflet in two without even looking at what was being offered this time.

But then she stopped, because she quickly realised this wasn't yet another leaflet offering house cleaning, or pizzas, or assistance with injury claims, but just a regular piece of plain paper, folded in half.

She unfolded the paper and stared down at the words, hand-written in blue.

'What the...?'

RIP Dean Harland. Now you're a killer too, DI Stephens. Just like your brother. And just like me.

Dani froze for a couple of seconds as the words sank in. Then she grabbed the door handle, threw open the door, and burst barefoot out into the corridor.

Chapter Forty-One

Dani sprinted along the corridor outside her apartment. All was quiet, not a soul in sight, but that note had been slipped under her door all of ten seconds before. Whoever had left it couldn't have gone far. Dani had taken little time to properly digest the scribbled words on the piece of paper that she was still clutching in her hand, but she knew damn well she wanted to catch whoever had left it.

She skidded around the corner to the lift and looked up to see the red screen blinking four, then three. That had to be the person who'd left the note, still heading down.

Dani rushed to the stairwell and crashed open the door, bounding down the steps two at a time. Twice her socks on the slippery bare concrete almost caused her to fly head over heels but, gripping hold of the handrail, she managed to keep her footing, just.

On the ground floor, out of breath, she flung open the door and raced into the foyer. She looked over to the lift. The doors were open, the lift waiting. No one was in sight inside. She turned the other way. The outer security doors were closed. The place was entirely deserted.

She thought about heading outside, but her own wariness got the better of her. What if the person who'd left that note was still upstairs even? Feeling more vulnerable than she cared to admit, Dani quickly moved back up to her apartment, remaining on high alert as she went.

Back in the safety of her home, after a thorough search inside to check she was alone, and with the door locked and bolted,

Dani went and sat on the sofa and stared at the handwritten note, unfolded on the coffee table in front of her.

For minutes she simply stared at the writing. Should she call the police? But who would she call? Easton? Jason? McNair? None of those options was appealing, for different reasons.

The more she considered the note, the more spooked she felt. But as Dani worked the swirling thoughts in her head over and over, she finally determined a plan.

There was, of course, the distinct possibility that the note was nothing more than a wind-up, someone goading Dani after seeing her in the press conference, and then reading about Dean Harland's death. She'd received plenty of such taunting mail over the last couple of years. There really were some sick weirdos out there. Most of them were harmless.

Most, but not all of them…

Dani went into the desk in the spare bedroom and pulled out a plastic wallet from the drawer. She put the note inside. Yes she'd handled it already, but she hadn't had any inkling what it was when she'd first picked it up. Her fingerprints on the note were easily explainable, but she had to do her best to preserve the note properly now. There could still be trace evidence on the paper that could prove vital in identifying who wrote it.

If she showed it to the police. *The police.* Like she wasn't one of them anymore.

Dani heard a clank at the lounge window and jumped in shock. She stared over at the glass. The blackness outside was interspersed with the yellow and orange glow from apartments across the canal. There was nothing else she could see, nothing to hear. Was it a small bird flying into her window? A giant moth, lured by the lights in her apartment?

Dani moved over to the window and pressed her face up against the glass so she could see onto the balcony. She realised her heart was thudding in her chest.

What would she actually do if there was a person standing out there, staring right back at her?

She had no idea. Luckily, it was a moot point. There was nothing and no one outside.

Then Dani jumped again when she heard faint footsteps behind her. She whipped around and held her breath…

Nothing.

Perhaps the sound had come from outside the apartment?

She could see out into the dark hallway, and as she stared at the band of light seeping in under the front door it was suddenly distorted.

Someone was definitely out there.

Dani rushed forwards, through the lounge, into the hallway. She threw open the door and sprang out into the corridor. She looked up and down. She was panting with anticipation, fear too. But the corridor was quiet. Just like it had been before when the note had been slipped into her home.

No one was in sight. But *someone* had been there. Dani knew that for sure. And it certainly wasn't the first time she'd felt a presence over the past few days.

Feeling anything but bold and courageous this time, Dani quickly retreated to the safety of her apartment and slammed the door shut, then locked and double-checked the door. She moved through the apartment in a frenzy, flipping every single light on, propping open all the doors, closing all the curtains. Then she went from room to room, once again satisfying herself that she was, in fact, alone.

When she'd finished her search, Dani grabbed a dining chair and lugged it out into the hallway where she propped it under the handle to the front door. Then she walked back into the lounge and curled up on the sofa.

Her eyes darted intermittently between the front door, and the note on the coffee table. Who'd left that note and why, she simply had no idea.

One thing was for sure, she wouldn't be getting much sleep tonight.

Chapter Forty-Two

Steven Grant woke up on Thursday morning feeling tired and groggy. Even after his usual quiet catch-up Wednesday, he didn't feel at all rested, and could scarcely believe there were still two full working days before the weekend. He knew why he was feeling so wiped out though: Ethan. Grant and Mary had heard nothing from him for days. The police still wanted to speak to him in connection with the deaths of at least two of his friends – if *friends* was the right word.

Even if Grant knew where Ethan was, he wasn't sure he'd tell the police. Ethan was still his son, and he would protect him if he could. *He* wanted to confront Ethan first and find out exactly what was happening, before he decided whether to let the police at him.

The whole situation was taking a toll on Mary too, though she'd been surprisingly relaxed the last couple of days. Perhaps she'd upped her meds again.

Grant got up from the bed and left Mary sleeping. After fixing himself a quick breakfast he was out of the house not long after eight. It was a cold, dark, foggy and drizzly autumn morning. The kind of morning that could suck any happiness out of even the most hardy and optimistic of people.

Out on the drive Grant headed to his car and pressed the unlock button on his key fob. He was intent on getting in and getting warm, until he heard a voice call out.

'Morning, neighbour!'

The cheery voice riled Grant. He looked out across the street to see Francis standing at the edge of his driveway, his set of pristine golf clubs propped up by his side. Grant had his hand on the door handle as Francis stepped forwards and crossed the road.

'Morning,' Grant said, deciding it best to at least play along for a few seconds rather than blank the guy. 'Another day, another game of golf, eh?'

Did the man never have anything else to do? Work, for example?

'Got to get the practice in,' Francis said, stopping at the edge of Grant's driveway, much to Grant's relief. 'I know you didn't enjoy yourself much last time, but you're always welcome to join me again.'

'Thanks. I'll bear it in mind. You waiting for a lift or something?'

Grant noticed there was still no sign of the Range Rover that Julie had taken off in a few days ago. He felt a slight satisfaction at the thought that she'd absconded with it for good. Though Mary had suggested a far more ghoulish explanation for her sudden disappearance.

'Car's in for a valet,' Francis said. 'Nice to keep it as new.'

'Yeah, I'm sure. You have a good one.'

'You too, mate.'

Grant turned and got into his car. As he made his way off the drive he nodded and smiled at Francis, who was back next to his clubs. Francis nodded in return, but the look he gave Grant was far from friendly.

What was going on with that bloke?

Grant arrived on campus in good time and spent the first couple of hours of the day reading through the research paper of one of his PhD students. He'd hoped to get through it all in that time, but it was in such a muddled and confused state that he managed less than a third of it before the clock wound around to eleven a.m., when he had a meeting scheduled. The meeting overran until nearly one, and after that it was back-to-back lectures, and he had no chance to get back to the research paper before the clock ticked along to four p.m. and his final lecture of the day.

The lecture theatre was already filling up when he arrived with thirty seconds to spare, and he quickly got himself set up and ready, feeling a little flustered and underprepared.

As Grant opened up the lecture he stared out across the faces in the room. He noticed there was no sign of Jessica Bradford. She'd missed the Monday lecture too, which was particularly strange given her previous keen interest, and her request the last time he'd seen her for some more of his time to discuss her thesis. Despite his previous discomfort at her fan-girling, he was quite disappointed that one of his few keen students was once again absent.

Regardless, he carried on and was soon well into his stride, until another face caught his attention. A woman. She stood out among the other people in the room. Most obviously, she was older than the other students, who were virtually all eighteen and nineteen, just a handful of more mature students in their twenties. Ok, she wasn't *old*, probably in her thirties, so younger than Grant, but she looked old among everyone else there. Grant didn't think he recognised her, but he did feel like he knew *what* she was. There was a serious and slightly world-weary look about her that only certain people had. Police.

Feeling more on edge, Grant carried on the lecture as best he could, but he was hyper-aware of the woman, who remained seated throughout, her gaze never leaving Grant.

As he closed off the lecture, the students quickly stampeded towards the exit. It was five p.m. after all, and the poor sods were likely shattered at such a late finish to their short day. The woman, however, was clearly going nowhere. As Grant gathered his things, she got up from her seat and came down the steps towards the podium.

'Professor Grant?' she asked.

'Yes, can I help you?'

'I'm Detective Inspector Dani Stephens, from West Midlands Police. Do you think we could chat in private?'

'Is this about Ethan again?'

'Not exactly.'

Grant frowned. 'Ok, right. Let's go to my office.'

He slung his laptop bag over his shoulder and made his way up the stairs and out of the theatre. DI Stephens followed him out, neither of them saying a word as they traipsed through corridors towards Grant's office.

Once inside, Grant shut the door behind him and moved over to the desk where he began shuffling the many scattered papers into some semblance of order.

'Sorry about the mess,' he said.

'A cluttered desk is a cluttered mind,' said Stephens.

Grant smiled. 'Indeed. And if a cluttered desk is a sign of a cluttered mind, of what, then, is an empty desk a sign?'

'Einstein, right?'

'Indeed. Please, take a seat.'

Stephens sat and continued to look around the room, at the messy bookshelves filled with all manner of reference books. Grant sat down at his desk and studied her for a few moments, waiting for her to say whatever she'd come to say.

'I remember reading about you years ago,' Stephens said.

Grant sighed. 'Yes. Many people do.'

'I wasn't very old then. I didn't properly think about what happened to you. What you went through.'

'It's an experience I would never wish upon another human being.'

'What? The fame and the fortune from a bestselling book? They made a TV documentary too, didn't they?'

Grant chuckled. 'Very good, Detective. I'm sure you can imagine my *fame* was rather short-lived, nothing more than a flash in the pan really, if you pardon the cliché. In many ways I'm thankful for that. I'm guessing you haven't come here today just to talk about my past, though?'

'Actually, in a way I have.'

Grant frowned, confused.

'Ok. So what exactly do you want to speak to me about?'

'Something I believe you're particularly knowledgeable about,' Stephens said.

'Which would be?'

'Serial killers.'

Chapter Forty-Three

'Detective, are you here on official police business?' Grant asked.

Dani did her best to remain steady. She'd expected this question. She hadn't shown Grant her police ID – she didn't have it anymore. She'd spoken to Grant's wife already the previous week, so *she* knew Dani really was a detective, but Grant himself had never seen or spoken to her before. Up until that question he'd taken it on trust that Dani was who she said she was, and was acting in an official capacity.

She could lie now, and tell him it was official business, but based on the fact that he'd already shown her to his office and given her a seat, and the problematic situation he was in with his son, she got the sense from Grant that he'd respond better if she told him the truth. Plus she figured that given the shared near-death experiences in their pasts, he may be happy to indulge her.

'No,' Dani said. 'This is personal business. Very personal, actually. You've probably heard of my brother. Ben Stephens.'

Grant's eyes narrowed as his gaze moved from Dani's face and up to the scar above her ear, then back again. 'Wait, you're—'

Dani held her hand up to interrupt Grant's all too familiar eureka moment. She was sure Grant was used to that himself.

'Yes. That's me,' she said, in a flat voice. 'My twin brother is a murderer. He killed his first wife, hid it for years, then when his life began to unravel went on a killing spree taking five other lives before he tried to kill me by smashing my head against a doorframe and cracking my skull open with an ornament a family member bought him as a wedding present.'

Grant didn't react at all to her words.

'I was in a coma. I suffered what the doctors call a Traumatic Brain Injury. I've spent two years recovering, and I'm getting better, but I'll never be the same person I used to be. I'm still here though, while my brother will now spend the rest of his life in prison. In that respect, you could say our experiences, our close shaves with death, are quite closely aligned.'

'Close shaves with death?' Grant said. 'I'm not sure I'd quite describe my own experience in that way. Are you familiar with what happened to me?'

'As familiar as most people, I guess.'

Grant's face screwed up in anger. Not at Dani, but at the memory of what had happened to him, she assumed. 'Then you'll know my *close shave with death*, as you put it, involved me being kidnapped and tortured. I was held in a grimy barn for nearly three weeks and very nearly starved. I had to watch as that bastard brought in two more victims to cut apart, in front of my eyes. I was his plaything. He would talk to me like I was his companion, asking for my thoughts and analysis on what he was doing, asking me to explain what it all meant, in a psychoanalytical sense. Whenever I refused to play along he'd beat me or cut me. So, other than that we both nearly died, I'm not sure the experiences are all that similar really.'

Dani couldn't find any words to respond to that. Grant had spoken at pace and with venom, and even though Dani didn't believe that anger was directed at her, she still regretted her own choice of words and wished she could start over.

Had she already blown her chance of help from this man?

After a few seconds of silence Grant defused and he sat back in his chair. His eyes locked onto Dani who held his stare.

'I'm sorry,' he eventually said. 'It's a subject that will always be raw. I shouldn't have been so flippant. Yes you've been close to death too, and I'm sure your experience was quite harrowing.'

'The most harrowing part has been the two years that have followed.'

'I'm sure. Tell me what you want to know.'

'That lecture you gave just now, about the characteristics of a killer… I have to say I was fascinated.'

Grant half-smiled. 'Let me guess. As you were listening you were trying to place your brother in among what I was saying.'

Dani felt herself blush. The fact was, she had. Was she that obvious?

'Mr Grant—'

'Call me Steven, please.'

'Ok. Steven, do you think every serial killer, one way or another, has a trigger? Something in their past that causes them to take that path?'

'Detective—'

'Dani is fine.'

Grant smiled again. 'Dani, then. The debate over nature versus nurture is one that could go on ad infinitum. I've already discussed it at length several times this last week in fact.'

Dani raised an eyebrow but didn't push Grant on what he meant by that.

'Honestly,' he said, 'I'm not sure there is an answer, nor what you could gain from it if there was. That said, it is true that many well-known serial killers had experiences in their childhood that could be linked to their future destructive behaviour. Abuse, trauma, loss.'

'But you don't think that's always the case?'

'I'm not sure it matters what I think. Though I will say this: for starters, not all killers are caught and analysed. Those *famous* killers, the ones who the layman know – Fred West, Peter Sutcliffe, Jeffrey Dahmer – they get picked apart largely for the simple fact that it's easy to do so. We know who they are, we know of their crimes. They were all over the media, they have movies and TV serials about them. Then, based on those cases, everyone begins to assume that all killers are the same. I'm sure you know the profile I'm talking about. Nut jobs who were abused as children, who hurt animals when they were kids before moving onto bigger prey as adults. You, for one, should know the answer isn't as simple as that.'

Dani winced at the comment. Grant was certainly right there. Dani had gone through in her own mind thousands of times what it was that could have turned her brother into a killer. As a child, even as an adult, Ben had appeared about as normal as anyone else. The conclusion that Dani had come back to again and again was that there must have been *something* that changed him; that made him capable of killing without apparent remorse, though she'd never figured out what that something was.

'I'm really not sure why this is important to you,' Grant said. 'Perhaps if you're more specific then I can properly help you.'

'I've dealt with murder for years,' Dani said. 'But those killers you mentioned before, they're almost so extreme they're not real world. The deaths I see are gang crime, domestics, drunken brawls, robberies gone wrong. But serial killers... I'd never really even thought about that. Until... my brother.'

'In real life it's best to assume that every conceivable connotation of good and evil is possible,' Grant said. 'First off, there are killers we *know* are out there, who just haven't been caught. You must know what I mean by that? I'm sure you've known murder cases go cold. But there are also murderers out there who simply fly so low under the radar that we don't even know of their existence. Serial killers do exist, Dani. They're out there.'

An eerie feeling washed through Dani as she took in Grant's words. His appearance, his voice, his manner, weren't creepy – in fact Dani thought he was handsome, in a fatherly, older guy sort of way – but the fervour with which he spoke about such ghastly things was quite unsettling.

'Let me explain myself a bit more clearly,' Grant said. 'You've heard of Harold Shipman, haven't you?'

'Of course,' Dani said. 'He was a doctor. Believed to have killed over two hundred elderly patients.'

'Making him one of the most prolific known killers of all time,' Grant added. 'It's believed he killed his victims over a span of more than twenty years before he was caught. And his method, it has to be stated, was simplistic. Yet to some extent it was faultless too, allowing him to carry on killing for many years. These weren't gruesome murders that captured the attention of the press or the police. There was no crime scene clean-up to think about, per se. For years no one suspected a thing, because his victims were all old people anyway, and he was a respected doctor, a respected member of the community. His signature on someone's death certificate, recording that they died of natural causes, or from some other age-related ailment, bore a lot weight.'

'But he *was* caught,' Dani said. 'It took many years but the police did get him in the end.'

Grant huffed. 'No offence, but I'm not sure I'd say it was down to some super-brain detective. Many people have suggested Shipman may well have *wanted* to get caught. That he was out of control and was ready to give himself up.'

'Did *he* ever say that?'

'Not that I'm aware. Suspicion about him first arose when a local funeral parlour queried the coroner about the unusually high number of Shipman's elderly patients who were being cremated there. Isn't that such a simple oversight by him? Why didn't he move location so that there was never such a build-up of evidence in one place, connected to one surgery? Surely that would have been obvious to someone who *really* wanted to keep going.'

'But just because he got away with murder for many years before that, doesn't mean he was a genius.'

'Certainly not. I would point out though, that even that initial suspicion didn't bear much weight with the police. They passed off those concerns saying there was insufficient evidence of a crime. He went on to kill three more people in exactly the same way as before. He could have called it a day when he knew the police were closing in, but apparently he couldn't stop himself. Do you know *how* the police finally got him?

'No.'

'He forged the will of his last victim, completely excluding the old lady's children and grandchildren, but giving Shipman several hundred thousands of pounds. He'd never done that before. Was that last move a sign that he was incredibly reckless? It's possible. But if he was so reckless I doubt he would have been able to kill undetected for so long.'

'So you really think he *wanted* to be caught at the end?'

'It's not unusual. Going back to the characteristics of serial killers – the known ones at least – it's quite common for them to crave attention. Often they're loners. Killing, for them, brings a feeling of great power. But sometimes it's not enough just to experience that feeling in the moment. They need to share it with others. One of the ways a killer can do that is to get caught.'

'And another is to leave notes,' Dani said, feeling her heart thump a little faster.

Grant studied her for a few moments, as though he sensed the words were important to her.

'Yes,' he said eventually. 'That's also relatively common. Calling cards, if you will, but also sometimes out and out taunts. Have you heard of the BTK killer?'

'Actually, no. I may investigate murder for a living, but reading up on serial killers has never been much of a hobby.'

Dani thought she saw a flicker of embarrassment on Grant's face, as though her words had made him feel slightly ashamed of his obvious passion for the subject. He wasn't derailed for long though.

'The BTK killer – an acronym for bind, torture, kill – was a notorious American serial killer,' Grant carried on. 'He killed ten people between 1974 and 1991. Gruesome killings, as you can imagine from his moniker. Yet he remained free for years, *despite* the fact that he regularly left taunting notes for the police, admitting and explaining what he'd done. These notes were often left in public places, because he absolutely wanted attention for being a serial killer. If he'd never left the notes? Maybe the deaths wouldn't have been linked at all. Perhaps he could have carried on killing with impunity.'

'The notes led to him being caught then?'

'Not exactly. His last confirmed victim was in the early nineties, and for years after that he went silent. No letters, no murders that we know of, and no progress from the police in finding him. He'd got away with it all. Then, in 2004 or 2005 I think, for no obvious reason other than he was missing the attention, and again, perhaps he *wanted* to be caught, he began leaving notes again. He wasn't killing anymore, that we know of, but just leaving notes. And he got sloppy. He sent a floppy disk to a local TV station. From the metadata on there the police managed to track him down. He openly admitted to his crimes at trial. He never tried to hide a thing.'

Dani sat back in her seat and let out a long sigh. Given the subject of the conversation, she felt the inanimate object stuffed inside her jacket pocket weighing her down, as though it was a great burden.

'I know it's not to everyone's taste,' Grant said, 'but you've probably gathered I can talk about this subject until the cows come home.'

Dani smiled. 'Yes. I had noticed.'

'But I'm sure it would be easier if you told me what you really need from me, rather than have me blather on about famous serial killers.'

'That's fair,' Dani said. 'Although you've already done a pretty good job of setting the scene for this.'

Grant looked puzzled as Dani reached inside her jacket pocket and her hand came back out clutching the plastic wallet with the unfolded piece of paper inside. She passed it across the desk for Grant to see. Then she stared at the professor as he took in the scribbled words. He said nothing for a good while, just focused his eyes on the note.

'What is this?' he asked eventually.

'That's what I'm hoping you can help me with.'

Chapter Forty-Four

Given recent events at her home, Dani was already tense as she headed through the door to the apartment block and across the foyer to the lift. She'd never been agoraphobic or claustrophobic or anything like that, but after the scare she'd had on Tuesday evening, and the debilitating lack of sleep that had followed the last two nights, she was weary and on edge. As she stood and waited for the lift to arrive, she felt apprehensive.

Finally there was a clunk as the lift landed on the ground floor and the doors slid open. Dani took a step forwards then reeled back when two figures loomed out from the inside.

Her heart jumped before she realised it was just two young men. She didn't recognise them, but they were chatting and laughing and she quickly determined they were no threat. They paid her little attention as they moved out of the lift and off towards the exit. Dani looked back to the small, enclosed and empty space in front of her.

She decided to take the stairs.

By the time she reached the sixth floor her heart was thudding in her chest and she was out of breath. Once inside her apartment, Dani quickly checked all the rooms from top to bottom. She'd rarely felt so spooked, but simply couldn't shake the feeling of sinister eyes watching her wherever she went.

Finding nothing untoward inside, but still on edge, she went to the kitchen to make a mug of coffee. She put two heaped teaspoons into the cup and the liquid ended up thick and treacly. She hoped it contained enough caffeine to boost her low energy reserves for the next few hours.

As she sat down on the sofa in the lounge she took out her phone and checked through her missed calls and messages which had been steadily building through the afternoon. There was still nothing from Easton, and Dani was becoming increasingly agitated by that. Jason had texted to see how she was doing, and to say he would come around any time she wanted. Same old, then. She'd had two more texts and calls from him since then too, becoming more concise each time. The last text message said simply:

> We need to talk

She called him back, hoping his need to speak to her urgently was because he wanted to talk to her about the case. Had there been a breakthrough? She knew she also needed to tell him about the note. She should have done so before now really, but had been too thrown by it.

The call went unanswered. She didn't bother to leave a message.

Dani sat back and tried to get her jumbled thoughts into some sort of order. She couldn't manage it. Mostly she tried to avoid thinking about how once again her life felt like it was at rock bottom. After two years on the sidelines, two years in which her life had been torn apart and she'd longed for the day when things would go back to normal, here she was, less than two weeks back at work, and now it looked like even her career might be taken away from her.

If that happened, would she have anything positive in her life at all?

A noise from the hallway made her jump and shook the melancholy thoughts away.

It sounded like the front door closing softly. She shot up from the sofa and raced into the hallway – an instinctive reaction, though she had no plan for what she was going to do if some stranger was standing there in the apartment.

But the hallway was empty. Yet unless she was actually insane she'd definitely heard the noise. Had someone been in the apartment and left? She rushed to the front door and flung it open, the feeling of déjà vu washing over her. There was no one out there in the corridor. Dani slammed the door shut and locked it. Heading into the kitchen, she grabbed a rolling pin, then searched through every room, every cupboard, and every corner of the apartment.

There was no one there. No signs that anyone had been there either. She headed into the en suite.

'What on earth is wrong with you?' she asked herself, staring into the mirror.

She shook her head then moved back into the lounge and slumped back on the sofa, coffee cup in hand. After a few long sips the caffeine started to kick in and Dani grabbed her laptop to start yet another dig. She had plenty of reasons to mope, but as far as she was concerned, she still had something to offer to the police, and to the case she'd been assigned to.

Did anyone at work know she'd been accessing the system while suspended?

That thought didn't stop her, and she was soon scouring the HOLMES 2 system once more.

There were no new murder cases that jumped out, and reading the files for Reeve and Natalya, it seemed to Dani that little progress had been made on these since her suspension.

There was a new missing persons case that intrigued her though.

Her heart rate steadily increased as she read the details. Jessica Bradford. A nineteen-year-old who'd first been reported missing by her parents on Monday morning after they failed to get hold of her over the weekend. Jessica was a university student, last seen by her friends on Friday night out in Selly Oak, near to where she lived in the university halls of residence. By the look of the reports in the HOLMES 2 system, other than interviewing her friends and family and requesting CCTV, little had so far been achieved on the case.

Dani sat back and sighed, recalling the conversation she'd had with the Missing Persons team the previous week. They'd seemed almost blasé about the open cases they had, emphasising that there was nothing they could see that was untoward in the volume or patterns of disappearances. Yet here was another young woman who'd disappeared from the area without a trace. That couldn't be right.

Was Dani reading too much into it all?

She frowned as she stared at Jessica Bradford's details. Why hadn't she spotted that straight away?

Jessica was a first year undergraduate studying psychology. Dani hadn't thought much of that when she'd first read it. After all, there were close to thirty thousand students at the university studying all manner of subjects.

But psychology?

Dani opened the internet browser and started searching. After a few minutes she'd found the syllabus for Jessica's course, including the various mandatory and optional modules. Several were related to criminology. Steven Grant's area of expertise.

Dani didn't like that connection one bit. She thought about Grant for a few moments. She really couldn't fathom how he could be in any way responsible, given his own history at the hands of a killer. But what about Ethan, who was already linked to at least one dead person? Then there was that snoopy neighbour who lived opposite the Grants' house too…

A rattling noise from out in the hall shook Dani from her increasingly disturbed thoughts. The vivid and horrifying images of what might have happened to Jessica and others were still playing in her mind as she looked around the now darkened room, another wave of panic taking hold.

When she'd first started working on her computer it had still been light outside. Dani glanced at the time on her laptop: seven p.m.

Another noise came from the hall. Quieter. A scraping sound. A throbbing pain began to take hold at the front of her skull.

Dani got up from the sofa. Groggily, she moved out into the hall, heart already racing. She spotted the note on the floor. Not poking out from under the door like the last one, but in the middle of the welcome mat. Her heart lurched. Her legs felt weak.

She rushed over and picked up the note, trying her to best unfold it, with her trembling hands.

> Another one bites the dust. Are you enjoying this as much as I am yet? I came over to chat but you looked too busy. Maybe next time.

The note still in her hand, Dani's whole body was quivering as she reached for the door. She whipped it open and stuck her head out. The corridor was empty, yet again, but she heard the clunk as the lift doors closed.

Without thinking, Dani raced along. Just like the other night the red light above the lift blinked with each floor as it descended.

Dani raced down the stairs, pushing away all rational thoughts about why this was probably a really bad idea. She crashed through the doors at the ground floor and darted out into the foyer. Off to her right, the lift doors were just closing. With her eyes still on the lift, Dani started rushing towards the outer door and ran slap bang into a hefty figure…

Without even thinking, Dani grabbed the figure's wrist and swivelled herself around. She pulled the wrist up against the shoulder and strained the elbow and shoulder joint to the point of bursting. At the same time she heaved forwards and pushed the person up against the wall.

'Dani, what the hell are you doing?'

'Jason?' she said, as her brain finally caught up with her body's instinctive defensive reaction. 'What are you doing here?'

'What do you think! I came to see you. I've been calling for days. You called back earlier but my battery went.'

'How did you get inside?'

'Someone else was coming out. The door was open. Jesus, Dani, let go of my arm!'

Dani did so, and Jason turned to her and rubbed his stricken limb. Thoughts cascaded through Dani's mind. Jason being there at that moment was convenient, to say the least. But the coincidence was more plausible than the note having been from him.

Wasn't it?

Dani looked up and noticed Jason staring down at her hand. She slipped the note she was still clutching behind her back, out of sight. He didn't say anything about it.

'Who opened the door?' Dani asked.

'What door?'

'The door to the bloody building, Jason! Who let you in? Describe them to me.'

'I… I don't know,' Jason looked over his shoulder, to the door and through the glass to the outside. There was certainly no one in sight anymore. 'I wasn't really paying attention. It was just some guy. He didn't look suspicious or anything. What's going on, Dani?'

She turned away. 'Nothing.'

'Yeah, of course not. You've just taken to heavy-handedly policing your apartment block for a spot of fun.'

Dani turned and glared at Jason and the thin smile that had accompanied his light-hearted comment quickly faded.

'I came to see if you're ok,' he said.

Dani snorted. The answer to that one was plain for anyone to see.

'Why don't we go upstairs?' he suggested.

'Nah,' Dani said. 'I think I'll lurk down here for a few hours more. In case there are any more invaders.'

She pulled her fists up to her body, like a boxer on the defensive.

The quizzical look on Jason's face suggested he wasn't quite sure whether she was being serious or not.

Dani shook her head in disbelief.

'Come on then,' she said, turning away and moving towards the lift.

But there was no way Dani could relax, even once they were both safely inside her apartment. She stood in the hallway, her mind in turmoil.

'Dani, seriously, what's going on?' Jason said.

Dani said nothing, just focused on keeping her hands steady as she held the note out for Jason to see.

Chapter Forty-Five

The forensics team left two hours later. They'd done what they could to take fingerprints from door frames and other surfaces, and shoe prints from the floors. Jason had helped Dani search through the apartment. Again. Nothing seemed to be missing. Nothing had been moved, even. There was no sign of forced entry. Had the person who'd written the note really been inside?

Dani was still feeling terrified as she and Jason sat down at the small dining table and began to eat a takeaway which Jason had ordered.

'I can't believe you didn't tell me about the first note,' he said, shaking his head.

Dani didn't respond.

'You don't always have to tackle your problems alone.'

Dani rolled her eyes. Typical of Jason to try and steer the conversation back there.

'The note suggests he was watching you,' Jason said.

'I mean, the curtains were open. But…'

'But he could have been in your apartment.'

'I just don't know.'

'Dani, what is going on here?'

'What do *you* think?'

'I think you've got someone sending you threatening notes. Regardless of whether it's someone with an axe to grind or someone who's actually dangerous, we still need to find out who it is so, if nothing else, we can stop them hassling you.'

'You messaged earlier to say we needed to talk,' Dani said.

Jason shifted in his seat and looked at her. 'You know I'm not supposed to talk to you about the case.' His tone wasn't particularly strong.

'Then why was it so important for you to speak to me?'

'Because of... you know. Because of you being suspended. And because of what happened to Harland. I wanted to make sure you were ok.'

'Yeah, well, I'm not ok. You've seen that for yourself. So was that it?'

'No, actually,' Jason said, more tersely. 'I wanted to see you. Because I give a shit. Is that ok with you?'

Dani said nothing.

'But,' Jason continued, 'what I said was that I'm not *supposed* to talk to you about the case. The way I see it, though, you have a right to know. It clearly affects you after all.'

Dani felt herself relax a little more, and the small grin on Jason's face suggested he knew he'd won her over for now.

'Well go on then,' Dani said.

'It seems, Detective Inspector, that perhaps you did the world a great big favour with Dean Harland.'

'*I* did the world a big favour?' Dani said, her face contorting. 'What the fuck does that mean? I didn't do anything to him!'

Jason flushed, obviously realising his choice of words had been poor.

'Sorry, Dani, that's not what I meant. Of course it wasn't your fault, what happened to him. What I meant was that it looks like it may well have been him.'

'Who killed Reeve and Natalya?'

'Yeah.'

Dani should have been pleased to hear that. But she wasn't. What about Jessica Bradford? The other missing women?

'What's led to that then?' she asked.

'We may have found the murder weapon.'

'You're kidding?'

'Nope. In Harland's apartment. One of the knives in the kitchen.'

'Harland's apartment?'

'The one in Handsworth. Seems from what we've found that Harland was the main tenant, even though the agreement was in the name of Colton. Our conclusion is that Colton is nothing but an alias that both Harland and Reeve were using to hide their drug-drug-related activities.'

Dani didn't know what to say.

'We scoured that apartment from top to bottom. Bagged all the knives for testing. One of them had blood traces on it. There was also a stash of old clothes in a suitcase, all looked clean enough – it's not like they were blood-soaked or anything – but the forensics team used luminol on them and found blood traces there too. They haven't had the full results back yet but if the blood matches the victims, it looks like Harland was our man.'

'Why do you think it was Harland and not Ethan Grant?'

'What?'

'You're assuming the knife and the clothes are Harland's? But Grant lived there too, didn't he? Have you even found him yet?'

'There's no evidence he lived there.'

'Other than his mother gave us that address.'

Jason shrugged. 'It's not just me toeing this line. Fletcher is too.'

'But you don't know for sure that Harland is the killer.'

'Not for sure, no.'

'And you don't know yet that the knife really is the murder weapon either. Just that it's a knife with blood on it. Could be from a damn steak.'

'Jesus, Dani, are you a defence lawyer all of a sudden?'

'No. I'm just not sure why you were making it sound so cut and dried. It sounds anything but.'

'Look, Reeve was a bad apple. Harland was too. A known low-level drug dealer, and a thug with a string of petty offences. If we can prove those clothes and that knife were linked to the murders, then we've got him. Grant is just a spoiled rich kid pulled into a bad world, if you ask me.'

'That doesn't mean it wasn't him.'

'No. I guess not,' Jason said. 'But maybe Grant is already dead. Harland could have knocked him off too.'

'Except no body has been found.'

'Not yet, no.'

'So maybe Ethan did a runner because he knows we're onto him.'

'It's possible, Dani,' Jason said, by now sounding fed up that Dani was challenging him so hard.

'And what about Jimmy Colton?'

'Like I said, we've found nothing to suggest he's a real person. Most likely he's an alias that Reeve and Harland used for whatever reasons.'

'Well we need to find those reasons then, surely? Otherwise his name, his existence, is just another loose end. A loose end that could mean much more.'

'I know that. I'm just giving you the low down on where we're at. I'd thought you'd want to know.'

'Yeah, but why are you doing that, Jason? You said we needed to talk, as though there'd been a massive breakthrough or something. Or because you needed my help. But it looks like all you've got at the minute is a couple of bits of circumstantial crap, and clearly you've already made your own minds up about what that means. Really, I'm not sure why you bothered.'

'I wanted to tell you where we'd got to because I thought it might help you,' Jason said, his tone now hard, clearly agitated by Dani's questioning. 'If Harland is the killer then—'

'Help me? Harland still got killed out on that road. Even if he turns out to be a murderer, I've still got to live with what happened, with what I *saw*, and with the knowledge that it was my actions that led to his death. And it's not going to stop McNair and Baxter if they want rid of me.'

'You don't know that.'

'Yes I do. This was never about Harland. It's about them not wanting me on the force.'

'Why the hell would you think that?'

'I just do.'

The two of them went silent for a few moments as they both focused on eating in a bid to overcome the awkwardness.

'Look, I'm sorry,' Dani said after a couple of minutes, when she felt her anger subsiding. 'I appreciate you trying to help me. But those notes. They must mean something.'

'Maybe they do. But you must know it's just as likely they're from some stalker, as it is that they're from someone who's actually involved in these murders.'

'Do you honestly believe that?'

Jason said nothing to that. Dani looked away, still thinking.

'I went to see Professor Steven Grant today,' she said.

'Ethan Grant's dad?'

'The one and the same.'

'You're suspended and you're off out speaking to the father of someone who is possibly a murder suspect?'

Dani gave Jason a hard look. 'A minute ago you said he wasn't a suspect. That he might even be a victim.'

'Ok, but he *is* a person of interest, whichever way you look at it. McNair will hang you out to dry if she knows you're interfering with the investigation.'

'Yeah, but you're not going to tell her. Are you?'

Jason humphed. 'Of course I'm not. But that doesn't mean it won't come out. I'm not threatening you; I just don't want you getting into even more trouble.'

'Thanks. But anyway, I didn't go to speak to Grant about his son. I went to speak to him about the note.'

'Why did you… wait, oh, come on, Dani. Reeve and Harland were into drugs, they were in with a seriously bad crowd. We know Natalya knew Reeve too. Perhaps they both got caught up in some drug-related feud. It could even be that Harland killed her too, in a dispute with Reeve. Do you really think there's a serial killer out there?'

'I've been a homicide detective far longer than you have, so don't you dare talk to me like I'm some fanciful idiot.'

Jason held his hands up. 'Do you know how crazy this sounds, though? I know you went to see Ben the other day, but—'

'This is absolutely nothing to do with Ben! If anyone else had received these notes it would be taken for what it is. You know this is exactly why I sat on the first one.'

And Dani truly did feel hurt by his blasé and somewhat churlish response.

'Ok, I'm sorry,' he said. 'It's just that… a serial killer? Is that really what you're saying to me?'

'Yes.'

'Why would a serial killer knock off Reeve like that?'

'I've no fucking idea.'

Dani thought it best not to also mention about the ominous presence she'd both seen and sensed several times over the last few days. It was clear Jason already thought she was losing it, even without that added extra.

Was she losing it?

'There's something not right about these murders, Jason.'

'I don't get it, though,' Jason said. 'If the notes are from the killer, why the hell would they even bother sending them? What's the point?'

Which was the exact question Dani had been through in detail with Grant earlier in the day. To him, a murder expert, the note made perfect sense, and he'd given several explanations, each of them backed up with analysis and facts and real life examples. Having said that, Dani had been a keen and willing listener and Grant had basically told her what she wanted to hear. Trying to now remember everything she'd been told by Grant and relay it to Jason – a clear sceptic – was far less simple.

'And there's more,' she said. 'There are still other missing persons cases that could be connected here.'

'I've already been through all that with Fletcher. There's nothing to link any of those other cases with Natalya or Reeve or Harland or Grant.'

'What about Grace Agnew? She was Reeve's girlfriend. What if she's dead too? How does that fit your theory?'

Jason said nothing now.

'And Jessica Bradford?' Dani said.

'Who?'

'A new case. She went missing just days ago. She's a uni student, and I'm pretty sure one of her lecturers is Steven Grant.'

'So now you're saying Steven Grant is—'

'What I'm saying is, there's something not right here. There are connections that need investigating properly.'

Jason chewed on that for a few moments but said nothing of it, nor did he ask how Dani knew about the Jessica Bradford case.

'Maybe I am crazy,' she said, 'but can you do me a favour at least?'

She'd hoped Jason would give an immediate *yes*. The time it took him to do so suggested his agreement was some way from binding.

'I've no doubt McNair will try to gloss over these notes,' Dani said. 'But do everything you can to get to the bottom of them. Check out the women on the missing persons list again. Jessica Bradford in particular. What's happened to her? See if there's anything to connect them to each other, to Reeve, to Ethan Grant. Natalya was being held somewhere. You have to find where. Above all, just keep me informed. I can still help.'

Jason let out a long sigh.

'Ok. Leave it with me. But don't get your hopes up that we'll find anything. And if you want my advice—'

'No, Jason. I really don't. But thanks all the same. I honestly think there's something else happening here. Something much bigger than two young people being stabbed to death because they're mixed up in drugs. I'm certain our killer's still out there. I'm certain the notes are from him. And I'm certain that if we don't catch him, then he's going to kill again.'

Chapter Forty-Six

To say his conversation with Dani Stephens was a turn-up for the books was something of an understatement. For years Steven Grant had felt he'd had something to offer to the police, but they'd shunned him as though he were simply a morbid nutter, much the same way the Chief Superintendent had on the golf course last week. What was his name again? Baker? Baxter?

Arsehole.

Dani Stephens, though, had recognised Grant's worth, although she wasn't exactly operating with her superiors' knowledge. From what she'd told him, and she'd really been quite open and honest, she'd been put on leave from the force pending a disciplinary investigation. Apparently they felt she might be to blame for Dean Harland's death – Harland being yet another of Ethan's acquaintances. Apparently.

Dani's suspension should have seen her down tools, but then she'd received that note.

That note.

Of course Grant had readily emphasised to Dani that the note was most likely the work of a wind-up merchant. She got that, so she said. But Grant could tell she didn't really want to believe that explanation. Truth be told, neither did he.

He'd tried his best to get through the rest of that damn research paper and his other admin before leaving for home but had been unable to shake the intrigue of the conversation with Dani Stephens from his mind. It was gone eight p.m. when he arrived back home and darkness had long descended.

As Grant turned the car onto his drive he noticed that Francis's Range Rover was back where it belonged, its dark polished metal gleaming in the electric haze from the overhead streetlights. Perhaps that was the end of the excitement there then.

For once there was no sign of the snoopy neighbour himself.

Grant parked up on his drive and headed inside. The downstairs of the house was quiet and he called out to Mary. She responded that she was reading, and Grant headed up the stairs and to their room where he found Mary lying on top of the bed in her dressing gown, her Kindle in her hand. Her face was caked in what could have been white paint, for all Grant knew, but was undoubtedly some ridiculously expensive moisturiser.

'Long day?' Mary said.

'You could say that.'

'There's some dinner on the side for you.'

'Thanks.'

'Just some pasta.'

'That's more than fine.'

Grant moved over and sat down next to his wife on the bed.

'Where's Annie?'

'Sleep over.'

'On a Thursday night?'

'Teacher training tomorrow.'

Grant rolled his eyes. 'Sleeping over at a girl's house, I hope.'

'That's what she told me, but you never know.'

Grant grimaced at the unwelcome thoughts forming in his mind, of his daughter doing things she shouldn't be doing. Mary looked amused at his reaction. He quickly banished the images. He knew sooner or later his teenage daughter would succumb to the world of boys and sex, but he still hoped that would be at some point way in the future rather than now.

'Anything from Ethan?' he asked.

He noticed Mary slump slightly at his question. The mere mention of their son sucked the life out of both of them.

'No,' she said.

'Me neither.'

'This'll be about the first day this week that I've not heard from the police either.'

Grant chuckled. 'Yeah, about that…'

'What?' Mary said, sitting upright, expectantly.

'I had a visitor today at work.'

'The police?'

'Detective Inspector Dani Stephens.'

'What? The one who came to see me here the other day? What did she want? Ethan?'

'No, not Ethan.'

'You know it's funny,' Mary said. 'I told her the two of you would have a lot to talk about. Do you remember her from the papers?'

'Yeah. And you're right, we did have a lot to talk about.'

'Well go on then, tell me.'

'Apparently she wants my help.'

Mary now looked quite impressed. And gratified, as though this was all her doing.

'These weren't exactly her words, but the impression I got was that Detective Stephens thinks there's a serial killer on the loose in Birmingham.'

'Does she now?' Mary said, laughing mockingly.

Grant felt a little offended, though he wasn't sure why. He explained about the note Dani had brought with her. He went over their conversation, and Mary seemed keenly interested. It was true Grant felt immensely lucky to have found a woman in Mary who had tolerated his oddities over the years. Mary always at least humoured him, even if she didn't really enjoy discussing his subject of interest.

Dani Stephens had.

Maybe that was because the detective was forever trying to analyse why her brother – her twin brother at that – was a sociopath.

'Well good for you, Steven. Now you're an official asset to the police.'

'Not exactly,' Grant said.

'How do you mean?'

'It seems she's acting on her own. She's been suspended.'

Grant briefly explained what he knew about that. Mary didn't say much in response.

'Do the police think Ethan killed that man?' Mary asked. 'Paul Reeve?'

Grant shrugged. 'She didn't say that, exactly. But they know he's connected somehow.'

Mary opened her mouth to say something else but Grant put his finger on her lips.

'That's enough about Ethan. I've managed to get through most of today without thinking about him.'

'Yeah. Why don't you go get your pasta, then come back up to bed.'

Grant smiled, then got up. He headed downstairs to the kitchen where his bowl of cold spaghetti was sitting next to the microwave. He slung it in to cook on high for two minutes, then went to find some parmesan in the fridge. As he closed the door he realised there was someone standing right there in the doorway off to his left.

He spun to face the figure. His heart lurched…

It was Mary.

'Jesus!'

She put a finger to her lips.

'There's someone out the front,' she whispered.

'What?'

He put the block of cheese down then moved through the hall and into the dining room. Standing behind the curtains, he peered out and scanned the driveway, the street outside and the houses on the other side of the road.

'I don't see anything,' he said.

He turned back to Mary who looked less than convinced.

'I'm telling you, there was someone out there! In the front garden. Staring up at the house.'

'Why were you even looking out the window?'

'I heard a noise! Like a scraping or rustling.'

Grant looked at her questioningly.

'Do you think I'm making this up?'

'No, I—'

'For fuck's sake, there was someone out there, spying on us! I bet it was that bloody Ed Francis.'

Grant turned back to the window and stared over at the Francis house. The lights were on in the downstairs front room, the flicker of a TV evident behind the curtains, but he saw no signs of anyone either within the room or outside of the house.

'You're absolutely sure?' Grant said.

'Of course I'm bloody sure,' Mary scolded. 'Why else would I say it?'

Wait, was that a shadow moving across Francis's drive? His security light hadn't come on, though. Grant did his best to focus on the dark space, but the more he looked, the more the thin shadows and glow from the streetlights jumped and danced at random.

He really couldn't be sure.

'Steven, just go and check, will you?'

'Fine,' Grant said.

He headed out of the room and across the hall to the cupboard under the stairs. He opened the door and soon spotted what he was looking for among the clutter. A black wooden baseball bat. Grant had bought it for his son while at a convention in Chicago years ago. The bat had always been more an ornament than a plaything, and had long been consigned to the darkness. He'd spotted it the other day for the first time in an age. It was the first thing Grant could think of grabbing in that moment.

Mary saw him lugging the bat towards the front door. 'Steven?'

'Just in case,' he said, not looking at her.

He stood into his shoes without doing them up, and before he could talk himself out of it, he opened the front door and headed into the darkness, laces flapping. He was only two steps from the house when his movement triggered the security light fixed up above the front door. It lit up most of the drive in bright white light, though Grant knew the corners of the front garden, which contained numerous shrubs and trees, were out of its reach.

Grant stomped across the soggy drive and over into one of the dark corners. He gripped the bat tightly. Was he really ready to clobber someone with it?

He never found out, because despite his careful search, he couldn't find anyone out there at all, or even any signs someone had been there.

After a couple of minutes, by which point he was shivering, Grant traipsed back over to the house. As he stepped through the open front door, Mary was still in the hallway, waiting in expectation.

'Whoever was out there, they're long gone,' Grant said, though he still wasn't particularly convinced anyone had been there at all.

Mary said nothing to that. Grant turned to shut the door. As he did so his gaze inevitably sought out the Francis house across the road. As he pushed the door shut, he was certain he saw the curtains of the downstairs front room twitch.

Chapter Forty-Seven

Day 527

Since my seizure I've been such a mixed bag of emotions. One day I'm up, the next I'm down. The psychiatrist has upped my anti-depressant meds though I don't always take them. It feels like cheating. And I feel like I'm losing my mind. My DVLA assessment was cancelled, because of the seizure. I'll have to wait several more months for that now. Which means I can hardly plan to be back on Force CID any time soon either. I'm devastated. I'm angry. And yet, inside, I know I'm getting better. I really can take care of myself now. My physical responses, my decision-making and all manner of cognitive abilities are flying high in the tests I still endure. My lack of emotion and empathy is still an area requiring more work, but despite everything I feel so much more like me again. Just an unhappier version of me.

If it wasn't for that damn seizure. If I hadn't pushed myself so far, so fast…

Life for me and Jason continues to be fraught. He's been working long hours. On a murder investigation that's really gotten under his skin. He's not around much, and when he is around he doesn't want to talk about it, and I think we both know that he's not really needed in my home now like he was when I first came out of hospital.

I've tried telling him this. I don't mean it nastily. It's not that I don't care for him. I do. And now that my emotions are more rounded I'm immensely grateful to him for sticking by me for so long. But time has moved on. My recovery continues but I want my independence back.

Jason had already come home from work tonight in a foul mood. I knew it wasn't the best time to broach the subject again, but then when would be a good time? So I did it anyway.

'So it's over,' he says, looking down at the floor. 'That's really what you want?'

He sounds calm though I know he's seething. We've just been through two minutes of yelling and this is just a moment's respite.

'I don't know,' I say. 'I just need space.'

'After everything I've done for you. This is what I get.'

'I never asked you for anything!' I shout, feeling the calm dissipating.

'You always were selfish. Welcome back to earth, Dani Stephens.'

He gets to his feet. I'm immediately riled by his heartless comment, however much I might deserve it. I jump up too.

'And you're a mind-numbingly boring arsehole busybody. There's nothing of worth going on in your life so you've infected mine! But I don't need you here anymore. I don't want you here! I've got my own life to lead, and I can do it without you, thank you very much.'

'So now I've been holding you back all this time. Well fuck you very much. I'm out of here.'

Jason storms out of the lounge. I hear him banging and rummaging in the spare room. I'm in despair. I didn't want to hurt him, I hadn't intended that outburst at all – yet another fuck-up caused by my damn TBI. I didn't want it to end like this. The truth is, I'm in two minds still. I need him in my life. But not like we are. More than anything I just wish we could start over. I don't want him to be Jason my carer, who watches over me and judges me and thinks I need my nappy changing. I want him to be my boyfriend. A lover. But I don't know how to explain that, or how we could ever recover that even if I could – real, natural affection has been absent from our relationship for so long.

Moments later he stands in the lounge doorway, a filled holdall over his shoulder. He glares at me and I just stand there and wait for him to say something. Anything. Will it be anger, regret or sorrow that he comes at me with? Will he plead to stay?

In the end he says nothing.

'Just go!' I shout, when the silence becomes unbearable.

He only hesitates for a second before he turns to leave.

Chapter Forty-Eight

'This is good, Dani,' Scholz said.

Dani frowned. 'Good? What the hell is good about any of this?'

She sat back in the chair, arms folded, and stared across the desk. Scholz's cheeks flushed ever so slightly at her challenging response.

'Rightly or wrongly, Dean Harland was killed because of actions that I took,' she said. 'I've got to live with that knowledge, but more importantly I've got to live with what I *saw.*'

'I understand that must be difficult b—'

'I've got a damn stalker who may or may not be a killer, harassing me and—'

'I—'

'—*and* until the disciplinary investigation is over, my whole life is basically in limbo. I can't move on at all, can I? For all I know in a few days' or weeks' time my entire career could well be over. What on earth am I supposed to do then?'

Scholz rubbed his hands together nervously. He looked just a little uncomfortable with Dani venting. It was quite unlike her to be so open in her therapy sessions, but today she just needed to get it all off her chest and had been talking pretty much non-stop for the best part of the hour session.

'What I mean is—'

'Sorry, but how exactly is any of this good?' Dani asked again.

Now Scholz sat back in his seat and smiled.

'Dani, your emotional responses… they're… well, what do you think?'

Dani thought about that one for a moment. She thought about everything that had happened in the last few days. The murders. Harland. Jason coming back into her life – kind of. The trips to see Ben. Spending time with her nephew and niece.

She huffed.

'You're undoubtedly going through a very difficult time right now,' Scholz said, 'but to me, what I see is that you resuming the role of the *old* Dani – detective, aunt, sister – has actually brought a lot of the old *you* back. Angry outbursts aside, perhaps. I must say in all of our sessions together I've never seen such an array of emotional responses from you.'

Dani huffed again. 'Anger. Fear. Bitterness. Resentment. Great. I'm really chuffed at how things are turning out for me.'

'Don't be so hard on yourself. Sadness, which I'm sensing a great deal of, is a very important emotion too. And I also sensed pride, even joy, when you were talking about Harry and Chloe earlier.'

'So what are you saying? I should feel like I'm in a good place now? The way I see it, my drugged-up isolation was a walk in the park compared to the last few days.'

'I'm saying you're still recovering from a very serious brain injury, and a very traumatic period in your life, but you're making improvements in some critical aspects of your mental wellbeing all the time.'

'Only some aspects?'

Scholz sighed and looked more serious again. 'Well I can still sense that your morale and motivation is extremely low. Bordering on worryingly so. I'd certainly recommend not reducing your anti-depressant medication any further just yet. But, like you said, you're having a very hard time at work. You *have* to make sure you're making the most of the positives in your life right now. Friends. The children. Even… Jason.'

Dani tried her best to show no reaction to that one. She checked her watch and was glad to see there were only two minutes left. They both sat in silence for a few moments. Scholz continued to stare at her, studying her. The silence quickly grew uncomfortable. Dani checked her watch again.

'I've got to go,' she said.

She got up from the chair. Scholz stayed in his seat on the other side of the desk.

'Good luck,' he said. 'I really mean that.'

'Yeah. Today, I think I'm going to need it.'

–

Dani headed on foot the short distance across Colmore Row towards HQ. The conversation with Scholz had all but disappeared from her mind, and she wasn't just feeling nervous, as she headed through the revolving doors at the main entrance; she felt like an absolute outsider. A week had passed since she'd been suspended from duty. She'd not spoken to McNair or Baxter or any other senior officer since then. Now she was back for her first formal disciplinary meeting with the West Midlands Police Professional Standards department.

That fact, at least, was a good first sign. The IOPC had the ability and discretion to carry out such investigations themselves, and certainly would for the most serious matters of police misconduct. The fact that the IOPC had passed the investigation back to Professional Standards at her own force was therefore an indication that they didn't feel their clout was warranted.

Or was it just that the case against Dani was so cut and dried that they didn't want to waste resources?

She'd been given the option of taking a colleague or other representative from the Police Federation into the meeting with her but chose not to. She had nothing to hide, and wouldn't hold back. She'd tell whoever was there exactly what had happened the day Dean Harland lost his life.

She headed over to the reception desk, the moment feeling all too similar to her first day back on the force all of twelve days before. Except this time she didn't recognise either of the two security guards on duty behind the front desk, nor did they recognise her.

She waited in the reception area, wondering who would come to fetch her this time, hoping that no one she knew would pass by and notice her there.

She should have known that wouldn't happen.

After she'd been waiting for barely sixty seconds, DS Easton walked through the revolving doors from the outside, coffee cup in one hand, sandwich in the other. Dani was caught in two minds as to whether to look away, and hope he did the same. She didn't. She was staring over at him as he caught her eye. He grimaced. At least that's what Dani thought the look was, it certainly wasn't a smile.

'Hey,' Dani said.

'Dani,' Easton said, taking two steps closer to her as he approached the security gates.

'You've been ignoring my calls,' Dani said.

Easton stopped and hovered. Dani could tell he was hugely uncomfortable.

'I get it,' Dani said. 'McNair's scared you off, right? Told you that if you talk to me, if you go anywhere near me you'll be in the shit too.'

He didn't say anything to that, just rubbed his neck nervously.

'I'm not asking you to lie for me,' Dani said. 'I never would. Just tell them the truth.'

He checked his watch. 'Sorry, I've really got to go.'

He turned and headed away.

Moments later Dani saw a frumpy woman coming towards her from the other side of the gates. Dani didn't recognise her, but when the woman locked eyes with her she knew who she was. Dani got to her feet.

–

'Is there anything else you'd like to tell us about the events leading up to Dean Harland's death?' asked the frumpy woman, who it turned out was DCI Barlow from Professional Standards. Dani had never met her before, nor the fresh-faced man sat next to her in the small conference room, DS Sturridge.

'No, I've told you everything,' Dani said.

They'd already been in the room for more than an hour, and Dani was pleased with herself for remaining calm, professional and relaxed despite the barrage of questions and nitpicking that she'd already endured.

'Are you absolutely sure, DI Stephens?' Sturridge asked.

Dani locked eyes with him but tried her best not to glare.

'Yes. I'm sure.'

Sturridge looked at Barlow. Barlow looked at Sturridge and gave a slight nod. Sturridge shuffled the papers in front of him.

'Is there a problem?' Dani asked, just about keeping her tone level.

'DI Stephens, as you can probably imagine, we've spoken to a great deal of witnesses from last week,' Barlow said. 'After all, the foot chase took place in the early evening on busy streets.'

Barlow left the statement hanging, as though Dani was supposed to understand the point being made.

'So? What are you trying to tell me?' Dani said. 'Are you implying my version of events differs from that of the witnesses you've spoken to?'

Once again she thought about Easton. What had *he* said? But Dani had told nothing but the truth, so what was the issue?

Barlow looked to Sturridge again. The young DS held up a piece of paper and read out the words: '*Please, help me. You've got to help me.*'

Sturridge stopped, and looked up at Dani. She didn't move a muscle. Her whole body was rigid, even though her brain was on fire.

'*Help me. She's going to kill me.*'

Another dramatic pause.

'*They want to kill me. Help.*'

Dani wasn't sure how much longer she could hold her emotions in. And it was anger – and quite strangely, fear – that was winning out.

'Did you, at any point, hear Dean Harland say or shout out any of those phrases?' Barlow asked.

'No,' Dani said, her tone surprisingly measured. 'Absolutely not.'

'We have more than one witness who has asserted that these were the words Dean Harland said before he was killed.'

'No,' Dani said, shaking her head, now more in disbelief. 'That's just not true.'

But then a flash of doubt swept through her. How far ahead had Harland been? Could he have shouted out like that, and she just hadn't heard? Had she been too focussed on getting to him?

'Can you think of a reason why Harland would say those things?' Barlow asked.

'I've no idea,' Dani said. 'The witnesses are lying.'

Barlow raised her eyebrows. 'Lying.'

'Yes! They're lying, that did not happen.'

'Why would the witnesses lie to us?'

'I don't bloody know!' Dani shouted, finally losing her cool. 'Why don't you ask them?'

Who the hell were these witnesses anyway?

Dani thought back to the chase. The woman with the pram. Other nearby pedestrians. The teenagers at the flats. Was it them? Causing trouble for the sake of it?

'DI Stephens?' Barlow said. 'Do you have anything else to add?'

'No. I'm all done.'

–

Dani walked back out onto the street outside HQ, her head heavy and numb. Thick drops of rain pelted down from the dark afternoon sky but Dani stood there staring into space.

'Dani, what are you doing?'

It was Jason. He came from behind and put a hand under her armpit, pulling her along, away from HQ.

'You're soaked through,' he said, lifting a golfing umbrella up over both of their heads.

'I'm not crazy,' Dani said. 'Am I?'

'What? No, Dani, you're not.'

Then what the hell was that all about with Harland and the witnesses? She wondered. Her memories felt so clear but were they really?

'Let's get out of the rain,' Jason said. 'We can grab a coffee.'

'I'd rather have something a bit stronger.'

Jason said nothing to that.

He led them around the corner to a coffee shop Dani hadn't been to before, that was decked out in the increasingly ubiquitous shabby-chic style. She couldn't remember what the unit had been in the past – a sandwich shop perhaps? They ordered their drinks and took a seat on a worn brown leather sofa in a quiet spot in the corner. Dani wrapped her hands around the large mug, still deep in thought.

'How did it go?' Jason asked, breaking the silence.

'I really don't know,' Dani said. 'I told them the truth. That's all I can do.'

But was what she'd told really what happened? Was it her version of events that was wrong? Was her mind playing tricks on her like it had so many times in the recent past?

Jason wisely chose to not try and make the situation better than it really was, staying silent instead.

'I saw Easton in the foyer,' Dani said. 'He clammed up so tight when he spotted me I thought he'd had cement for breakfast.'

'The guy's actually alright,' Jason said. 'He's got a promising future.'

'He's working with you now?'

'Yeah. You heard about Fletcher, didn't you?'

The look on Dani's face indicated she hadn't.

'There was a complication so they delivered the baby early.'

'When?' Dani said.

'Wednesday night, but I only found out this morning. Last I heard all's fine, though the baby's still in hospital. Her name's Erika.'

Dani rolled her eyes. At herself. She and Fletcher had not exactly been on the best of terms recently, but she still wished she'd known. She would have sent a message at least.

'But I've spoken to Easton. He's not going to screw you over.'

'Then why could he barely look me in the eye earlier?'

'He's a young guy who's thinking about his career. He's not going to challenge McNair and Baxter, is he? He'll give Professional Standards the plain, simple truth when asked. He's not going to stick the knife in. He's doing what they're asking by not talking to you.'

'Yet you're talking to me.' Dani said.

Jason shifted in his seat. 'I guess my position with you is a little more complicated.'

Dani didn't ask what he meant by that. She thought again about the meeting with Barlow and Sturridge and what the witnesses had said they'd heard Harland shout. What did it mean? She debated whether to talk to Jason about it. She decided she couldn't.

'Have you made any progress?' she asked, trying to push the thoughts away.

'Not exactly. Still no sign of Ethan Grant. We've now traced Natalya's final movements as best we can using CCTV. We did manage to find one more capture, and given the direction she was running in, we've honed in on three industrial estates with various business premises and lock-ups. It's a long search but we're doing what we can to see if we can find any evidence of her being held at one of those sites.'

'What about residences? It's equally possible she was held in a home.'

'Yeah, we're working on it, but it's not a fast process. Toxicology is back but there's not much to tell. We've also had prelim results back from forensics both on the crime scenes, and at Natalya's home, though we're still yet to formally ID her.'

'And?'

'And pretty much nothing. No sign of any kind of struggle at Natalya's. No indication of anyone being there who couldn't be explained.'

Dani sighed. 'And Jessica Bradford?'

'I've spoken to Missing Persons about her. They couldn't add anything that you didn't already know.'

'That's it?'

'No. I've followed up with her parents and two of her friends too. It looks like a complete red herring. Her parents received a phone call from her two days ago. They've had texts too. She'd buggered off to Prague or Budapest or somewhere with some guy she's met. Her friend showed me the Facebook post.'

Dani shook her head in disbelief. She'd felt sure there was more to Jessica's story.

'Missing Persons are going to follow up when she's home to make sure everything is ok. They won't take any chances, but there's not much else they or we can do right now.'

Dani sighed again. It seemed the investigation was simply hitting dead end after dead end.

'Did they figure out what happened to Mrs Staunton?'

'She was injected with a tranquiliser, just as you suspected, but there was no evidence found of the intruder, other than the prints in the grass. But those're next to useless. All we can tell from them is that the person was wearing a shoe size probably between seven and ten.'

Dani shook her head.

'We've still got more to come back from the lab, but that's where we're at.'

'And nothing more on the other missing persons cases either?'

'Nothing. Those women have just disappeared. No trace of what happened to them.'

Which Dani still didn't like at all, particularly given Paul Reeve was directly linked not just to Natalya, but to Grace Agnew as well.

'What about other deaths?' Dani said, as a thought sprang to mind.

'How do you mean?'

'Other murders we've investigated that shared any similarities to Reeve's and Natalya's deaths? Solved or unsolved.'

Jason looked a little worn out now by her relentless grasping. 'Where are you going with this?'

'You know where. Can you check for me? Please?'

Though the reality was, she'd already performed similar checks on HOLMES 2 with no luck.

Jason sighed. 'I'll check.'

They went silent for a couple of moments as Dani's brain whirred. Her thoughts began to take shape but for some reason she wasn't sure she wanted to share them with Jason.

She saw him check his watch for the umpteenth time.

'If you've somewhere to be, it's ok,' she said.

He gave her an uncertain look.

'Honestly, it's fine,' she said. 'I appreciate you spending the time with me. We'll catch up again later.'

She had somewhere else she wanted to be anyway. She knew exactly who she wanted to speak to next.

Chapter Forty-Nine

Dani took a train over to University station and walked the short distance to the University of Birmingham campus, though it turned out to be a wasted trip. Steven Grant wasn't there; he had already finished his last lecture of the day and headed home. Which was where Dani went next.

Even after their chat earlier, she could sense that Jason wasn't quite aligned with her thinking, that he was helping her more because he wanted to support her than anything else. But Dani felt sure she was close to uncovering something big. She just needed a lead to follow. Those notes meant something. To consider the writer of the notes as a real and imminent danger was the right thing to do, and to delve into a deep and dark world of murder in order to identify that person was absolutely necessary to Dani. Not because it would help to smooth over her relationship with the senior team at the police if she solved the murder cases, but because the case was personal for her. The notes had been left for *her*. Perhaps she was even a target.

–

Dani stepped from the taxi outside the Grants' house, opened the gate and headed up the gravel drive. The last time she'd visited, she and Easton had come away with an address for Ethan Grant. The series of events which had followed on that day had seen Dean Harland killed out on a dual carriageway in Handsworth, and Dani suspended from the police. She felt slightly apprehensive about what might be the result of this visit.

The rain had stopped and it was still light outside as Dani crunched across the gravel to the front door, though the thick cloud in the sky meant that daytime was struggling to keep hold, and likely wouldn't for much longer. Any remnants of summer now appeared well and truly over and autumn was without doubt in full swing.

Dani rang the bell then knocked on the door and only had to wait a few moments before it was opened and a skinny little teenage girl poked her head out.

'Can I help you?' she asked.

'Is your dad home?'

'Yes.'

The girl just stood there.

'Do you think I could speak to him?'

'Who are you?'

'I'm Dani Stephens.'

Dani surprised herself by using her actual name rather than her police title. That was new. Was that the way of the future now?

The child still looked less than convinced, but a moment later Dani heard an adult voice and Mary Grant came into view from the kitchen.

'Ah, Detective Stephens,' Mary said, 'Steven mentioned you were coming.'

Dani had called Grant's mobile before she'd left the university. Grant hadn't sounded thrilled that she wanted to speak to him again, but he hadn't put up much of a fight either, and suggested she go to the house. The young girl rolled her eyes and turned and disappeared off somewhere.

'Steven!' Mary bellowed, before turning back to Dani. 'He is here. Just pottering upstairs. Come and sit down.'

Mary showed Dani through into the lounge and she sat on a sofa.

'So how is the investigation going?' Mary asked. She remained standing by the doorway, and Dani sensed by her casual tone that this was simply small talk until Grant arrived, rather than her really taking a keen interest.

'Into the killings? We have a number of leads.'

'I'm sure. Must be quite something having to unpick all of the evidence. An analytical mind, I think that's what you call it, isn't it?'

'Mrs Grant, have you heard from Ethan at all yet? It's still very important that we speak to him.'

'No,' Mary said. She hung her head and Dani couldn't quite read what the reaction meant. Was it embarrassment, or was she trying to conceal a lie?

Dani didn't get the chance to press any further, because a second later Grant came into the room, and Mary promptly shot off back to do whatever she'd been doing when Dani first knocked on the door.

Grant offered Dani a drink but she politely declined and he showed her across the hall into his study where he shut the door. He took a seat at the brown leather chair behind the grand mahogany desk and Dani sat at the simpler wooden chair the other side. She looked around the room. Glass cabinets took up two of the walls, filled with textbooks and ornaments and photo frames. Academic certificates covered another wall.

'I've been thinking about the last conversation we had,' Dani said.

'About Ethan?' Grant asked, looking at her with suspicion.

'No. Not exactly. We talked last time about what that note could mean.'

'We talked at length, yes.'

He made it sound as though he'd felt hassled by that, which wasn't how Dani remembered it.

Dani briefly told him about the second note, including the words and the context. He sat listening attentively, not making a sound.

'Before, we really only talked about the motivation for someone to send a note like that,' Dani said. 'About how it's either an out and out taunt by a killer who thinks they're untouchable, or a clue left by someone who's ready to be caught.'

302

'Those are two of the more obvious possibilities.'

'I'm not sure though that really helps me to get any closer to understanding who this killer is. The thing is, if there really is a serial killer on the loose here…' Dani felt herself cringe slightly at her own words, it still sounded so outlandish, '…then why is the only thing we have those damn notes, and the stabbings of a young man and a young woman, both of which, it could be said, were quite simple attacks?'

'I'm not sure what you're getting at?'

'What I'm getting at is that those notes were possibly sent by a killer. *The* killer.'

'Yes, that's possible.'

'And, please don't think I'm mad, but I've felt almost like I've been stalked these last few days. Like someone's always watching me.'

'Which could be the alternative explanation for the notes. That you simply have a stalker intent on winding you up and causing you grief.'

Dani felt riled by him saying that; she'd thought he was one person who'd indulge her. She'd come here to have the conversation out in full though, so she wouldn't stop now.

'Yes, that's possible,' Dani said, 'but I don't think it's true. I think the murder of the young woman, Natalya, was a mistake.'

'A mistake?'

'An accident, perhaps. Maybe the killer panicked. But he hadn't meant to kill Natalya. At least not then, not like that. She'd been tied up somewhere. There were cuts and sores on her wrists and ankles. She'd been bound, but escaped.'

The look of concern on Grant's face was growing as she delved into the detail. She realised she was breaking multiple rules in divulging such information to him, but she felt justified. Plus, she believed not only that she could trust him, but that he could help too.

But then thoughts of Jessica Bradford still sat uncomfortably at the back of her mind. Could she really trust him?

'And what about the man?' Grant said. 'Paul Reeve.'

'That's what I don't get still. It's possible he was the one who killed Natalya, but then why would someone kill him afterwards?'

'The answer might be simple. Maybe you have more than one suspect here. It's not unheard of for killers to act as teams. Fred and Rose West, for example.'

Dani hadn't really considered that possibility, but she had to admit it made a certain amount of sense. That wasn't necessarily where she'd been going, but for a few moments she sat there thinking about it, before she got herself back on track.

'Or maybe he was killed to frame someone else,' Dani said.

'But you don't have someone else,' Grant said. 'Do you?'

'Really, the point I was getting to, is that this feels to me like more than just out of control drugs related violence.' She thought again about the notes. About the intruder at Mrs Staunton's house. About the shadow following her around.

'What if there are other victims?' Dani asked. 'Take Reeve out of the question, but think about Natalya. Her life in a dark world. She was an illegal immigrant, we believe. An escort. Very few people knew about her, and those that did know her knew very little. She was such an easy target for someone who can make people… disappear.'

Dani left that thought out there, not sure if Grant was picking up on where she was headed or not.

'So you're saying you think there are other victims, similar to Natalya?'

'It's a theory. An assumption. But so far we have no bodies. But we do have a list of missing women.'

'Which is quite a leap to take.'

Dani ground her teeth. Why was Grant now having a sudden change of heart since their last conversation?

'Maybe it is,' she said. 'Except one of the missing women is linked to Paul Reeve too. Potentially that's two dead women who were both close to him, but then why is he dead too? Whatever the answer to that one, I can't get past the possibility that there are more victims out there. Does the name Jessica Bradford mean anything to you?'

Something flashed across Grant's face – fear? – but was gone as quickly as it'd come.

'I don't think so,' he said, pursing his lips.

'She was a student at the university. She went missing last week. A psychology student. I believe some of the modules she took were yours.'

Grant shrugged. 'Some of my modules have well over a hundred participants. I rarely get to know each and every student. Are you saying she's linked to the other people you're investigating?'

'I don't know yet. But I will find out.'

Dani stared resolutely at Grant for a few seconds until he looked away, down at the desk.

'Coming back to my point,' Dani said, 'about the person who sent those notes to me. If it is the killer, then it's someone who really cares about what they're doing. Someone who takes time and effort finding victims and making sure they leave as little evidence as they can. My guess is that stabbing someone to death in the street isn't really their regular thing. It's just too... easy, and ordinary.'

Grant huffed, as though he was feeling both frustrated and lost.

'My point is,' Dani said, 'why hasn't this killer been on the radar before now?'

'It could be that this is just the start. Natalya was his first victim.'

'His,' Dani said.

'Excuse me?'

'You said his. People always say *his* when talking about unidentified murderers. Even I do it. It's just interesting that you, the expert, do it as well.'

'It's simple probability. It depends exactly which statistics you look at, but rarely have I seen a study where the proportion of male versus female serial killers is given as less than ninety percent.'

'Fair enough. What I was getting at though is that perhaps what we're dealing with here is a killer who's been very careful in the past. A killer who leaves as little evidence as they can. This isn't someone like my brother, where rage or revenge or something like that was a driving force behind his actions and he simply lost control.'

'You think that's what made your brother a killer?'

'I think that's what ultimately caused his actions, yes. None of his targets was random. In his mind, they had all wronged him one way or another. Maybe, though, the killer had always been inside him, waiting to come out.'

'Indeed. Some people would say there's a killer inside us all, somewhere.'

'That's basically what he said,' Dani said. For a few moments she felt slightly derailed as the thoughts about whether she was affected by the same personality defects as her brother whirred in her mind once more.

'So what was the point again?' Grant said. 'Have you said it already?'

'No. What is it that links all of the known serial killers who've been caught? What finally brought them to everyone's attention?'

'Evidence?'

'Exactly. Evidence that links the killer to the deaths of the victims. Deaths. People. Bodies.'

'Some killers are convicted without bodies being found.'

'But I'm guessing those cases are few and far between, right?'

Grant nodded. 'On balance, yes.'

'So if you're a killer who doesn't want to get caught, if you want to fly so far under the radar that no one even connects the dots in the first place to suggest there might be a killer out there, what's the best way to do it?'

'I'm sensing you're about to tell me the answer to that yourself.'

'I am. The answer is, you don't leave *any* evidence. No victim. No body. No killer. In fact, no trace that a murder took place at all.'

Chapter Fifty

'You've been thinking about this a lot,' Grant said.

'It's my job to think about it,' Dani answered, slightly disappointed by Grant's tepid reaction to her thinking. 'There must be some killers out there who fit that mould?'

'But by your very definition, we wouldn't know about such killers. It's a major flaw in my field of science. We only ever get to analyse the killers who get caught. Or, at the very least, the ones whose crimes we know about.'

'I understand that, but there must be something in what I said that rings true to you? Killers who tried to make their victims disappear completely. No body, no evidence, no crime. Burning. Quick Lime. Acid. Those methods have all been used before, haven't they?'

Grant raised an eyebrow. 'You really have been doing your homework, haven't you?'

'No, not homework. Just thinking. This, speaking to you, is the homework. Assume Natalya was a mistake. Without her body, we would likely never have known she was missing at all. She had no real friends or family. The people who knew her would have assumed she'd just run off somewhere else. It's only because she escaped, and then because the killer was spooked when he caught up with her, that we have a body. But there are other missing women too. What if they're victims of this same killer?'

Grant sighed, but Dani sensed he was coming around to the idea more.

'I need you to tell me what you can about a killer like the one I described. How could we catch a killer like that, who leaves no trace of the victims?'

Grant shrugged. 'It's pure simple luck, most often.'

Dani waited for Grant to expand and felt herself becoming more agitated when he didn't. The last time they'd spoken he'd been ready and willing to talk about anything and everything to do with murderers. Was he simply uncomfortable broaching the subject in that level of detail because he was at home with his wife and daughter, and didn't want his morbid interests to be overheard by them? Dani figured that wasn't such an outlandish reaction.

She wasn't giving up though.

'Please, just indulge me here,' Dani said.

'Ok,' Grant said, and his eyes focused beyond her. Checking the door was closed and the coast clear?

'Have you heard of John Childs?' Grant asked.

'No.'

'He was a contract killer. An assassin. Not necessarily a master in the art of killing, but more a brute who bludgeoned and stabbed his victims to death in horrific attacks. His method of disposal, however, was very effective. He dismembered the bodies and burned the remains in the fireplace of his London home. This was in the 1970s, and no traces of the victims were ever recovered.'

'No traces? So no bones or anything? Just from burning in a household fireplace?'

'You'd have to work methodically to burn only small pieces of the body at a time, which creates its own issue. If you're dismembering bodies you've got a lot of blood and other mess to clean up. But if constructed and lit effectively then a fire is easily good enough to break down every element of a body, and all you're left with is a pile of ash. Same as in a cremation. The police actually demonstrated Childs's technique by burning the body of an eleven stone pig in that same fireplace.'

'Then how was he caught? Trace evidence from the murder scenes themselves?'

'No. Like I said, this was the 1970s, so blood and DNA analysis was nothing like it is today. He was caught because he was a hired gun, not a carefully calculated killer. So although there were no bodies, there *was* evidence. The people who hired him, for starters, who had links to the people who disappeared. The police did their jobs and got to the truth through old-fashioned methods. Motives, circumstances, interviews and confessions. Like I said, you don't always need a body to prove, in a legal sense, that someone has been killed.'

Dani digested those words for a moment. She felt slightly flummoxed by the story of Childs, because she'd been moving well away from the idea of her killer being a paid assassin working for gangs. Yet Childs had been just that. And Reeve had been involved in drugs.

Everything came down to the notes. Those notes. A gangland assassin wouldn't send those. The notes had to be the clue to the killer's motives… and identity.

'What about other methods I mentioned then?' Dani said. 'Quick lime? Acid?'

Grant sighed as though a little bored by the conversation, like he'd had to cover these bases multiple times already. 'Obviously I'm no chemist or biologist, but my understanding is that both *could* be used, to limited ends. Quick lime really wouldn't be effective at all though. There are different types of lime for different precise purposes but in all cases if you bury a body in quick lime, or slaked lime or chlorinated lime, you may get some immediate or short term dissolving of tissue, but long term, given certain conditions, the lime can actually *prevent* putrefaction, which the killer really wouldn't want. You'd effectively be mummifying the corpse.'

'Seriously?'

'Seriously. Don't believe everything you see on TV, which I'm presuming is where you're taking some of your knowledge.'

Dani felt offended by Grant's words but she said nothing. It was true she'd never worked a case where a killer had gone to such lengths to dispose of a body and yes, she did take a lot of what she knew from fiction – TV, film, books.

'Have you heard of Henry Wainwright?' Grant asked.

'No.'

'In the late nineteenth century he killed his mistress, and packed her away in a sack of chlorinated lime which he stored in his Whitechapel workshop. A year later he was moving premises and so it came time to move that sack. His landlord saw him doing this and offered to help. During that process the sack somehow came open and the landlord caught a glimpse of a human hand and arm. He alerted the police, and Wainwright was caught. The body had been preserved so well that even a year after the poor woman's murder, the police were able to prove her identity.'

'Ok, so not lime then. What about acid?'

'It's not unthinkable, but you can have similar problems to lime, really. You'd have to find the right acid mix for starters, and you'd have to be able to either buy it or mix it in sufficient quantity to allow it to do its work properly, which may well leave an evidence trail in itself. Then you'd need a way of disposing of all the acid afterwards without arousing suspicion. John Haigh tried it. You heard of him?'

'Actually, yes,' Dani said, feeling a slight triumph. 'The Acid Bath Murderer.'

'Indeed.'

'But wasn't his method *almost* foolproof?'

'Almost, yes. When the police first took an interest in him, it wasn't because they thought he was a murderer at all. They were pursuing him for theft and fraud, and when searching his workshops they found belongings of his victims. He eventually confessed to the murders.'

'So if he hadn't been stupid enough to be involved in petty crime, and if he'd not kept those belongings, he may have gotten away with it.'

'Maybe. Maybe not for much longer though. The acid he used to dissolve the corpses turned into a thick sludge. Bodies don't just disappear in acid, they dissolve into it. Haigh stored the sludge in oil drums. I'm not sure of the overall effectiveness of the method, to be honest. That sludge is going to be pretty suspicious to say the least, unless you use a vast quantity of acid in the first place so that it remains dilute enough to dispose of easily. Plus there's the risk that some body parts would remain. Teeth, bone. Gall stones or kidney stones, if the victim was unlucky enough to have such afflictions, as was the case with one of Haigh's victims.'

Grant finished his spiel. Dani's brain was working overtime going over what he'd said, and trying to make sense of it all.

'Bodies can be fed to animals,' Grant said, as though thinking out loud now, and warming back into his role once more. 'Plenty of animals, pigs for example, will crunch through bones happily enough.'

'Like Robert Pickton?' Dani said. Grant gave her an impressed look.

'Exactly. He was thought to have killed as many as forty-nine women. Many he fed to his pigs, but it was also alleged that he minced some of the victims and sold their remains as meat.'

Dani winced at the disgusting words.

'In his case, some DNA traces of the victims did still remain. Pigs won't clean up every last morsel, or every drop of blood. They're messy animals. And some of the bone fragments, teeth, would pass through in the pigs' faeces, but it would still take a lot of effort to identify those traces and match them to victims. To all intents the bodies have disappeared.'

Dani thought about that one.

'Or you could have a simple case of burying the bodies,' Grant said. 'Out of sight, out of mind. Plenty of killers have employed that method over the years, as I'm sure you'll know.'

'Like Fred and Rose West,' Dani said. 'And the Moors Murderers.'

'Two duos, I might add, coming back to the earlier point. In both those cases, the murders were covered up to varying degrees by burying the bodies. In the case of the Moors Murderers, at least one of the victims' bodies still hasn't been found, decades later, such is the remoteness of the moors where Brady buried the corpses.'

The room fell silent and Dani realised she was beginning to feel queasy with all the talk of death and corpses and sadistic murderers.

'I'm sure you realise that this is an area I take great interest in, but from your point of view it's all just hypothetical,' Grant said. 'I'm really not sure at this stage, unless you have *something*, some evidence of a crime – other than Reeve and Natalya of course – how any of this can help you with your case.'

'Actually it's all helping,' Dani said. 'Knowledge is power, as they say.'

There was a knock on the door and Dani spun around to see Mary standing there. She had a slight look of disquiet on her face.

How long had she been there for?

'Your tea's nearly ready,' she said. 'Annie needs to eat before she goes to dance class.'

'Oh, right. Dani—'

'It's fine,' Dani said, getting to her feet. 'That's enough talk of the dead for one day. Thank you for speaking to me at such short notice.'

'That's really no problem at all,' Grant said. 'I want to help you here in any way that I can.'

'It was nice to see you again, Detective,' Mary said, before turning and heading off once more.

Grant got up from his chair and Dani followed him out into the hallway.

'You have a beautiful home,' Dani said, looking around the grand space.

'Thank you. It'll soon be a hundred years old. We've been here a long time ourselves now, over fifteen years. Since Annie was just a baby. It feels a bit big with the three of us. When Annie leaves I'm really not sure what we'll do.'

Dani looked around. Adjacent to the open door leading into the kitchen was a plain-looking door. It caught Dani's eye because it had a small padlock clasped over an outer bolt.

'Is that where you keep the dead bodies then?' Dani joked.

'What?'

Dani nodded over to the locked door.

'Oh, ha, yeah. The basement. No. You won't find any dead bodies down there. Dead bodies don't need locking in. That's trying to keep the monsters out.'

'Monsters?'

'Sounds kind of silly now. There was a massive storm a few years ago that blew out the single slit window down there. The noise of the wind whistling through was horrendous. Naturally Ethan told Annie that monsters lived down there.'

'As brothers tend to do,' Dani said.

'Indeed. The only solution was to put the lock on, to show Annie the house was still safe. I'm not sure she's ever been down there since. We don't need the lock anymore, of course. Just never got around to taking it off.'

Dani felt her phone vibrating and she apologised and took it out of her pocket. She recognised the number from earlier in the day.

'I really should take this,' Dani said. 'Thanks for your time.'

'Of course. Let me show you to the door.'

She answered the phone as Grant walked over with her. He opened the door, Dani smiled at him then headed out.

—

Two hours later, with the clouds finally parting to reveal the sun just moving down below the tree line in front of her, Dani was sitting on a bench on the leafy university campus looking out across emerald fields that were cluttered with students playing impromptu games of football, rugby and frisbee.

'Like I told the other detectives, I guess I don't really know her that well.' Georgia Draper said.

Nineteen years old, with dyed black hair and piercing eyes, Georgia was supposedly one of Jessica Bradford's closest friends at university, but the girls had only known each other a few short months.

'At first I thought maybe she'd just gone home for some reason. Then I noticed those Facebook posts.'

'And who's this guy she's gone with?'

Georgia shrugged. 'I've really no idea. She never mentioned him to me before.'

'And you've still not seen or heard from her directly?'

'Not that I can remember.'

The way Jason had relayed the story earlier in the day made it sound like all was fine and dandy. But Dani was far from agreeing.

'What do you know of Professor Grant?' Dani asked.

Georgia shrugged. 'Never talked to him before. He's one of our lecturers. Jess was way more into that stuff than me.'

'How do you mean?'

'I only took that module because she was. I couldn't really care less. It's all a bit… weird, isn't it?'

'Murder? Yes I guess so.'

'But Jess is really into it. She's got the professor's book and everything. It was written before we were even born, but she's well into it. Even went to talk to him about it a couple of times.'

'Sorry?'

'What?'

'Jess did what?'

'She was talking to Professor Grant. Went to his office one day so they could discuss killers. How weird is that?'

'So they knew each other?'

Georgia's face turned sour. 'Knew each other? What do you mean? I'm not saying they were shagging or anything like that.'

Dani felt her phone vibrating in her bag, the fifth time it'd done so in the last couple of minutes.

'Sorry, just give me a second.'

She fished it out and saw it was Jason.

'I'll just be a moment.'

She answered the call.

'Where are you?' Jason asked.

'Why?'

314

'I'm at your apartment.'

'My apartment?'

'I need to speak to you, Dani. We've got some results.'

'From the notes?'

'Yeah. And some more from Harland's apartment.'

She felt a surge of anticipation, though Jason's tone worried her.

'And?'

'And we found nothing on the notes. Nothing at all except for your fingerprints.'

'Damn,' Dani said. 'And the other stuff?'

'Well, that's the thing. The blood traces from Harland's flat did match with Reeve. Not with Natalya though.'

'So that knife really was the murder weapon?'

'It looks like it. For Reeve at least. The thing is though, Dani, we found no fingerprints or hair or anything else to directly link the knife or clothes to Harland. Or Ethan Grant, for that matter.'

'Really? That's odd.'

'It is. And that's not the oddest part. Because we *did* find some prints on the knife, and also some hairs in that pile of clothes.'

'Whose?

'They're yours, Dani.'

Chapter Fifty-One

'Where's Annie?' Grant asked as he sat down at the kitchen table.

Mary was by the counter, spooning out stew onto two plates.

'She's coming,' Mary said. 'Just getting ready.'

'Going out again?'

'She's a teenager.'

'She's never here anymore. You don't think she's got a boyfriend, do you?'

'Does it really matter if she has?'

Grant said nothing to that.

'Come on, Steven. It's going to happen sooner or later.'

'That's not it,' Grant said. 'I'm not an idiot. It's *who* she's hanging out with that I'm bothered about.'

'What does that mean?'

'It means it wasn't that long ago she was telling us how Ethan and his lowlife friend Jimmy were hooking up with her friends. And not just hooking up, but having sex with them too. The thought of Annie… I can't even bring myself to say it.'

Grant's mood sank further with the talk of Ethan and his no-good friends.

What had that boy got himself mixed up in?

Mary placed a dinner plate overflowing with boiled vegetables and stew in front of Grant, then took the seat opposite and set down her plate, containing a slightly smaller portion. Grant took a deep inhalation of meaty vapour. It smelled sublime and he felt his tummy rumble with anticipation.

'You like her, don't you?' Mary said, her eyes on her food.

'Annie?'

'No, you idiot,' Mary said. 'That detective. You like her.'

'I'm intrigued by her.'

'What, because she's so messed up?'

'What makes you think she's messed up?'

'Because of what happened to her.'

'You're saying I only like people who are messed up in the head?'

'Or perhaps it's the woman in authority you like the idea of. You always like it when I take charge.'

Mary gave him a seductive look.

'Ugh,' came Annie's voice. 'You two are *so* disgusting.'

Grant spun around in his seat, his cheeks burning. Annie barged through and went to the fridge, grabbed a can of Coke, then turned back for the door again.

'Honey, your tea's here.'

'It's ok, Mum. I'll eat at Susan's. Thanks though.'

Grant was about to chastise his daughter but when he turned back to Mary he saw she didn't looked fazed in the slightest. Seconds later Grant heard the front door open and then close.

'What was that all about?' Grant asked.

Mary shrugged.

'So we've got the house to ourselves tonight?' he said.

'We do.'

'How about... you know?'

Mary smiled.

'Perhaps,' she said. 'But on one condition.'

'What condition?'

'I need you to do something for me first.'

'Which is?'

'I want you to go and see Ed Francis.'

Grant deflated, and Mary's face took on a more serious look.

'What the hell for?' Grant asked.

'Oh, Steven, come on, don't be like that.'

'I'm not being like anything. I'm just not sure why you want me to go over there. Has he been snooping again?'

'He's always bloody snooping. Three times today I've seen him. But there's no sign of Julie still.'

'Ah, so that's it.'

'What do you mean, *that's it*?'

'The car's back now,' Grant said.

'Yeah, but she's not.'

'So you think he's strangled her and buried her in the garden?'

'Not funny, Steven. I'm serious. I don't like him. He's creepy as hell and he's up to something. Just go over there, take a look around the house, see if anything's off.'

'Yeah, ok. *Hi Ed*. Oh, hi, Steven, what can I do for you? *Oh, you know, just wanted to take a look around your home. See if you've left any evidence of you murdering your wife lying around.* Oh, right, yeah. Come on in then.'

'Well that's good,' Mary said, sullen now. 'You've rehearsed your lines, so it looks like you're all set to go.'

She got up from the table and came around and grabbed Grant's plate.

'Hey, I'm not finished with that.'

'You are now.'

She strode over to the bin, flipped the lid and dropped the remains of Grant's tea into the black bag. Grant opened his mouth to protest but found the restraint to let it go.

'Well, off you go then,' Mary said.

Grant got up from his chair. He moved over to Mary and planted a kiss on her lips.

'You, my dear, really are quite something.'

Mary said nothing to that. Grant made his way to the front door, slipped on his loafers then headed out into the cold and clear night, not bothering with his coat. Across the street Francis's car was parked up on the drive. Lights were on in the house. Grant was almost surprised not to see Ed Francis's face stuck up against one of the windows. When he reached the front door Grant rang the bell and waited. After a few seconds he wondered if his call would go unanswered.

Should he ring again or head back home?

He turned and looked across at his own house. He was sure he could see Mary's outline in their bedroom window. Just then the door opened and Grant spun back around.

'Ed, how you doing?'

Francis looked slightly annoyed, as though he'd been rudely interrupted, but on seeing Grant he quickly brushed his agitation to one side.

'Steven, what a surprise. What can I do for you?'

Francis had on a pair of jeans and a buttoned shirt that was half hanging out of his trousers. The sleeves were rolled up to his elbows. His cheeks were flushed from exertion.

'Bit of an embarrassing one,' Grant said.

'Need some sugar?'

'Almost, but not quite. Light bulbs.'

'Light bulbs?'

'Yeah.'

Grant fought hard to keep his manner passive and relaxed. Light bulbs? He wasn't quite sure where that bright idea had come from. He'd initially thought about saying screwdriver, but what if Francis kept all his tools in the garage? Mary wanted him to snoop in the house. Light bulbs had been a spur of the moment thing.

'What kind of light bulbs?' Francis asked, looking a little suspicious.

Grant moved his hands together, indicating the size.

'You know the ones. About this big. Don't know the name. The ones you get in table lamps and that.'

'Have you got the old one so I can see?'

'No, it broke.'

'It's only seven o'clock, you know. You'd probably find them over at Tesco.'

'Yeah, probably. Just thought if you had some, would save the bother.'

'Right. Well, I may do. Come in and we'll take a look.'

Francis seemed less than impressed with the disturbance but he moved to the side and ushered Grant through nonetheless. It was the first time Grant had been in the house, and his first impression was that it was sparsely furnished. From the hall he had a glimpse of the kitchen, a dining room and a lounge. All the furniture you would expect was there, but little in the way of the knick-knacks that normally cluttered family homes; paintings, picture frames, ornaments.

'Through here,' Francis said, leading Grant through to the sleek and modern kitchen that was pristine and so tidy it almost seemed unused. They headed on into a small utility room.

Grant kept alert as he walked through. For what, exactly, he wasn't quite sure. One thing he did know, was that there was no sign at all of Julie Francis. Not even a photo of her.

'You're on your own tonight?' Grant asked.

Francis gave him a look. 'Yeah.'

'Not seen Julie for a few days. She working away or something?'

'No.'

Grant wasn't sure what else to say to that. Francis bent down to a cupboard, opened the door and started rummaging around.

'I've got these,' Francis said, handing Grant a small box without looking up from the cupboard. 'Or these. Or these.'

Grant looked at the three different types of bulb in his hands. The first one was most like the type he'd described to Francis at the door.

'This one's perfect,' he said.

'Just the one?' Francis asked.

'Two would be ideal.'

'You got it.'

Francis gave him another one and took the unwanted boxes back, then shut the cupboard.

'Anything else, neighbour?' Francis said as he straightened up. 'Some sticky tape? A couple of screws?'

'I think I'm all good. Thanks for these.'

'Any time. I'd offer you a drink, but I really was just in the middle of something. Maybe next time though, right?'

'Yeah, next time.'

Grant followed Francis back out through the kitchen and into the hall. Other than the lounge, dining room and kitchen there was one other doorway there. That door was ajar a couple of inches and as Grant passed he tried his best to peek inside.

No, it was too dark. He couldn't see anything. Not even if it was another room beyond that door, a simple cupboard, or the entrance to a basement. Francis's house was a similar age and style to Grant's so it would probably have one.

He continued to look around, and spotted something past the open door of the lounge. On a small bookcase that was only partly filled, the spine of one of the books caught his eye. He'd seen that damn book enough times to recognise it anywhere.

Grant stopped walking. 'You've got my book.'

Francis stopped too and turned, his forehead creased, his eyes beady – clear signs his agitation was growing.

'Yeah. *The Essence of Evil*. Not read it all yet. It's not my usual thing, I must say.'

Grant took a step forwards, towards the lounge, intending to get a better look inside. Francis stepped past him and darted in. He went to the bookcase and picked the book out, then quickly leafed through it. As if satisfied with his inspection he tossed the book to Grant who caught it one-handed.

He looked down. The edges of the book were clearly aged, the inner pages yellowed. The book was old, and well-thumbed. Grant thought it looked like the one Jessica Bradford had shown him the other week. Frowning, he opened the cover, to take a look at the title page. It wasn't there. Torn out.

'Got it from a charity shop,' Francis said. 'Twenty pence. Can you believe it? Looks like it's been read a hundred times over, but still, can't argue with that price.'

'No, absolutely not.'

Francis moved forwards and took the book out of Grant's hands. He placed it on a side table then turned back to Grant.

'I really do need to get back to what I was doing,' Francis said.

'Of course. Thanks for the bulbs.'

'Anything to help a neighbour and friend.'

Francis showed Grant out and he made his way back across the street. What he'd seen, and the words Francis had spoken, swam in his head.

Friend? Grant wouldn't call Francis a friend. Not at all. Quite what his neighbour was though, Grant really couldn't be sure.

Chapter Fifty-Two

She wasn't sure if she'd been asleep or not when she heard the footsteps coming down the stairs. She was drowsy, groggy, but she didn't think it was from lack of rest; she must have been drugged.

The footsteps got louder, closer. Her heart drummed in her chest, the tempo upping with each beat and with each tap of the feet on the solid floor.

How long had she been here now? With the sack over her head most of the time, and no evidence of any natural light coming into the room, it was virtually impossible to know.

Memories of the night in the bar, last Friday, flashed in her mind as she listened to the footsteps coming down. The last thing she could remember was walking for a taxi, on her own, but that memory was foggy and patchy. Had she already been drugged by that point? She certainly hadn't hooked up with anyone in that bar, but could only assume that was how she'd come to be in this ghastly place.

She held her breath when she realised the footsteps had stopped, right by her. When the sack was removed from her head she thought her heart had burst right out of her chest and for a few moments she could do nothing but try to get her breathing under control. As ever, she could see little of the room beyond because of a bright white light blaring into her eyes. The place smelled dank and was echoey. All she could make out other than the light was the shadowy outline of shelving filled with nondescript items. It wasn't a big place. A store room? A cellar?

'Good evening, Jessica,'

A voice as smooth as silk. No hint of strain or animosity. Quite caring and kind, which only made it all the more chilling.

Jessica Bradford tried to scream, to moan, but all that came out was a pathetic whimper. A fabric gag stuffed in her mouth prevented anything more. She was sitting on the cold, hard floor, arms behind her, handcuffed around a metal post. She still had on the same mini skirt and lycra top that she'd worn to the bar however many days ago it'd been, though her clothes were now dirtied and torn, revealing even more of her cleavage, and her knickers and legs had been soiled more than once.

The figure in front of her, cast in shadow from the glare of the light, moved forwards and pulled the gag from Jessica's mouth, then stepped over to a workbench barely visible at the side of the room. She realised now, as her eyes continued to adjust, that her small handbag sat atop the wooden worktop.

'What do you want from me?' Jessica murmured, after taking a few moments to compose herself. 'They'll find me,' she said, now showing a bit more fight.

Of course, she'd already begged and pleaded and shouted and threatened plenty since she'd been here, but it had made no difference and now her efforts were far more half-hearted and desperate.

'Who will?'

'My friends. My family,' she said. 'The police. Whatever you do to me, they're going to find me. And then they'll find you. But if you let me—'

'Uh-uh, not another word. Please don't attempt to make promises that you can't possibly keep. If I let you go you won't tell anybody? I mean, Jessica, come *on*. Have you any idea how silly that sounds? Do you really expect that *I* would ever believe that?'

'I promise,' Jessica sobbed.

'No. That's enough of that. And you're wrong about them finding you. Very wrong.'

'They'll find me!' Jessica blasted. 'My parents will never stop looking.'

'Now that's two different statements, Jessica. One is *possibly* true, the other absolutely isn't. Perhaps your mum and dad really will keep on looking, once they realise you haven't jetted off with a new love. But they'll never find *you*. Not even a trace.'

The figure picked up Jessica's handbag and started rummaging through the contents.

'I read an amazing story recently, about a man and a woman who were hiking in Yellowstone National Park in America. I've never been but I really would love to go. Anyway, these two were hiking, but they decided to head off the beaten track, going beyond warning signs which indicated the dangerous nature of the landscape. Perhaps they were daredevils and wanted to see something that all the other tourists don't get to see. They wanted to go hot potting. Have you heard of that?'

The figure paused and turned back to Jessica. She made no attempt to answer the question either with words or gesture. She was too scared to.

'I hadn't,' the figure said. 'Hot potting is when people go for a dip in a thermal spring or a geyser. Apparently it's quite a thrill. Yellowstone is famous for springs and geysers, if you didn't know. The whole point though, is that this area of the park was off limits for a good reason. Those springs weren't created by Mother Nature as a reward for eager tourists. They're unforgiving and deadly. The temperature of the water can be close to boiling, and it's often very acidic.

'Anyhow, the poor chap goes to dip his toe to test the water. He slips, he falls. What happens? He gets boiled and burned alive by that hot acidic water. His companion is there, filming the whole thing on her mobile phone, their perfect getaway taking quite an unexpected turn.'

The figure pulled out Jessica's small leather purse and stepped to the large glass jar sitting at one end of the worktop. The figure put on a heavy-duty rubber glove and lifted the lid off the jar, which was half-filled with liquid.

'The man was dead within seconds. He had absolutely no chance of survival. The friend raised the alarm immediately but due to a turn in the weather, the rescue team couldn't even attempt to recover what was left of him. When they returned a day or two later, do you know what they found?'

The figure turned to Jessica and waited for a response. Once again no words passed her lips.

'They found absolutely nothing. No trace of the man whatsoever. No skin, no flesh, no bones, no teeth, no clothes. The acid had dissolved him. Whatever atoms used to be a man were just part of that deadly acidic mixture.'

The figure took the purse in its gloved hand and lifted it towards the jar.

'And remember what I'm talking about there is just a *natural* mixture of water and acid from dissolved rocks. Imagine how much more powerful a heavily concentrated and deliberately manufactured substance could be. Imagine what *that* kind of substance would do to a human body.'

The figure moved the purse down inside the jar and the outer edges of it touched the liquid which sizzled and bubbled. Jessica began to shudder and tremble with fear. She felt her bladder release, began to whimper and plead, incoherently.

Carefully, the figure dropped the purse into the jar and placed the lid back on top. The acid fizzed and frothed ferociously as it worked on devouring the leather, fabric and plastics that had been thrown its way.

'So, Jessica, coming back to my point. When you say they'll *find* you, perhaps now you can understand why that really is never going to happen. Because quite soon, there will be absolutely nothing left of you to find.'

Chapter Fifty-Three

The whole way in the taxi from Knowle, Dani fretted about what would await her when she arrived at her apartment. It wasn't just what Jason had said to her on the phone, but the way he'd said it. Like he didn't trust her. Like he really thought she had something to do with the murders. Like he half expected her to do something stupid now.

But then, could she really trust him? What she'd just learned from Georgia Draper put quite a different spin on the tale of Jessica Bradford. Someone was lying to her. Was it Steven Grant, who definitely had lied about Jessica? Jason? Someone else within the police?

She got out of the taxi outside her apartment block without incident. There were no flashing lights, no gaggle of policemen and policewomen lying in wait to haul her into jail. Just Jason, standing by the outer doors to the building, his head ducked down into the collar of his thick overcoat.

'Dani, about bloody time. I'm freezing my bollocks off here.'

'It was your choice to wait there,' Dani said, with not an ounce of sympathy.

She moved past Jason and opened the door then stepped inside, not bothering to turn to look whether he would follow. She walked over to the lift and pressed the button, her eyes focused only on the closed lift doors. When they opened she looked around to see that Jason was indeed right there behind her.

They rode up without speaking, and Dani kept her eyes front and centre, though she felt Jason watching her the whole time. They exited on the sixth floor and walked in silence to Dani's apartment. Only once they'd both stepped inside and Jason had shut the door behind him, was the silence finally broken.

'You've got some explaining to do,' Jason said.

Dani didn't like the way he said it. 'Do I?' She stomped away, into the lounge. Jason followed a step behind.

'Yes, you bloody do. What's going on, Dani?'

Dani stopped halfway into the lounge and looked over at the dark windows, the orange of streetlights and the apartments across the water visible beyond the glass. She didn't turn to face Jason.

'I really have no idea.'

'You're going to need to think of a better explanation than that.'

She spun around. 'An explanation for what?'

'For the notes.'

'What? Of course you found my prints on them, I picked the damn things up! Are you saying you think I wrote them?'

'Did you?'

Dani glared at Jason as hard and as coldly as she could. 'I'm not even going to answer that.'

'And what about the things at Harland's house? The knife? The clothes? Jesus, Dani, your fingerprints are on a murder weapon.'

'I've... I've no idea how that happened.'

'You searched that apartment, didn't you? The day Harland was killed?'

'It wasn't a search. I just had a look around.'

'And did you pick anything up? That knife? It wasn't in your notes that you did anything like that.'

Dani slumped, confusion taking over. 'I don't think so but... no, I really don't think I did.'

'*Don't think?*'

'No, I didn't, ok!'

'You're absolutely sure? You're on your meds still, aren't you? Could they have clouded your recall?'

Dani's face screwed in anger. She was about to bite back, but really, she didn't know what the right answer was. Had she taken her meds that day? Were her memories solid and… real? There were plenty of times since the accident when she'd hallucinated, or where reality had blurred, but that had all been many months ago. Hadn't it?

'I'm as sure as I can be,' Dani said, sounding anything but. 'Unless I really am going mad.'

She dropped down onto the sofa, her head a muddled mess. All of those times she'd thought she was being watched. Her leaps to believing there was a serial killer out there. Was it all the meds talking? Or was it even just her mangled brain?

'Jessica Bradford knew Steven Grant,' she said.

'What?'

'Grant said the name meant nothing to him, but her friend told me the two of them had had a one-on-one meeting not long ago.'

'Dani, what the hell? You're suspended. Do you have any idea how much shit you'll be in if McNair knows you've been out speaking to witnesses?'

'I'm not going to sit around while a murderer is out there taunting me!'

'But Jessica Bradford's not even missing, never mind a murder victim. We've already been over that.'

'Not missing? Then where the bloody hell is she?'

Dani slumped back. Her head was pounding. She couldn't take this anymore. She shot up from the sofa and stormed out and into the en suite, slamming the door behind her. She turned on the taps in the sink then opened the cupboard and stared at the pill bottles.

She wanted to be strong, but she really needed the release. She needed the clarity of mind, too. She grabbed two different bottles, opened one and threw some pills into her hand and then into her mouth without even seeing how many she'd grabbed. She ducked her head under the water, swallowed, then did the same with the next bottle. She slammed the bottles onto the side, shut off the taps then stared at herself in the mirror for a few seconds. Ashamed.

When she found the strength to come back out, Jason was standing right there in the hallway, arms folded, glaring at her grumpily.

'You really think that's going to help? Maybe that's why you're in this mess in the first place.'

'I don't know what's going on, Jason.'

'No. And neither do I.'

'But I didn't have anything to do with Reeve's death. You can't possibly think I did?'

'Of course I don't.'

His tone wasn't particularly convincing and Dani took little comfort in it. She moved forwards and past him, into the kitchen. She headed for the fridge; the bottle of vodka her next stop. As she reached forwards for the handle Jason's arm came in front of her, pinning the fridge door shut.

'That's not going to help.' His voice was stern.

'I was going for some chilled water, idiot.'

She let go of the handle and turned to look at him. He hadn't bought the lie.

'So what now then?' she asked.

'How do you mean?'

'Am I under suspicion?'

'Not yet.'

'Not yet? That's not a great answer. Does McNair know?'

'No. These results came directly to me. I've not passed the forensic results on to her, and they haven't been logged in the system yet. Look, you need to be one hundred percent straight with me here. I'll only help you if you tell me everything.'

'There's nothing to tell! What are you expecting me to say?'

'That you fucked up? That you went around that flat gung-ho, picking up things right, left and centre without recording your movements. That you didn't find anything of note, because at the time neither Harland or Grant were suspects in your case. That you then forgot to write up in your notes exactly what you'd seen and done in that flat so we could properly eliminate any fingerprints you left. Maybe because you were too traumatised by what happened to Harland that day, or maybe because of your meds. You made a mistake. The notes created a false impression of what you did in the flat, but at the time you had no reason to suspect that the place was a crime scene, and you thought nothing of it.'

Dani said nothing to Jason's statement. She just stood and stared at him, trying to read his face. What did he mean exactly? Was that a story he believed himself? Or just the one he was prepared to tell to help Dani out?

But it was all bullshit.

What about the story in which Dani had never picked up that knife? In which she'd barely even searched that place and her notes from that day – that damn day, that she could remember nearly every second of – were one hundred percent accurate. The story in which someone was trying to frame her, or at least direct suspicion her way to make her life even more difficult and miserable than it already was.

What about that story? Would Jason believe that one?

The problem was, this wasn't just about Jason. She saw no way of convincing the likes of McNair and Baxter of the truth.

'That's right,' Dani said. 'That's exactly what happened.'

She hung her head.

'Good,' Jason said. He put his hand out onto Dani's shoulder. It was an understanding touch, the first warmth he'd shown to her thus far. 'If you want, that's the story that McNair will get. But, Dani, I don't believe it for a second. So now you need to tell me what you really think is happening here.'

Chapter Fifty-Four

Dani sipped her coffee, then sat it back down on the kitchen table. She was already feeling calmer as the drugs took effect, even though she knew more medication perhaps wasn't the best solution, under the circumstances. It was absolutely a good thing she hadn't made it to the vodka bottle too. Jason was opposite, holding his mug of coffee in both hands. Dani guessed he was still trying to get some warmth in them after being outside in the cold so long while she made her trip back from Knowle.

'So you really think someone is trying to set you up?' Jason said.

'It's the only explanation that makes sense.'

'Why?'

Flashes of Dani's conversations with Grant went through her mind.

'Because they can,' she said. 'It's all about power and control. This killer is showing how good he is. And how far off the mark we are. Putting me in the centre of the mess is entertainment.'

'Why you?'

'Why not? I was the lead detective on the case. And everyone knows I have a dark past.'

'If there's a mastermind killer out there, which I think is where you're going, I still don't get why Reeve became a part of this.'

'No. Nor me. And there's still something I don't like about the other missing women, and Jessica Bradford's disappearance in particular.'

Jason sighed as though bored and frustrated with Dani's relentlessness. He looked at his watch and glanced at his phone. Not for the first time.

'Please, Jason, something isn't right.'

'I can take another look at it,' he said.

'And what about other suspicious, unexplained deaths? Did you find any that could be linked.'

'It's not an exact science, but on the face of it, no. There're plenty of stabbings and shootings and other deaths linked to drugs and gangs in the area over the last five years. That's how far I went back. But all of them made sense, if that makes sense. Either we know the killers, or there were witnesses, or there's CCTV evidence, or solid forensics, or clear motives. There's always something.'

'We still have those other missing persons cases. Obviously we know Grace Agnew was linked to Paul Reeve. That can't be a coincidence. Are there others?'

'We haven't found any other links, and we simply can't explain what's happened to Grace. I've done the rounds with friends and family, for her and for others, and I'm really not sure where we can go next. The whole point is that the Missing Persons team have no evidence of what happened.'

Dani paused, thinking.

'What is it?' Jason asked.

'Someone out there wants to cause *me* trouble. I don't know who they are, or why they're targeting me, but I feel like they're watching me, following me.' Dani felt goose pimples rising on her arms. 'The more I think about it, the more I think they really must have been in my apartment too.'

'You're safe now,' Jason said. 'I'm here.'

Dani said nothing to that, just sighed, and a further silence followed. There was a gnawing in her mind as she struggled to process a thought that wasn't quite taking hold.

'Jessica Bradford aside,' she said, 'what do you really make of those missing persons cases? What do you think happened to those women?'

'Same as you. Most likely they're all dead. Murdered, though? And by the same person? I just don't know. And I've no idea how we even go about investigating them any further. Not on the information we have. I want to believe you, Dani, and I want to help, but other than Grace Agnew I still don't see anything specific to link those cases to Reeve and Natalya or to Harland and Ethan Grant, and Jimmy Colton. Or to the notes you were sent.'

'But maybe the answer is a simple one,' Dani said, sounding as frustrated as she was feeling. 'This is a killer who switches M.O. That's the whole point. He *knows* that we won't pull all of these seemingly unconnected people together. Because we can't. The evidence just isn't there to do so.'

'Look, I'm not saying I don't believe you...' Jason said. The fact he needed to say that, Dani thought, suggested it wasn't true. '...I just don't see this as clearly as you do, and I'm really trying my hardest.'

'The killer doesn't want to be caught,' Dani said, following a train of thought from her conversations with Steven Grant.

'What? Of course he doesn't.'

'No, Jason, there's no *of course*. Some killers *do* want to get caught. They want the attention, or they've had enough, or they're looking for atonement.'

'Is this what that professor has been feeding you?'

'Yes. It is. Some killers send notes like the one I received as a way of reaching out, a cry for help. But not this one.'

'Which leads us where?'

'You were right. There's nothing in those missing person cases. Nothing at all. It would be a waste of time to pursue them further.'

'Then what?'

'Perhaps to catch this killer we have to keep playing *his* game.'

'His game? What does that even mean? From what I gather you're suggesting to me that this killer planted evidence to try and frame you—'

'Maybe to frame me, or maybe just to cause me grief.'

'Then what's the next step in that game? We have you arrested and locked up?'

He said it as though he thought it was a ridiculous idea, but then his expression changed to one of concern.

'Dani, seriously?' he said.

It was him who'd suggested it, but was it really so outlandish? Was her arrest what the killer wanted? But how would it even work in practice? Jason was the only person Dani had confided in. McNair would likely be far less open to what Dani was saying, and it was even more unlikely that she'd ever buy such a madcap ruse, so how would Jason sell the idea to the DCI? Would he have to tell her that he really thought Dani was responsible?

What if it all went wrong and she never got out?

'I mean, I guess it could work,' Jason said, looking ponderous now.

She stared at him for a few seconds and felt a sudden chill, though she couldn't put her finger on why.

'Dani? Is that what you want?'

She didn't answer him. Her mind was too busy desperately trying to grasp an answer that made sense.

Jason's phone pinged. It was in his hand in a flash.

'I'm really sorry, I have to go,' he said.

'Seriously? After everything we've just talked about?'

'I know, I know—'

'Are you going to tell McNair?'

'About having you arrested?'

'About the forensics findings? About any of this?'

'I can hold off for now. If that's what you're asking.' He got to his feet. 'But I'll come back later so we can finish this. Think about what I said.'

Dani said nothing. Her mind was still too busy. She showed Jason out but didn't speak a word as she did so. When she'd shut and locked the door she remained standing in the hallway for a few moments.

Something was bugging her.

No, that wasn't true. Not something. Pretty much everything.

And where the hell was Jason going so urgently after everything they'd just talked about?

There was one way to find out, she guessed.

She grabbed her shoes, her coat, her keys, and was soon out of the door and running down the corridor.

Chapter Fifty-Five

Steven Grant lay back in the bed, panting heavily. His brow, chest and back were covered in a thin film of sweat from the exertion. Mary flopped down beside him in the bed and slung an arm over his naked torso.

'Fuck. Me,' she said, through laboured breaths.

'I thought I just did.'

He looked over at her and smiled. She pecked him on the lips, then got up from the bed.

'Just going to freshen up,' she said, before sauntering seductively into the en suite.

Grant watched her the whole way, enjoying the view. He closed his eyes and let out a contented sigh.

He didn't intend to, but before she'd come back out, he drifted happily off to sleep.

Not for long though. Grant's eyes shot wide open when he heard a shout. His head jumped up off the pillow. He spotted Mary – her dressing gown now on – standing by the window, a hand over her mouth. Grant looked at the bedside clock, then back at Mary. It was only ten p.m. He'd been asleep for all of five minutes, though it was long enough for his mind to be foggy.

'What's going on?' he asked.

'There's someone out there.'

'This again?'

Grant pushed himself up in the bed, leaning the weight of his torso on one elbow. He was still trying to overcome his sleepiness, nowhere near as alert or bothered as Mary wanted him to be.

'Well don't just sit there!' she yelled.

'All right, all right, I'm coming.' Grant forced himself out of the bed. 'Why were you at the window anyway?'

'I wasn't at the window! I heard a noise. Banging. I went to look.'

Grant was still struggling to believe this was all happening again, but Mary certainly seemed adamant. He grabbed his dressing gown before heading over to her. He pushed the curtains aside and peered out. He really couldn't see a thing; it was too dark out there. The security light at the front of the house hadn't tripped.

'Probably a cat or a fox or something,' he said.

'It wasn't a damn fox. I saw someone, on the drive.'

'You're sure?' Grant felt a glimmer of doubt; Mary was so insistent.

'Yes, I'm sure!'

'Fine. Let me go and take a look.'

Grant slung on his clothes and fetched the baseball bat, which this time was more conveniently placed underneath his side of the bed. He made his way downstairs, slipped on his shoes and headed out through the front door, holding the bat behind him as he walked across the gravel so that he wouldn't look like a lunatic in the bright glare of the security light which he knew he'd trigger.

Except the light didn't go on.

What the hell?

After a few steps Grant tensed and he pulled the bat up in front of him, holding it in striking pose. He turned this way and that, searching in the darkness, the illumination from the streetlights beyond not reaching the drive at all. With every slight gust of wind, and every swaying branch he heard, he became more jittery and on edge.

But he could see no one at all.

Really not wanting to be out there in the dark any longer than necessary, Grant turned and walked with more purpose back to the open front door.

That was when the thought struck him: *I left the door open!*

He rushed into the house and quickly closed the door behind him, still holding the bat at the ready.

'Mary!' he called, not far from panic.

'What?' she said, coming into view at the top of the stairs. The strain in her voice matched his.

But she was fine and Grant relaxed a little.

'Did you see anything?' she asked.

'No.'

Grant was about to put the bat down when he heard a noise in the kitchen. His anxiety level peaked once more.

'Mary, wait there.'

Grant squeezed his hands tightly around the bat and edged forwards. The sound came again. Like a gentle rattle. Something tapping on glass? On a window? When Grant reached the doorway he stopped and peered around the space in front of him. The lights in the kitchen were off and he stayed there for a few moments, letting his eyes adjust to the dark.

There was no sign of movement. No sign of anyone.

He took a hand off the bat and quickly flipped the lights on.

The kitchen was empty, everything as they'd left it. There really was no one there. It was all in his mind. He was making an issue out of the natural creaks and strains of the house, and the noise of the wind outside.

But then the sound came again, and this time Grant could place it more clearly. He looked over to the patio doors and saw that a loose branch from the ivy at the back of the house was gently swaying in the wind, and tapping on the window every now and then.

Then a voice came from behind him…

'What is it?' Mary whispered.

Grant jolted at the shock of her standing right there behind him. He spun and his heart thumped so hard in a sudden wave of panic that he thought it might actually burst out of his rib cage.

'Sorry, did I scare you?'

'Yes, you bloody did!' he hissed. 'There's nothing here. Just a branch on the doors.'

'Did you check out the back?'

'No.'

'Could you? Please?'

Grant let out a long deep sigh then nodded. He knew it wouldn't be that difficult to quickly check, but the fact was, he was genuinely rattled. He moved over to the patio doors and turned the key, then pressed down on the handle. The door released and Grant pushed it open and stepped out into the cold, though only a couple of inches from the threshold. He really wasn't intending to venture too far.

He saw movement out of the corner of his eye… A dark shadow moving towards him… For the second time in a few moments Grant thought his heart might actually explode, but this time he was ready. Almost. The bat was in his grasp. Grant turned to where the shadow was. He crouched, moving into a defensive position and pulled the bat behind his head, ready to uncoil his arms and attack…

The figure came forwards. Split-seconds moved ever so slowly as Grant's brain worked to decipher what was unfolding in front of him. The bat began to arc forwards…

The shadowy figure loomed, but then, all of a sudden, it was out of the shadows, lit up by the light seeping out from the kitchen.

Grant could now see his face clearly. He pulled his arms back, abruptly stopping the bat's trajectory.

'You?!'

Ethan Grant said nothing, just gave his father a crooked half smile.

Chapter Fifty-Six

Dani headed down the stairs and cautiously opened the doors at the bottom to peer out. There was no sign of Jason, but then she heard the outer door to the apartment block clink shut. She moved out into the foyer and caught a glimpse of his figure outside, heading away around the corner.

He hadn't seen her.

When Dani had arrived home earlier she'd not seen Jason's car, but she guessed he'd driven to hers and knew where he usually tried to park on the one-way street outside. With any luck he'd still be stuck in the one-way system by the time she caught up.

She rushed to the car park and swung her car out and over to the electronic gates which seemed to open painfully slowly. When they'd parted just enough for her to squeeze through she floored it, with barely a glance for any traffic. At the last second she saw headlights approaching from the right. She didn't bother to slow or to stop as her car shot out through the narrow space into the road. The other driver honked the horn but Dani just ignored it and carried on and picked up speed as she tried to close the distance to Jason.

She managed it. He was waiting at a set of traffic lights barely two hundred yards from her apartment, two cars between him and her. In the nighttime, he'd have no idea it was her car behind him as long as she kept her distance. She just needed to try and be discreet enough not to rattle him.

As she began to follow him, the same rumbling thoughts that she'd had in the apartment about what Jason could be up to were still nagging away at her, though a sense of guilt was also building.

Why was she following him? He was the one person who seemed to be on her side still, despite everything. And not just despite what was happening to her in her work, but despite all of the shit that had gone between them – mostly shit that she'd thrown at him, in all honesty.

She tried to push that thought away. Yes Jason was on her side, or so he said, but there was also plenty he wasn't telling her. He could have been open and honest about whatever out of hours appointment he now had, but he'd chosen to keep the truth from her. She wanted to know why.

They were soon heading out of the centre of Birmingham and east on the A41, a route that was by now increasingly familiar to Dani. She immediately began to wonder if Jason's destination would once again be Knowle, where she'd last come from herself earlier that day.

Of course, that was Dani putting two and two together, but if Jason was going to Knowle to see Steven Grant, why hadn't he just said so?

As she continued along, that final destination became an ever increasing reality, and with each turn they took, Dani's confusion and suspicion grew. Thus far on the journey the traffic in the early nighttime had been light enough to enable Dani to stay close, though not so light as to make it obvious she was following, though now that they were entering quiet suburbia, the task was becoming harder all the time.

Not wanting to draw Jason's attention, Dani decided to drop back one more, but doing so meant that Jason's car was out of sight more and more frequently as he took a series of left and right turns. When Dani next turned right, there was no sign of his car up ahead at all and she had a momentary wave of panic. She pushed her foot down. Relying on instinct, she sped up and took the next two turns on memory, retracing her earlier steps.

Sure enough, she soon had Jason's car in sight again. It surely couldn't be a coincidence that they were now so close to the Grants' house?

After just one more turn, Dani's deduction was confirmed. She slowed and turned her headlights off. The Grants lived on a cul-de-sac and if she followed Jason onto that road he was sure to spot her car straight away. Instead, she crawled to the junction and brought her car to a stop once she'd got a good enough view from around the corner.

Further ahead, Jason's car was pulled up by the side of the road. He was just getting out.

Dani's already turbulent thoughts were only further troubled when he didn't head left across the road, but instead right, and up the drive of Ed Francis's house.

'Seriously?' Dani said out loud.

A few moments later Jason stepped inside the house, though Dani couldn't see from her angle who had opened the door for him.

What the hell was going on?

Dani shut off her engine. Should she get out?

No. What was the point? She could hardly go and sneak up to the window to get a look.

Could she?

Instead she sank low in her seat and simply sat there as her brain whirred away, unhappily.

With the engine off she was soon cold and shivering. What on earth was she doing? Why hadn't she just stayed at home in the warmth and relative safety of her apartment?

Though was her home really safe now?

Dani tried to shake away the unwelcome thoughts, though she really didn't have anything more positive to put in their place. Minutes late, her ringing phone finally stole her attention away, though the sparse relief was short-lived when she pulled the phone from her pocket and saw who was calling. Jason.

'Hey,' she said.

Did he know?

'Dani, are you still at home?'

'Of course,' she said.

'I'm really sorry, something has come up. I don't know when I'm going to get back to yours.'

'Something's come up?'

'Yeah.'

'What?'

He sighed. 'I can't really say. Not yet. But I'll explain all soon, I promise.'

Why was he holding back on her?

Dani opened her mouth to say just that but he'd already hung up. Less than impressed, she thumped the phone down onto the seat next to her as she glared over at Jason's car.

What should she do now?

The reality was, there was so little she *could* do.

Of course she could just head home and wait for Jason to come back. Why wasn't she doing that?

Her phone chirped again soon after, this time with a message. Dani fully expected it to be Jason once again, but was surprised to see it was from Easton, of all people.

> Sorry about this morning, Dani. I know everything will work out in the end.

She really didn't know what to make of that and didn't bother to respond.

She remained in the car for more than half an hour more, getting colder, more tired and more anxious with every minute that passed. In that time several pedestrians, mostly dog walkers, had strolled past her car, more than one gazing suspiciously inside. She really couldn't just sit there all night.

And she didn't have to. Because finally up ahead she saw Jason striding down the drive and back to his car.

Dani found herself in a sudden panic. If she stayed where she was Jason would surely spot her car as he passed it, even in the dark.

344

She fired the engine up and as Jason ducked into his car she pushed the gearstick into reverse and pressed the accelerator and her car rolled back. She continued fifty yards, to the turning for the next street and wound her car around the bend. Then she sat and waited with her engine idling and her headlights still off. Once Jason had passed by in front she'd follow again.

Except that seconds soon turned to two minutes and he still hadn't gone by.

Surely he couldn't be sitting in his car outside Ed Francis's house still.

Dani pulled her car forwards again and rolled it slowly along and back up to the junction where she'd been parked earlier. There was no sign of Jason's car at all now.

She cursed under her breath. She'd made the most basic of mistakes. She'd always come and gone to the Grants' house from the same direction, and had simply assumed Jason would similarly retrace his steps on leaving. But he hadn't. At the end of the Grants' road, he'd gone in the other direction. To where, who knew, but one thing was abundantly clear. Dani had lost him.

Chapter Fifty-Seven

Steven Grant had been sitting in the front room on his own for two hours. Mary was still in the kitchen with Ethan, talking. Grant hadn't wanted to be a party to that. He hadn't yet figured in his own mind what he really wanted to say to his son. What questions he wanted to ask, or what answers he wanted, or hoped, to hear.

Grant was surprised at how relaxed, almost happy, Mary was at the sudden reappearance of their miscreant offspring. He wasn't feeling quite so at ease. But Ethan *was* still their boy, Grant knew, and it was a father's duty to always protect a son.

Wasn't it?

Yet Grant's mind remained in turmoil over what he should do.

For starters, they couldn't keep Ethan holed up in their home forever. For whatever reason, the police were out there, still looking for Ethan. That point had been made clear to both Grant and Mary on more than one occasion. And *out there* wasn't some vague expression of location. Right now, the police were *literally* out there.

Not long ago, as Grant was sitting in the darkened front room, staring out at the nighttime street outside, he'd spotted a car pull up on the road. The man who'd stepped out, his face caught in the streetlight, was DI Jason Barnes. Yet another detective, snooping around. Why always a different one?

Grant hadn't met Barnes before but he'd seen him in the local paper the other day in a piece about the growing knife crime in the city. He was another murder detective, like Dani Stephens.

When Grant had first spotted Barnes emerge from the car he'd been ready to shout out to Mary. His mouth had been open but then he'd quickly shut it again when Barnes didn't come onto their drive – as he'd expected – but instead crossed the road and went up Ed Francis's drive.

Francis had opened the door and hadn't looked particularly happy to see his visitor, but had nonetheless invited Barnes into the house eventually.

The policeman had been inside Francis's house for close to an hour before leaving as quietly as he'd turned up. What was all that about? He knew there was something odd going on with Francis; there was something about the man, about his life, that didn't add up. Yet Grant really didn't know what the problem with him was, or what he could or should do about it.

Grant was shaken from his tumbling thoughts when a shadow appeared in the doorway. He turned. Ethan. His hands were casually slung into his pockets, but he was standing tall, looking confident and relaxed, like he was in control of this situation now. As though the problems that had been burning inside him for so long were now extinguished, once and for all.

'Dad,' Ethan said. 'We need to talk.'

'About what?'

'I think you know.'

Yes, Grant thought he knew too.

'Ok, give me a minute.'

Ethan turned and walked away. Grant looked over at Ed Francis's house one more time. All remained quiet. Grant was absolutely certain that wouldn't be the case for much longer.

Chapter Fifty-Eight

Dani was still trying to shake the earlier chill from her failed spying attempts, and was heavily wired on caffeine two hours later back at her apartment. There'd been no call or text or anything from Jason in that time and she was becoming increasingly anxious and angry about what he was up to. She'd called him twice since she'd arrived back but he hadn't answered and however much she wanted to, she wouldn't call again and risk arousing his suspicions.

Rather than mope, she'd put her time to good use, scouring back through the HOLMES 2 system to identify any new information on the murder and missing persons cases, hoping that doing so would spark a eureka moment, but also trying to figure out if there was any explanation for what Jason was up to.

So far on her endless and roundabout search she'd found next to nothing and her brain was quickly wearing out.

Although…

She re-opened the notes on the system related to the house-to-house enquiries performed following Natalya's murder. The last Dani had heard about that, nearly every address they'd targeted had been covered off, except for a few residences where the owners or tenants were away, and a few industrial units that were seemingly empty.

But there was more. Dani delved back into the detail. She read through the notes compiled by various DCs and DSs. She opened up Google Maps on her laptop and plotted the streets, the residences and the industrial estates.

At the last team briefing Dani had given before her suspension she'd told the team to widen the house-to-house, and their review of CCTV, but she'd never seen the results of that until now. The latest notes had only been entered into HOLMES 2 that afternoon. A small retail park in Moseley had several industrial units, but also had a privately operated CCTV which included a camera angled to the street outside. Officers had attended the estate, spoken to the owners of each of the businesses and performed brief searches of the premises. Except for one unit. A unit that didn't appear to be in use and was owned by the same registered company that was the listed owner of the estate. The same company was also responsible for the CCTV.

The comment at the end of the notes was simply that further investigation was required to identify the directors of the company and contact them in order to secure the CCTV images and access to the unit if that was deemed necessary.

Most likely a search of that nature would be carried out by the in-house team of data analysts, though responsibility for ensuring that happened was stated on the system as belonging to DI Barnes.

She again looked at the map. Those units were several streets away from where Natalya was killed, and it certainly wasn't a straight route from A to B given the only previous CCTV image they'd found of her. But it also wasn't an unthinkable route, given that she was literally running for her life.

Dani sat back in the chair as her brain raced. Was that the lead Jason was now following?

She picked up her phone. Still no calls or messages from him. She bit the bullet and called him again. Still no answer. Her call went straight to voicemail.

She sent him a message.

We need to talk. Something's happened.

Would he see that as a cry for help from her and feel duty bound to call back?

There was no immediate response. What was he doing?

Unable to set her mind at ease, Dani was soon back rummaging through the case files. But she was only wasting time now. She couldn't get thoughts of Natalya out of her mind. And what about the other missing women? Grace Agnew? Jessica Bradford? Were they still alive?

Natalya had been bound. She'd been running for her life when she was killed. Finding where she'd been kept wasn't just important for finding the murderer, it was important for finding any victims who were still alive.

Dani couldn't sit there knowing even a few minutes might make all the difference.

–

Five minutes later Dani was back in her car and heading out of the city centre once more with the address in Moseley plugged into her sat nav. The traffic, past midnight, was light and the journey took all of ten minutes before Dani pulled into a small industrial estate that consisted of just five units erected with breeze blocks and corrugated steel. Not surprisingly given the time, there were no indications of life within any of the premises. Dani glanced at the signage above each unit and soon found the one she was looking for. She gasped when she spotted the single car parked up outside. Jason's.

She checked her phone again. Still nothing from him.

What the hell was he doing here?

She called Jason again. Straight to voicemail. She really wasn't liking the situation at all.

Should she call for backup?

No. She couldn't. Who would she call and what would she say?

She took a few deep breaths to calm her nerves and then stepped from the car. She went around to the boot and opened it up, taking out the socket wrench from the small toolkit next to the spare tyre. It was better than nothing, and she still couldn't be sure what she was about to walk in on.

She walked tentatively over to Jason's car, looking around her as she went. There was no one else about at all. The whole area was dark and eerily quiet. Isolated.

She headed on past Jason's car to the main door of the unit it was parked by. She tried the handle. It was unlocked. She opened the door. It was dark inside and she could see and hear nothing. With the wrench at the ready in one hand, she took her phone in the other and turned on the torch. It did a lousy job of lighting up the space in front of her.

'Jason?' she shouted out. Nothing.

She shone the torch up to her left and right, looking for a light switch. There it was, just a step away on the right. She moved to it, flipped on the lights...

Then noticed the shadow creeping over her shoulder.

Dani spun around, ready to attack with the wrench.

'Whoa! Dani?'

Jason. Her arms flinched but she held back from smashing his head with the wrench. Just.

'Jason, what the hell are you doing here?' she said, ready to collapse from fright.

'Me? What are *you* doing here?' His tone was scathing.

'Tell me what's going on. Please.'

'Why are you here, Dani?'

Was there any point in lying? She quickly explained. The look on his face went from one of confusion and concern to one of outright anger.

When she'd finished he didn't say a word. He just stood there, glaring and shaking his head.

'It's not in here,' he said after a few moments. 'Come on, this way.'

He walked out. Dani hesitated, but only for a moment. She flicked off the lights and closed the door behind her. Outside, Jason was hanging by the corner of the unit in a veil of darkness. She'd never before thought Jason had anything even close to a dark side. Was it the situation or Jason that was creeping her out now?

'Jason, please, just tell me what's going on. You're scaring me.'

'I'm sorry. I'm not meaning to. But you have to see this, Dani. Before anyone else does.'

Jason disappeared around the side of the unit. Dani cautiously followed, though she realised the wrench was now wobbling in her shaky hands.

When she rounded the corner she saw there was a side entrance to the unit.

'It's down here,' Jason said, then headed on through the doorway.

'What's down there?' she asked, her words as shaky as her hands.

'Come on,' he called, his voice echoing.

Despite her nerves, Dani followed him in, down the steps and into a basement level underneath the unit, glancing over her shoulder every other step to make sure there was no one else behind her. There wasn't.

A single overhead light was on in the basement. The space looked like a workshop, filled with all manner of racking and tools.

'Jason?'

He was standing over by one of the shelves with his back to her.

As he turned around, she saw he was wearing plastic gloves.

'Why haven't you called for backup? For forensics?'

'Have you seen this?' he held out his hand. He was clutching a pendant.

Dani didn't move from the spot.

'I've seen photos from Rebecca Hargreaves, of her and Natalya together. Natalya always wore this necklace.'

He placed it back on the shelf then took another item.

'A student's union card for Jessica Bradford,' Jason said.

Dani gulped.

Jason held up a small plastic wallet. 'A railcard for a Grace Agnew.'

Dani was speechless.

'It's all here, Dani. All of it. You were right.'

'Jason.' Dani's voice was strong and stern. 'We have to call this in.'

He shook his head. Took something else from the shelf.

'And this?'

Dani's face fell as she stared at the object in Jason's hand. She felt shock. Anger. Betrayal. Terror. A whole mix of emotions struggled to take hold.

'My diary,' she said. 'But how…?'

But Dani already knew how. It had been taken the day the second note had been left. So someone really had been in her apartment.

Someone. Or was the answer far simpler than that? After all, there were only two people who knew about her diary…

'You know,' Jason said, 'even though I was utterly confused when I saw this here, it was heartening when I started to read through. For a few moments I forgot where I was. What I was doing here. My head was with you again, back in the hospital. Back in the apartment after you'd been sent home. I knew you were writing this at the time, but I never saw your problems through your eyes before.'

The diary had become a real solace for Dani after her TBI. At the suggestion of one of her doctors she'd written at length about her recovery, about her mixed emotions, about her troubles finding herself again and reconnecting with the world and with Jason.

'But then I got to the most recent chapters.'

He tossed the book over to her. She caught it. Confused, she flicked through to the back pages. She hadn't written anything in the diary for months. Not since the day she'd kicked Jason out of her apartment. But sure enough, there was a whole host of new entries she'd not seen before. Dani frowned.

'That's your writing,' Jason said. 'Isn't it?'

Dani said nothing. Was it her writing? It looked like it could be. But she couldn't remember writing any of it. She read some of the gruesome words. Gory details through a killer's eyes. Grace Agnew. Natalya. Jessica Bradford. It was all there.

Her brain started to blur. What was happening to her?

'I didn't do it,' Dani said. 'You must know I didn't kill any of them?'

Jason said nothing.

'You must know it's not me!'

'You're right. I know it wasn't *you*. Not the Dani I know. But—'

'There is no other *me*! I'm not a fucking schizo with split personalities!'

Jason didn't say anything. His silence made her question her own strong words. She wasn't mad. Was she?

'If you need help, Dani… I'm here for you.'

She didn't know what to say. What to do. She dropped the diary and turned for the door. She just had to get out.

'No, Dani!' Jason shouted.

She ran up the stairs, out into the cold night, a thousand thoughts blurring in her mind. She didn't kill those women. She couldn't have. But then… her brother was a murderer. Was there a killer in her too?

With her confused brain consumed by those demented thoughts, she didn't see the figure standing outside until it was too late. She had no time to react as the gloved hand sprang forwards, a small black object sticking out from its grasp. The taser pressed into Dani's side and a surge of electricity rushed through her body, knocking her clean off her feet.

She landed on the cold paving slabs with a painful thud. In a daze, she was only vaguely aware of the sound of a scuffle above her, before another body flopped down right next to her.

Unable to move, Dani stared into Jason's eyes, as both their bodies twitched uncontrollably. She heard but couldn't see the figure move up behind her.

The taser stabbed into her back and the pulse of electricity that surged through her seemed even more powerful than before, sending both her brain and her heart into a panic. Sparks and stars danced in front of Dani's twitching eyes.

But not for long. Seconds later, everything turned black.

Chapter Fifty-Nine

The first thing Dani saw when she opened her eyes was Jason. Her head was bowed forwards and turned to the side. She was sitting on the cold hard floor of the basement, her legs out in front of her. She tried to move, to fully sit up, but realised she couldn't. Her hands were behind her, linked together – metal handcuffs? – and wrapped around a hard object of some kind. A metal pole, was Dani's best guess.

She tried to pull her head up to look around the room but it was heavy, and even moving a few millimetres sent a searing pain through her neck and down her spine. Was that because she'd been sitting in the awkward position for so long, or was it the after effects of the taser?

Dani's eyes remained focused on the forlorn figure of Jason. He was lying on the ground in front of her, his eyes closed, his body hog-tied; wrists and ankles clasped together with plastic cable ties. Two sets, no, three, all linked together. He had a large gash up above his eye; the smear of red blood on his face glistened in the electric light.

The light. It was so bright.

Dani fought through the pain in her body and lifted her head as best she could to survey the room she was in. Was it the same basement still, or a different room altogether? She could just about make out the shelves, a workbench. A single overhead bulb, like before. But that was emitting only a dull orange glow, yet there was a piercing white light in front of her that was almost impossibly bright to look at, like staring into the sun. It was so bright and glaring that Dani couldn't even see where exactly in front of her it was coming from, and she could see nothing of what lay beyond.

'Jason,' Dani murmured, looking back at him, her tongue and lips struggling to form the word. She focused, tried again. 'Jason. Can you hear me?'

She saw the slightest of twitches from him. Heard the slightest of groans.

Then she heard a noise from across the room in front of her. Dani's head whipped around and she cringed in pain.

'Who's there?'

Nothing. Silence.

'Who the fuck are you?' Dani screamed, finding a strength that surprised her.

She heard a long but calm sigh. Then movement. The first thing she saw were the shoes. Shining brown loafers. Because of the position of that bright spotlight Dani could make out nothing of the figure the shoes belonged to. Not until he took two more steps forwards. Finally his whole body was visible, the spotlight now on his back and creating a long shadow that swept forwards onto Dani.

She looked up into his eyes. She'd never met him in person, but she'd seen enough pictures of him to recognise him instantly.

It was Ethan Grant.

Chapter Sixty

'DI Stephens,' Ethan said, his manner calm and confident, though his face was twisted in a grimace as he stared at Dani. 'I understand you've been looking for me.'

Dani's mind whirred with so many conflicting questions that nothing would stick.

'So what's the plan?' she said, sounding way more direct and focussed than she had any right to be. 'You set me up for killing Reeve already. Now those poor women too?'

Ethan laughed. 'You mean the diary? Do you like that touch? When I starting reading it in your apartment, I just knew what I had to do with it. I mean, look at you. You're so fucked up. I bet even you thought for a few moments that maybe you really were a murderer. Like your loser brother.'

Dani winced. Ethan was right. She had doubted herself when she'd read those gruesome words in her diary.

Ethan moved over to the workbench off to his right where a variety of tools were laid out. A large glass jar half filled with clear liquid was on the worktop. Grim thoughts fired through Dani's mind. Her conversations about serial killers with Steven Grant replayed in her head. Methods for disposing of bodies. How a killer could leave no trace.

But Ethan Grant was barely an adult. Could he really do such a thing?

Dani looked down at Jason. His eyes were still closed. Was he conscious? Did he understand what was happening?

'You've got a lot to be thankful to DI Barnes for,' Ethan said as he turned back to face her. 'I felt sure that by now you would have been locked up for Paul Reeve's murder, and I can only assume it's *his* blind love for you which has saved your skin. For now. Unfortunately, the reward for DI Barnes's loyalty isn't quite going to be what he hoped for.'

'You're fucking crazy,' Dani said. 'No one will believe this.'

'Believe what? That the twin sister of a sociopath is herself a sociopath? It's not so hard to comprehend really. No, you're one crazy bitch all right. Not only did you kill Paul Reeve and three innocent young women – quite why, no one really knows – but when the heat on you got too much you turned on your former boyfriend. After that… you just disappeared.'

The finality with which Ethan Grant delivered that final word sent a chill right into Dani's core.

Ethan grabbed an object from the workbench he was standing by. A wallet? He started flipping through the contents. He put it down and picked up a thick rubber glove, then took the wallet and stepped over to the glass jar and lifted off the lid.

'You're going to like this next bit.'

Ethan moved the wallet down inside the jar and as it touched the liquid it began to foam and froth as the acid ate away at the material. Ethan looked at Dani, smiling when he saw the look of horror on her face. He carefully dropped the wallet into the jar and placed the lid back on top as the acid consumed the remainder of the object.

'Quite something, isn't it?' Ethan said. 'Dani Stephens, serial killer. Disappeared into the night.'

'Tell me, Ethan,' Dani said. 'How many people have you killed exactly?'

The continued strength in her voice surprised Dani, as did the question itself. Of all the burning questions she could ask in that moment, she really wasn't sure why that was the first to come from her lips. Was she simply looking to latch onto facts and concrete information, to help her try and work out and make sense of the whole situation?

But the reality was that Ethan Grant was a teenager still, had only recently left home, and even before he opened his mouth to answer, that realisation caused a horrible feeling to creep over Dani.

'Just two, actually,' Ethan said. He winked at Dani. 'So far, that is.'

Thoughts crashed through Dani's weary brain.

'Natalya,' Dani said as the pieces started to fall together and Steven Grant's words echoed in her mind once more. 'And Reeve? But not the others.'

Ethan's slight grin told her the answer. Dani frowned, still deep in thought as the sequence of events continued to take shape in her mind. She thought through everything that had happened over the last few days. The last few months, even. The turmoil she'd gone through because of what her brother had done. The feelings of guilt and shame and anger and that need for revenge and to lash out that she'd tried so hard to keep hidden away. She thought about the visits to see Ben, the conversations and ideas about what made him a killer. She thought of Reeve and Natalya, their pale bodies in the morgue. The other bodies – Jessica Bradford, Grace Agnew, others? – who hadn't been found. Lastly, she thought of those conversations she'd had with Steven Grant, the murder expert.

Steven Grant. The murder expert. The damaged soul.

'There's someone who's been waiting to say hello,' Ethan said, as though he'd been party to Dani's thoughts.

He turned and crept out of sight. Dani heard the door at the top of the stairs open and close, and then all was silent.

She wasn't going to sit there and wait for the next act. She squirmed and bucked against her restraints. No, there was simply no way she could get free of the cuffs on her wrists.

But Jason on the other hand...

'Jason!' Dani hissed, her voice a loud whisper. She was quite sure they were now alone in the room but she remained cautious nonetheless.

Not even a murmur from Jason.

'Jason, wake up!' Dani said.

If she could wake him, he could help. He only had simple cable ties securing his wrists and ankles. Yes, those things were damn secure, but if you knew how…

And Dani did.

The only problem was, Jason was out of it.

Was he drugged?

'Jason, please,' Dani said, her voice pleading and desperate.

He shivered and opened his eyes a fraction. His hands twitched.

'Please,' Dani said again.

Then she heard the door opening, somewhere beyond the spotlight. She heard footfalls, coming down the steps. More than one set.

Moments later Ethan Grant came back into view, a horrible smirk on his face.

'DI Stephens… oh, and DI Barnes too. You're awake. Well, that's great, you're just in time.'

Dani looked down at Jason. His eyes were now fully open but he remained listless. She looked back up to Ethan. She'd already prepared herself for the face of the person who would step forwards next to him.

But how wrong she was.

The figure came into view.

Not Steven Grant at all, but his wife, Mary.

Chapter Sixty-One

Mary stepped forward in front of her son.

'What the fuck is going on here?' Jason slurred, finally coming around to the reality of the situation.

Mary looked from Dani and down to him.

'Did Dani not fill you in?' she said. 'And I thought you two were playing so nicely together.'

'You?' was the only word that came out of Dani's lips.

Mary raised an eyebrow and shook her head. 'Wow, you must have thought long and hard about that one.'

'I… I don't get it,' Dani said.

'Well of course you don't, Detective. That's why you're sitting on the floor like that, and why I'm not.'

Dani again looked down at Jason. He was shaking his head in confusion, but at least he appeared more lucid now. Jason was their only hope of getting out alive.

'Does Steven know what you're going to do to me?' Dani asked.

Steven Grant. Dani had been certain that it would be him making the grand entrance. After all, he had a morbid interest in murderers. He had a direct connection to Jessica Bradford, which he'd lied to Dani about. He had first-hand experience of being at the mercy of a killer. Did he know what Mary was?

'Steven?' Mary said, a little perturbed. 'You're on first name terms with my husband now? Does DI Barnes know you've developed something of a crush on the professor? Or was it not my husband, but the subject of death that pulled you in?'

Dani again thought back to her conversations with Grant. What makes a killer? Nature or nurture. The answer was complex. Impossible to test. Yet Dani saw a slim window of opportunity.

She knew what she had to do.

'Ethan,' Dani said. 'Don't let her do this. Don't follow her path.'

'I know you didn't mean to kill Natalya. It was a mistake.'

Dani saw Ethan clenching his jaw. She was right. 'She was your first, wasn't she? What happened, Ethan? Did you get scared? Did you panic and give her the opportunity to escape?'

Mary turned to Ethan who gave his mother a sheepish look. He held his tongue.

'You had no choice but to kill her in the open. And then Reeve? Were you trying to cover your tracks? Hoping the police would link the deaths and put them down to gang violence? Why? Was Reeve getting too close to the truth?' The flinch on Ethan's face suggested perhaps that was the answer. 'What about Harland? Did he know too?'

'Dean?' Ethan said. 'No, DI Stephens, his death is on you, not me.'

'Well done,' Mary said. 'Very perceptive, Dani. You're right, I've been working with Ethan, *trying* to teach him. But he's so impatient. And naturally, he has his own views and ideas. He just needs reining in sometimes. What happened with that young girl… he very nearly ruined everything. Until *you* came into the mix. It's just a shame for you that you've figured all this out too late.'

'Ethan. You're not like *her*!'

'Oh, come off it,' Mary scolded. 'You're not going to suddenly break through to him. This is what he is.'

Dani stared at Ethan and the blank stare he gave Dani in return was almost lifeless. Except for a faint flicker of something. Regret?

'Ethan's always been trouble,' Mary continued, then she sighed. 'He's always been *my son*. There's nothing we, or he, can do about that. It might have taken him some time to realise the truth, but now he knows. He's not going to fight against it anymore.'

Yet Dani had seen something in Ethan's eyes. She was certain she had.

'This next part should be of interest to you, Dani,' Mary said. 'I—'

A piercing chime cut Mary off and she glared over to her side. She took two steps forwards and Dani caught a glimpse of a faint light coming from one of the shelves. The source of the light was concealed by boxes and plastic containers. What was it? A small CCTV monitor?

'What is *he* doing here?' Ethan said, sounding more exasperated than anything else as he looked over his mother's shoulder.

Mary remained unflustered though it was clear the interruption was not welcome.

'Let me deal with this,' Mary said as she turned away. 'If either of them move, kill them. It'd be a shame to spoil the best part, but we never take chances.'

Ethan nodded and Mary moved out of sight. Dani heard her walking up the stairs and then opening and closing the outer door.

'Ethan, who is it?' Dani asked. 'Who's here?'

Ethan said nothing. He pulled out a metal chair and sat down, then glared over at Dani.

'Your dad?'

Ethan shook his head slowly.

'The police?'

Ethan smiled and shrugged.

'They're going to catch up with you sooner or later. You must realise that? Even if I don't make it out of this alive, you can see how close we've come. We won't be the last.'

'No. You won't be the last. You're right about that.'

'You don't have to do this. You're not a killer, Ethan. Don't let her corrupt you like that. She's insane!'

'I used to think that too,' Ethan said. 'Do you know how old I was when I found out the truth?'

Dani didn't answer.

'I was fourteen. I'm not sure I was supposed to, but I could almost sense Mum's relief. But I was confused. For a long time. Can you imagine the fights we've had over the years? But I know now that it wasn't me fighting with her. Not really. It was me fighting with myself. I've been in denial for too long. I *am* just like her. I was born this way, and there's nothing I can do about it.'

'That's not true, Ethan. It's simply not true. There's always a choice. Always another way. And your dad? He's not a killer. You're as much him as you are *her*.'

Ethan's face took on a hard edge at the mention of his dad. What did that look mean?

Dani looked over at Jason. He'd been so quiet through the conversation. Too quiet. Dani soon saw why. She knew exactly how to break through plastic cable ties. The most obvious way was to cut through them. But really you didn't need a saw or a knife or anything as heavy duty as that. A bog standard shoelace would do the trick if you created enough tension. It was one of the many survival techniques Dani had picked up over the years, which she'd become even more interested in following her near-death experience at the hands of her own brother.

It seemed Jason knew a thing or two as well. While Dani was talking, he was discreetly working on the cable tie between his wrists. Dani had to keep Ethan distracted.

'But how does she do it?' she asked.

'Do what?'

Dani looked over at the glass jar on the workbench, which was on the other side of the room to where Jason was.

'You're not going to get rid of a body with that, are you?' Dani said. 'You couldn't even fit an arm in there. So where's the rest?'

'Well that's the thing,' Ethan said. 'This is what *you* get to see. A glimpse of your fate. It's for aesthetic purposes more than anything.'

'And for your twisted pleasure.'

'Something like that. I hate to break it to you, but you won't leave this room alive. Though you will leave it resembling a human being.'

'So this is just where you imprison your poor victims. Why? Just to humiliate them?'

Ethan said nothing to that.

'You take the bodies out of here and dispose of them somewhere else?' Dani said, thinking furiously. 'Surely that just increases the chances of you making mistakes? You're leaving evidence here, there and everywhere, Ethan. You're taking unnecessary risks. You must know you're going to get caught eventually?'

'Really? Then why has no one figured it out yet, then? I'd say, as a plan, it's pretty well oiled.'

'And you really think *you* can go through with it all? You stabbed Natalya and Reeve to death, but those were simple, frenzied attacks. You fucked up. Do you really think you can hack a body apart and then carefully and precisely dispose of each part without making more mistakes?'

'I wouldn't be here if I didn't,' Ethan said, quite coldly. 'I'm used to dead bodies, Detective. It's not something that many fourteen-year-olds have to see, but as a boy it *was* something I became used to. Too used to.'

'Ethan, you must realise that's not *ok*. No teenage boy should have to witness that!'

'She didn't mean for me to see. But it's one of those memories that never dulls. A defining moment. You know the strangest part? I wasn't even that scared. To this day I don't even know whose body it was. That was never important.'

Dani daren't look at Jason. She didn't want to do anything to alert Ethan, but she could see small movements out of the corner of her eye. She had to keep Ethan talking.

'Natalya. Her death makes sense,' Dani said. 'You had her down here, but she escaped. But Reeve? What happened, Ethan?'

Ethan gave her a resolute look but said nothing.

'Did he see something he shouldn't have?' Dani asked. 'Or was it that he was suspicious because two women he'd known were killed?'

Still Ethan said nothing, though the steady look on his face suggested perhaps Dani's deduction on Reeve was right. But Ethan wasn't going to give her anything more on that subject. She had to try something else.

'I can't believe this is what your dad wants for you.'

'You know nothing about him,' Ethan sneered, Dani doing her best to try and hide her relief that she'd got him talking once more.

'Actually I think I do,' Dani said. 'I know what he went through. And you have a sister too, don't you? Surely she's not part of this?'

'Annie? What makes you so sure she's different? She's young, but she'll be part of this if that's what Mum wants.'

Dani shook her head in disbelief.

'Does your dad know?'

Ethan didn't answer. It seemed like he was about to look down to Jason…

Dani burst out laughing and Ethan's eyes fixed on her in a cold stare.

'Your dad. Is that why your mum married him? Because of his past? Because he was a victim of a murderer?'

Once again Ethan said nothing.

'Fuck, Ethan, she's so twisted. Your dad is nothing but another plaything for her. And she's probably been using his knowledge of killers all this time just to keep one step ahead. Ethan, she's crazy. But you can still save yourself. Save your sister from that life too.'

'I'm not stupid,' Ethan suddenly said. His eyes were still fixed on Dani's, but she realised straight away that his words weren't aimed at her. 'DI Barnes. I'm talking to you.'

Dani's heart pounded. Before another word was spoken, Jason jumped to his feet. Dani was still looking over at Ethan. She saw his hand move for the jar.

'No!' Dani screamed.

She wasn't sure if her instruction had been for Ethan or Jason, but she knew what was coming. Ethan's hand reached behind the jar and he swept it forwards. The open container hurtled off the workbench. All manner of horrors flashed before Dani's eyes. Jason was no slouch though. He must have known what Ethan was planning.

Jason ducked, sidestepped and held up his arm as the jar flew through the air towards him. The glass brushed his side and smashed to the ground and acid sprayed everywhere, fizzing and spitting against anything it touched. Jason roared in pain as his clothes sizzled and frothed, but he didn't stop moving. He barrelled into Ethan and the two of them tumbled to the floor, knocking over the spotlight in the process. For the first time Dani could properly make out the small, dank space in front of her again.

Dani felt burning and looked down at her foot. Her shoe was sizzling, the leather bubbling up and melting. Dani screamed and heaved her legs into her body, away from the creeping acid on the floor. She kicked her shoes against each other, trying to remove them. She managed it, but the deadly mixture had already eaten a patch of her sock underneath and all that remained of the skin below was a bloody red mess.

The pain was immense, but Dani was in pure survival mode. Superficial acid burns wouldn't stop her, and it seemed they weren't about to stop Jason either. He was grappling with Ethan on the floor. Dani couldn't tell how badly burned Jason was, but he was fighting with animal instinct. He somehow wormed his way on top of Ethan and, despite the younger man's attempts to get him off, Jason rained blows down onto Ethan's head.

Then, as it looked like Ethan may have the strength to shake his foe off, Jason decided to fight dirty. He grabbed Ethan's head and slammed it on the concrete floor beneath them. Once. Twice. Three times.

Ethan's eyes rolled. He was either dead or unconscious.

The next second Jason jumped up. He remained where he was, staring down at Ethan while his chest heaved in and out. He was in a trance. But they had no time to dwell. Mary would be back any second.

'Jason, get me the fuck out of here!'

Chapter Sixty-Two

Jason pulled himself away from Ethan Grant. He looked at Dani and then carefully moved around the spilled acid and over to her. Dani could see now that the acid had burned away much of his clothes down one side. The bloody, pulpy mess underneath was clearly evident. Yet he almost seemed oblivious as he moved forwards towards Dani with purpose. He was running on nothing but adrenaline.

He crouched down and tugged at her hands.

'I can't get these off,' Jason said. 'I'll go and get help.'

'No!' Dani said 'You're not leaving me here alone. You can't.'

'I'm not sure what else to do!'

'Stand by the fucking door with a wrench in your hand. Take her damn head off when she comes back in!'

Jason huffed at that.

'Over there,' Dani said, nodding into the far corner where some of the racking looked like it contained tools. 'There must be something you can use to pick the cuffs.'

'I've never done that before,' Jason said.

'No, but I'm guessing you've never sawn through plastic cable ties with a shoelace while hog-tied either?'

'No. But I did see the YouTube video for that one.'

Jason almost smiled.

'And I've seen plenty on how to pick locks. Come on, Jason, hurry!'

He stood and jumped over the acid pool and limped to the corner. After rattling about for a few seconds, he turned around.

'Even better,' he said, holding up a set of bolt cutters.

He gingerly moved back over and behind Dani. She heard him straining as he heaved down on the cutters. There was a crunching sound and Dani pulled at her wrists but they were still held firmly together.

'Jason?'

'Fuck's sake. Those things bent the cutters. But… just let me try one more time.'

Jason heaved again and this time she heard a snap. But when she pulled her hands, she still couldn't move them forwards.

The next thing she knew the cutters were hurtling through the air in front of her. They clattered against the racking at the end of the room.

'Useless!' Jason shouted. He came back in front of Dani, his face contorted in a painful grimace as he clutched his stricken side with his good arm. 'The chain is almost cut through, you can probably pull them off now, but you need to work them properly.'

Jason quickly explained the technique, which was much the same as an alternative technique for snapping cable ties. He instructed her to pull the cuffs down, twist the wrists so her palms were facing outwards, then pull out and down in one sharp motion.

'Got it,' Dani said. She'd seen those videos too.

She tried and cried out in pain when all that happened was that the cuffs dug into the flesh on her wrists.

'It's almost there, Dani, do it again.'

She pulled and tugged again. No luck. Then again and again. She felt blood pouring down over her hands and her fingers. The pain was making her delirious. She imagined the flesh on her wrists peeled right back.

But she had no choice. She had to keep trying.

'One more time!' Jason said.

Then she saw Ethan move. His eyelids flickered. Then opened. He began to shift, like a coiled snake waiting to unfurl.

'Dani, come on!' Jason shouted.

Tears streaming, Dani heaved one more time and her hands shot forwards in front of her. Before she could even process relief or the pain that was now consuming her, Ethan Grant was up on his feet, rage in his eyes.

Dani lunged for him.

They clattered to the floor and Ethan screamed as he landed in the acid. There was ferocious anger in his eyes. Even though Dani was on top he grabbed her neck and began to choke her. His strength was too much. She couldn't breathe at all.

She stared into his evil eyes. In desperation, Dani channeled the inner rage that had eaten away at her over the last two years and pushed her thumbs into Ethan's eye sockets, using every ounce of animal strength she had. The inner rage that had been such a detriment to her life over the last two years was breaking out.

She wouldn't try to stop it this time.

She pushed with her thumbs as hard as she could, venom and hatred bursting from her. Blood oozed out of Ethan's eye sockets.

'Dani!' Jason shouted.

She barely heard him. She crashed Ethan's head into the floor again and again. It was a scene of bloody horror. Dani would never have imagined she could stand to even watch something like that, never mind do it.

But she could. Because she knew for damn sure that Ethan Grant deserved no better.

Jason had grabbed hold of her trying to pull her up and away. Eventually he managed it.

Dani clambered to her feet. Ethan's eyes were now two dark holes. Blood streamed from them. Dani thumped her heel down into Ethan's face then kicked him in the side and used her foot to heave him over. The side of his face landed in the bubbling pool of acid and he found the strength to scream as the skin and flesh on his cheek fizzed and melted.

Not long after that, the screaming stopped. Ethan Grant went silent and still.

'Dani, we have to go.'

Dani tried to clear the torment from her mind. She nodded.

As they ran for the staircase at the far end, Dani suddenly changed course. She moved over and grabbed the broken cutters. The blade mechanism was wrecked but it was still a big lump of metal.

They moved cautiously up the stairs then stopped at the closed door. Jason looked at Dani. She nodded and held up the cutters. Jason pulled on the handle and crashed open the door.

They barrelled out into the night. But everything was dark and quiet.

Jason stepped forwards past her.

'Mary, no!' Dani heard a man call out. Steven Grant?

There was a crackle of static and Jason collapsed to the ground.

Dani spun around, saw the dark object coming towards her chest and dodged it, rolling down onto the ground. She sprang back up, arced the cutters behind her and swung forwards ferociously. The contact was solid and sent a jolt up her arm and into her neck.

There was a thud as the figure collapsed to the ground. Dani didn't let up. She lifted the cutters above her head, swung down and crashed the metal onto the fallen figure. There was a sickly crack and squelch as the metal smashed into the target.

'No, Dani, stop!'

Dani spun around again, to where the voice had come from.

'Whoa, whoa, Dani.'

She paused. It was Steven Grant. He held his empty hands up in the air. His face was panicked.

'It's ok, Dani. It's me. I'm here to help you.'

Dani said nothing, just held the cutters aloft, ready to strike again. Grant held out a hand to Dani, but she wasn't buying his good samaritan act. She edged backwards, moving closer to where Jason was groaning on the floor. She looked across at the figure she'd felled. It was hard to see clearly in the darkness, but she was sure it was Mary. Whether she was alive or not, Dani had no clue.

'You stay away from me,' she said to Grant.

'Dani? Come on, it's me. I'm not going to hurt you.'

'No. You leave that to your bitch of a wife and your low-life son.'

Even in the darkness, Dani saw the twitch on Grant's face. A chink in his accommodating facade?

'I came here to stop her. To stop them both. You have to believe me. This isn't what I want.'

'How did you even know we were here?' Dani asked. A wave of revulsion washed through her. She'd sat as a guest in his home just days before. Had he known then what Mary was planning?

'Ethan told me!' Grant said. 'Seriously, Dani, you have to believe me. Why else would I turn up like this? What do you think Mary and I were doing just now? She didn't know I was coming. We were arguing. I was telling her she had to stop. She had to turn herself in!'

'But did you know!' Dani screamed, so hard it made her lungs burn. 'How many other people has she killed?'

Grant didn't have an answer for that.

'And Ethan?' Dani said. 'Nature versus nurture, right?'

'He's my son,' Grant said. '*Our* son.'

'But you don't need to worry about Ethan anymore,' Dani said with a sneer. 'He won't cause trouble for anyone now.'

Grant's face twitched again. He knew what she meant. And Dani knew she was playing a dangerous game taunting him like that. But she had to push. Because if there was any chance he really hadn't known about his wife and son's dark secrets, and that he really did want to help – a flicker of hope – then she had to find out, and fast.

Grant took a step forwards. Dani tightened her grip on the bolt cutters further.

'Another step and I'll smash this into your skull,' she said. 'Then I'll do it again and again until I'm certain you can't hurt me anymore.'

'Dani, I'm here to help. I really am. Please, let me.'

Hearing a murmur, Dani turned to Jason. His face was covered in blood. The open wound he'd already had up above his eye was now gaping.

'Jason?'

Dani bent down and shook him gently, one eye still on Grant. He bent down next to Mary who was unmoving.

'Don't touch her!' Dani shouted, straightening back up.

'I need to see if she's ok!'

'No. You don't.'

Grant slowly rose back to his feet, his face creased with anger. Mary still didn't move at all.

'Jason, come on, you need to get up,' Dani prodded him with her foot.

'I can help,' Grant said. 'My car's here. I'll get you both away.'

Jason went to sit up and Dani bent down again and put her hand under his armpit to help haul him up, the cutters still gripped tightly in her other hand. Despite his increasingly battered body, Jason was coming around again and was soon able to take his own weight. Dani took a quick glance around her. She spotted Grant's car parked between hers and Jason's. She had no idea where her own keys were.

'Take out your car keys and throw them over,' Dani said.

Grant didn't respond.

'Give me something, Steven. For fuck's sake, your wife is a murderer and was about to chop us up and dissolve our bodies! If you really want me to believe that you're here to help then you need to do as I say.'

'Fine. Fine,' he said. He reached into his trouser pocket, pulled out a set of keys and tossed them over. They bounced off Jason's leg and onto the floor.

'We're going now,' Dani said. 'Don't try to follow us.'

Grant didn't move or even respond.

'Maybe you should go and check on your son,' Jason said, as he bent down to pick up the keys. 'At least, what's left of him.'

Dani saw the look on Grant's face change, rage bursting through. He lunged forwards.

'Jason!'

But Jason was too injured. He tried to defend himself, but it only took a simple stab from Grant, the taser gripped in his outstretched hand – had he picked it up from Mary?

Jason's body pulsed as it crumpled to the ground once more.

Dani surged forwards, a cry of fury erupting as she swung the cutters through the air. Grant had enough time to lift his arm up to protect his head but the huge impact still sent him reeling back and he shouted out in pain. The blow had been easily hard enough to shatter the bones of his lower arm.

The taser clattered away. But Grant wasn't finished. With Dani's body still twisted from the momentum of the blow, Grant barrelled into her midriff and they both tumbled to the floor and Dani lost grip of the cutters.

Her head smacked off the concrete and her vision blurred. She tried to move but couldn't. The slivers of moonlight coming through the tall windows of the warehouse danced in front of her.

'He's my son,' Grant said, tears rolling down his cheeks. 'My only son.'

Dazed, Dani's vision blurred. Ben? Standing over her. That hideous ornament in his hand that he'd tried to kill her with. She'd been lying on the floor then, in the lounge of the home he'd shared with his wife and kids. He'd wanted to kill Dani. He'd bludgeoned her. But he'd never checked that she was dead before rushing off to kill Gemma. He should have made sure he finished her off.

Suddenly the image – hallucination? – flickered and Dani realised it wasn't Ben standing over her, but Steven Grant. And he wasn't about to make the same mistake as Ben had. His face was creased with venom. She'd killed his son. Had she killed Mary too? It didn't matter what Ethan and his mother were. Steven Grant still loved them. He lifted the bolt cutters above his head…

Then his eyes widened and his body jerked and jolted. He lurched forwards, much like Jason had moments earlier when he'd been tasered. He kept coming. Right for Dani.

All she could do as Steven Grant descended upon her was to hold up a hand to her face. It did little to soften the blow as Grant's heavy body slammed down onto her, winding her in the process, and sending her to the brink of unconsciousness.

She couldn't breathe. Grant's listless mass was covering her face. She began to drift. She was going to suffocate.

Then she heard a muffled voice that gave her the focus she needed.

'Dani. Are you ok?'

Jason.

Chapter Sixty-Three

Two months later

'You'll receive a formal letter confirming the decision shortly,' McNair said.

Dani nodded in response, her eyes flicking between her boss and Chief Superintendent Baxter who were both sat over the other side of the desk in the meeting room. The internal investigation into Dean Harland's death had been concluded in her favour. The investigation had found that Harland, along with Reeve, was a low-level drug dealer with a history of criminality, which was the likely explanation for why he had run from Dani that fateful day.

The witness evidence against Dani had been disregarded after several inconsistencies were identified, not in the least the fact the witnesses all turned out to be associates of Harland and Reeve and Grant, and most of them hadn't even been in the area at the time. Ultimately Professional Standards had determined that Dani's actions, under the circumstances, were reasonable and justified. Dani wondered if what had happened recently out at that warehouse had had any bearing on the result. After all, the investigation into the deaths of Mary Grant and Ethan Grant was still only just getting started. Perhaps the police thought the circumstances of their deaths would be a clear-cut opportunity to remove Dani from the force. Unlike her son, Mary had been pulled from the scene in Moseley alive, but brain dead from the blows to the head. Her life support had been turned off a few days afterwards and her death, like that of her son, had to be investigated.

'Is he talking yet?' Dani asked.

'Who?'

'Steven Grant.'

Baxter and McNair shared a look, as though weighing up whether they were prepared to tell Dani anything.

'Not really,' Baxter said, his decision to answer the question rather than brush it off taking Dani by surprise. 'Of course there's going to be a lengthy investigation into how many victims Mary Grant killed over the years, and we'll likely need to look beyond the West Midlands, given she only moved here in her thirties—'

'You think she was a killer even before she met Grant?'

'At this stage we honestly don't know. Though I would say her choice of husband is quite telling, wouldn't you?'

Dani certainly would. She'd had the same thought back on that fateful night. Had Mary chosen Grant because she took some twisted pleasure in knowing his dark past? Similarly, was that the reason why Dani was apparently chosen for those notes and to be set-up for the murders?

'Quite ironic really that the one man who could help us to analyse and explain the things that Mary and Ethan have done is keeping his mouth shut out of loyalty to his dead wife and son,' Dani said.

'We'll keep trying,' Baxter said. 'Perhaps Grant will have second thoughts on his silent treatment when he realises just how long he's going to be behind bars.'

'You know, it's almost poetic justice that Mary spent so long trying to convince her son that he was a natural born killer, only for him to blow the whole operation open.'

'How do you mean?'

'Reeve and Natalya. They weren't Mary's M.O., and the killings weren't to her standards, not by far. Ethan was raw and naive. I'd bet anything those notes I received were from him. To Ethan Grant this was all a sick game. He was impulsive and reckless, compared to Mary's cold calculation.'

'Ok, DI Stephens, I think I need to stop you there,' Baxter said, sounding more stern now. 'You know of course that the investigation into the Grants is at a very early stage and we'll be taking formal statements from you in due course. I'd caution you to not go spouting your conjecture any further outside these walls.'

Dani's cheeks reddened. She got the point. As in the case of Harland, Ethan and Mary had died at the hands of an active officer, and their deaths, and her conduct, had to be thoroughly investigated, no matter who the dead people were, or what they'd done.

The fact was, she didn't feel in the least bit bad that both Ethan and Mary Grant were no longer breathing. As far as Dani was concerned they both got what they deserved, and she'd simply been fighting for her life in those moments at the warehouse. Would that be the police's ultimate conclusion too?

'Though…' Baxter said, before taking a large inhalation. 'I shouldn't really say this, but I've got your back, Stephens. Everyone knows what happened and appreciates what you did. I'm sure the IOPC will come to the right conclusion.'

The comment flummoxed Dani and for a few seconds she just stared at Baxter.

'Well, go on then,' he said. 'I have got other things to do today. McNair will show you out.'

'Yes, sir. Thank you, sir.'

Dani got to her feet and headed for the door. With McNair at her side they walked in silence along the corridor of the top floor of HQ to the lifts.

'Can we stop on the second floor?' Dani asked when they stepped inside the lift.

'I'm supposed to take you down to reception.'

'And you will. But I want to wait for Barnes first. Please?'

'Sorry, Dani.'

Dani sighed but didn't bother to push.

On the ground floor McNair showed Dani through the security gates then made herself scarce. Dani sat down and was waiting for less than ten minutes before Jason appeared, coming out of one of the lifts beyond the gates. He wasn't alone. A casually dressed man was walking with him. Dani had to double take when she realised who it was. Ed Francis.

Or, to give him his real name, DS Kendrick – an undercover officer from DCI Fairclough's Organised Crime team. Jason had been brought into the loop on the day he'd gone to Francis's – Kendrick's – house, after Kendrick had called to inform Jason that he'd spotted Ethan Grant returning to the family home.

From what she'd been told by Jason – well, no one else was telling her anything, were they? – Fairclough's team were investigating a drug ring. Call it coincidence that the top dogs in that ring were the players supplying Reeve and Harland, and Ethan Grant had been on their radar because of that, even before Natalya and Reeve were killed. Their apparent previous lack of interest in the murder cases was out of their desire to protect their ongoing undercover operation.

Obviously they'd no idea exactly what the Grants were. Kendrick had been trying to get close to Steven Grant because they thought he was involved with the gang. He was under suspicion for money laundering, of all things. Apparently Ethan Grant wasn't too careful with how he was using mummy and daddy's money, and several of their bank accounts and investments had been flagged up for investigation. Which was in part how Jason had eventually traced the fact that Mary Grant was the owner of that warehouse, through a whole series of offshore shell entities. All of this had come to a head that night when Jason had arranged to meet with Kendrick to discuss the findings.

Kendrick shook Jason's hand then scuttled back off towards the lifts and Jason came limping over to Dani. As well as surface burns to his skin and the gash above his eye, the muscles on his left leg had been damaged too. He'd been out of hospital little more than two weeks. The skin grafts were still healing, though they appeared to have been a success.

He'd taken a battering, that was for sure. As had Dani. Many people had commented that it was a miracle they'd both survived.

Dani had never believed in miracles. Maybe it was about time she did.

Jason gave her a half smile when he reached her. His face certainly looked far more at ease than it had two hours earlier when he'd gone into his own disciplinary briefing.

'I thought you were supposed to be having a disciplinary meeting,' Dani said. 'Not catching up with undercovers?'

Jason smiled. 'I was. But I saw Fairclough and Kendrick by chance after. They didn't say this exactly, but my sense is that the whole force is rooting for us on this one.'

Dani said nothing to that. She was thoroughly confused by the change of heart towards her. But then that was police politics. If it worked out in her favour this time, she wouldn't argue.

Across the way, Dani saw Easton. He waved to her to get her attention and gave her a half smile. Dani looked at Jason who just shrugged. Easton came over.

'Dani…'

'Aaron. Long time no see.'

'Yeah,' he rubbed the back of his neck. 'Dani, I'm sorry. About everything. I was just—'

'You were just doing what McNair told you to. I get it.'

'No hard feelings?'

'Why would there be?'

Easton gave her another sheepish look. He glanced at Jason who just nodded.

'See you around?' Easton said to Dani.

'You never know.'

He turned and headed back towards the security gates.

'Come on,' Jason said. 'Let's get you home.'

Chapter Sixty-Four

This is the first entry in my new diary that Jason has bought me. I came to depend on the last one so much during my recovery. I realise now that the release of writing about my life helps me to escape the many torments I've had to endure. Writing in this new diary will help me as my recovery continues.

As I'm writing this, I stare out of the window across the canals and the numerous other blocks of new-build apartments. It's the last time I'll do so. At one time I felt proud and happy living in this apartment, but there are too many scars, too many bad memories now to ever go back. I need to go forwards.

The intercom rings and I peel myself away. I walk into the hall and look at the screen. Jason.

I buzz him in, then stare at the screen as I always do now. After a few seconds it goes blank. No one has followed him in.

I stand by the door, waiting for him, an uncomfortable feeling enveloping me. I hear the lift clunking away. I hear the doors opening. When I hear the footsteps in the corridor I grab the wrench from the sideboard. I hold it tightly in both hands and wait for the soft rap on the door.

Will I ever shake off this paranoia?

'Jason?' I say.

'Yeah. It's me.'

I look into the peephole. He's standing back, in clear view. He knows all about my new habits. He looks left and right then smiles at me. I take one hand from the wrench and unlock, then open, the door.

'It's ok,' he says. 'Ready for the last supper?'

He holds up the bag containing our dinner. I glance past him, along the corridor, one last check to make sure he's definitely alone. I nod and step back to let him in. When he's inside with the door shut I finally put the wrench down on the floor. That's where it'll stay. I'm not taking that with me.

After we've finished our food we head back to the hallway. Jason goes to pick up the largest of the three packed suitcases. He groans as he picks it up.

'You sure you can manage that?' I ask, genuinely concerned for him.

'Yeah,' he says, his voice sounding strained. 'One side of me is good, at least.'

I grab the other two cases and Jason opens the door. I look around the empty space of my apartment one more time. Then I walk out.

We make our way along the corridor towards the lift.

'Steven Grant was released from hospital this morning,' Jason says.

'How do you know that?' I ask.

'Baxter told me. They're going to charge him with murder. The CPS think he was close enough to the crimes to be considered a direct accomplice.'

I say nothing to that. Grant has never admitted to knowing about Mary and Ethan's crimes. I don't know what the truth is, but I'll watch keenly to see what plays out at trial.

I feel little pride in having brought an end to Mary Grant's reign of terror. Just sadness and frustration that we may never know the full truth about who she killed. Grace Agnew? Jessica Bradford? The evidence found in the warehouse suggests they were likely her last victims, together with Paul Reeve and Natalya, whose lives were taken by Ethan's less experienced hands. But how many came before them?

More importantly, why?

Perhaps she was a natural-born killer. It was in her DNA. Steven Grant himself might have explained that to be the case. The same for his own son. The apple doesn't fall far from the tree, after all, although there is no doubt in my mind that Ethan was nothing like the monster that his mother was. To Ethan Grant, killing was a game. He taunted me with those notes, and in trying to make me take the fall for his mistakes. I don't think he ever understood the seriousness of what he was involved in, perhaps because he'd been brainwashed at such a young age, and violence and killing was normalised for him. Mary Grant on the other hand...

was she the epitome of true evil? To her, killing was a way of life. A source of power and satisfaction, despite the fact that no one knew of her existence as a killer until her son began to draw attention.

What about Annie Grant? She's just a teenage girl, and a good kid from what I hear. She's currently under the care of Grant's sister and her husband who live not far from Birmingham. I wonder, and in many ways, fear what will become of her. Even if she is 'normal', how can her life ever recover from what has happened?

I know one thing for sure, I'll be keeping a close eye on her fate.

And what does all this mean for me? My brother, too, is a killer, and now I've taken two lives with my own hands. Was that pure survival? Was it because of my TBI and my damaged frontal lobes and my newfound anger – which I still feel rumbling away inside, even if I feel more adept at controlling the outbursts now?

Have I always been capable of such violence?

Perhaps Ben was right after all. There really is a killer inside everyone.

One thing that's clear to me is that I don't regret what I did, even if it does disturb me to know what I'm capable of. Ethan and Mary Grant are buried six feet under, and as far as I'm concerned, it's good riddance.

Jason and I make our way down in the lift and haul the luggage across the street to Jason's car.

'Give me the keys,' I say. 'You shouldn't really be driving.'

'I'm fine,' Jason says.

'I don't give a damn. I'm driving. I know you can take care of me, but I can take care of you too.'

Jason says nothing. For so long he's watched out for me. Even when I was pushing him away. Even when I hated him for treating me like an invalid during my recovery. Or like a child. I now see that he did it only out of love. I need to show him I can care for him too. That my love for him is as unwavering as his is for me.

He grabs the keys and slings them over to me. I catch them and we dump the suitcases in the boot and get into the car. I fire up the engine. I look back up at the apartment block.

'I should have done this months ago,' I say.

That apartment represents the darkest part of my life, I realise, and the feelings of anger, depression, alienation and reclusiveness would never go away if I stayed.

'Yeah, but you've always been so damn stubborn, DI Stephens.'

'And you've always been such a charmer.'

'You're getting out now,' Jason says. 'A fresh start. With me. That's the main thing.'

I say nothing to that. I take one last look up to the sixth floor of the apartment block, then say goodbye to that place, and that part of my life, once and for all.

A Letter From Rob

Thank you for reading *The Essence of Evil*. It's always a great pleasure and relief to finally send a book out into the world after so many months of work and revisions, and this book in particular has been in the works for a very long time!

The Essence of Evil is the first book in the DI Dani Stephens crime series, and I hope you've enjoyed the first glimpse into her dark and troubled world, and feel sufficiently invested in her, like I do, to read more!!

I hope you enjoyed *The Essence of Evil*, and I'm always grateful for reviews if you could spare a few minutes to write and post one online.

If you've followed my writing career to date, you'll know that until now, I've very much concentrated on writing action based thrillers with embattled heroes, but I've long been fascinated by police and crime thrillers too, both in book and in TV/film, and a couple of years ago I put myself to the challenge of writing one. I mean, why not?!

Dani Stephens as a character came to me in something of a random brain wave, and I really can't pinpoint now what sparked her creation. I do know that I quickly decided that she was a character I wanted to put some serious effort into. Even within my action thrillers, I've always enjoyed writing strong female characters, and I knew that with Dani I just had to give her the leading role. With her dark back story, it was clear to me that this first book should be all about exploring what it is that makes someone a killer.

But how to go about writing a police procedural when I've zero experience of murder investigations, save for reading a few detective books and watching *Line of Duty*?! First port of call was an eye-opening meeting with the Homicide team at West Midlands Police, where they walked me through the ins and outs of a typical murder investigation – typical from the point of view of procedure at least.

Of course, I wasn't interested in writing about a 'typical' murder, so I've also spent many an hour online researching some pretty horrific crimes of years gone by, carried out by some of the most notorious serial killers we know of. Not a procedure for the faint of heart, and my internet searches must look seriously suspicious right now!

You'll also notice the setting of this book is entirely within and around Birmingham – a far cry from my previous globetrotting thrillers which often span multiple continents! I currently live in Sutton Coldfield, and both my kids were born here, and my current home town features fleetingly in this book. All of the locales referred to in *The Essence of Evil* are real places that I'm familiar with (to varying degrees, and quite a few road names are made up!), and if you're wondering about Dani, she actually lives in my old apartment by the canals near Brindleyplace!

I also welcome direct comments and feedback, and you can reach me via my website (where you can also sign up to my newsletter), and on social media, links as follows:

Website: www.robsinclairauthor.com

Twitter: @rsinclairauthor

Facebook: fb.me/robsinclairauthor

All the best

Rob Sinclair

Acknowledgments

Firstly, I'd like to express my immense gratitude to everyone who's taken the time to read my work, including readers, writers, reviewers and bloggers – I wouldn't be an author without you!

A special mention goes to Camilla and Roya for their help in finding Dani Stephens a suitable home, to Keshini and Michael for their enthusiasm in bringing this series to life, and to everyone else at Canelo and Hera who have helped pull *The Essence of Evil* into such great shape.

Thanks to Detective Superintendent Payne and Detective Inspector Hines from Force CID at West Midlands Police for shedding light on their hard and harrowing jobs, and finally to my family for their ongoing patience and encouragement, particularly when I'm in the midst of writing about vile killers!

Books By Rob Sinclair

The Sleeper series

Sleeper 13
Fugitive 13
Imposter 13

The Enemy series

Dance with the Enemy
Rise of the Enemy
Hunt for the Enemy

The James Ryker series

The Red Cobra
The Black Hornet
The Silver Wolf
The Green Viper
The White Scorpion

Others

Dark Fragments